❈ HANS ❈ CHRISTIAN ANDERSEN
EIGHTY FAIRY TALES

Translated by R. P. Keigwin
Introduction by Elias Bredsdorff
Illustrations by Vilhelm Pedersen and Lorenz Frølich

HANS CHRISTIAN ANDERSEN

EIGHTY FAIRY TALES

Pantheon Books, New York

Library of Congress Cataloging in Publication Data

Anderson, H. C. (Hans Christian), 1805–1875.
Eighty fairy tales.
(Pantheon fairy tale and folklore library)
Reprint. Originally published: 80 fairy tales.
Odense [Denmark]: Skandinavisk Bogforlag, c1976.
Summary: Includes the well-known tales as well as less
familiar ones such as "The Gardener and the Squire," "The
Story of a Mother," "In a Thousand Years Time," and "The
Shadow."

1. Fairy tales—Denmark. [1. Fairy tales. 2. Short sto-
ries] I. Keigwin, R. P. (Richard Prescott), 1883–   .II.
Pedersen, Vilhelm, 1820–1859, ill. III. Frølich, Lorenz,
1820–1908, ill. IV. Title. V. Title: 80 fairy tales. VI. Series.
PT8116.E5 1982   839.8'136 [Fic]   82-47882
ISBN: 0-394-52523-X   AACR2

Display design by Naomi Osnos

Manufactured in the United States of America
First American Edition

Contents

Introduction

Hans Christian Andersen's fairy tales and stories have had their important place in world literature since the middle of the nineteenth century and have been translated into well over a hundred languages. The first four tales were published in Denmark in 1835, and the first English translations appeared in 1846. Within a short time, Andersen had become a household word both in Britain and in the United States. In 1875, on the occasion of his seventieth birthday, the London *Daily News*, a paper founded by Dickens, paid homage to Andersen:

> It has been given to *Hans Andersen* to fashion beings, it may almost be said, of a new kind, to breathe life into the toys of childhood, and the forms of antique superstition. The tin soldier, the ugly duckling, the mermaid, the little match girl, are no less real and living in their way than *Othello*, or *Mr. Pickwick*, or *Helen of Troy*. It seems a very humble field in which to work, this of nursery legend and childish fancy. Yet the Danish poet alone, of all who have laboured in it, has succeeded in recovering, and reproducing, the kind of imagination which constructed the old fairy tales.

Hans Christian Andersen was more a creative writer than a collector of folk tales. It is somewhat misleading to bracket him, as is often done, with the German brothers Jakob and Wilhelm Grimm, or with Asbjørnsen and Moe, the two Norwegian collectors of traditional folk tales. Nevertheless, a few of Andersen's tales, especially among the early ones, were based on traditional Danish folk tales he had heard as a child. Two months before the publication of his first four tales Andersen wrote to a friend: "I have set down a few of the fairy tales I myself used to enjoy as a child and which I believe aren't well known. I have written them exactly as I would have told them to a child."

This group includes "The Tinderbox," "Little Claus and Big Claus," "The Travelling Companion," "The Wild Swans," "The Swineherd" (all of them published in 1835–1838), and two later ones, "Simple Simon" (1855), with the subtitle "A Nursery Tale Retold," and "Dad's Always Right" (1861) (which begins: "Now listen! I'm going to tell you a story I heard when I was a boy..."). There are also elements of folk tales in "The Princess and the Pea" and in "The Garden of Eden." Three of the tales have literary sources: "The Naughty Boy" (based on a poem by Anacreon), "The Emperor's New Clothes" (based on a fourteenth-century Spanish story), and the narrative frame of "The Flying Trunk" (taken, with a few modifications and a complete change of style, from a French eighteenth-century work). As for the rest, the remaining 144 tales (out of a total of 156) are entirely Andersen's own invention, though this does not mean, of course, that he did not use themes or features from other sources.

Andersen entitled his tales *Eventyr og Historier*, thus making a deliberate distinction between *Eventyr*, fairy tales containing a supernatural element, and *Historier*, stories which lack that element. Thus "The Little Mermaid" is a fairy tale, "The Emperor's New Clothes" a story. But the dividing line is not always so clear, nor is Andersen always consistent. For instance, in spite of its title, "The Story of a Mother" is not so much a story as a fairy tale. Andersen first used the term *Historier* in 1852; until then he had consistently used the term *Eventyr*. In his autobiography, he explains that he had gradually come to regard the word *Historier* as a truer description of his tales in their full range and nature: "Popular language puts the simple tale and the most daring imaginative description together under this common designation; the nursery tale, the fable and the narrative are referred to by the child as well as by the peasant, among all common or garden people, by the short term: stories."

Throughout, Andersen's style was unique, and far removed from that of the traditional folk or fairy tale.

Since Andersen was writing primarily for children, he took great pains not to use words they might have difficulty in understanding, and he showed great ingenuity in paraphrasing complicated words and ideas. In "The High Jumpers" he speaks of "the man who writes the almanac," meaning a professor of astronomy. He writes "a student who was studying to become a parson" instead of a "student of theology." If he does use a word children may not know, he takes care to explain it: thus, he says about one of his characters that "he went in for conjuring and learnt to talk with his stomach, which is called being a ventriloquist."

Few writers employed truisms to such deliberately humorous effect as Andersen. Witness the opening lines of "The Nightingale": "You know of course that in China the emperor is a Chinese and his subjects are Chinese too."

Another of Andersen's special talents was that of conveying abstract ideas through a tangible reality. In "The Tinder Box," after the soldier has lifted the third dog down on to the floor and seen the chest full of gold coins, the amount of money is explained in terms which are fully comprehensible to a child: "There was enough for him to buy the whole of Copenhagen, all the sugar-pigs that the cake-women sell, and all the tin soldiers and rocking-horses in the world."

Expressions like "everybody" and "the whole world" seemed too abstract to Andersen, so that he often added something more tangible to them. For their jumping competition the three high jumpers "invited the whole world, and anyone else who liked, to come and watch the sport." What could convey a better impression of open admittance? Perhaps the best example is the reward the Snow Queen promises Kay if he is able to combine the letters correctly: not only does she promise him his freedom but also "the whole world and a pair of new skates." The genius of Andersen's conception is clear, for that expression is imbued with both humour and a deep understanding of children's minds.

Some of Andersen's best tales are understood at two levels, by the child and by the grown-up person. Andersen himself once explained that his tales "were told for children, but the grown-up person should be allowed to listen as well." This is certainly true of such masterpieces as "The Little Mermaid," "The Emperor's New Clothes," "The Nightingale" and "The Snow Queen." But there are other tales which might actually appeal more to adults than to children. "The Story of a Mother," "The Bell," and "The Shadow" are all examples of this sort of story, for the true philosophy of these tales is beyond the comprehension of most children. In particular, "The Shadow" is an extremely sophisticated story open to many different interpretations; it could have been written by Kafka.

Andersen himself was a man of deep and apparently irreconcilable contrasts, and the same contrasts are to be found in his fairy tales and stories. "The Bell" and "The Shadow," for instance, have themes which, at first glance, seem quite similar, and yet they express two very different philosophies. "The Bell" is an optimistic story about the triumph of goodness and the victory of genius. In contrast, "The Shadow" tells a pessimistic story in which the learned man, a dedicated scholar and lover of truth and beauty, is beheaded, while his Shadow, the parasite, steals his fame and is rewarded by marrying the princess.

In a much-quoted comment concerning his tales, Andersen said: "They lay in my thoughts like a seed-corn, requiring only a flowing stream, a ray of sunshine, a drop of wormwood, for them to spring forth and burst into bloom." The autobiographical element is obvious in many of the tales. It is not difficult to see Andersen as the ugly duckling, or as Mr. Larsen in "The Gardener and the Squire," yet he frequently appears in other tales in many different disguises. He is the soldier in "The Tinder Box"; he is the sensitive princess who can feel one pea through twenty mattresses and twenty featherbeds; he is the student in "Little Ida's Flowers"; he is the little mermaid, the outsider who came from the depths and was never really accepted in the new world into which he moved; he is the little boy in "The Emperor's New Clothes" who could see that the emperor had nothing on; he is the poet in "The Naughty Boy"; and I could cite many more examples. As a Danish critic once said, Andersen wrote more self-portraits than Rembrandt ever painted.

Andersen put not only himself but also his friends and enemies into his tales, and scholars can point to many personal elements in them. But for the large majority of readers all over the world, children as well as adults, who read his tales with little or no knowledge of the author's life and background, most of this information is irrelevant. One can enjoy his fairy tales and stories without any background knowledge whatsoever. If this were not so, Andersen would never have been translated into most living languages, and even in Denmark he would have been largely forgotten by now.

Some of Andersen's tales were written in a matter of hours, or in the course of a few evenings; others took much longer. In 1844, writing to a friend about "The Snow Queen," he noted that "it came out dancing over the paper." He began writing this tale, one of his longest fairy tales, on December 5, 1844, and it was published in book form (together with "The Fir Tree") on December 21. The whole process of writing, setting up type, printing, binding, and publishing was done in the course of sixteen days.

On the other hand, "The Marsh King's Daughter," another long fairy tale, was rewritten six or seven times before Andersen was certain that he could not improve upon it.

Andersen is not easy to translate, and many of the early English translations of Andersen are shockingly bad. Yet many of them are still being reprinted today (though often without any mention of the translator's name), partly because age has made them sacrosanct, and partly because publishers do not have to pay royalties on them. Some of the early translators did not know Danish at all and translated from mediocre German versions. Others, who were able to boast on the title-page that their version was "translated from the original Danish," had such limited knowledge of the language that their translations reflect the most appalling mistakes.

In 1949 I treated some of these translations, which were then still being reprinted, in an English journal under the heading "How a Genius Is Murdered." As a result of the publicity surrounding that article, I was approached by a Danish publishing firm in Andersen's native town of Odense which wanted to commission a new translation of some eighty of Andersen's tales. They asked me if I knew of a qualified translator who might be willing to undertake such a task. I immediately asked my old friend R.P. Keigwin if he would be willing to do it. Keigwin possessed both an extensive knowledge of Danish and a very fine sense of style. In 1935, he had been responsible for an excellent translation of the first four tales by Andersen, published in the centenary of their first publication in Denmark. Keigwin understood the difficulty of the task: Andersen's language is full of colloquialisms, special Danish idioms, untranslatable puns and an intimacy between writer and reader which is strengthened by the frequent use of certain Danish adverbs that defy translation. In his preface to the 1935 volume, Keigwin wrote of Andersen:

He sprinkled his narrative with every kind of conversational touch— crisp, lively openings, to catch the listener's attention at a swoop; frequent asides or parentheses; little bits of Copenhagen slang; much grammatical licence; and, above all, a free use of particles—those nods and nudges of speech, with which Danish (like Greek) is so richly endowed. So completely did Andersen maintain the conversational tone in his *Tales* that you are quite shocked when you occasionally come across some really literary turn.

Not all of Andersen's 156 fairy tales and stories are masterpieces, and R.P. Keigwin's translation includes a little over half their total number. Personally, I think that his is the best available version of Andersen's tales, taking into consideration both the quality of the translation and the choice of tales and stories.

"The True Wizard of the North" was the term that E.V. Lucas, the English critic, said he would rather apply to Hans Christian Andersen than to Walter Scott, "because whereas Scott took men and women as he found them, [Andersen], with a touch of his wand, rendered inhuman things — furniture, toys, flowers, poultry — instinct with humanity." Robert Lynd, another British literary critic, wrote about Andersen: "He can make the inhabitants of one's mantelpiece capable of epic adventures and has a greater sense of possibilities in a pair of tongs or a door-knocker than most of us have in men and women."

There has been a tendency in both Britain and the United States to regard Andersen as being only a writer for the nursery, with the implication that he cannot be taken seriously as a literary figure. Or, as the Austrian writer Egon Friedell once put it: "The great public had adopted the same attitude to Andersen as a certain Prussian lieutenant of the guard did to Julius Caesar when he said that he could not possibly have been a great man since he had only written for the lower Latin forms. Similarly, since Andersen is so great an author that even children can understand him, the grown-ups have concluded that he cannot possibly have anything to offer them."

Let me conclude by quoting Andersen's own definition of the literary genre in which he was, and still is, the unsurpassed master:

In the whole realm of poetry no domain is so boundless as that of the fairy tale. It reaches from the blood-drenched graves of antiquity to the pious legends of a child's picture-book; it takes in the poetry of the people and the poetry of the artist. To me it represents all poetry, and he who masters it must be able to put into it tragedy, comedy, naive simplicity, and humour; at his service are the lyrical note, the childlike narrative and the language of describing nature.... In the folk tale it is always Simple Simon who is victorious in the end.... Thus also the innocence of poetry, overlooked and jeered at by the other brothers, will reach farthest in the end.

Elias Bredsdorff

The Tinder-Box

Left, right! Left, right!... Down the country road came a soldier marching. Left, right! Left, right!... He had his knapsack on his back and a sword at his side, for he had been at the war, and now he was on his way home. But then he met an old witch on the road. Oh! she was ugly-her lower lip hung right down on her chest. »Good evening, soldier,« she said, »what a nice sword you've got, and what a big knapsack! You're a proper soldier! Now I'll show you how to get as much money as you want!« »Thank you very much, old dame!« said the soldier.

»Do you see that big tree over there?« said the witch, pointing to a tree near by. »It's quite hollow inside. Now, you must climb right up it, and then you'll see a hole; slip through this, and you'll come deep down into the tree. I will tie a rope round your waist, so that I can haul you up again, as soon as you give me a shout.«

»But what am I to do down in the tree?« asked the soldier.

»Fetch money!« answered the witch. »For, mind you, when you get down to the bottom of the tree, you will find yourself in a large passage. It's quite light there, because hundreds of lamps are burning there. Next, you will see three doors; you can open them all right, for the key's in the lock. If you go into the first room, you will see in the middle of the floor a big chest, with a dog sitting on it which has got eyes as big as tea-cups; but never you mind about that! I'll give you my blue-check apron, and you can spread it out on the floor. Then go along quickly and lift off the

11

dog and put it on my apron; open the lid of the chest and take just as many pennies as you like. They are all copper, but if you would rather have silver, then you must go into the next room. There sits a dog with eyes as large as mill-wheels, but never you mind about that! Put the dog down on my apron, and help yourself to the money! And yet, if it's gold you want, you can get that too-as much as ever you can carry-if only you go into the third room. But this time the dog which is sitting on the money-chest has two eyes each one as big as the Round Tower ...Something like a dog, I can tell you! But never you mind a bit about that! Just put the dog down on my apron, and then it won't do you any harm, and you can take as much gold out of the chest as you like.«

»That doesn't sound at all bad,« said the soldier. »But tell me, old witch, what am I to give you? Because I expect you'll be wanting your share!«

»No,« said the witch, »Not a single penny will I take. You've simply got to bring me an old tinder-box that my grandmother forgot when she was last down there.«

»Oh, come on, then! let me get that rope round my middle!« said the soldier.

»Here it is«, said the witch, »and here's my blue-check apron.«

Then the soldier crawled up the tree, let himself down, plump! through the hole, and now he was standing, as the witch had said, down in the great passage where the hundreds of lamps were burning.

Then he unlocked the first door. Ugh! there sat the dog with eyes as big as tea-cups and glared at him.

»You are a nice chap, you are!« said the soldier. He put it down on the witch's apron and took just as many copper pennies as he could stuff into his pocket. Then he shut the chest, put the dog up again and went into the second room. Bless my soul! there sat the dog with eyes as big as mill-wheels.

»You shouldn't stare at me so!« said the soldier; »You'll strain your eyes.« And then he put the dog down on the witch's apron; but when he saw such piles of silver in the chest, he threw away all the coppers he had got and filled up his pocket and his knapsack with nothing but silver. And now he went into the third room!...Oh, but it was horrible! The dog in there had actually got two great eyes as big as the Round Tower, and they were going round and round in its head like wheels!

»Good evening!« said the soldier; and he touched his cap, because never in his life had he seen such a dog. But after he had looked at it for a bit, he thought to himself, »Enough of that!« and went and lifted the dog down on to the floor and opened the chest – why, goodness gracious, what a lot of gold there was! There was enough for him to buy the whole of Copenhagen, all the sugar-pigs that the cake-women sell, and the tin-soldiers and whips and rocking-horses in the world. Yes, yes, plenty of money in there – my word, there was!

12

So at once the soldier emptied out all the silver coins from his pockets and his knapsack and put in gold instead; yes, and he filled up everything with gold, his pockets, his knapsack, his cap and even his boots, so that he could hardly walk. Now he had got some money! He put the dog back on the chest, slammed the door, and then shouted up through the tree, »Hi, mother, haul me up again, will you?«

»Have you got the tinder-box?« asked the witch.

»Oh no! that's true, I had clean forgotten it,« said the soldier; and he went straight back and fetched it. The witch hauled him up out of the tree, and there he was again, standing on the road with his pockets, boots, cap and knapsack bulging with money.

»What are you going to do with this tinderbox?« asked the soldier.

»That's no business of yours!« answered the witch. »You've got your money; now just give me my tinder-box!«

»Rubbish!« said the soldier. »Tell me at once what you want to do with it – or I'll have out my sword and cut your head off.«

»No,« said the witch.

So he cut off her head...There she lay!

But the soldier tied up all his money in her apron and made a bundle of it, to go on his back. He put the tinder-box in his pocket and went straight on into the town.

It was a fine town, and he put up at the finest inn. He ordered the very best rooms and the food he was most fond of; for, now that he had all that money, he was a rich man. The servant who had to clean his boots thought, well, this was a funny old pair of boots for such a rich gentleman to have; but he hadn't yet bought any new ones. The next day he went out and got some good boots and some really smart clothes. And now the soldier had become quite a fashionable gentleman, and they told him all about the sights of their town, and about their King, and what a pretty Princess his daughter was.

»Where is she to be seen?« asked the soldier.

»She just isn't to be seen,« they all answered. »She lives in a big copper castle with lots of walls and towers all round it. No one but the King is allowed to go to her there, because a fortune-teller once said that she is to marry a common soldier, and the King doesn't like that at all.«

»My word! I should like to see her,« thought the soldier; but of course he couldn't possibly get leave to.

And now he lived a merry life.

He was always going to the theatre, or driving in the Park; and he gave away lots of money to the poor. That was very nice of him; you see, he remembered so well from the old days how awful it was to be absolutely penniless. But now he was rich and well-dressed, and so he made lots of friends who all said what a fine fellow he was - a real gentleman - and the soldier liked that very much. But as he was spending money every day and never getting any back, at last he had only got twopence left; and so he had to move from the fine rooms he had been living in and go and live in a little poky attic right under the roof. He had to clean his own boots and mend them with a darning-needle, and none of his friends ever came to see him, for there were such a lot of stairs to climb.

One evening, when it was quite dark and he couldn't even buy himself a candle, he suddenly remembered that there was a little bit of candle left in the tinder-box that he had got for the old witch out of the hollow tree. He got out the tinder-box and the bit of candle; but just as he was striking a light and the sparks flew up from the flint, the door sprang open, and the dog he had seen down in the tree with eyes as big as tea-cups stood before him and said »What are my lord's commands?«

»I say!« said the soldier. »This must be a queer sort of tinder-box, if I can get whatever I want like that.« »Bring me some money,« he said to the dog; then flick! and away it went, and flick! here it was back again, with a large bagful of pennies in its mouth.

And now the soldier realised what a splendid tinder-box it was. One stroke brought before him the dog which sat on the chest with the copper money; two strokes, the dog with the silver; and three strokes, the dog with the gold. The soldier lost no time in changing back into the fine rooms and the smart clothes, and of course all his friends remembered him again at once and were tremendously fond of him.

And then one day he thought to himself »There's something queer about this, that no one's allowed to see the Princess. She's supposed to be so very lovely, according to all these people; but what's the good of that, if she has to sit the whole time inside the copper castle, the one that has all those towers? Can't I possibly manage to see her somehow? Now then, where's my tinder-box?« So he struck a light and flick! there stood the dog with the eyes as big as tea-cups.

»Of course I know it's the middle of the night«, said the soldier, »but all the same I would like to see the Princess, that I would! Just for half a jiffy!«

The dog was out of the door in a flash and, before the soldier had time to think about it, there was the dog again with the Princess lying asleep on his back; and she looked so lovely that anyone could see she was a real princess; and the soldier simply couldn't resist, he had to kiss her — he was a soldier all over.

Then the dog scuttled back again with the Princess, but in the morning, when the King and Queen were at breakfast, the Princess said she had had such a curious dream in the night, about a dog and a soldier. She had ridden on the dog's back, and the soldier had kissed her.

»That's a pretty tale, if you like!« said the Queen.

And so one of the old ladies-in-waiting was told to sit up the following night by the Princess's bed and see if it was really a dream or not.

The soldier did so long for another look at the pretty Princess; and so up came the dog by night and took her and dashed off at full speed. But the old lady-in-waiting put on her overboots and ran just as fast after them, and when she saw them disappear into a big house she thought to herself, »Now I know where it is,« and chalked up a big cross on the door. Then she went home to bed, and the dog came back too with the Princess. But when it saw a cross had been chalked on the door where the soldier was living , the dog also took a bit of chalk and put a cross on every door in the town. That was a clever idea, because now, you see, the lady-in-waiting couldn't find the right door, as there were crosses on the whole lot of them.

Early in the morning the King and Queen, the old lady-in-waiting and all the Court officials sallied forth in order to see where it was the Princess had been.

»Here's the house!« said the King, when he saw the first door with a cross on it.

»No, it's there, darling!« said the Queen, catching sight of the second door with a cross on it.

»But here's another – and there's another!« they all kept saying. Whichever way they turned, there were crosses on the doors. So then they soon realized that it was no good searching any longer.

But the Queen, you know, was a very clever woman, who could do more than just drive out in a coach. She took her great golden scissors and cut up a large piece of silk and sewed the pieces together into a pretty little bag, which she filled with the finest buckwheat flour. She fastened the little bag to the Princess's back, and then she snipped a little hole in the bag, so as to sprinkle the flour wherever the Princess went.   At night, up came the dog once more, took the Princess on his back and ran off with her to the soldier, who loved her so dearly and did so wish he were a prince and could marry her.

The dog never noticed how the flour kept leaking out all the way from the castle to the soldiers's window, where it ran up the wall with the Princess. The next morning it was quite plain to the King and Queen where their daughter had been going; so they took the soldier and put him in prison.

There he sat. Ugh! how dark and dreary his cell was! And, beside, they kept saying to him »To-morrow you're going to be hanged!« That didn't sound at all cheerful, and the worst of it was he had left his tinder-box at the inn. In the morning, through the iron bars of his little window, he watched people hurrying out of the town to see him hanged. He heard the drums and saw the soldiers marching past. Everyone was afoot. Among them was a cobbler's boy in leather apron and slippers; he was trotting along so fast that one of his slippers came off and flew right against the wall where the soldier sat peeping out between the iron bars.

»I say! you young cobbler, you don't need to hurry like that,« the soldier said to him, »They can't begin without me. But look here – if you will kindly run along to where I've been living and fetch me my tinder-box; you shall have twopence for your trouble; but mind you get a move on!« The cobbler's boy was very glad to earn twopence, so he sprinted off for the tinder-box, brought it to the soldier, and – well, now listen to what happened!

Outside the town a high gallows had been built, and round about it stood the soldiers and thousands and thousands of people. The King and Queen sat on a beautiful throne opposite the judge and all his councillors.

Already the soldier had climbed the ladder; but just as they were going to put the rope round his neck he reminded them that, before being executed, a criminal always had the right to ask for one harmless favour. He said he would so like to smoke a pipe of tobacco – after all, it would be the last pipe he could smoke in this world.

Now, the King didn't like to say no to that; so the soldier took his tinder-box and struck a light – one, two, three! – and there stood all three dogs: the one with eyes as big as tea-cups, the one with eyes like mill-wheels, and the one which had eyes as big as the Round Tower.

»Save me now from being hanged!« said the soldier; and then the dogs flew at the judges and all the councillors, and seized some by their legs and others by their noses, and tossed them so high into the air that when they came down they were dashed to pieces.

»I won't be tossed!« said the King; but the biggest dog picked them both up, King and Queen, and sent them hurtling after the others. Then the soldiers got frightened, and the people all shouted out: »Soldier boy, you shall be our King and have the pretty Princess.« And they put the soldier into the King's coach, and all three dogs went dancing in front of it and cried out »Hurrah!« And the boys whistled on their fingers, and the soldiers presented arms. The Princess came out of the copper castle and was made Queen, and how pleased she was! The wedding-feast lasted for a week, and the dogs sat at table with everyone else and kept rolling their great big eyes.

Little Claus and
Big Claus

There were two men in one village, who both had the very same name; they were both called Claus. One of them owned four horses, the other only one; and, to tell them from each other, people called the man who had four horses Big Claus, and the man who had only one horse Little Claus. Now let us hear how these two got on; for this is a true story.

All through the week Little Claus had to plough for Big Claus and lend him his one horse; in return, Big Claus gave him the help of all his four horses, but only once a week, and that was on Sunday. My word! How Little Claus did crack his whip over all five horses! They were as good as his – for that one day. The sun shone so pleasantly, and the church-bells were all ringing for church; the villagers went by in their Sunday best, with their hymn-books under their arms, to hear the parson preach, and when they looked at Little Claus ploughing with five horses, he was so delighted that he cracked his whip once more and cried out: »Gee up, all my horses!«

»You mustn't say that,« said Big Claus; »there's only one horse, you know, which is yours.« But when some more people went past on their way to church, Little Claus forgot that he wasn't to say that and cried out again: »Gee up, all my horses!«

»Look here, will you kindly give over?« said Big Claus. »The next time you say that, I'll give your horse a clump on the head and kill him on the spot; and that'll be good-bye to him.«

»I promise you I won't say it again,« said Little Claus. But when some more people went by and they nodded good-morning to him, he was so delighted and felt that it must look so smart for him to have five horses to plough his field with, that he cracked his whip and cried out: »Gee up, all my horses!«

»I'll gee up your horses for you!« said Big Claus, and he took the mallet for the tetherpeg, and gave Little Claus's one horse such a clump on the forehead that it fell down stone dead.

»Oh, dear! Now I haven't a horse at all,« said Little Claus and began to cry. By and by he flayed the dead horse and took the hide and gave it a thorough drying in the wind. Then he stuck it in a bag, which he threw over his shoulder, and went off to the next town to sell his horse-hide.

He had a long way to go, and it led through a big, gloomy wood. Presently a terrible storm got up, and he quite lost his way. It was evening before he could find it again, and he was much too far from the town or from home to be able to reach either before night fell.

Close to the road stood a large farmhouse; the windows had the shutters up outside, but yet a gleam of light showed over the top of them. »I daresay I can get leave to spend the night there,« thought Little Claus and went up and knocked at the door.

The farmer's wife came and opened it; but when she heard what he wanted, she told him to be off, as her husband was not at home, and she didn't take in strangers.

»Oh, well, in that case I must find a bed out of doors,« said Little Claus, and the farmer's wife shut the door in his face.

Near by was a big haystack, and between this and the house a little shed had been built, with a flat thatch roof to it.

»I can sleep up there,« said Little Claus, catching sight of the roof; »that will be a lovely bed, and I shouldn't think the stork will fly down and bite my legs;« for a real live stork was standing up there on the roof, where it had its nest.

Little Claus now crawled up on to the shed, where he lay and wriggled himself to get really comfortable. The wooden shutters didn't quite cover the windows up at the top, and so he was able to see right into the room.

There was a large table laid with wine and roast meat and oh! such a delicious-looking fish. The farmer's wife and the parish clerk were sitting at table all by themselves; and she kept filling up his glass for him, and he kept helping himself to the fish – he was very fond of fish.

»If only I could get a taste af that!« thought Little Claus, craning out his neck towards the window. Heavens! What a gorgeous cake he could see in there! It was really a wonderful spread.

Then he heard someone riding along the road towards the house. It was the farmer himself, coming home.

Now, although he was an excellent man, the farmer had the strange failing that he never could bear the sight of a parish clerk; if he ever set eyes on a clerk, he flew into an absolute rage. And that was just why this clerk had called in to pass the time of day with the farmer's wife, when he knew that her husband was away from home; and the good woman set before him all the nicest things to eat that she could find. And now, when they heard the husband coming, they got so scared that the woman begged the clerk to creep into a big empty chest which stood over in the corner. So he climbed in, for he knew quite well that the poor man couldn't bear the sight of a parish clerk. The woman quickly hid away all the delicious food and wine inside her oven, because if her husband had seen it he would have been sure to ask what it all meant.

»Oh, dear!« sighed Little Claus up on the shed, when he saw all the food disappearing.

»Is that somebody up there?« asked the farmer, peering up at Little Claus. »What are you lying up there for? Much better come along o'me into the house!«

Little Claus then explained how he had lost his way and asked if he might stop the night.

»Why, certainly,« said the farmer, »but first we must have a bit o' something to eat.«

The farmer's wife gave them both a most friendly welcome, laid a long table and gave them a large bowl of porridge. The farmer was hungry, and he ate with a good appetite; but Little Claus couldn't help thinking about the lovely roast meat, the fish and the cake which he knew were inside the oven.

Under the table, at his feet, he had placed his sack with the horse-hide in it; for we mustn't forget, it was the hide which he had brought away with him from home, in order to sell it in the town. He didn't care for the porridge at all; and so he trod on his bag, and the dry hide inside it gave out quite a loud squeak.

»Sh!« said Little Claus to his sack; but at the same time he trod on it again, and it gave out a still louder squeak.

»Why, what ever have you got in that there bag?« asked the farmer.

»Oh, it's a wizard,« said Little Claus. »He says that we shouldn't be eating porridge; he has conjured the whole oven full of meat and fish and cake.«

»You don't say so!« said the farmer, and in a twinkling he opened the oven and saw all the delicious food which his wife had hidden away, though he thought himself that the wizard had conjured it there. His wife didn't dare say a word; she put the food straight on the table, and they both made a good meal off the fish and the meat and the cake. Presently Little Claus trod on his bag once more and made the hide squeak.

»What's he say now?« asked the farmer.

»He says,« answered Little Claus, »that he has also conjured us three bottles of wine, and they're in the oven too.« So the wife had to bring out the wine she had hidden, and the farmer drank and became quite merry; he felt he'd give anything to own a wizard like the one Little Claus had got in his bag.

»Can he also make the devil appear?« asked the farmer. »I should so like to see him, now that I'm feeling so cheerful.«

»Certainly,« said Little Claus, »my wizard can do whatever I like to ask him – can't you, old man?« and at the same time he trod on the bag so that it squeaked. »Did you hear him? He says, yes, of course he can; but the devil's so hideous that you'd better not see him.«

»Oh I'm not afraid. What d'you think he'll look like?«

»Well, you'll find he's the very image of a parish clerk.«

»Ugh!« said the farmer, »that's hideous and no mistake! You know, I can't bear the sight of parish clerks; but never mind, I know it's the devil this time, so I reckon I'll put up with it for once. I'm full o' pluck just now – but don't let him come too near!«

»Now I'll ask my wizard,« said Little Claus, treading on the bag and turning his ear to it.

»What's he say?«

»He says you may go up and open the chest which is standing over there in the corner, and you'll see the devil squatting inside; but mind you hold on to the lid, or he'll slip out.«

»Come and help me hold it, then!« said the farmer, going across to the chest in which his wife had hidden the real clerk, who sat there trembling with fear.

The farmer raised the lid a little way and peeped in under it: »Ugh!« he shrieked and jumped back from the chest. »Yes, I saw him right enough; he looked the dead spit of our clerk – oh, it was horrible!«

They had to have a drink after that, and they went on drinking far into the night.

»You must sell me that wizard,« said the farmer. »Ask what you like for him! I tell you what, I'll give you a whole bushel of money straight away.«

»No,« said Claus. »I can't do that. Just think of the profit I can make out of this wizard.«

»Oh, but I'm fair crazy to have him,« said the farmer, and he begged and pleaded till at last Little Claus said yes. »You've been very kind and given me a good night's lodging, so it doesn't make much odds. You shall have the wizard for a bushel of money, but full measure, mind you!«

»Right you are!« said the farmer. »But you must take that there chest with you; I won't have it another hour in the place – he may be in there yet, for all we can tell.«

Little Claus gave the farmer his sack with the dry hide in it, and got a whole bushel of money, full measure, in exchange. What's more, the farmer gave him a large barrow on which to wheel away the chest and the money.

»Good-bye!« said Little Claus, and off he went trundling his money and the great chest with the clerk still in it.

On the other side of the wood ran a deep river, where the current was so

strong that you could hardly swim against it. A big bridge had lately been built across it, and Little Claus halted when he got to the middle and said out aloud, so that the clerk in the chest could hear him: »Hang it all! What ever am I to do with this stupid chest? It's so heavy, you'd think it was full of stones. I'm sick and tired of wheeling it, so I'll just tip it into the river. Then, if it sails home to me, very good; and if it doesn't – well, it can't be helped.«

Then he took hold of the chest by one of the handles and tilted it a bit, as though he meant to hurl it down into the water.

»Stop! Stop!« shouted the clerk from inside the chest. »Let me out! Oh do let me out!«

»Good gracious!« said Little Claus and pretended to be frightened. »He's still inside! I must push him into the river at once, and then he'll drown!«

»No! No!« shouted the clerk. »I'll give you a whole bushel of money, if you'll let me out.«

»Ah, that's another story,« said Little Claus and opened the chest. The clerk quickly crept out, pushed the empty chest into the water and went to his home, where Little Claus was given a whole bushel of money. He had already got one out of the farmer, so there he was now with his wheelbarrow chock-full of money.

»There! I got rather a good price for that horse!« he said to himself, when he came home to his own room and turned out all the money in a big heap on the floor. »Big Claus will be very annoyed when he hears how rich I've become out of my one horse; but all the same I won't tell him straight away.«

Presently he sent a boy along to Big Claus to borrow a bushel measure.

»I wonder what he wants that for?« thought Big Claus, and he smeared the bottom with tar, so that a little of whatever was measured might stick to it; and, sure enough, when the measure came back, there were three new silver florins sticking to it.

»Hullo, what's this?« said Big Claus, and ran straight off to Little Claus. »Where did you get all this money from?«

»Oh, that was for my horse-hide that I sold yesterday.«

»That's a wonderful good price!« said Big Claus; and he ran home, took an axe and gave all his four horses a clump on the forehead. Then he stripped off the hides and trundled them away into the town.

»Hides! Hides! Who'll buy my hides?« he shouted through the streets.

All the shoemakers and tanners came running up and asking how much he wanted for them.

»A bushel of money apiece!« said Big Claus.

»Are you mad?« they all asked him. »Do you suppose we keep money in bushels?«

»Hides! Hides! Who'll buy my hides?« he shouted again; but to everyone who asked him the price he answered: »A bushel of money.«

»He's trying to make fools of us,« they all said; and then the shoemakers took their straps and the tanners their leather aprons and began to give Big Claus a good beating.

»Hides! Hides!« they mocked at him, »we'll give you a hide that'll bleed like a pig! Out of the town with him!« they shouted; and Big Claus had to bolt for his life – he'd never had such a drubbing.

»All right!« he said, when he got home. »Little Claus shall pay for this. I'll beat his brains out.«

But at Little Claus's home his old grandmother had just died. It's true she had always been very cross and unkind to him; still, he was very much grieved and took the dead woman and laid her in his own warm bed, to see if he couldn't bring her to life again. She was to lie there all night, while he himself would sit over in the corner and sleep on a chair; it wouldn't be the first time he had done that,

During the night, as he was sitting there, the door opened and Big Claus came in with an axe. He knew quite well where Little Claus's bed was, so he went straight up to it, and, thinking the dead grandmother was Little Claus, gave her a great clump on the forehead.

»There now!« he said. »you're not going to make a fool of me again;« and he went back home.

»What a very wicked man!« said Little Claus to himself. »It's clear that he meant to kill me. Anyhow, it's a good thing for the old dame that she was dead already, otherwise he would have taken her life.«

And now he dressed up the old grandmother in her Sunday clothes, borrowed a horse from his neighbour, harnessed it to the cart and set up the old grandmother in the back seat, so that she couldn't fall out when he drove faster, and away they bowled through the woods. By sunrise they were outside a large inn, where Little Claus drew up and went inside to get something to eat.

The landlord of the inn had plenty of money and was a very kind man too; but he was hot-tempered, as if he were full of pepper and snuff.

»Good morning!« he said to Little Claus. »You're out early to-day in your best clothes.«

»Yes,« said Little Claus, »I'm off to town with my old grandmother. She's sitting out in the cart; can't get her to come in here. Will you take her a large glass of honey-wine? But you must speak rather loud, for she's a bit deaf.«

»Right you are!« said the landlord and poured out a large glass of honey-wine, which he took out with him to the dead grandmother who was propped up in the cart.

»Here's a glass of honey-wine from your grandson, lady,« said the landlord. But the dead woman never said a word nor moved a muscle.

»Can't you hear?« cried the landlord at the top of his voice; »here's a glass of honey-wine from your grandson!«

Once more he shouted it out, and yet again after that; but as she never stirred, he lost his temper and threw the glass right into her face so that the wine ran down over her nose and she toppled over backwards into the cart; for she was only propped up and not fastened in.

»Hi! What's this?« cried Little Claus, rushing out and seizing the landlord by the throat. »You've been and killed my grandmother! Just look, there's a big hole in her forehead!«

»Oh, dear! That's a bit of bad luck!« cried the landlord, wringing his hands. »That all comes of my hot temper. Dear, kind Little Claus, I'll give you a whole bushel of money and bury your grandmother as if she was my own, if only you'll not say a word. Otherwise they'll cut off my head, and that is so disagreeable!«

So Little Claus got a whole bushel of money, and the landlord buried his old grandmother as if she had been his own.

As soon as Little Claus got back home with all his money, he sent his boy along to Big Claus to ask if he'd lend him a bushel measure.

»Hullo, what's this?« said Big Claus. »Didn't I kill him? I really must see about this myself.« And he went over to Little Claus with the measure.

»Why, where ever have you got all this money from?« he asked, and my goodness! how he opened his eyes when he saw all the fresh money that had come in.

»It was my grandmother you killed, not me,« said Little Claus. »It's she I've just sold and got a bushel of money for.«

»That's a wonderful good price,« said Big Claus and hurried home, took an axe and quickly killed his old grandmother. Then he placed her in the cart, drove into the town where the doctor lived, and asked if he wanted to buy a dead body.

»Whose is it and where did you get it?« asked the doctor.

»It's my old grandmother,« said Big Claus. »I killed her to get a bushel of money.«

»Good gracious!« said the doctor, »you don't know what you're saying. Don't go babbling like that, or you may lose your head!« And then he told him frankly what a dreadfully wicked thing he had done, and what a bad man he was, and that he ought to be punished. This made Big Claus so frightened that he rushed straight out of the surgery into the cart, whipped up the horses and made for home. But the doctor and the rest of them thought he was mad, and so they left him to drive where he liked.

»You shall pay for this!« said Big Claus, once he was out on the high-road. »Yes, you shall certainly pay for this, Little Claus!« And, as soon as he got home, he took the biggest sack he could find, went along to Little Claus and said: »You've been and fooled me again! First, I killed my horses, and then my old grandmother. It was your fault both times, but you shan't fool me any more!« And he caught hold of Little Claus by the waist, thrust him into the sack, slung him over his shoulder and called out to him: »Now I'm going to take you out and drown you!«

There was some distance to go before he came to the river, and Little Claus was no light weight to carry. The road went past the church; and the sound of the organ playing and the people singing was so beautiful that Big Claus put down his sack, with Little Claus inside it, near by the church-door and thought it would be nice to go in and listen to a hymn first before he went any further. Little Claus couldn't possibly get out, and everybody was in church; so in he went.

»Oh, dear! Oh, dear!« sighed Little Claus inside the sack. He wriggled and wriggled, but he couldn't possibly manage to get the string unfastened. Just then an old cattledrover came up. His hair was as white as chalk, and he leaned on a big stick, as he drove a whole herd of cows and bullocks in front of him; these ran up to the sack, in which Little Claus was sitting, and overturned it.

»Oh, dear!« sighed Little Claus, »I'm so young to go to heaven!«

»And poor me!« said the drover. »I'm so old and I can't get there!«

»Open the sack!« called out Little Claus. »Crawl in here instead of me, and you'll soon get to heaven!«

24

»Ah! I'd give anything for that,« said the drover, and he unfastened the sack for Little Claus, who jumped out at once.

»You'll mind the cattle, won't you?« said the old man, as he crawled into the bag. Little Claus tied it up and went on his way with all the cows and bullocks.

Soon after, Big Claus came out of church and put the sack over his shoulder again. Sure enough, he noticed that it seemed lighter; for the old drover wasn't more than half the weight of Little Claus. »How light he's become! No doubt it's because I listened to a hymn.« Then off he went to the river, which was a deep one, and threw the sack with the old drover inside it right out into the stream and shouted after him, thinking of course that it was Little Claus: »There now! You shan't fool me any more!«

Then he turned homeward, but when he came to the cross-roads he met Little Claus driving off with all his cattle.

»Hullo, what's this?« said Big Claus, »didn't I drown you?«

»Yes, you did,« said Little Claus. »You threw me into the river barely half an hour ago.«

»But where did you get all those fine cattle from?« asked Big Claus.

»They're sea-cattle,« said Little Claus. »I must tell you the whole story; and by the by, thank you so much for drowning me. I'm in luck's way now; I'm really rich, I can tell you!...

»I was very frightened, as I lay inside the sack with the wind whistling round my ears, when you threw me down off the bridge into the cold water. I sank straight to the bottom, but I didn't hurt myself, because down there grows the finest, softest grass. As I came down on this, the bag at once opened, and the most lovely girl dressed in pure white, with a green garland on her wet hair, took my hand and said: 'Is that you, Little Claus? Here are a few cattle for you to go on with. About four miles further up the road there's another drove of them, which I'll make you a present of'...

»Then I could see that the river was a great high-road for the sea-people. Down there at the bottom they walked and drove straight out of the sea, and then right away inland to where the river rises. It was delightful down there – what with flowers and the freshest grass, and fishes swimming about in the water and darting past my ears as birds do in the air up here. What fine folk there were, and what cattle to be met with along the hedges and ditches!«

»But why have you come up to us again in such a hurry?« asked Big Claus. »I wouldn't have done that, if it was so beautiful down there.«

»Ah, but that's just where I've been rather cunning,« said Little Claus. »You remember I told you what the sea-maiden said – that about four miles further up the road (and by the road she means of course the river, as she can't go anywhere else) there's another drove of cattle waiting for me. Well, I know how the river keeps winding in and out; it would be a very roundabout way, you know. So, if you can do it, it's much shorter to come up on land and drive straight across to the river again. You see, I save almost half the distance that way and get to my sea-cattle more quickly.«

»Oh, what a lucky man you are!« said Big Claus. »Do you think I shall get some sea-cattle too, if I go down to the bottom of the river?«

»I should just think you would!« said Little Claus; »but I can't carry you as far as the river in the sack, you're too heavy. If you will go there yourself and then crawl into the bag, I'll throw you into the water with the greatest of pleasure.«

»Thanks very much,« said Big Claus, »but if I don't find any seacattle when I get down there, I'll give you such a beating, I can tell you!«

»Oh, no; don't be so cruel!« So they went off to the river. The cattle were thirsty and, when they saw the water, they trotted off as fast as they could so as to get down and have a drink.

»Look what a hurry they're in,« said Little Claus. »They're longing to get down to the bottom again.«

»Yes, but help me first,« said Big Claus, »or you'll get your beating!« And then he crawled into the big sack, which had been lying across the back of one of the herd. »Better put a stone in, or else I'm afraid I mayn't sink,« said Big Claus.

»I expect you'll sink all right,« said Little Claus. Still, he put a big stone in the sack, tied the string tight and then gave it a good push – plomp! – there was Big Claus out in the river, and he sank straight to the bottom.

»I'm afraid he won't find his cattle,« said Little Claus – and drove off home with what he had.

The Princess and the Pea

Once upon a time there was a Prince, who wanted to have a Princess of his own, but she must be a proper Princess. So he travelled all over the world in order to find such a one, but every time there was something wrong. There were plenty of Princesses, but he could never quite make out if they were real Princesses; there was always something that wasn't quite right. So he came back home and was very much upset, because he did so long for a real Princess.

One evening a terrible storm blew up. There was lightning and thunder, the rain came pouring down – it was something dreadful! All at once there was a knock at the city gate, and the old King went out to open it.

It was a Princess standing outside. But goodness! what a sight she was with the rain and the weather! The water was running all down her hair and her clothes, and in at the tip of her shoes and out again at the heel; and yet she declared she was a real Princess.

»Well, we shall soon see about that!« thought the old Queen. She didn't say anything, but she went into the bedroom, took off all the bedclothes and placed a pea on the bottom of the bed; then she took twenty mattresses and laid them on top of the pea, and then again twenty of the softest featherbeds on top of the mattresses. That's where the Princess had to sleep for the night.

In the morning they asked her how she had slept. »Oh, dreadfully badly!« said the Princess. »I hardly had a wink of sleep all night! Goodness knows what there was in the bed! I was lying on something so hard that I'm simply black and blue all over. It's perfectly dreadful!«

So then of course they could see that she really was a Princess, because she had felt the pea right through the twenty mattresses and the twenty feather-beds. Nobody but a real Princess could have such a tender skin as that.

And so the Prince took her to wife, because now he knew that he had a proper Princess. And the pea was sent to the museum, where it is still to be seen, unless someone has taken it.

There, that's something like a story, isn't it?

Little Ida's Flowers

My poor flowers are quite dead!« said little Ida. »Yesterday evening they were so pretty, and now their leaves are all drooping. Why is it?« she asked of the student who was sitting on the sofa. She was very fond of him, because he knew the most lovely stories and could cut out such amusing pictures – hearts with little dancing ladies inside them, flowers, and great castles with doors that opened. He was a very jolly student.

»Why do the flowers look so unwell today?« she asked once more, pointing to a whole nosegay that was quite withered.

»Ah! don't you know what's the matter with them?« said the student. »The flowers were at a dance last night, that's why they're hanging their heads.«

»But flowers can't dance!« said little Ida.

»Can't they!« said the student. »When it's dark and we are all asleep, they go hopping round quite gaily; almost every night in the year they have a dance.«

»Are children allowed to join in?«

»Certainly,« said the student, »tiny little daisies are allowed to, and lilies-of-the-valley.«

»Where do the loveliest flowers dance?« asked little Ida.

»You've often been out of town, haven't you, to look at all the beautiful flowers in the garden of the great castle where the King lives in summer? Then you must have seen the swans which swim up to you, when you offer them bread-crumbs. There are wonderful dances out there, I can tell you!«

»I was out in that garden yesterday with my mother,« said Ida, »but the leaves were all off the trees, and there wasn't a single flower left. Where are they? I saw so many there last summer.«

»They are inside the castle,« said the student. »You see, directly the King and all his Court come back to town, the flowers at once run up from the garden into the castle and make merry. You should just see them! The two finest roses go and sit on the throne – they are King and Queen. All the red cockscombs line up on both sides and bow – they are gentlemen-in-waiting. Then come all the prettiest flowers, and there is a grand ball. The blue violets are young naval cadets, and they dance with the hyacinths and crocuses, whom they call Miss. The tulips and the large yellow lilies are old dowagers, who keep an eye on the dancing and see that everybody behaves.«

»But look here,« asked little Ida, »isn't there anyone to scold the flowers for dancing at the King's castle?«

»Nobody really knows what's going on,« said the student. »Sometimes, it's true, the old castle-steward, who is on watch there, comes along at night with his great bunch of keys but as soon as the flowers hear the keys rattle, they don't make a sound, but hide behind the long curtains and poke their heads out. 'I can smell flowers in here', says the old steward, but he can't see them.«

»What fun!« said little Ida, clapping her hands. »But shouldn't I be able to see the flowers either?«

»Oh, yes!« said the student. »You must just remember, next time you go out there, to peep in at the windows. You'll be sure to see the flowers. I did to-day. I saw a long yellow daffodil lolling on the sofa and pretending she was a maid-of-honour.«

»Can the flowers in the Botanical Garden go out there too? Can they go all that way?«

»Ra-ther!« said the student, »because they can fly, if they want to. You've seen lots of pretty butterflies, haven't you? Red ones and white ones and yellow ones – they almost look like flowers, don't they? They were flowers once, but then they jumped off their stalks high into the air and kept flapping their petals as if they were little wings, and away they flew. And as they behaved nicely, they got leave to fly about by day as well – they didn't have to go back and sit still on their stalks – and so at last their petals grew into real wings. You've seen that, of course, yourself. All the same, it's quite possible that the flowers at the Botanical Garden have never been out to the King's castle and that they have no idea of the fun that goes on there at night. Well, now I'm going to tell you something which will quite astonish the Professor of Botany who lives close by – you know him, don't you? When you go into his garden, you're to tell one of the flowers that there's a grand ball out at the castle. This flower will be sure to pass the news on to the others, and so they will all fly away. Then, if the Professor walks out into his garden, there won't be a single flower left and he won't have the slightest idea what has become of them.«

»But how can the flowers tell the others about the ball? Flowers can't talk, can they?«

»No, not exactly,« answered the student; »but they do it by signs. Surely you've noticed them, when it's a bit windy – how the flowers keep nodding and fluttering their green leaves; that means as much to them as if they talked.«

»Does the Professor understand their signs, then?« asked Ida.

»I should just think he does! Why, one morning he went into his garden and saw a great stinging-nettle making signs with its leaves to a lovely red carnation; it was saying, 'You are so attractive, and I am so fond of you!' But the Professor can't bear that sort of thing, and he at once rapped the stinging-nettle over its leaves – for they are its fingers – but in doing this he stung himself and, ever since, he has always been afraid to touch a stinging-nettle.«

»What fun!« said little Ida, with a laugh.

»Fancy filling a child's head with such rubbish!« said the grumpy old Councillor, who had come to pay a visit and was sitting on the sofa. He never could bear the student and always got cross when he saw him cutting out those comic figures which were so amusing – sometimes it was a man hanging from a gibbet, with a heart in his hand because he was a stealer of hearts, sometimes an old witch riding on a broomstick, with her husband perched on the bridge of her nose. The Councillor couldn't bear that sort of thing, and he always used to say just what he said now: »What rubbish to put into a child's head! All stuff and non-sense!«

But little Ida was most amused at what the student had said about her flowers, and she thought about it for a long time. The flowers drooped their heads because they were tired out from dancing all night. No mistake about it, they were ill. So she took them along to her other playthings, which stood on a nice little table where she kept all her treasures in a drawer. Her doll, Sophie, lay sleeping in her little bed, but Ida said to her: »You really must get up, Sophie, and be content with sleeping in the drawer to-night. The poor flowers are ill, and so they must sleep in your bed, then perhaps they will get well again.«She picked up the doll, which looked cross and never said a word, because it was annoyed at having to give up its bed.

Ida laid the flowers in the doll's bed, tucked them well up and told them to lie quite still while she made them some tea; then they would be well enough to get up next morning. She pulled the curtains close round the little bed, so that the sun shouldn't shine into their eyes.

All that evening she couldn't stop thinking about what the student had told her and, now that it was time to go to bed herself, she had first to take a peep behind the curtains drawn across the window, where her mother's beautiful flowers were standing. They were hyacinths and tulips, and she whispered to them quite softly: »I know perfectly well where you're going to-night!« But the flowers pretended they didn't understand a word, and they never stirred a leaf;but little Ida knew perfectly well what they were up to.

When she had got into bed, she lay for a long time thinking how jolly it would be to see the beautiful flowers dancing out there at the King's castle. »I wonder if my flowers really went too.« But then she fell asleep. In the middle of the night she woke up again; she had been dreaming about the flowers and the student whom the Councillor scolded because he filled her head with rubbish. There wasn't a sound in the bedroom where Ida lay, the night-light was quietly burning on the table, and her father and mother were asleep.

»I wonder if my flowers are still lying in Sophie's bed,« she said to herself; »I should like to know!« She sat up in bed and looked over at the door which stood ajar. In there lay the flowers and all her playthings. She listened carefully, and then it was just as though she heard a piano being played in the next room, but quite softly and more beautifully than she had ever heard before.

»That must be the flowers all dancing in there!« she said. »Oh dear, how I should like to. see them!« But she didn't dare get up for fear of waking her father and mother. »If only they would come in here!« she said. But the flowers never came, and the music went on playing so beautifully that she couldn't stay where she was any longer, it was too lovely. She crept out of her little bed and went softly across to the door and peeped into the next room. Oh, it was really too amusing, what she saw in there.

There was no night-light of any sort, but all the same it wasn't a bit dark, for the moon was shining through the window on to the middle of the floor – it was almost as clear as daylight. All the hyacinths and tulips were standing on the floor in two long rows; there wasn't one left in the window, where the pots stood empty. Down on the floor all the flowers were dancing round so nicely together, actually doing the Grand Chain, and holding each other by their long green leaves as they swung round. But over at the piano sat a tall yellow lily, which little Ida was sure she had seen last summer for she remembered the student saying: »Isn't it like Miss Lena!« Everybody had laughed at him, but now Ida, too, thought that the long yellow flower really was like Miss Lena. It had just the same way of sitting at the piano, and of turning its sallow oval face first to one side and then to the other, while it nodded time to the pretty music. Nobody noticed little Ida.

Next she saw a big blue crocus jump on to the middle of the table, where her playthings were lying, and go straight up to the doll's bed and pull aside the curtains. There lay the sick flowers but they sat up at once and nodded to the others that they would gladly come down and join in the dancing. The old chimney-sweep, whose lower lip had broken off, stood up and bowed to the dainty flowers, which didn't look in the least ill, but jumped down among the others and enjoyed themselves like anything.

Suddenly something seemed to fall down off the table. Ida saw that it was the teaser she had been given for the carnival; it had jumped down, because it felt it was really one of the flowers. It certainly looked fine with its paper streamers, and at the top of it was a little wax doll, wearing just such a wide awake hat as the Councillor went about in. The teaser, on its three red wooden legs, hopped right in among the flowers and stamped away like anything, for it was dancing the mazurka, and that's a dance the other flowers couldn't manage, because they were too light to stamp properly.

All at once the wax doll at the end of the teaser seemed to grow bigger and taller; it whirled round above its own paper flowers and shouted at the top of its voice: »What rubbish to put into a child's head! All stuff and nonsense!« The wax doll was the very image of the Councillor, all sallow and grumpy, in his wide-awake hat, but the teaser's paper flowers kept curling round his thin legs, and then he shrank together and became a little shrimp of a wax doll again. It was such fun to watch, and little Ida couldn't help laughing. The teaser went on dancing and the Councillor had to dance as well. It made no difference whether he grew large and lanky or remained the little yellow wax doll in the big black hat, he had to keep on dancing – till at last the other flowers, and especially those which had been lying in the doll's bed, begged him off, and the teaser stopped. At the same moment there was a loud knocking inside the drawer, where Ida's doll, Sophie, was lying among a lot of other playthings. The chimney-sweep ran along to the edge of the table and, lying full length on his stomach, he managed to work the drawer a little way open. Sophie sat up and looked around her in utter astonishment. »Why, there's a dance going on here!« she said. »Why didn't anyone tell me about it?«

»Will you dance with me?« said the chimney-sweep.

»I should think so! You're a fine one to dance with!« – and she turned her back on him. Then she sat down on the drawer, thinking that one of the flowers would be sure to come and ask her for a dance; but nobody came. She kept coughing – ahem! ahem! – it made no difference, not a soul came up to her. So the chimney-sweep danced by himself, and he didn't get on at all badly either.

And now, as none of the flowers seemed to notice Sophie, she let herself fall down, plump! on to the floor. It was a terrific thud. All the flowers came running up and stood round her, asking if she had hurt herself. They all behaved so nicely to her, especially the flowers who had been lying in her bed; but she hadn't hurt herself in the slightest, and all Ida's flowers said: »Thank you for the lovely bed« and made a great fuss of her

and took her along to the moonlight in the middle of the floor and danced with her, while the other flowers made a ring round them. Sophie was delighted, and told them they were quite welcome to keep her bed, as she didn't a bit mind sleeping in the drawer.

But the flowers answered: »Thank you very, very much, but we can't live very long; we've only got till to-morrow. But please tell little Ida to bury us out in the garden where the canary was buried; then we shall sprout up again next summer and be far prettier.«

»Oh, no! You mustn't die,« said Sophie, as she kissed the flowers. At the same moment the drawing-room door opened, and a whole throng of beautiful flowers came dancing in. Ida couldn't make out where they came from, but of course they were all the flowers which had come in from the King's castle. Two lovely roses, wearing little crowns of gold, led the way; they were the King and Queen. Next came the most charming stocks and carnations, bowing in every direction. There was a band playing, too – great poppies and peonies blowing away on pea-shells till they were purple in the face, and harebells and little white snowdrops tinkling along as if they had real bells. It was such funny music. After that came a lot of other flowers, and they all danced together – the blue violets and the red daisies, the ox-eyes and the lilies-of-the-valley. And it was pretty to see how the flowers all kissed each other. At last they said good-night to one another, and little Ida also crept away to bed, where she dreamt of all she had seen.

When she got up next morning, she went straight along to the little table, to see if the flowers were still there. She drew back the curtains of the little bed – yes, there they all lay together; but they were quite withered, much more than they were yesterday. Sophie was still in the drawer where Ida had put her; she was looking very sleepy.

»Do you remember what you were to tell me?« asked little Ida; but Sophie looked very stupid and didn't say a word.

»You're very naughty,« said Ida, »and yet they all danced with you«.

Then she took a little cardboard box, which had a pretty design of birds on it, and taking off the lid she placed the dead flowers inside it. »There's a nice coffin for you,« she said, »and later on, when my Norwegian cousins arrive, they will help me to bury you out in the garden, so that you can sprout up again next summer and become still prettier.«

The Norwegian cousins were two lively boys called Jonas and Adolph, whose father had just given them new bows and arrows, and they brought these with them to show to Ida. She told them all about the poor dead flowers, and they got leave to bury them. The two boys walked in front with the bows over their shoulders, and little Ida followed with the dead flowers in the pretty box. Out in the garden they dug a small grave. Ida first kissed the flowers, and then she placed them, box and all, in the earth; and, as they hadn't any guns or cannons, Adolph and Jonas fired a salute over the grave with their bows and arrows.

Thumbelina

There was once a woman who did so want to have a wee child of her own, but she had no idea where she was to get it from. So she went off to an old witch and said to her, »I would so dearly like to have a little child. Do please tell me where I can find one.«

»Oh, that!« said the witch, »Nothing easier. Take this barleycorn – mind you, it's not the kind that grows out in the fields or that the fowls are fed with. Put it in a flower-pot, and see what happens!«

»Thank you very much«, said the woman, giving the witch a shilling. She went straight home and planted the barleycorn, and in no time there came up a lovely great flower which looked just like a tulip, only the petals were shut tight as though it were still in bud.

»It *is* a pretty flower,« said the woman, and she gave the lovely red and yellow petals a kiss; but directly she kissed it, the flower burst open with a pop. It was a real tulip – that was plain enough now – but, sitting on the green pistil in the middle of the flower, was a tiny little girl. She was delicately pretty and no taller than your thumb, so she was given the name of Thumbelina.

A nicely varnished walnut-shell did for her cradle, blue violet petals for her mattress, and a rose-leaf for her counterpane. That was where she slept at night; but in the daytime she played about on the table, where the woman had put a plate with a wreath of flowers. These dipped their stalks down into the water, in the middle of which floated a large tulip petal where Thumbelina could sit and row herself from one side of the plate to the other, using a couple of white horsehairs as oars. It was a most charming sight. She could sing, too, in the sweetest little voice you ever heard.

One night, as she lay in her pretty bed, a hideous toad came hopping in through a broken pane in the window. It was a great ugly slimy toad, and it jumped straight down on to the table where Thumbelina was lying asleep under her red rose-leaf.

»She would make a nice wife for my son,« thought the toad, and she snatched up the walnut-shell in which Thumbelina was sleeping and hopped off with her through the window into the garden.

There was a wide brook running through it, but the bank was swampy and muddy, and here the toad lived with her son. Ugh! wasn't he ugly and horrible – just like his mother! »Koax, koax, brekke-ke-kex« was all he could say, when he saw the pretty little girl in the walnut-shell.

»Sh! Not so loud, or you'll wake her,« said the old toad. »She might yet run away from us, for she's as light as swan's-down. Let's put her out in the brook on one of those broad water-lilies. She's so small and light that its leaf will be like an island for her. She can't escape from there, and in the meantime we'll get the best room ready under the mud for you two to live in.«

There were quite a lot of water-lilies growing on the water with their broad green leaves which seem to be floating on the surface. The biggest of them all happened to be the furthest away, but the old toad swam out and placed the walnut-shell on it with Thumbelina still sleeping inside.

Early the next morning the poor little thing woke up and, when she saw where she was, she began to cry bitterly, for the big green leaf had water all round it and she couldn't possibly reach the bank.

The old toad stayed down in the mud and decorated her room with rushes and yellow water-lilies, so as to make everything quite snug for her new daughter-in-law. Then she swam out with her son to the water-lily where Thumbelina was standing, for they wanted to fetch that fine walnut bed and put it up in the bridal-chamber before she came herself. The old toad made a low curtsey to her in the water and said, »Here's my son – he's to be your husband. You'll have a lovely home together down in the mud.«

»Koax, koax, brekke-ke-kex!« was all that the son could say.

Then they took the pretty little bed and swam away with it. But Thumbelina sat all alone on the green leaf and cried, for she didn't want to live with the horrible toad or to marry her ugly son. The little fishes, swimming down there in the water, had caught sight of the toad and heard what she said. So they poked their heads out of the water; they were so anxious to have a look at the little girl. Directly they saw her, they found her charming, and they couldn't bear to think that she must go and live with the ugly toad. No, that must never happen! They all swarmed together down in the water round the green stalk that held the leaf she was standing on and gnawed it through with their teeth; where-upon the leaf floated away with Thumbelina down the brook, far away where the toad could never reach her.

Thumbelina went sailing past all sorts of places, and the little birds
perched in the bushes saw her and trilled out, »What a pretty little lady!«
The leaf that carried her floated further and further on; and thus it was
that Thumbelina began her journey abroad.

A dainty little white butterfly kept on fluttering round and round her,
till at last it settled on the leaf, for it had taken a great liking to Thumbelina; and she too was pleased, because the toad couldn't reach her now
and she was sailing through such a lovely part of the brook. The sunshine gleamed on the water like the finest gold. Then she took her sash
and tied one end of it round the butterfly, while the other end she made
fast to the leaf; and this at once gathered speed – and so did Thumbelina
because, you see, she was standing on the leaf. Just then a large cockchafer came flying up and, catching sight of her, clutched her round her

slender waist and flew with her up into a tree. But the green leaf went floating on and the butterfly with it, because it had been tied to the leaf and couldn't manage to free itself.

Gracious, what a fright it gave poor Thumbelina, when the cockchafer flew up into the tree with her! Still, what upset her even more was the thought of the pretty white butterfly that she had tied to the leaf; for unless it could manage to free itself, it would certainly starve to death. But that didn't worry the cockchafer in the slightest. He settled beside her on the largest green leaf in the tree, gave her some nectar from the blossoms and said how pretty she was, although she wasn't a bit like a cockchafer. Later on, all the other cockchafers living in the tree came to call on her. They stared at Thumbelina, and the young lady cockchafers shrugged their feelers – »Why, she's only got two legs,« they said. »What a pitiable sight!« »She hasn't any feelers,« they went on. »She's so pinched in at the waist – ugh! she might almost be a human. Isn't she ugly!« exclaimed all the lady cockchafers. And yet Thumbelina was really so pretty. And that's what the cockchafer thought who had carried her off; but when all the others kept saying how ugly she was, then at length he thought so too and would have nothing to do with her; she could go where she liked. They flew with her down from the tree and sat her on a daisy. There she cried and cried, because she was so ugly that the cockchafers wouldn't have her; and all the time she was as beautiful as can be – as exquisite as the loveliest rose-petal.

Right through the summer poor Thumbelina lived quite alone in that enormous wood. She took blades of grass and plaited herself a bed, which she hung under a large dock-leaf, so as to be out of the rain. She got her food from the honey in the flowers, and her drink from the morning dew on the leaves; and in this way summer and autumn went by. But now came winter – the long, cold winter. All the birds that had sung to her so beautifully now flew away; the trees and flowers withered; the great dock-leaf she had been living under furled itself into nothing but a faded yellow stalk. She felt the cold most terribly, for her clothes were by this time in tatters, and she herself was so tiny and delicate, poor Thumbelina, that she would surely be frozen to death. It began snowing, and every snowflake that fell on her was like a whole shovelful being thrown on us, for we are quite big and she was no taller than your thumb. So she wrapped herself up in a dead leaf, but there was no warmth in that, and she shivered with cold.

On the fringe of the wood where she had now come to was a large cornfield; but the corn had long been harvested, and only the bare barren stubble thrust up from the frozen earth. It was just like an entire forest for her to walk through – oh, and she was shivering with cold! At length she came to the field-mouse's door. It was a little hole down below the stubble. There the field-mouse had a fine snug place to live in, with a whole roomful of corn and a splendid kitchen and dining-room. Poor Thumbelina stood just inside the door like any other wretched beggar-girl and asked for a little bit of barleycorn, for she hadn't had a scrap to eat for two days.

»You poor mite!« said the field-mouse, for at heart she was a kind old thing. »Come you in and have a bite with me in my warm room.«

As she at once took a liking to Thumbelina she made a suggestion. »You're quite welcome to stay with me for the winter,« she said, »as long as you'll keep my rooms nice and tidy and also tell me stories, for I'm so fond of stories.« And Thumbelina did what the kind old field-mouse asked for and was extremely comfortable there.

»I dare say we shall have a visitor before long,« said the field-mouse. »My neighbour generally pays me a call once a week. His house is even snugger than mine, with goodsized rooms, and he wears such a lovely black velvet coat. If only you could get him for a husband, you'd be comfortably off. But his sight's very bad. You must tell him all the nicest stories you know.«

Thumbelina took no notice of all this; she had no intention of marrying the neighbour, for he was a mole. He came and called in his black velvet coat. He was so rich and clever, according to the field-mouse, and his home was twenty times the size of the field-mouse's. He was very learned, but he couldn't bear sunshine and pretty flowers; he said all sorts of nasty things about them, never having seen them. Thumbelina had to sing, and she sang both »Ladybird, ladybird, fly away home« and »Ring-a-ring-o'roses«; and the mole fell in love with her because of her pretty voice, but he didn't say anything – he was much too cautious a man for that.

He had lately dug a long passage for himself through the earth, leading from his house to theirs. Here the field-mouse and Thumbelina were invited to stroll whenever they cared to. But he told them not to be afraid of the dead bird lying in the passage; it was a whole bird with beak and feathers, that had evidently only just died as the winter began and was now buried in the very spot where he had made his underground passage.

The mole took a bit of touchwood in his mouth – for in the dark that shines just like fire - and went ahead to give them a light in the long dark passage. When they came to where the dead bird was lying, the mole tilted his broad snout up to the ceiling and thrust through the earth; making a large hole through which the light could penetrate. In the middle of the floor lay a dead swallow with its pretty wings folded close in to its sides, and head and legs tucked in beneath its feathers. The poor bird must have died of cold. Thumbelina felt so sorry for it; she was very fond of all the little birds that had sung and twittered for her so sweetly right through the summer. But the mole kicked at it with his stumpy legs, saying, »That won't chirp any more! How wretched it must be to be born a little bird! Thank goodness no child of mine ever will be. A bird like that has of course nothing but its twitter and is bound to starve to death when winter comes.«

»Just what I'd expect to hear from a sensible man like you,« said the field-mouse. »What has a bird to show for all its twittering, when winter comes? It must starve and freeze. But I suppose that's considered a great thing.«

Thumbelina didn't say a word, but when the other two turned their back on the bird, she stooped down and, smoothing aside the feathers that lay over its head, she kissed its closed eyes. »Who knows – this may be the very one,« she thought, »that used to sing so beautifully to me last summer.«

The mole now filled in the hole where the daylight shone through and saw the two ladies home. But that night Thumbelina simply couldn't sleep; so she got up, and plaited a fine big blanket of hay, which she carried down and spread all over the dead bird, and she took some soft cotton-wool she had found in the field-mouse's room and tucked this in at the sides, so that the bird might lie warm in the cold earth.

»Goodbye, you lovely little bird,« she said. »Goodbye, and thank you for your beautiful singing last summer, when all the trees were green and the sun was so bright and warm.« Then she laid her head up against the bird's breast – but at the same moment she got such a fright, for she heard a kind of thumping inside. It was the bird's heart. The bird wasn't dead; it had been lying numb and unconscious and now, as it grew warm again, it revived.

You see, in autumn the swallows all fly away to the warm countries, but if there's one that lags behind it gets so cold that it falls down dead. There it lies, where it fell, and the cold snow covers it over.

Thumbelina was all of a tremble from the fright she had, for the bird was of course an immense great creature beside her, who was no taller than your thumb. However, she took courage and tucked the cottonwool still more closely round the poor swallow and fetched a curled mint leaf that she had been using herself for a counterpane and spread this over the bird's head.

The following night she again stole down to the bird, and this time it had quite revived; but it was so feeble that it could only open its eyes for a short moment to look at Thumbelina, standing there with a bit of touchwood in her hand, for she had no other light.

»Thank you, my darling child,« said the sick swallow. »I'm lovely and warm now. I shall soon get back my strength and be able to fly again, out in the warm sunshine.«

»Ah, but it's so cold out of doors,« she said. »It's snowing and freezing. Stay in your warm bed; I'll look after you all right.«

Then she brought the swallow some water, in the petal of a flower, and the bird drank it and told her how it had torn one of its wings on a bramble and therefore couldn't fly as fast as the other swallows when they flew far, far away to the warm countries. At last it had fallen to the ground, but it couldn't remember anything after that and had no idea how it came to be where it was.

The swallow now remained here all through the winter, and Thumbelina took care of it and grew very fond of it. Neither the mole nor the field-mouse heard anything at all about this; they had no liking for the poor wretched swallow.

As soon as spring had arrived and the sun had begun to warm the earth, the swallow said goodbye to Thumbelina, who opened up the hole that the mole had made in the roof of the passage. The sun came shining in so pleasantly, and the swallow asked if she would like to come too; she could sit on its back, and they would fly far out into the green forest. But Thumbelina knew that it would grieve the old field-mouse, if she left her like that.

»No, I can't,« said Thumbelina. »Goodbye goodbye, you dear kind girl,« said the swallow, as it flew into the open sunshine. Thumbelina gazed after it with tears in her eyes, for she was so fond of the poor swallow.

»Tweet-tweet!« sang the bird and flew off into the woods...

Thumbelina felt so sad. She was never allowed to go out into the warm sunshine. The corn that had been sown in the field above the field-mouse's home was certainly very tall; so that it was like a dense wood for the poor little girl, who after all was only an inch high.

»You will have to start making your wedding trousseau this summer,« the field-mouse told her, because by now their neighbour, the tiresome tedious mole in the black velvet coat, had proposed to her. »You'll need to have both woollens and linen – something for every occasion – when you're married to the mole.«

So Thumbelina had to spin from a distaff, and the field-mouse engaged four spiders to spin and weave day and night. Every evening there was a visit from the mole, who always kept on about how, when summer was over, the sun wasn't nearly so warm, whereas now it scorched the earth till it was as hard as a stone. Yes, and when the summer had ended there was to be his wedding with Thumbelina. But she wasn't at all pleased, for she found the mole such a terrible bore. Every morning, as the sun rose, and every evening as it set, she stole out to the door, and when the wind parted the ears of corn so that she could see the blue sky, she thought how lovely and bright it was out there and did so wish she could catch sight of the dear swallow once more; but the bird never came again and had evidently flown far off into the beautiful green forest.

Now it was autumn, and Thumbelina had the whole of her trousseau ready.

»Your wedding will be in four weeks' time,« the field-mouse told her. But Thumbelina wept and said she wouldn't marry the tedious mole.

»Hoity-toity!« said the field-mouse. »Don't you be so pig-headed, or I'll bite you with my white teeth. Why, he's a splendid husband for you. The Queen herself hasn't anything like his black velvet coat. His kitchen and cellar are both of the best. You ought to thank Heaven he's yours.«

The wedding-day arrived. The mole was already there to fetch Thumbelina. She would have to live with him deep down under the earth and never come out into the warm sunshine, for he didn't care for that. The poor child was very sad at having to say goodbye to the beautiful sun, which she had at least been allowed to look at from the doorway when she was living with the field-mouse.

»Goodbye, bright sun!« she said and, stretching out her arms to it, she also took a few steps out from the field-mouse's dwelling; for the harvest was in, and nothing was left but the dry stubble. »Goodbye, goodbye,« she said, throwing her tiny arms round a little red flower standing near. »Remember me to the dear swallow, if you happen to see it.«

»Tweet-tweet!« she heard suddenly over her head. She looked up, and there was the swallow just passing. How delighted it was to see Thumbelina! She told the bird how she disliked having to marry the ugly mole and to live deep down under the earth where the sun never shone. She couldn't help crying at the thought.

»The cold winter will soon be here,« said the swallow. »I'm going far away to the warm countries. Will you come with me? You can sit on my back. Just tie yourself on with your sash, and away we'll fly from the ugly mole and his dingy house, far away across the mountains, to the warm countries, where the sun shines more brightly than it does here and there's always summer with its lovely flowers. Dear little Thumbelina, do come with me – you who saved my life when I lay frozen stiff in that dismal cellar.«

»Yes, I'll come with you,« said Thumbelina. She climbed on to the bird's back, setting her feet on its outstretched wings and tying her sash to one of the strongest feathers. Then the swallow flew high up into the air, over lake and forest, high up over the great mountains of eternal snow. Thumbelina shivered in the cold air, but then she snuggled in under the bird's warm feathers, merely poking out her little head to look at all the loveliness stretched out beneath her.

And at last they reached the warm countries. The sun was shining there much more brightly than with us, and the sky looked twice as far off. On walls and slopes grew the finest black and white grapes, in the woods hung lemons and oranges; the air smelt sweetly of myrtle and curled mint, and the most delightful children darted about on the roads playing with large gay-coloured butterflies. But the swallow kept flying on and on, and the country became more and more beautiful, till at last they came upon an ancient palace of glittering white marble standing among vivid green trees beside a blue lake. Vines went curling up round the tall pillars, and right at the top were a number of swallow's nests. One of these was the home of the swallow that had brought Thumbelina on its back.

»Here's my house,« cried the swallow.

»But you see those beautiful flowers growing down here? You shall now choose one of them yourself, and then I'll put you on it, and you can make yourself as cosy as you like.«

»That will be lovely,« she said, clapping her little hands.

A large white marble column was lying there on the ground just as it had fallen and broken into three pieces, but in among these were growing the most beautiful white flowers. The swallow flew down with Thumbelina and placed her on one of the broad petals – but what a surprise she got! There in the middle of the flower sat a little man as white and transparent as if he had been made of glass. He wore the neatest little gold crown on his head and the most exquisite wings on his shoulders; he himself was no bigger than Thumbelina. He was the guardian spirit of the flower. Each flower had just such a little man or woman living in it, but this one was King of them all.

»Goodness, how handsome he is!« whispered Thumbelina to the swallow. The little monarch was very frightened of the swallow, which of course seemed a gigantic bird beside one so small and delicate as himself; but when he caught sight of Thumbelina he was enchanted, for she was much the prettiest little lady he had ever seen. So he took the gold crown off his head and placed it on hers. At the same time he asked her what her name was and whether she would be his wife; if so, she would become Queen of all the flowers. Well, he would be a proper husband for her, quite different from the son of the old toad and from the mole with the black velvet coat. So she said yes to the handsome King, and from every flower there appeared a lady or a gentleman that was the most dapper little creature imaginable. Each one brought a present for Thumbelina, but the best of them all was a pair of beautiful wings from a large white fly. These were fastened to her back, so that she too could flit from flower to flower. There was such rejoicing, and the swallow sat up above in its nest and sang for them as well as it could, but the poor bird was really too sad at heart, for it was very fond of Thumbelina and would have liked never to be parted from her.

»You shan't be called Thumbelina,« said the guardian spirit of the flower to her. »It's an ugly name, and you are so pretty. We will call you Maia.«

»Goodbye, goodbye,« said the swallow and flew away again from the warm countries, far away back to Denmark. There it had a little nest above the window where the man lives who can tell fairy tales, and there it was that the swallow sang »Tweet-tweet!« to him... And that's where the whole story comes from.

The Little Mermaid

Far out at sea the water's as blue as the petals of the loveliest cornflower, and as clear as the purest glass; but it's very deep, deeper than any anchor can reach. Many church steeples would have to be piled up one above the other to reach from the bottom of the sea to the surface. Right down there live the sea people.

Now you mustn't for a moment suppose that it's a bare white sandy bottom. Oh, no. The most wonderful trees and plants are growing down there, with stalks and leaves that bend so easily that they stir at the very slightest movement of the water, just as though they were alive. All the fishes, big ones and little ones, slip in and out of the branches just like birds in the air up here. Down in the deepest part of all is the sea King's palace. Its walls are made of coral, and the long pointed windows of the clearest amber; but the roof is made of cockle-shells that open and shut with the current. It's a pretty sight, for in each shell is a dazzling pearl; any single one of them would be a splendid ornament in a Queen's crown.

The sea King down there had been a widower for some years, but his old mother kept house for him. She was a clever woman, but proud of her noble birth; that's why she went about with twelve oysters on her tail, while the rest of the nobility had to put up with only six. But apart from that, she was deserving of special praise, because she was so fond of the little sea Princesses, her grandchildren. They were six pretty children, but the youngest was the loveliest of them all. Her skin was as clear and delicate as a rose-leaf, her eyes were as blue as the deepest lake, but like the others she had no feet; her body ended in a fish's tail.

All the long day they could play down there in the palace, in the great halls where living flowers grew out of the walls. The fishes would swim in to them, just as with us the swallows fly in when we open the windows; but the fishes swam right up to the little Princesses, fed out of their hands, and let themselves be patted.

Outside the palace was a large garden with trees of deep blue and fiery red; the fruit all shone like gold, and the flowers like a blazing fire with stalks and leaves that were never still. The soil itself was the finest sand, but blue like a sulphur flame. Over everything down there lay a strange blue gleam; you really might have thought you were standing high up in the air with nothing to see but sky above and below you, rather than that you were at the bottom of the sea. When there was a dead calm you caught a glimpse of the sun, which looked like a purple flower pouring out all light from its cup.

Each of the small Princesses had her own little plot in the garden, where she could dig and plant at will. One of them gave her flower-bed the shape of a whale, another thought it nicer for hers to look like a little mermaid; but the youngest made hers quite round like the sun, and would only have flowers that shone red like it. She was a curious child, silent and thoughtful; and when the other sisters decorated their gardens with the most wonderful things they had got from sunken ships, she would have nothing but the rose-red flowers that were like the sun high above, and a beautiful marble statue. It was the statue of a handsome boy, hewn from the clear white stone and come down to the bottom of the sea from a wreck. Beside the statue she planted a rose-red weeping willow, which grew splendidly and let its fresh foliage droop over the statue right down to the blue sandy bottom. Here the shadow took on a violet tinge and, like the branches, was never still; roots and treetop looked as though they were playing at kissing each other.

Nothing pleased her more than to hear about the world of humans up above the sea. The old grandmother had to tell her all she knew about ships and towns, people and animals. One thing especially surprised her with its beauty, and this was that the flowers had a smell – at the bottom of the sea they hadn't any – and also that the woods were green and the fishes you saw in among the branches could sing as clearly and prettily as possible. It was the little birds that the grandmother called fishes; otherwise, never having seen a bird, the small sea Princesses would never have understood her.

»As soon as you are fifteen,« the grandmother told them, »you shall be allowed to rise to the surface, and to sit in the moonlight on the rocks and watch the great ships sailing past; you shall see woods and towns.« That coming year one of the sisters was to have her fifteenth birthday, but the rest of them – well, they were each one year younger than the other; so the youngest of them had a whole five years to wait before she could rise up from the bottom and see how things are with us. But each promised to

tell the others what she had seen and found most interesting on the first day; for their grandmother didn't really tell them enough – there were so many things they were longing to hear about.

None of them was so full of longing as the youngest: the very one who had most time to wait and was so silent and thoughtful. Many a night she stood at the open window and gazed up through the dark-blue water, where the fishes frisked their tails and fins. She could see the moon and the stars, though it's true their light was rather pale; and yet through the water they looked much larger than they do to us, and if ever a kind of black cloud went gliding along below them, she knew it was either a whale swimming above her or else a vessel with many passengers; these certainly never imagined that a lovely little mermaid was standing beneath and stretching up her white hands towards the keel of their ship.

By now the eldest Princess was fifteen and allowed to go up to the surface.

When she came back, she had a hundred things to tell; but the loveliest, she said, was to lie in the moonlight on a sandbank in a calm sea and there, close in to the shore, to look at the big town where the lights were twinkling like a hundred stars; to listen to the sound of music and the noise and clatter of carts and people; to see all the towers and spires on the churches and hear the bells ringing. And just because she couldn't get there, it was this above everything that she longed for.

Oh, how the youngest sister drank it all in! And, when later in the evening she stood at the open window and gazed up through the dark-blue water, she thought of the big town with all its noise and clatter, and then she seemed to catch the sound of the churchbells ringing down to her.

The following year, the second sister was allowed to go up through the water and swim wherever she liked. She came to the surface just as the sun was setting, and that was the sight she found most beautiful. The whole sky had looked like gold, she said, and the clouds – well, she just couldn't describe how beautiful they were as they sailed, all crimson and violet, over her head. And yet, much faster than they, a flock of wild swans flew like a long white veil across the water where the sun was setting. She swam off in that direction, but the sun sank, and its rosy light was swallowed up by sea and cloud.

The year after that, the third sister went up. She was the boldest of them all, and she swam up a wide river that flowed into the sea. She saw delightful green slopes with grape-vines; manors and farms peeped out among magnificent woods; she heard all the birds singing; and the sun was so hot that she often had to dive under the water to cool her burning face. In a small cove she came upon a swarm of little human children splashing about quite naked in the water. She wanted to play with them, but they ran away terrified, and a little black animal came up; it was a dog. She had never seen a dog before. It barked at her so dreadfully that she got frightened and made for the open sea. But never could she forget the magnificent woods, the green slopes and the darling children, who could swim on the water although they had no fishes' tails.

The fourth sister was not so bold. She kept far out in the wild waste of ocean, and told them that was just what was so wonderful: you could see for miles and miles around you, and the sky hung above like a big glass bell. She had seen ships, but a long way off, looking like sea-gulls. The jolly dolphins had been turning somersaults, and enormous whales had spirted up water from their nostrils, so that they seemed to be surrounded by a hundred fountains.

And now it was the turn of the fifth sister. Her birthday happened to come in winter, and so she saw things that the others hadn't seen the first time. The sea appeared quite green, and great icebergs were floating about; they looked like pearls, she said, and yet were much larger than the church-towers put up by human beings. They were to be seen in the most fantastic shapes, and they glittered like diamonds. She had sat down on one of the biggest, and all the ships gave it a wide berth as they sailed in terror past where she sat with her long hair streaming in the wind. But late in the evening the sky became overcast with clouds; it lightened and thundered, as the dark waves lifted the great blocks of ice right up, so that they flashed in the fierce red lightning. All the ships took in sail, and amidst the general horror and alarm, she sat calmly on her floating iceberg and watched the blue lightning zigzag into the glittering sea.

The first time one of the sisters went up to the surface, she would always be delighted to see so much that was new and beautiful; but afterwards, when they were older and could go up as often as they liked, it no longer interested them; they longed to be back again, and when a month had passed they said that, after all, it was nicest down below – it was such a comfort to be home.

Often of an evening the five sisters used to link arms and float up together out of the water. They had lovely voices, more beautiful than any human voice; and when a gale sprang up threatening shipwreck, they would swim in front of the ships and sing tempting songs of how delightful it was at the bottom of the sea. And they told the sailors not to be afraid of coming down there, but the sailors couldn't make out the words of their song; they thought it was the noise of the gale, nor did they ever see any of the delights the mermaids promised, because when the ship sank the crew were drowned, and only as dead men did they come to the palace of the sea King.

When of an evening the sisters floated up through the sea like this, arm in arm, their little sister stayed back all alone gazing after them. She would have cried, only a mermaid hasn't any tears, and so she suffers all the more.

»Oh, if only I were fifteen!« she said. »I'm sure I shall love that world up there and the people who live in it.«

And then at last she was fifteen.

»There, now you'll soon be off our hands,« said her grandmother, the old Dowager Queen. »Come now, let me dress you up like your sisters;« and she put a wreath of white lilies on her hair, but every petal of the flowers was half a pearl. And the old lady made eight big oysters nip tight on to the Princess's tail to show her high rank.

»Oo! that hurts,« said the little mermaid.

»Yes,« said the grandmother, »one can't have beauty for nothing.«

How she would have liked to shake off all this finery and put away the heavy wreath! The red flowers in her garden suited her much better, but she didn't dare make any change. »Goodbye,« she said, and went up through the water as light and clear as a bubble.

The sun had just set, as she put her head up out of the sea, but the clouds had still a gleam of rose and gold; and up in the pale pink sky the evening star shone clear and beautiful. The air was soft and fresh, and the sea dead calm. A large three-masted ship was lying there, with only one sail hoisted because not a breath of wind was stirring, and sailors were lolling about in the rigging and on the yards. There was music and singing, and as it grew dark hundreds of lanterns were lit that, with their many different colours, looked as if the flags of all nations were flying in the breeze.

The little mermaid swam right up to the porthole of the cabin and, every time she rose with the swell of the wave, she could see through the clear glass a crowd of splendidly dressed people; but the handsomest of them all was a young Prince with large dark eyes. He couldn't have been much more than sixteen; it was his birthday, and that's why there was all this set-out. As the young Prince came out on to the deck where sailors were dancing, over a hundred rockets swished up into the sky – and broke into a glitter like broad daylight. That frightened the little mermaid, and she dived down under the water; but she quickly popped up her head again, and look! it was just as if all the stars in heaven were falling down on her. Never had she seen such fireworks. Great suns went spinning around, gorgeous firefishes swerving into the blue air, and all this glitter was mirrored in the clear still water. On board the ship herself it was so light that you could make out every little rope, let alone the passengers. Oh, how handsome the young Prince was; he shook hands with the sailors, he laughed and smiled, while the music went floating out into the loveliness of the night.

It grew late, but the little mermaid couldn't take her eyes off the ship and the beautiful Prince. The coloured lanterns were put out, the rockets no longer climbed into the sky, and the cannon were heard no more; but deep down in the sea there was a mumbling and a rumbling. Meanwhile the mermaid stayed on the water, rocking up and down so that she could look into the cabin. But the ship now gathered speed; one after another her sails were spread. The waves increased, heavy clouds blew up, and lightning flashed in the distance. Yes, they were in for a terrible storm; so the sailors took in their sails, as the great ship rocked and scudded through the raging sea. The waves rose higher and higher like huge black mountains, threatening to bring down the mast, but the ship dived like a swan into the trough of the waves and then rode up again on their towering crests. The little mermaid thought, why, it must be fun for a ship to sail like that – but the crew didn't. The vessel creaked and cracked, the stout planks crumpled up under the heavy pounding of the sea against the ship, the mast snapped in the middle like a stick, and then the ship gave a lurch to one side as the water came rushing into the hold. At last the little mermaid realized that they were in danger; she herself had to look out for the beams and bits of wreckage that were drifting on the water. One moment it was so pitch dark that she couldn't see a thing, but then when the lightning came it was so bright that she could make out everyone on board. It was now a case of each man for himself. The young Prince was the one she was looking for and, as the ship broke up, she saw him disappear into the depths of the sea. Just for one moment she felt quite pleased, for now he would come down to her; but then she remembered that humans can't live under the water and that only as a dead man could he come down to her father's palace. No, no, he mustn't die. So she swam in among the drifting beams and planks, with no thought for the danger of being crushed by them; she dived deep down and came right up again among the waves, and at last she found the young Prince. He could hardly swim any longer in the heavy sea; his arms and legs were beginning to tire, the fine eyes were closed, he would certainly have drowned if the little mermaid had not come. She held his head above water and then let the waves carry her along with him.

By morning the gale had quite gone; not the smallest trace of the ship was to be seen. The sun rose red and glowing out of the water and seemed to bring life to the Prince's cheeks, but his eyes were still shut. The mermaid kissed his fine high forehead and smoothed back his dripping hair. He was like the marble statue down in her little garden; she kissed him again and wished that he might live.

Presently she saw the mainland in front of her, high blue mountains with the white snow glittering on their peaks like nestling swans. Down by the shore were lovely green woods and, in front of them, a church or a convent – she wasn't sure which, but anyhow a building. Lemon and orange trees were growing in the garden, and tall palm trees in front of the gate. At this point the sea formed a little inlet, where the water was quite smooth but very deep close in to the rock where the fine white sand had silted up. She swam here with the handsome Prince and laid him on the sand with his head carefully pillowed in the warm sunshine.

Now there was a sound of bells from the large white building, and a number of young girls came through the garden. So the little mermaid swam further out behind some large boulders that were sticking out of the water and covered her hair and breast with seafoam, so that her face wouldn't show; and then she watched to see who would come to the help of the unfortunate Prince.

It wasn't long before a young girl came along. She seemed quite frightened, but only for a moment; then she fetched several others, and the mermaid saw the Prince come round and smile at those about him; but no smile came out to her, for of course he didn't know she had rescued him. She felt so sad that, when he was taken away into the large building, she dived down sorrowfully into the sea and went back to her father's palace.

Silent and thoughtful as she had always been, she now became much more so. Her sisters asked her what she had seen on her first visit to the surface, but she wouldn't say.

Many a morning and many an evening she rose up to where she had left the Prince. She saw the fruit in the garden ripen and be gathered, she saw the snow melt on the peaks, but she never saw the Prince, and so she always turned back more despondent than ever. Her one comfort was to sit in the little garden with her arms round the beautiful marble statue which was so like the Prince. She never looked after her flowers, and they grew into a sort of wilderness, out over the paths, and braided their long stalks and leaves on to the branches of the trees, until the light was quite shut out.

At last she could keep it to herself no longer, but told one of her sisters; and immediately all the rest got to know, but nobody else – except a few other mermaids who didn't breathe a word to any but their nearest friends. One of these was able to say who the Prince was; she, too, had seen the party that was held on board the ship, and knew where he came from and whereabouts his kingdom was.

»Come on, little sister!« said the other Princesses. And with arms round each other's shoulders they rose in one line out of the sea, just in front of where the Prince's castle stood. It was built in a glistening stone of pale yellow with great flights of marble steps; one of these led straight into the sea. Splendid gilt domes curved above the roof, and between the pillars that went right round the building were lifelike sculptures in marble. Through the clear glass in the tall windows you could see into the most magnificent rooms; these were hung with sumptuous silk curtains and tapestries and their walls were covered with large paintings that were a delight to the eye. In the middle of the biggest room was a huge splashing fountain; its spray was flung high up to the glass dome in the ceiling, through which the sun shone down on to the water and the beautiful plants growing in the great pool.

Now she knew where he lived, and many an evening and many a night she would come to the surface at that spot. She swam much closer to the shore than any of the others had ever dared. She even went up the narrow creek under the fine marble balcony that threw its long shadow across the water. Here she would sit and gaze at the young Prince, who imagined he was quite alone in the clear moonlight.

Often in the evening she saw him go out to the strains of music in his splendid vessel that was dressed with flags. She peeped out from among the green rushes and, when the wind caught her long silvery veil and someone saw it, they fancied it was a swan spreading its wings.

On many nights, when the fishermen were at sea with their torches, she heard them speaking so well of the young Prince, and that made her glad she had saved his life when he drifted about half-dead on the waves; and she thought of how closely his head had rested on her bosom and how lovingly she had kissed him. But he knew nothing whatsoever about that, never even dreamed she existed.

Fonder and fonder she became of human beings, more and more she longed for their company. Their world seemed to her to be so much larger than her own. You see, they could fly across the ocean in ships, climb the tall mountains high above the clouds; and the lands they owned stretched with woods and meadows further than her eyes could see. There was so much she would have liked to know, but her sisters couldn't answer all her questions, and so she asked the old grandmother, for she knew all about the upper world – as she so aptly called the countries above the sea.

»If people don't drown,« asked the little mermaid, »can they go on living for ever? Don't they die, as we do down here in the sea?«

»Yes, yes,« said the old lady, »They, too, have to die; their lifetime is even shorter than ours. We can live for three hundred years, but when our life here comes to an end we merely turn into foam on the water; we haven't even a grave down here among those we love. We've no immortal soul; we shall never have another life. We're like the green rush – once it's been cut it can't grow green again. But human beings have a soul which lives for ever; still lives after the body is turned to dust. The soul goes climbing up through the clear air, up till it reaches the shining stars. Just as we rise up out of the sea and look at the countries of human beings, so they rise up to beautiful unknown regions – ones we shall never see.«

»Why haven't we got an immortal soul?« the little mermaid asked sadly. »I would give the whole three hundred years I have to live, to become for one day a human being and then share in that heavenly world.«

»You mustn't go worrying about that,« said the grandmother. »We're much happier and better off here than the people who live up there.«

»So then I'm doomed to die and float like foam on the sea, never to hear the music of the waves or see the lovely flowers and the red sun. Isn't there anything at all I can do to win an immortal soul?«

»No,« said the old lady. »Only if a human being loved you so much that you were more to him than father and mother – if he clung to you with all his heart and soul, and let the priest put his right hand in yours as a promise to be faithful and true here and in all eternity – then his soul would flow over into your body and you, too, would get a share in human happiness. He would give you a soul and yet keep his own. But that can never happen. The very thing that's so beautiful here in the sea, your fish's tail, seems ugly to people on the earth; they know so little about it that they have to have two clumsy supports called legs, in order to look nice.«

That made the little mermaid sigh and look sadly at her fish's tail.

»We must be content,« said the old lady. »Let's dance and be gay for the three hundred years we have to live – that's a good time, isn't it? – then one can have one's fill of sleep in the grave all the more pleasantly afterwards. To-night we're having a Court ball.«

That was something more magnificent than we ever see on the earth. In the great ballroom walls and ceiling were made of thick but quite clear glass. Several hundred enormous shells, rose-red and grass-green, were ranged on either side, each with a blue-burning flame which lit up the

54

whole room and, shining out through the walls, lit up the sea outside as well. Countless fishes, big and small, could be seen swimming towards the glass walls; the scales on some of them shone purple-red, and on others like silver and gold ... Through the middle of the ballroom flowed a wide running stream, on which mermen and mermaids danced to their own beautiful singing. No human beings have voices so lovely. The little mermaid sang the most sweetly of them all, and they clapped their hands for her, and for a moment there was joy in her heart, for she knew that she had the most beautiful voice on earth or sea. But then her thoughts soon returned to the world above her; she couldn't forget the handsome Prince and her sorrow at not possessing, like him, an immortal soul. So she crept out of her father's palace and, while all in there was song and merriment, she sat grieving in her little garden. Suddenly she caught the sound of a horn echoing down through the water, and she thought, »Ah, there he is, sailing up above – he whom I love more than father or mother, he who is always in my thoughts and in whose hands I would gladly place the happiness of my life. I will dare anything to win him and an immortal soul. While my sisters are dancing there in my father's palace, I will go to the sea witch; I've always been dreadfully afraid of her, but perhaps she can help me and tell me what to do.«

So the little mermaid left her garden and set off for the place where the witch lived, on the far side of the roaring whirlpools. She had never been that way before. There were no flowers growing, no sea grass, nothing but the bare grey sandy bottom stretching right up to the whirlpools, where the water went swirling round like roaring mill-wheels and pulled everything it could clutch down with it to the depths. She had to pass through the middle of these battering eddies in order to get to the sea witch's domain; and here for a long stretch there was no other way than over hot bubbling mud – the witch called it her swamp. Her house lay behind it in the middle of an extraordinary wood. All the trees and bushes were polyps, half animals and half plants. They looked like hundred-headed snakes growing out of the earth; all the branches were long slimy arms with supple worm-like fingers, and joint by joint from the root up to the very tip they were continuously on the move. They wound themselves tight round everything they could clutch hold of in the sea, and they never let go. The little mermaid was terribly scared as she paused at the edge of the wood. Her heart was throbbing with fear; she nearly turned back. But then she remembered the Prince and the human soul, and that gave her courage. She wound her long flowing hair tightly round her head, so that the polyps shouldn't have that to clutch her by, she folded both her hands across her breast and darted off just as a fish darts through the water, in among the hideous polyps which reached out for her with their supple arms and fingers. She noticed how each of them had something they had caught, held fast by a hundred little arms like hoops of iron. White skeletons of folk who had been lost at sea and had sunk to the bottom looked out from the arms of the polyps. Ship's rudders and chests were gripped tight, skeletons of land animals, and – most horrible of all – a small mermaid whom they had caught and throttled.

Now she came to a large slimy open space in the wood where big fat water-snakes were frisking about and showing their hideous whitish-yellow bellies. In the middle was a house built of the bones of human folk who had been wrecked. There sat the sea witch letting a toad feed out of her mouth, just as we might let a little canary come and peck sugar. She called the horrible fat water-snakes her little chicks and allowed them to sprawl about her great spongy bosom.

»I know well enough what you're after,« said the sea witch. »How stupid of you! Still, you shall have your way, and it'll bring you into misfortune, my lovely Princess. You want to get rid of your fish's tail and in its place have a couple of stumps to walk on like a human being, so that the young Prince can fall in love with you and you can win him and an immortal soul« – and with that the witch gave such a loud repulsive laugh that the toad and the snakes fell to the ground and remained sprawling there. »You've just come at the right time,« said the witch. »Tomorrow, once the sun's up, I couldn't help you for another year. I shall make you a drink, and before sunrise you must swim to land, sit down on the shore and drink it up. Then your tail will divide in two and shrink into what humans call 'pretty legs'. But it'll hurt; it'll be like a sharp sword going through you. Everyone who sees you will say you are the loveliest human child they have ever seen. You will keep your graceful movements – no dancer can glide so lightly – but every step you take will feel as if you were treading on a sharp knife, enough to make your feet bleed. Are you ready to bear all that? If you are, I'll help you.«

»Yes,« said the little mermaid, and her voice trembled; but she thought of her Prince and the prize of an immortal soul.

»Still, don't forget this,« said the witch: »once you've got human shape, you can never become a mermaid again. You can never go down through the water to your sisters and to your father's palace; and if you don't win the Prince's love, so that he forgets father and mother for you and always has you in his thoughts and lets the priest join your hands together to be man and wife, then you won't get an immortal soul. The first morning after the Prince marries someone else, your heart must break and you become foam on the water.«

»I'm ready,« said the little mermaid, pale as death.

»Then there's me to be paid,« said the witch, »and you're not getting my help for nothing. You have the loveliest voice of all down here at the bottom of the sea. With that voice, no doubt, you think to enchant him; but that voice you shall hand over to me. I demand the best that you have for me to make a rich drink. You see, I have to give you my own blood, in order that the drink may be as sharp as a two-edged sword.«

»But if you take my voice,« said the little mermaid, »what shall I have left?«

»Your lovely form,« said the witch, »your graceful movements, and your speaking eyes. With those you can so easily enchant a human heart... Well, where's your spunk? Put out your little tongue and let me cut it off in payment; then you shall be given the potent mixture.«

»Go on, then,« said the little mermaid, and the witch put the kettle on for brewing the magic drink. »Cleanliness before everything,« she said, as she scoured out the kettle with a bundle of snakes she had knotted together. Next, she scratched her breast and let her black blood drip down into the kettle; the steam took on the weirdest shapes, terrifying to look at. The witch kept popping fresh things into the kettle, and when it boiled up properly it sounded like a crocodile in tears. At last the brew was ready; it looked like the clearest water.

»There you are!« said the witch and cut off the little mermaid's tongue; she was now dumb and could neither sing nor speak.

»If the polyps should catch hold of you, as you go back through the wood,« said the witch, »throw but a single drop of this drink on them, and their arms and fingers will burst into a thousand pieces.« But the little mermaid had no need to do that. The polyps shrank from her in terror when they saw the dazzling drink that shone in her hand like a glittering star. So she quickly came through the wood, the swamp and the roaring whirlpools.

She could see her father's palace; the lights were out in the great ballroom. They were all certain to be asleep in there by this time; but she didn't anyhow dare to look for them, now that she was dumb and was going to leave them for ever. She felt as if her heart must break for grief. She stole into the garden, picked one flower from each of her sisters' flower-beds, blew a thousand finger kisses towards the palace, and rose then through the dark-blue sea.

The sun was not yet up, as she sighted the Prince's castle and climbed the magnificent marble steps. The moon was shining wonderfully clear. The little mermaid drank the sharp burning potion, and it was as if a two-edged sword pierced through her delicate body – she fainted and lay as though dead. Then the sun, streaming over the sea, woke her up, and she felt a sharp pain. But there in front of her stood the handsome young Prince. He stared at her with his coal-black eyes, so that she cast down her own – and saw that her fish's tail had gone and she had the sweetest little white legs that any young girl could wish for; but she was quite naked and so she wrapped herself in her long flowing hair. The Prince asked who she was and how she had come there, and she could only look back at him so gently and yet so sadly out of her deep-blue eyes; for of course she couldn't speak. Then he took her by the hand and led her into the castle. Every step she took, as the witch had foretold, was as though she were treading on sharp knives and pricking gimlets; but she gladly put

up with that. By the side of the Prince she went along as lightly as a
bubble; and he and all of them marvelled at the charm of her graceful
movements.

Costly dresses were given her of silk and muslin; she was the most
beautiful in all the castle. But she was dumb; she could neither sing nor
speak. Lovely slave-girls in gold and silk came out and danced before the
Prince and his royal parents; one of them sang more beautifully than all
the rest, and the Prince clapped his hands and smiled at her. This sad-
dened the little mermaid, for she knew that she herself had sung far more
beautifully. And she thought, »Oh, if only he knew that I gave my voice
away for ever, in order to be with him!«

Next, the slave-girls danced a graceful gliding dance to the most delightful music; and then the little mermaid raised her pretty white arms,

lingered on the tips of her toes and then glided across the floor, dancing as no one had danced before. She looked more and more lovely with every movement, and her eyes spoke more deeply to the heart than the slave-girls' singing.

Everyone was enchanted, and especially the Prince, who called her his little foundling. Still she went on dancing, although every time her foot touched the ground it felt as though she was treading on sharp knives. The Prince said that she must never leave him, and she was allowed to sleep on a velvet cushion outside his door.

He had boys' clothes made for her, so that she could go riding with him on horseback. They rode through the sweet-smelling woods, where the green boughs grazed her shoulders and the little birds sang among the cool foliage. She went climbing with the Prince up high mountains and, although her delicate feet bled so that others could see it, she only laughed and went on and on with him, until they could see the clouds sailing below them like a flock of birds migrating to other lands.

Back at the Prince's castle, when at night the others were asleep, she would go out on to the broad marble steps and cool her tingling feet in the cold sea-water; and then she would think of those down there in the depths of the sea.

One night her sisters rose up arm in arm singing so mournfully as they swam on the water. She made signs to them, and they recognized her and told her how unhappy she had made them all. After that, they used to visit her every night; and once, in the far distance, she saw her old grand-mother who hadn't been above the water for many years, and also the sea King wearing his crown. They both stretched out their hands towards her, but they didn't venture in so near to the shore as the five sisters.

Day by day she became dearer to the Prince. He loved her as one loves a dear good child, but he didn't dream of making her his Queen; and yet she had to become his wife, or else she would never win an immortal soul, but on his wedding morning would be turned to foam on the sea.

»Do you like me best of all?« the little mermaid's eyes seemed to say, when he took her in his arms and kissed her lovely brow.

»Yes,« said the prince, »You're the dearest of all, because you have the kindest heart. You are the most devoted to me, and you remind me of a young girl I once saw but shall probably never see again. I was sailing in a ship that was wrecked; the waves drove me ashore near a sacred temple where a number of young girls were serving. The youngest, who found me on the beach and saved my life – I only saw her twice. She was the only one I could ever love in this world, but you are so like her that you almost take the place of her image in my heart. She belongs to the holy temple, so that fortune has been kind in sending you to me. We will never part.«

»Ah, little does he know that it was I who saved his life,« thought the mermaid; »that I carried him across the sea to the temple in the wood;

that I waited in the foam and watched if anyone would come. I saw the pretty girl he loves better than me« – and the mermaid sighed deeply, for she didn't know how to cry. »The girl belongs to the sacred temple, he says; she'll never come out into the world, and they'll never meet again. I am with him. I see him every day. I will take care of him, love him, give up my life to him.«

But now the Prince was getting married they said – married to the pretty daughter of the neighbouring King, and that was why he was fitting out such a splendid ship. The Prince was going off to take a look at his neighbour's kingdom – that was how they put it, meaning that it was really to take a look at his neighbour's daughter. A large suite was to go with him, but the little mermaid shook her head and laughed. She knew the Prince's thoughts far better than all the others. »I shall have to go,« he said to her. »I shall have to visit the pretty Princess, as my parents are so insistent. But force me to bring her back here as my wife, that they will never do. I can't love her. She's not like the beautiful girl in the temple, as you are. If I ever had to find a bride, I would rather have you, my dear mute foundling with the speaking eyes,« and he kissed her red mouth, played with her long hair and laid his head against her heart, so that it dreamed of human happiness and an immortal soul.

»You've no fear of the sea, have you, my dumb child?« he asked, as they stood on board the splendid ship that was to take him to the neighbouring kingdom. And he told her of stormy gales and dead calms, of strange fishes at the bottom of the ocean, and all that the diver had seen there; and she smiled at his tales, for she knew better than anyone else about the bottom of the sea.

At night, when there was an unclouded moon and all were asleep but the helmsman at his wheel, she sat by the ship's rail and stared down through the clear water; and she seemed to see her father's palace, with her old grandmother standing on the top of it in her silver crown and gazing up through the swift current at the keel of the vessel. Then her sisters came up on to the water and looked at her with eyes full of sorrow, wringing their white hands. She beckoned to them and smiled and would have liked to tell them that all was going well and happily with her; but the cabin-boy came up at that moment, and the sisters dived down, so that the boy felt satisfied that the white something he had seen was foam on the water.

Next morning the ship sailed into the harbour of the neighbouring King's magnificent capital. The church-bells all rang out; and trumpets were blown from the tall battlements, while the soldiers saluted with gleaming bayonets and flying colours. Every day there was a fête. Balls and parties were given one after another, but nothing had yet been seen of the Princess; it was said that she was being educated abroad in a sacred temple, where she had lessons in all the royal virtues. At last she arrived.

The little mermaid was eager for a glimpse of her beauty, and she had to admit that she had never seen anyone more charming to look at. Her complexion was so clear and delicate, and behind the long dark lashes smiled a pair of trusting deep-blue eyes.

»It's you!« cried the Prince. »You who rescued me, when I was lying half-dead on the shore.« And he clasped his blushing bride in his arms. »Oh, I'm too, too happy,« he said to the little mermaid. »My dearest wish – more than I ever dared to hope for – has been granted me. My happiness will give you pleasure, because you're fonder of me than any of the others.« Then the little mermaid kissed his hand, and already she felt as if her heart was breaking. The morrow of his wedding would mean death to her and change her to foam on the sea.

All the church-bells were ringing, as the heralds rode round the streets to proclaim the betrothal. On every altar sweet oil was burning in rich lamps of silver. The priests swung their censers, and bride and bridegroom joined hands and received the blessing of the bishop. Dressed in silk and gold, the little mermaid stood holding the bride's train; but her ears never heard the festive music, her eyes never saw the holy rites; she was thinking of her last night on earth, of all she had lost in this world.

That same evening, bride and bridegroom went on board the ship; the cannon thundered, the flags were all flying, and amidships they had put up a royal tent of gold and purple, strewn with luxurious cushions; here the wedded couple were to sleep that calm cool night.

The sails filled with the breeze and the ship glided lightly and smoothly over the clear water.

As darkness fell, coloured lanterns were lit, and the crew danced merrily on the deck. The little mermaid could not help thinking of the first time she came up out of the sea and gazed on just such a scene of joy and splendour. And now she joined in the dance, swerving and swooping as lightly as a swallow that avoids pursuit; and shouts of admiration greeted her on every side. Never had she danced so brilliantly. It was as if sharp knives were wounding her delicate feet, but she never felt it; more painful was the wound in her heart. She knew that this was the last evening she would see the Prince for whom she had turned her back on kindred and home, given up her beautiful voice, and every day suffered hours of agony without his suspecting a thing. This was the last night she would breathe the same air as he, gaze on the deep sea and the star-blue sky. An endless night, without thoughts, without dreams, awaited her who had no soul and could never win one... All was joy and merriment on board until long past midnight. She laughed and danced with the thought of death in her heart. The Prince kissed his lovely bride, and she toyed with his dark hair, and arm in arm they went to rest in the magnificent tent.

The ship was now hushed and still; only the helmsman was there at his wheel. And the little mermaid leaned with her white arms on the rail and looked eastward for a sign of the pink dawn. The first ray of the sun, she knew, would kill her. Suddenly she saw her sisters rising out of the sea.

61

They were pale, like her; no more was their beautiful long hair fluttering in the wind – it had been cut off.

»We have given it to the witch, so that she might help us to save you from dying when to-night is over. She has given us a knife – look, here it is – do you see how sharp it is? Before sunrise you must stab it into the Prince's heart. Then, when his warm blood splashes over your feet, they will grow together into a fish's tail, and you will become a mermaid once more; you will be able to come down to us in the water and live out your three hundred years before being changed into the dead salt foam of the sea. Make haste! Either he or you must die before the sun rises. Our old grandmother has been sorrowing till her white hair has fallen away, as ours fell before the witch's scissors. Kill the Prince and come back to us! But make haste – look at that red gleam in the sky. In a few minutes the sun will rise, and then you must die.« And with a strange deep sigh they sank beneath the waves.

The little mermaid drew aside the purple curtain of the tent, and she saw the lovely bride sleeping with her head on the Prince's breast. She stopped and kissed his handsome brow, looked at the sky where the pink dawn glowed brighter and brighter, looked at the sharp knife in her hand, and again fixed her eyes on the Prince, who murmured in his dreams the name of his bride – she alone was in his thoughts. The knife quivered in the mermaid's hand – but then she flung it far out into the waves; they glimmered red where it fell, and what looked like drops of blood came oozing out of the water. With a last glance at the Prince from eyes half-dimmed in death she hurled herself from the ship into the sea and felt her body dissolving into foam.

And now the sun came rising from the sea. Its rays fell gentle and warm on the death chilled foam, and the little mermaid had no feeling of death. She saw the bright sun and, hovering above her, hundreds of lovely creatures – she could see right through them, see the white sails of the ship and the pink clouds in the sky. And their voice was the voice of melody, yet so spiritual that no human ear could hear it, just a no earthly eye could see them. They had no wings, but their own lightness bore them up as they floated through the air. The little mermaid saw that she had a body like theirs, raising itself freer and freer from the foam.

»To whom am I coming?« she asked, and her voice sounded like that of the other beings, more spiritual than any earthly music can record.

»To the daughters of the air,« answered the others. »A mermaid has no immortal soul and can never have one unless she wins the love of a mortal. Eternity, for her, depends on a power outside her. Neither have the daughters of the air an everlasting soul, but by good deeds they can shape one for themselves. We shall fly to the hot countries, where the stifling air of pestilence means death to mankind; we shall bring them cool breezes. We shall scatter the fragrance of flowers through the air and send them comfort and healing. When for three hundred years we have striven to do the good we can, then we shall win an immortal soul and have a share in mankind's eternal happiness. You, poor little mermaid, have striven for that with all your heart; you have suffered and endured, and have raised yourself into the world of the spirits of the air. Now, by three hundred years of good deeds, you too can shape for yourself an immortal soul.«

And the little mermaid raised her crystal arms towards God's sun, and for the first time she knew the feeling of tears.

On board the ship there was bustle and life once more. She saw the Prince with his pretty bride looking about for her; sorrowfully they stared at the heaving foam, as if they knew she had thrown herself into the waves. Unseen, she kissed the forehead of the bride, gave a smile to the Prince, and then with the other children of the air she climbed to a rose-red cloud that was sailing to the sky.

»So we shall float for thee hundred years, till at last we come into the heavenly kingdom.«

»And we may reach it even sooner,« whispered one. »Unseen we float into human homes where there are children and, for every day we find a good child who makes father and mother happy and earns their love, God shortens our time of trial. The child never knows when we fly through the room and, if that makes us smile with joy, then a year is taken away from the three hundred. But if we see a child who is naughty or spiteful, then we have to weep tears of sorrow, and every tear adds one more day to our time of trial.«

The Emperor's New Clothes

many years ago there lived an Emperor who was so tremendously fond of fine new clothes that he spent all his money on being elegantly dressed. He took no interest in his army or the theatre or in driving through the country, unless it was to show off his new clothes. He had different clothes for every hour of the day and, just as you might say of a King that he was in the council-chamber, so it was always said of the Emperor: »He's in his wardrobe.«

There was plenty of fun going on in the city where the Emperor lived. Strangers were continually arriving, and one day there came two swindlers. They made out they were weavers and could weave the very finest stuffs imaginable. Not only were colours and design unusually attractive, but the clothes made from their material had the peculiarity of being invisible to anyone who wasn't fit for his post or who was hopelessly stupid.

»I say! They must be wonderful clothes,« thought the Emperor. »If I had some, I could find out which of my statesmen were unfit for their posts and also be able to tell the clever ones from the stupid. Yes, I must have some of that stuff woven for me at once.« And he paid down a large sum of money to the swindlers straight away, so as to enable them to start work.

And they did; they put up a couple of looms and pretended to be working, though there was absolutely nothing in the loom. They coolly demanded the most delicate silk and the finest gold thread, which they promptly stowed away in their own bags; and then they went on working far into the night at their empty looms.

»Well, now, I wonder how they are getting on with the work,« said the Emperor to himself. But there was one point that really made him feel rather anxious, namely, that a man who was stupid or quite unfit for his post would never be able to see what was woven. Not that he need have any fears for himself – he was quite confident about that – but all the same it might be better to send someone else first, to find out how things were going. Everyone in the city had heard of the mysterious power possessed by the material, and they were all eager to discover how incapable or stupid his neighbour was.

»I'll send my honest old Prime Minister to the weavers',« thought the Emperor. »He's the best one to see what the stuff looks like, for he has plenty of sense and nobody fills his post better than he does.«

So off went the honest old Premier to the workshop where the two swindlers sat busy at their empty looms. »Lor' bless my soul,« thought the Minister with eyes starting out of his head. »Why, I can't see anything!« But he was careful not to say so.

The two swindlers begged him to take a closer look – didn't he find the colours and design most attractive? They then pointed to the empty loom but, although the poor old Minister opened his eyes wider and wider, he couldn't see a thing; for there wasn't a thing to see. »Good Lord!« he thought, »Is it possible that I'm stupid? I never suspected that, and not a soul must hear of it. Can it be that I'm unfit for my post? No, it will never do for me to say that I can't see the material.«

»Well, what do you think of it?« asked the one who pretended to be weaving.

»Oh, it's charming! Quite exquisite!« said the old Minister, looking through his spectacles. »What a pattern and what colouring! I shall certainly tell the Emperor how pleased I am with it.«

»Ah, we're glad to hear that,« said the swindlers, and they then gave details of the colours and the peculiar design. The old Minister listened carefully, so as to be able to repeat all this when he came back to the Emperor – which he duly did.

The swindlers now demanded more money, more silk and more gold thread, for these would be required for weaving. They put it all into their own pockets – not a thread came into the loom – while they went on working the empty frames as before.

By and by, the Emperor sent another honest official to see how the weaving was getting on and whether the stuff wouldn't soon be ready. The same thing happened to him as to the Minister: he looked and looked but, as nothing was there but the empty looms, he couldn't see anything.

»There, isn't it a handsome piece!« said the swindlers, as they pointed out the beauty of the design which wasn't there at all.

»I know I'm not stupid,« thought the man, »so it must be my fine position I'm not fit for. Some people might think that rather funny, but I must take good care they don't get to hear of it.« And then he praised the material which he couldn't see and assured them of his delight in its charming shades and its beautiful design. »Yes, it's quite exquisite,« he said to the Emperor, when he got back.

The splendid material became the talk of the town. And now the Emperor himself said he must see it while it was still in the loom. Quite a throng of select people, including the two honest old officials who had been there already, went with him to where both the crafty swindlers were now weaving for all they were worth without the vestige of a thread.

»Look, isn't it magnificent!« said the two honest officials. »If Your Majesty will but glance - what a pattern, what colouring!« And they pointed to the empty loom, feeling certain that the others could see the material.

»What's this?« thought the Emperor. »I can't see anything - this is appalling! Am I stupid? Am I not fit to be Emperor? This is the most terrible thing that could happen to me... Oh, it's quite wonderful,« he said to them; »it has our most gracious approval.« And he gave a satisfied nod, as he looked at the empty loom; he wasn't going to say that he couldn't see anything. All the courtiers who had come with him looked and looked, but they made no more of it than the rest had done. Still, they all said just what the Emperor said - »Oh, it's quite wonderful!« - and they advised him to have some clothes made from this splendid new material and to wear them for the first time in the grand procession that was shortly taking place. »Magnificent!« »Delightful!« »Superb!« were the comments that ran from mouth to mouth; everyone was so intensely pleased with it. On each of the swindlers the Emperor bestowed a knight-hood, with a badge to wear in his button-hole, and the title of Imperial Weaver.

On the eve of the procession the swindlers sat up all night with some-thing like twenty lighted candles. People could see how busy they were finishing off the Emperor's new clothes. They pretended to take the stuff off the loom, they clipped away at the air with huge scissors, they worked at their needles without thread, and last they announced: »There! The Emperor's clothes are ready!«

Then the Emperor, with his most distinguished gentlemen-in-waiting, went in person to the weavers, who each put out his arm just as if he were holding something and said: »Here are the Breeches! Here is the Robe! Here is the Mantle!« And so on. »They are all as light as gossamer; you can hardly feel you have anything on - that's just the beauty of them.«

»Yes, indeed,« answered the gentlemen-in-waiting. But they couldn't see a thing, for there wasn't a thing to see.

»Now will Your Imperial Majesty be graciously pleased to take off your clothes?« said the swindlers. »Then we can fit you with the new ones, there in front of the big glass.«

So the Emperor took off the clothes he was wearing, and the swindlers pretended to hand him each of the new garments they were supposed to have made, and they took him at the waist as if they were fastening something on... it was the train, and the Emperor turned and twisted in front of the looking-glass.

»Goodness! How well they suit your Majesty! What a wonderful fit!« they all exclaimed. »What a cut! What colours! What sumptuous robes!«

The Master of Ceremonies came in with an announcement. »The canopy to be carried above Your Majesty in the procession is waiting outside.«

»All right, I'm ready,« said the Emperor. »Aren't they a nice fit!« And he turned round once more in front of the glass, for he really had to make them think he was gazing at his fine clothes.

The chamberlains who were to carry the train groped about on the floor as if they were picking the train up; and, as they walked, they held out their hands, not daring to let it be thought that they couldn't see anything.

There marched the Emperor in the procession under the beautiful canopy, and everybody in the streets and at the windows said: »Goodness! The Emperor's new clothes are the finest he has ever had. What a wonderful train! What a perfect fit!« No one would let it be thought that he couldn't see anything, because that would have meant he wasn't fit for his job, or that he was very stupid. Never had the Emperor's clothes been such a success.

»But he hasn't got anything on!« said a little child. »Goodness gracious, do you hear what the little innocent says?« cried the father; and the child's remark was whispered from one to the other.

»He hasn't got anything on! There's a little child saying he hasn't got anything on!«

»Well, but he hasn't got anything on!« the people all shouted at last. And the Emperor felt most uncomfortable, for it seemed to him that the people were right. But somehow he thought to himself: »I must go through with it now, procession and all.« And he drew himself up still more proudly, while his chamberlains walked after him carrying the train that wasn't there.

The Staunch Tin
Soldier

There were once twenty-five tin soldiers, all brothers, for they all came from one old tin spoon. »Shoulder arms! Eyes front!« – that's how they were, and they wore splendid red tunics with blue trousers. The very first thing they ever heard, when the lid was taken off the box in which they were lying, was - »tin soldiers!« It was a little boy who shouted this and clapped his hands. He had been given them for his birthday, and now he was putting them up on the table.

Each soldier was the image of the other, except for one who was a little bit different. He had only one leg, because he was the last to be made and there wasn't enough tin to go round. Still, there he stood, as firmly on his one leg as the others on their two; and, as it happened, he's the soldier this story is all about.

There were a lot of other toys on the table where the tin soldiers had been put up, but the one you noticed first was a beautiful paper castle; through its tiny windows you could see right into the rooms. In front of it were some small trees standing round a little mirror, which was sup-posed to represent a lake, with wax swans reflected in it as they swam. Everything was very pretty, and yet the prettiest of all was a little lady who was standing at the open door of the castle. She, too, was cut out of paper, but she was wearing a skirt of the clearest muslin and a narrow blue ribbon draped over her shoulder like a scarf, with a glittering spangle in the middle as big as the whole of her face. The little lady was holding out both her arms; you see, she was a dancer and, besides, she had kicked one of her legs so high in the air that the tin soldier couldn't make out where it was and imagined she only had one leg, like himself.

»That's the wife for me!« he thought to himself. »But she's so grand; she lives in a castle. I've only got a box, and there are twenty-five of us to that; it's no place for her. All the same, I must see if I can't get to know her.« Then he lay down at full length behind a snuff-box that was on the table. From here he could keep his eyes on the elegant little lady, who continued to stand on one leg without losing her balance.

Later in the evening, all the other tin soldiers went back into their box, and the people in the house went to bed. The toys now began to play games – visiting, fighting, dancing. The tin soldiers rattled in their box, because they wanted to join in, but they couldn't get the lid off. The nutcrackers turned somersaults, and the slate pencil had some fun on the slate. There was such a noise that the canary woke up and began to join in with some twittering in verse. The only two who didn't budge were the tin soldier and the little dancer. She stood perfectly upright on tiptoe with both arms stretched out, while he was just as staunch on his one leg; his eyes never left her for a moment.

Suddenly the clock struck twelve and – clack! flew the lid from the snuff-box, but do you suppose there was snuff in it? No, there was a little black goblin – it was a kind of Jack-in-the-box.

»Tin soldier!« cried the goblin. »Will you please keep your eyes to yourself!« But the tin soldier pretended not to hear.

»All right – you wait till tomorrow!« said the goblin.

And when tomorrow came and the children got up, the tin soldier was put away by the window; and, whether it was the goblin or the draught that did it, all at once the window flew open and the soldier fell out head first from the third storey. It was a terrible fall. There was his leg going straight up in the air, and he was left standing on his helmet with his bayonet stuck in between the paving-stones.

The maidservant and the little boy came down directly to look for him; but although they very nearly trod on him, they never saw him. If only the tin soldier had called out »Here I am!« they would have found him easily enough; but he didn't think it would be right to shout out, as he was in uniform.

Presently it began raining, more and more heavily, until it was a regular downpour. When it was over, two street-boys came by. »Gosh, look at that!« said one of them. »There's a tin soldier. Let's send him for a sail.« So they made a boat out of a newspaper, put the tin soldier aboard, and away he sailed down the gutter with the two boys running alongside and clapping their hands. Bless my soul, how the waves did rock in the gutter, and what a strong current there was! Well, after all, it had been a real soaker. The paper boat bobbed up and down, and now and then it whirled round so fast that the tin soldier became quite dizzy. But he kept staunch and never moved a muscle; he looked straight ahead, and still shouldered arms.

All at once the boat drifted in under a broad culvert; it was as dark as if he were in his box.

»I wonder where I'm coming to now«, he thought. »I'll swear it's all the fault of that goblin. If only the little lady were here in the boat, it could be twice as dark for all I'd care!«

Just then a great water-rat appeared, who lived under the culvert. »Where's your passport?« asked the rat. »Now then, show me your passport!«

But the tin soldier never said a word and clutched his gun more tightly than ever. The boat rushed on, and the rat after it. Ugh! How it ground its teeth and shouted out to sticks and straws: »Stop him! Stop him! He hasn't paid the toll! He hasn't shown his passport!«

But the current grew stronger and stronger; the tin soldier could already see daylight ahead where the culvert ended. But he could also hear a roaring sound that might well bring dismay to the bravest man. Just think of it – where the culvert ended, the gutter plunged straight out into a large canal. It was as dangerous for him as it would be for us to sail down a big waterfall.

By now he had come so near that there was no stopping. The boat dashed out, the poor tin soldier held himself as stiffly as he could; no one should say that he had moved an eyelid. The boat spun round three or four times and filled right up with water, until it was bound to sink. The tin soldier was now up to his neck; the boat sank deeper and deeper; the paper grew more and more sodden. At last the water closed over the soldier's head... He thought of the pretty little dancer whom he would never see again, and the old song rang in his ears:

»On, on, brave warrior!

On, where death awaits thee!«

At this moment, the paper went to pieces, and the tin soldier fell right through – but was instantly swallowed by a large fish. Oh, and how dark it was inside! Even worse than it was in the culvert, and so terribly cramped, too. But the tin soldier was still staunch, still shouldering arms, as he lay at full length.

The fish darted about, making the most terrifying twists and turns. Then at last it lay quite still; a lightning flash went through it, there was broad daylight, and someone called out: »A tin soldier!« The fish had been caught, taken to market and sold, and here it was in the kitchen, where the maid cut it open with a big knife. She picked up the soldier by the waist with her two fingers and carried him into the parlour, where everyone wanted to see this extraordinary man who had been travelling about inside a fish. But the tin soldier thought nothing of it. They set him up on the table, and there – well, what wonderful things can happen! The tin soldier found himself in the very same room as he had been in before. There they were – the same children, the same toys on the table, the same beautiful castle with the pretty little dancer who still stood on one leg and kept the other one high in the air – she, too, had been staunch. This touched the tin soldier, who could have wept tears of tin, only that would hardly have done! He looked at her, and she looked at him, but neither of them spoke.

Suddenly one of the small boys took and threw the soldier straight into the stove. He had no reason for doing this; of course, the Jack-in-the-box was behind it all.

The tin soldier stood in a complete glow; the heat that he felt was tremendous, but whether it came from the actual fire or from love, he had no idea. All his bright colours were gone, but no one could tell if this had happened on his voyage or was the result of grief. He looked at the little lady, she looked at him, and he could feel that he was melting, but he still stood staunchly with arms at the shoulder. Then a door opened, the draught caught the dancer, and she flew like a sylph right into the stove to the tin soldier, flared up in a flame and was gone. The tin soldier was melted down to a lump and, when the maid cleared out the ashes next morning, she found him in the shape of a little tin heart; but all that was left of the dancer was her spangle, and that was burnt as black as coal.

The Flying Trunk

There was once upon a time a merchant, who was so rich that he could pave the whole street, and most of a little alley, as well, with silver money. But he didn't do that, because he knew another way of using his money. If he paid out a penny, it brought him in a florin; that's the kind of merchant he was... And then he died.

All this money now came to his son, and he led a merry life. He went out dancing every night, made paper kites from banknotes and played ducks and drakes on the lake with gold pieces instead of pebbles. Money would soon go that way, and it did. At last he'd only got fourpence left, and nothing to wear but a pair of slippers and an old dressing-gown. His friends had nothing more to do with him now, as of course they couldn't be seen in the street with him; but one of them, who was good-natured, sent him an old trunk, saying, »Pack up!« Yes, that was all very well, but he hadn't got anything to pack, so he got into the trunk himself.

It was a comic sort of trunk. As soon as you pressed the lock, the trunk could fly. And fly it did. It zoomed away with him, up through the chimney, high above the clouds, further and further into the distance. The bottom kept creaking, and he was terrified that it might give way – dear me, that would have been a nice bit of acrobatics! And at last he came to the land of the Turks. He hid the trunk away under some dried leaves in a wood and walked off into the town. It was all right his doing that, for of course all the Turks went about in dressing-gown and slippers the same as he did. Then he met a nurse with a baby. »I say, you Turknanny,« he began, »what's this great castle here, close to the town, with the high windows?«

»That's where the King's daughter lives,« she answered. »It's been foretold her that she'll have an unhappy love-affair, and so no one's allowed to visit her without the King and Queen being there.«

»Thank you,« said the merchant's son; and he went back to the wood, got into his trunk, and flew up on to the castle roof, where he crawled in through the window to the Princess.

She was lying on the sofa, asleep. She was so pretty that the merchant's son felt he must kiss her. This woke her up, and she was very frightened, until he told her he was the Turkish God who had come down to her from the sky. She liked that very much.

Then they sat beside each other, and he told her stories about her eyes. They were the loveliest dark lakes, he said, where her thoughts went swimming like mermaids. And he told her stories about her forehead; it was a snowy mountain with the most wonderful rooms and pictures inside it. And he told her about the stork, which brings the dear little babies. Yes, yes, they were lovely stories that he told her. And then he proposed to the Princess, and she at once said yes.

»But you must come here on Saturday,« she said. »The King and Queen are coming to tea with me then. They will be so proud of my marrying the Turkish God; only be sure you have a really fine story to tell them, because my father and mother do so enjoy that. My mother likes a story to be goody-goody and correct, but my father likes it to be funny, so that he can laugh.«

»All right,« he said. »I shan't bring any other wedding present, but simply a story.« Then they said goodbye; but the Princess gave him a sword which was decorated with gold coins – and he had plenty of use for those.

So off he flew and bought himself a new dressing-gown; and then he sat in the wood and began to think out a good story. It had to be ready by Saturday and, after all, that's not so easy.

At last he was ready, and Saturday arrived.

The King, the Queen and all the Court were waiting at tea-time with the Princess. They received him most charmingly.

»Now will you tell us a story?« said the Queen. »One that goes deep and has a moral.«

»Yes, but one that'll make us laugh, mind you!« said the King.

»Very well,« said the merchant's son and began his story. So now we must listen very carefully.

Once upon a time there was a bundle of matches; they were tremendously proud of their high birth. Their family tree - that's to say, the tall fir-tree that each little matchstick came from – had been a huge old tree in the wood. And now the matches lay on the shelf between a tinder-box and an old iron cook-pot, and they told the other two about the time when they were young. »Ah, yes,« they said. »In those days, with the velvet moss at our feet, we really were on velvet. Every morning and evening we had diamond tea; that was the dew. And all day we had sunshine – if there was any sunshine – and all the little birds had to tell us stories. We could see, too, how well off we were, because the broad-leaved trees, they only wore clothes in summer, whereas our family could afford green clothes all the year round. But then the woodcutters arrived; that was the great upheaval, and our family was all split up. Our founder and head was given a place as mainmast on board a splendid ship that could sail round the world if she liked; the other branches went to other places and, as for us, we've got the task of lighting up for the common herd; that's how we gentlefolk come to be in the kitchen.«

»Well, things have gone differently with me,« said the cook-pot which stood alongside the matches. »Right from the time I first came out into the world, I've been scrubbed and boiled again and again. I've got an eye for the practical and, strictly speaking, I'm No. 1 in this house. My great delight, at a time like after dinner, is to sit clean and tidy on the shelf and have a nice chat with my friends. But except for the water-bucket, who now and then goes down into the yard, we spend all our time indoors. Our one newsbringer is the market basket, but that goes in for a lot of wild talk about the government and the people. Why, the other day there was an elderly jug so flabbergasted by what the basket said that it fell down and broke in pieces. It's an out-and-out radical, that basket, mark my words!«

»How you do chatter!« said the tinderbox; and the steel let fly at the flint, so that it gave out sparks. »Come on, let's have a cheerful evening!«

»Yes, let's discuss who belongs to the best family,« said the matches.

»No, I don't like talking about myself,« said the earthenware jar. »Let's have a social evening. I'll begin. I'll tell you about the sort of thing that we've all been through; then you can really enter into it, and that makes it so enjoyable. On the shores of the Baltic, where the Danish Beech-trees –«

»That's a splendid way to begin«, said all the plates. »Just the kind of story we like!«

»Well, that's where I was brought up, in a quiet family. The furniture was polished, the floor washed, and we had clean curtains every fortnight.«

»It does sound interesting the way you tell it,« said the broom. »One can hear at once that it's a lady telling the story; there's such a refined note running through it all.«

»That's just how I feel,« said the bucket, and it gave a little hop of sheer delight, and that meant »splash!« on the floor. Then the cook-pot went on with its story, and the end was every bit as good as the beginning.

The plates all rattled with joy, and the broom took some green parsley out of the bin and crowned the cook-pot with it, knowing this would annoy the others and »if I crown her to-day,« she thought, »then she'll crown me to-morrow.«

»Now I'm going to dance,« said the tongs and dance she did – my word, what a high kick! The old chintz on the chair in the corner fairly split himself looking at it. »Now may I be crowned?« asked the tongs, and crowned she was.

»After all, they're the merest riff-raff,« thought the matches.

The tea-urn was then supposed to give a song, but it had a cold, it said; it could only sing when it was on the boil. It was really just being rather superior; it never would sing except when standing on the table, in there with the master and mistress.

Over in the window lay an old quill pen that the maid generally wrote with. There was nothing remarkable about it except that it had been dipped much too far into the inkpot, but this made it very stuck-up. »If the tea-urn doesn't want to sing,« said the quill pen, »then it needn't. In a cage hanging outside is a nightingale – she can sing. It's true she's never had any lessons, but we won't find fault with that this evening.«

»I consider it quite out of place,« said the tea-kettle, who was the regular kitchen-singer and half-sister to the tea-urn, »that a foreign bird like that should be allowed to sing here. Is it patriotic? I leave it to the market basket to decide.«

»I'm disappointed, that's all,« said the market basket. »You've no idea how disappointed I am. Is this a suitable way to spend the evening? Instead of turning the house upside down, wouldn't it be better to put it straight? Then each one would find his proper place, and I should be cock of the walk. Very different to the way things are going now.«

»That's it, let's kick up a shindy!« they all exclaimed. Just then the door opened. It was the maid. They all stood still; no one uttered a syllable. But there wasn't a pot among them that didn't know perfectly well how much it could do and how elegant it was. »Yes,« they thought, »if we'd wanted, we could easily have turned it into quite a gay evening.«

The maid took the matches and struck a light with them – my goodness, how they spluttered and blazed! »Now,« thought the matches, »now everyone can see that we are the ones. This is where we shine, where we sparkle!« – and then they burnt right out.

»That was a lovely tale,« said the Queen. »I quite felt myself in the kitchen together with the matches. Yes, thou shalt certainly marry our daughter.«

»Ra-ther!« said the King, »thou shalt marry our daughter on Monday.« They said »thou« to him now because, you see, he was to be one of the family.

The wedding was all fixed and, the evening before, the whole town was lit up. Cakes and buns were thrown to be scrambled for by the crowd. The street boys stood on tiptoe and shouted hurrah and whistled on their fingers. There were great goings on.

»I suppose I'd better take a hand as well,« thought the merchant's son; and so he bought rockets and whizzbangs and every sort of firework you could think of, put them in his trunk and then flew up into the air with them.

Rootsch! How they went off! How they pooffed and popped! The Turks almost jumped out of their skins, and their slippers flew about their ears. Never before had they seen such a vision in the sky. They knew now that it really was the Turkish God who was to marry the Princess.

Directly the merchant's son landed in the wood again with his trunk, he thought, »I may as well walk into the town and hear how people have taken it.« It was natural enough that he should want to find that out.

Heavens, the way people talked! Every single person he asked gave his own version, but one and all were enchanted.

»I saw the Turkish God himself,« said one. »He had eyes like shining stars, and his beard was like a foaming torrent.«

»He flew off in a mantle of fire,« said another. »I saw the loveliest little cherubs peeping out from the folds.«

Yes, they were pretty things he listened to; and tomorrow was his wedding day.

He now went back to the wood to get into his trunk – but where was it? The trunk was burnt right up. The fireworks had left a spark which set fire to the trunk, and this was now in ashes. No more could he fly, no more could he go to his bride.

All day she stood on the roof and waited. She's waiting still – while he goes trudging round the world, telling stories. But they're not so jolly as the one he told about the matches.

Willie Winkie*)
(Ole Lukøje)

Nobody in the world knows so many stories as Willie Winkie... And he knows how to tell them, too – no doubt about that!

Late in the evening when children are sitting nice and quietly at a table or on their stools, that's when Willie Winkie comes along. He comes ever so softly up the stairs, for he goes in his stocking-feet, and he very gently opens the door. Then fft! he squirts sweet milk into the children's eyes – only the tiniest drop, yet always enough to stop them keeping their eyes open – and so they don't see him. He steals up just behind them and gently blows down their necks, and then their heads grow heavy. It's all right – it doesn't hurt them, because Willie Winkie is really most kind to children; all he wants is to see them quieten down, and for that it's best to get them to bed. They must be quite still before he can tell them stories.

When at last the children are asleep, Willie Winkie sits down on the bed. He's nicely dressed, and his coat's made of some sort of silk – though it's hard to say what colour it is, for as he turns about it's all shot with green and red and blue. Under each arm he carries an umbrella. One umbrella, with pictures on it, he holds over the good children, so that they have the loveliest dreams all night; and the other umbrella, without anything on it, he holds over the naughty children, so that they sleep like logs and when they wake in the morning haven't dreamt a thing.

Now you shall hear how Willie Winkie came every night for a whole

* The Mother Goose rhyme beginning:
»Wee Willie Winkie runs through the town,–« is almost as well-known to Danish children as our own, and »Willie Winkie« is translated and explained to them as 'Ole Lukøje'.

78

week to a little boy called Hjalmar, and the stories he told him. There are seven stories altogether, for there are seven days in the week.

Monday

»Now look here!« said Willie Winkie one evening, when he had got Hjalmar to bed. »First, I'm going to smarten things up« – and straight away all the flowers in the flower-pots became large trees stretching their long branches up under the ceiling and along the walls, until the whole room was turned into a lovely bower, and all the branches were full of blossom; every flower was prettier than a rose, with a delicious smell, and, if you cared to taste it, was sweeter than jam. The fruit all glistened like gold, and there were buns that were bursting with currants – you never saw anything like it! But all at once there began a most dreadful hullabaloo over in the drawer where Hjalmar kept his school-books.

»What's up now?« said Willie Winkie, as he went over to the table and opened the drawer. It was the slate that was in such distress, because a wrong figure had got into the sum so that it wouldn't come right. The pencil frisked and gambolled at the end of its string like a little dog; it wanted to help the sum, but didn't know how to.

Next, there was a howling set up from inside Hjalmar's copybook – it was simply ghastly to listen to! Running down every page were all the capital letters, each with a small letter beside it, a complete row of them the whole way down. They acted as a copy, and beside them were also some letters which imagined that they looked like the copy ones; Hjalmar had written these, and they straggled about almost as if they had tumbled over the ruled line they were supposed to stand on.

»Look here, this is how you ought to hold yourselves,« said the copy. »Look – sloping a bit like this, with a free swinging stroke.«

»Ah, we should so like to,« said Hjalmar's letters, »but we can't; we're feeling so bad.«

»Then you must have a dose of medicine!« said Willie Winkie.

»Oh, no!« they screamed – and at once stood up as straight as you could wish for.

»There! That's enough story-telling for the present,« said Willie Winkie. »Now I must put them through their drill – left, right – left, right!« And he drilled the letters until they stood up as firm and straight as any copy ones. But after Willie Winkie had gone and Hjalmar looked at them the next morning, they were just as miserable-looking as before.

Tuesday

Directly Hjalmar was in bed, Willie Winkie touched all the furniture in the room with his little magic squirt, and they immediately began to chatter. They all chattered about themselves, except the spittoon, which stood in silent annoyance that the others could be so conceited as to talk and think only of themselves and never have a thought for the one who, after all, stood so modestly in the corner and let himself be spat upon.

Over the chest of drawers hung a large painting in a gilt frame. It showed a landscape with tall venerable trees, flowers growing in the meadow, and a great broad stream curving round behind a wood, past many a castle, far out into the open sea.

Willie Winkie touched the painting with his magic squirt, and the birds in it at once began to sing. The branches stirred in the trees, and the clouds scudded along; you could see their shadow drifting over the fields.

Willie Winkie took little Hjalmar and lifted him up to the picture-frame, and Hjalmar put his feet into the picture, right into the tall grass; there he stood, with the sun shining down on him through the branches of the trees. He ran down to the water and got into a little boat that was lying there. It was painted red and white, and its sails shone like silver. Six swans, all with gold crowns down over their necks and a glittering blue star on their heads, towed the boat past the green woods, where the trees were telling tales about robbers and witches, and the flowers had stories of the dear little elves and of all they had heard from the butterflies.

The loveliest fishes, with scales like gold and silver, swam after the boat, leaping up now and then so that there was an answering splash in the water; and the birds flew behind in two long rows, red birds and blue birds, big ones and little ones. The gnats kept dancing round and the cockchafer repeated his »boom! boom!« - they all wanted to go with Hjalmar, and each of them had a story to tell.

Yes, it was a wonderful sail they went for. At one moment the woods were quite thick and dark, and then suddenly they were like a beautiful garden with flowers and sunshine, and there appeared great castles of glass and marble with princesses on the balconies who were all little girls that Hjalmar knew well and had played with. They reached out their hands, and each one was holding the nicest sugar-pig any sweet-shop could sell. Hjalmar caught hold of one end of a sugar-pig as he sailed past, and the princess held on tight to the other, so they each got a piece; she got the smallest and Hjalmar much the biggest. Little princes, with gold swords carried at the salute, were on guard at every castle, and they showered him with toffee and tin soldiers; they were proper princes! Sometimes Hjalmar was sailing through forests, and sometimes through what seemed to be immense halls or through the middle of a town. In this way he came to the home of the nurse who had looked after him when he was quite small. She had been so very fond of him, and now she nodded and waved her hand, singing the pretty verses she had made up herself and sent to Hjalmar.

Of you, dear Hjalmar, I often think
and how as a babe I kissed you
on forehead and mouth and cheek so pink –
my darling, how much I've missed you!
Your earliest words I heard you crow,
but soon from your side was driven.
God grant you his blessing here below,
sweet messenger sent from heaven!

And all the birds joined in her song; the flowers danced on their stalks, and the old trees nodded, just as if Willie Winkie were telling them stories too.

Wednesday

Goodness! how the rain was coming down outside! Hjalmar could hear it in his sleep, and when Willie Winkie opened a window, the water came right up to the sill. There was a complete lake outside, but a splendid - looking ship lay alongside the house.

»Hjalmar, my boy, will you come for a sail?« asked Willie Winkie. »Then you'll be able to go off to foreign parts to-night and be back again in the morning.«

And all of a sudden Hjalmar found himself standing in his Sunday best on board the splendid ship, and the weather at once became fine. She sailed through the streets, cruised round the church and finally came out into open sea. On and on they sailed, until the land was quite out of sight; and they came upon a flock of storks, who were also leaving home and were bound for the warm countries. They were flying one behind the other and had already flown a very long way. One of the storks was so tired that his wings could hardly bear him up any longer; he was the very last in the row, and he soon got a long way behind. Finally he sank with outspread wings lower and lower; he gave a few more beats with his wings, but that was no good; and then his feet touched the ship's rigging, he glided down the sail and plomp! there he was on the deck.

Then the ship's boy picked him up and put him in the hen-coop among hens, ducks and turkeys. The poor stork looked so sorry for himself amongst them.

»What a creature!« said all the hens.

And the turkey-cock puffed himself out as big as he could and asked who he was, and the ducks waddled backwards and nudged each other – »Quick, get quacking!«

Then the stork told about the warmth of Africa, and the pyramids, and the ostrich that ran like a wild horse through the desert; but the ducks never understood what he was saying and so they nudged each other again – »We all agree, don't we, that he's a stupid?«

»As stupid as can be!« said the turkey-cock with a gobble-gobble. At that the stork kept silent and thought about his beloved Africa.

»Those are nice lanky legs you have,« said the turkey. »How much a yard?«

»Quack, quack, quack!« chuckled the ducks. But the stork pretended not to hear.

»You may as well join in the laugh,« said the turkey to him; »it was very neatly put. Or was it perhaps too low for him? Heighho! He's a bit one-eyed; we must look to ourselves, if we want to have some fun.« And they clucked away, and the ducks kept quack-quack-quacking – it was terrible how funny they seemed to think it was.

But Hjalmar went over to the hen-coop, opened the door and called to the stork, who then hopped out on to the deck. He had now had a good rest and seemed to give Hjalmar a nod, in order to thank him. The next moment he spread out his wings and flew off to the warm countries. But the hens went on clucking and the ducks went on quacking, while the turkey-cock became quite red in the face.

»To-morrow we shall make soup of you!« said Hjalmar – and then he woke up. There he was, lying in his little bed. It really was an astonishing voyage Willie Winkie had arranged for him that night.

Thursday

»What do you think I've got here?« said Willie Winkie. »Now don't get frightened; I'm going to show you a little mouse« – and there was the dainty little creature in Willie Winkie's hand as he held it out to him. »It has come,« he said, »to invite you to a wedding. There are two little mice here to-night who are entering into matrimony. They live down under the floor of your mother's larder; it ought to be a charming affair.«

»But how am I to get through the tiny mousehole in the floor?« asked Hjalmar.

»Leave that to me,« said Willie Winkie; »I know how to make you small enough.« and he touched Hjalmar with his magic squirt, so that he at once became smaller and smaller and at last was no bigger than your finger. »Now we can borrow the tin soldier's clothes; I think they'll fit you, and it looks so smart to be wearing uniform at a party.«

»Ra-ther!« said Hjalmar, and the next moment there he was dressed as the most dapper-looking tin soldier.

»If you'll kindly take a seat in your mother's thimble,« said the little mouse, »I'll do myself the honour of pulling you along.«

»Good gracious! Miss Mouse,« said Hjalmar, »to think of me giving you all that trouble!« And off they drove to the mousewedding.

First, they made their way in under the floor by a long passage that was just high enough, and no more, for them to be able to drive along in a thimble, and the whole passage was lit up by touchwood.

»Doesn't it smell nice!« said the mouse that was pulling him. »The whole passage has been rubbed with bacon-rind; there's nothing to touch it!«

Now they entered the wedding-chamber. To the right stood all the little she-mice, twittering and tittering as if they were making fun of each other; to the left stood all the he-mice, stroking their whiskers with their paws. But out in the middle of the floor were the bridal pair, standing in a scooped-out cheese and kissing each other like anything in front of everybody. Well, after all, they were engaged and were going to be married almost at once.

More and more guests kept arriving, and the mice looked like trampling each other to death. The bride and bridegroom had stationed themselves in the middle of the doorway, so there was no getting either out or in. The whole room, like the passage, had been rubbed with bacon-rind, which was all the refreshment there was; but for dessert there was produced a pea in which a mouse belonging to the family had nibbled the name of the bridal pair – or rather, the first letter. That was considered something altogether out of the ordinary.

All the mice agreed that it was a lovely wedding and that they had talked with such interesting people.

Finally, Hjalmar drove home again. He had certainly been in very smart society; on the other hand, he had to put up with no end of a shrinking, to make himself small enough to get into a tin soldier's uniform.

Friday

»You'd never believe how many elderly people would like to get hold of me,« said Willie Winkie. »Especially the ones who've done something they shouldn't. 'Dear, kind Winkie,' they say to me, 'We can't shut our eyes at night, and so we lie awake and see our evil deeds sitting on the edge of the bed like hideous little goblins and squirting us with hot water. Do come and chase them away, so that we can get a good sleep!' And then they add with a deep sigh, 'We're only too glad to pay. Good-night, Winkie – the money's in the window.' But I don't do it for money,« said Willie Winkie.

»Now, what are we going to have to-night?« asked Hjalmar.

»Well, I don't know if you'd care to go to another wedding – quite a different sort to yesterday's I may say. Your sister's big doll – the one that looks like a man and is called Herman – is to marry the doll Bertha; and, as it's Bertha's birthday, there will be a lot of presents.«

»Yes, I know what that means!« said Hjalmar.»Whenever the dolls want new clothes, my sister lets them have a birthday or a wedding. That must have happened a hundred times.«

»Well, but to-night's wedding is the 101st time, and when Number 101 is over there won't be any more. That's why it's going to be so brilliant. Just look!«

And Hjalmar looked across at the table. There stood the little card-board house with lights in the windows, and all the tin soldiers were presenting arms outside. The bride and bridegroom were seated on the floor, leaning up against the leg of the table and looking very thoughtful, as indeed they might well do. But Willie Winkie draped himself in Grannie's black petticoat and married them! When the wedding was over, all the furniture in the room joined in singing the following beautiful song, which had been written by the pencil and went to the tune of the devil's tattoo: –

Our song shall greet like wind and weather these two that the priest has tied together; so poker-stiff they stand in tether, each of them made of chamois leather!

Hurrah for bride and groom together!

Hurrah for them both in wind and weather!

Next came the wedding presents; they had said they would rather not have any eatables, as their love was enough for them to live on.

»Which do you think?« said the bridegroom to his bride. »Shall we go and stay in the country, or shall we travel abroad?« They asked advice of the swallow, who was a great traveller, and of the old hen, who had hatched five broods of chicks. The swallow described the lovely warm countries, where the grapes hang in big heavy bunches and the air is so soft, and the colour on the hills is something quite unknown to us here.

»Still, they haven't got our garden cabbage!« said the hen. »I once spent the summer with all my chicks in the country; there was a gravel pit we could go and scratch in, and then we had the use of a garden where there were cabbages – such a green, they were! I can't imagine anything lovelier.«

»But one cabbage-stalk looks just like another,« said the swallow. »And then again, the weather here is so often bad.«

»Oh, well, we're used to that,« replied the hen.

»But it's so cold. It freezes.«

»That just suits the cabbages,« said the hen. »Besides, we get warm weather too, sometimes. Don't you remember, only four years ago, we had a summer that lasted five weeks! It was so hot here that you could hardly breathe ... And then we don't get all those poisonous creatures they have abroad; and we are free from brigands. Anyone who doesn't think our country is the best of all is a scoundrel; he doesn't really deserve to live here« – and tears came into the hen's eyes. »I've done a bit of travelling myself,« she added. »I've ridden over 50 miles in a coop. There's no fun at all in travel.«

»Yes, the hen's a sensible woman,« said the doll Bertha. »I don't want to go mountaineering either. It only means that first you go up and – then you go down. No, let's move out to the gravel pit and go for a walk in the cabbage patch.«

And that's how they left it.

Saturday

»Any stories for me to-night?« asked little Hjalmar, as soon as Willie Winkie had got him to bed.

»We haven't time for that this evening,« said Winkie, as he opened above him the umbrella with the prettiest pictures on. »Take a peep at those Chinese!« – and the whole umbrella looked like a great Chinese bowl with blue trees and bridges with pointed arches, where there were little Chinese who stood nodding their heads.

»We must have everything trim and tidy for tomorrow,« said Winkie. »You see, it's a holy day; it's Sunday. I must go up the church-tower and see if the little church-elves are cleaning the bells, so that they ring out nicely. I must get along to the fields and see if the breezes are blowing the dust off the grass and the leaves. And then – what is really my hardest task – I must have all the stars down and give them a thorough polish. I take them into my apron; but, first, each one of them has to be numbered, and the holes they fit into up there must also be numbered, so that they can find their right places again; otherwise, they wouldn't fit tight and we should get too many shooting stars, as they dropped out one after the other.«

»I say, look here, Mr. Winkie,« said an old portrait hanging on the wall of Hjalmar's bedroom. »I'm Hjalmar's great-grandfather. Thank you for telling the boy these stories, but you mustn't muddle him with wrong ideas. The stars can't be taken down and polished. A star is a globe, the same as the earth is; that's just the beauty of it.«

»Thanks very much, old great-grandfather!« said Willie Winkie, »Thanks very much! You're of course the head of the family – the Grand Old Man – but I'm older than you are. I'm an ancient heathen – the Romans and Greeks call me the Dream God. I visit the very best houses, continually, and I know how to get on with all sorts, both young and old. Now you can tell a story of your own.« And Willie Winkie picked up his umbrella and away he went.

»Dear, dear!« said the old portrait. »One mayn't even express one's opinion nowadays.«

And at that moment Hjalmar woke up.

Sunday

»Good evening,« said Willie Winkie, and Hjalmar nodded; but then he jumped up and turned his great-grandfather's portrait with its face to the wall, so that it shouldn't butt into the conversation as it did the day before.

»Please tell me some stories: the one about the five peas that lived in a pod, and the one about the cock-a-doodle-doo that made love to the hen-a-doodle-doo, and the one about the darning-needle who was so stuck-up that she fancied she was a sewing-needle!«

»Ah, but one can have too much of a good thing,« said Willie Winkie. »I'd rather show you something. I tell you what, I'll show you my brother. He never comes to anyone more than once and, when he comes, he takes them up on his horse and tells them stories. He only knows two: one is so utterly beautiful that no one on earth can imagine it, and the other is so ghastly and terrible – well, it's impossible to describe it.«

Then Willie Winkie lifted little Hjalmar up to the window and said, »Look, there's my brother. He's also called Death. You see, he's nothing like so horrid to look at as he is in pictures, where he's nothing but a skeleton. No, he has silver lace on his tunic – it's a splendid hussar uniform with a black velvet cloak flying behind him over his horse. Look how he gallops along!«

And Hjalmar saw how this other Winkie rode away, taking both young and old up on his horse. Some he placed in front of him, others behind; but he always asked them first, »What does it say in your report?« »Good,« they all answered. »Ah, but let me see it myself,« he said. Then they had to show him the report, and all the ones who had »very good« or »excellent« came to the front seat on the horse and were told the beautiful story. But those who had »moderate« or »poor« had to sit behind and hear the terrible story; they trembled and wept and tried to jump off the horse, but they couldn't do that because they had immediately grown fast on to it.

»But Death is a most wonderful Willie Winkie,« said Hjalmar. »I'm not a bit afraid of him.«

»No, and you needn't be,« said Willie Winkie. »Mind you get a good report, that's all.«

»Most instructive!« muttered the great-grandfather's portrait. »It does some good, after all, to express one's opinion.« And he was quite contented.

There! That's the story of Willie Winkie. Now this evening he can tell you some more himself.

The Swineherd

Once upon a time there was a prince who hadn't much money, but he had a kingdom; and though this was quite small, it was large enough to marry on, and marry he would.

Still, it was really rather bold of him to say straight out to the Emperor's daughter: »Will you have me?« But sure enough he did, for his name was famous everywhere, and there were hundreds of princesses who would only too gladly have taken him. But do you think she did? Well, now just listen. Growing on the grave of the Prince's father was a rose-tree – oh, such a lovely rose-tree. It only flowered every five years, and even then had but one solitary bloom. But this rose smelt so sweet that it made you forget all your cares and troubles. And the Prince also had a nightingale that could sing just as if it had all the loveliest tunes hidden away in its little throat. The Princess should have both the rose and the nightingale, he said; and so they were placed in big silver caskets and sent to her.

The Emperor had them brought before him in the great hall, where the Princess was playing »visitors« with her maids-of honour. They never did anything else and, when she saw the big caskets with the presents inside, she clapped her hands with glee.

»I do hope it's a pussy-cat,« she said... But then out came the lovely rose.

»Oh, isn't it pretty!« cried all the maids-of-honour.

»It's more than pretty,« said the Emperor, »It's handsome.«

But when the Princess touched it she nearly burst into tears. »Oh, Papa, what a shame!« she cried. »It's not artificial, it's real!«

»Come, let's first see what's in the other casket before we get annoyed,« suggested the Emperor. And then out came the nightingale. Its singing was so lovely that for the moment there wasn't a thing that could be said against it.

»*Superbe! Charmant!*« exclaimed the maids-of-honour, for they all talked French, the one worse than the other. »How the bird reminds me of Her late Majesty's musicalbox!« said an old courtier. »Dear me, yes! Exactly the same tone, the same expression!«

»So it is,« said the Emperor; and he cried like a child.

»All the same, I can't believe that it's real,« said the Princess.

»Yes, it is; it's a real live bird,« said the ones who had brought it.

»All right, then let it fly away,« said the Princess, and she wouldn't hear of the Prince being allowed to come.

But he wasn't going to be put off like that. He smeared his face with brown and black, pulled his cap down over his eyes and knocked at the door. »Good morning, Emperor!« he said. »I wonder if you've got a job for me here at the Castle.«

»Ah, well,« said the Emperor, »there are so many who come and ask that. But now, let me see – yes, I want some one to mind the pigs. We've such a lot of pigs.«

And so the Prince was appointed Imperial Swineherd. He was given a miserable little room down by the pig-sties, and there he had to live. But all day he sat working, and by the evening he had made a lovely little pot with bells round it and, as soon as the pot boiled, these tinkled charmingly; they played the old tune of –

»Ah, my dear Augustine,
Our dreams are all done, done, done!«

But the cunningest arrangement of all was that, if you held your finger in the steam from the pot, you could at once smell what was being cooked on every fire in the town. Well, of course, that was something quite different from a rose.

Presently the Princess came strolling along with all her court-ladies, and when she heard the music she stopped, looking so delighted; for she, too, could play »Ah, my dear Augustine« – it was the only tune she knew, and she played it with one finger.

»Why, that's *my* tune!« she said. »This pigman must be a man of taste. Look here, go in and ask him how much he wants for the instrument.«

So one of the court-ladies had to run in and see him; but she put on her clogs first.

»How much do you want for that pot?« she asked.

»I want ten kisses from the Princess,« answered the pigman.

»Goodness gracious!« said the maid-of-honour.

»That's the price; I can't take less,« said the pigman.

»Well, what does he say?« asked the Princess.

»I really can't repeat it,« said the maid-of-honour. »It's too dreadful.«

»Well, then whisper it« – and the maid-of-honour whispered it.

»Oh, how rude he is!« said the Princess and walked off at once. But when she had gone a little way, the bells began to tinkle so charmingly –

»Ah, my dear Augustine,
our dreams are all done, done done!«

»Come,« said the Princess, »ask him if he will take ten kisses from my ladies-in-waiting.«

»No, thank you,« said the pigman. »Ten kisses from the Princess, or I stick to my pot!«

»How horribly annoying!« said the Princess. »Well, then, you ladies'll have to stand in front of me, so that no one can see.«

The court-ladies went and stood in front of her, spreading out their dresses; and then the pigman had his ten kisses and she got her pot.

Goodness! What fun they had! Day and night the pot was kept on the boil. There wasn't a kitchen in the town where they didn't know what was being cooked, whether it was the Mayor's or the shoemaker's. The maids-of-honour danced about, clapping their hands with glee.

»We know who's going to have soup and pancakes, and we know who's going to have chops and jelly. It's so interesting.«

»Most interesting,« observed the high Stewardess.

»Yes, but not a word to anyone, mind you; for I'm the Emperor's daughter.«

»O, dear, no!« they all replied. »We shouldn't dream of it.«

The swineherd - that is to say, the Prince, but you see, they didn't know but what he was a regular pigman - couldn't let the day go by without making something. The next thing he made was a rattle. When you swung it round, it played all the waltzes and jigs and polkas that anybody had ever heard of.

»Now that really is *superbe*,« said the Princess, as she was passing. »I've never heard anything lovelier. Look here, go in and ask him what he wants for that instrument. But, mind, no kisses!«

»He wants a hundred kisses from the Princess,« said the lady-in-waiting who had been in to ask.

»The fellow must be mad,« said the Princess and began to walk off. But when she had gone a little way, she stopped. »Art must be encouraged,« she said; »after all, I'm the Emperor's daughter. Tell him he shall have ten kisses like yesterday, and my ladies-in-waiting will give him the rest.«

»Oh, but we couldn't bear to do that,« said the ladies.

»Nonsense!« said the Princess. »If I can kiss him, so can you. Remember, I give you wages and board« - and once more the maid-of-honour had to go in and see the pigman.

»A hundred kisses from the Princess,« he said, »or we stay as we are.«

»Stand in front!« she cried. And so all the court-ladies placed themselves in front, and the kissing began.

»What on earth are they all up to over there by the sties!« said the Emperor, who had just stepped out on to his balcony. He rubbed his eyes and put on his spectacles. »Why, it's the ladies-in-waiting, up to some game or other. Perhaps I'd better go and have a look« - and he gave a hitch to the back of his slippers, for he had trodden them down at the heel.

Phew! What a hurry he was in!

As soon as he came down into the courtyard, he crept along very quietly. And the maids-of-honour were so busy counting the kisses, for it had to be fair do's - he mustn't have too many kisses, nor yet too few - that they never noticed the Emperor, who now drew himself up on tiptoe.

»What's all this!« he said, when he saw them kissing; and he slogged them over the head with his slipper, just as the young pigman was having his eighty-sixth kiss. »Out you get!« said the Emperor, for he was furious, and both Princess and swineheard were turned out of his kingdom.

Look, there she sat crying, while the swineherd scolded and the rain came down in torrents.

»Poor me!« said the Princess. »If only I had accepted the handsome Prince! Oh, I am so unhappy!«

The swineherd went behind a tree, wiped off the black and brown from his face, threw away his old clothes and now stepped forward in princely robes that were so magnificent that the Princess couldn't help making a curtsey.

»My dear, I've come to despise you,« he said. »An honest prince you rejected. The rose and the nightingale were not to your taste. But the swineherd – you could kiss him for the sake of a musical box. Now you can have what you asked for!«

And with that he went into his kingsom, shut the door and bolted it; but she could stand outside if she cared to and sing –

»Ah, my dear Augustine,
Our dreams are all done, done, done!«

The Nightingale

You know of course that in China the Emperor is a Chinese and his subjects are Chinese too. The story I'm going to tell you happened many years ago, but that's just why you had better hear it now before it's forgotten.

The Emperor's palace was the finest palace in the world, made entirely of delicate porcelain. It was all so precious and fragile that you had to be tremendously careful how you touched anything. The garden was full of the rarest flowers, and the loveliest of these had little silver bells tied to them which tinkled so that no one should go by without noticing them. Yes, everything in the Emperor's garden was most carefully thought out, and it stretched so far that even the gardener had no idea where it ended. If you kept on walking, you found yourself in a glorious wood with tall trees and deep lakes. The wood went right down to the sea, which was blue and deep; big ships could sail right in under the branches of the trees. Here lived a nightingale that sang so beautifully that even the poor fisherman, who had so much else to see to, would stop and listen, when he was taking his nets in at night and suddenly heard the nightingale. »My word! that's lovely!« he said; but then he had to get on with his work and forgot about the bird. Yet when she sang again the following night and the fisherman was out there with his nets, »My word!« he repeated, »that is lovely!«

From every country in the world travellers came and marvelled at the Emperor's great city, his palace and his garden; but as soon as they heard

the nightingale, everyone said the same – »Oh, but that's the best of all!«
And when they got home from their travels, they had many tales to tell,
and clever people wrote books about the city and the palace and the
garden, yet they never forgot the nightingale; she was given the place of
honour. And the poets wrote the most lovely poems, all about the nightingale in the wood there beside the deep sea.

These books went all over the world, and so in course of time some of
them reached the Emperor. There he sat in his golden chair, reading and
reading; and now and then he nodded his head, for he was pleased to
come across such splendid descriptions of the city and the palace and the
garden. »But the nightingale is really the best of all,« said the book he
was reading.

»What's this?« thought the Emperor. »The nightingale? Why, I've
never heard of her! Is there such a bird in my Empire and, what's more, in
my own garden? Nobody's ever told me that – one has to read about it in a
book!« And, with that, he summoned his gentleman-in-waiting, who
was so grand that, whenever anyone of lower rank than himself ventured
to speak to him or to ask a question, he only answered »P!« – and that
means nothing at all.

»It says here that we have a most remarkable bird called a nightingale,«
said the Emperor. »They declare that there's nothing like her in all my
Empire. Why have I never been told of this before?«

»It's the first I've ever heard of her,« repeated the gentleman-in-waiting. »She's never been presented at Court.«

»I command her to be brought here this evening to sing to me,« said
the Emperor. »The whole world knows what I possess – and I know
nothing!«

»It's the first I've ever heard of her,« repeated the gentleman-in-waiting. »I shall look for her, and I shall find her.«

Find her? But where? The gentleman-in-waiting ran upstairs and
downstairs, through rooms and passages, but none of the people he met
had ever heard of the nightingale. So the gentleman-in-waiting hurried
once more to the Emperor and said it was obviously a story invented by
those who write books. »Your Majesty mustn't believe everything you
read. Most of it's just made up – what they call black art.«

»But the book I read it in,« said the Emperor, »was sent me by the high
and mighty Emperor of Japan, so it can't be untrue. I *will* hear the nightingale. She's to come and sing to-night, under my royal patronage; and
if she fails to appear, then every courtier shall be punched in the stomach
directly after supper.«

»Tsing-pe!« said the gentleman-in-waiting and ran up and down all
the stairs again, through all the rooms and passages; half the Court ran
with him, for they didn't a bit like the idea of being punched in the
stomach. They kept asking after this extraordinary nightingale that everybody knew about except the people at Court.

At last they came across a poor little girl in the kitchen, who said »Oh, golly – the nightingale? I know her well. My, how she can sing! Every evening I'm allowed to take home a few scraps from the table for my poor sick mother who lives down by the shore; and on my way back I often take a rest in the wood, and then I hear the nightingale singing. It brings tears to my eyes, just as if my mother were kissing me.«

»Little kitchen-maid,« said the gentleman-in-waiting, »you shall have a regular situation in the kitchen and be allowed to watch the Emperor eating his dinner, if only you'll take us to the nightingale. You see, she's to give a command performance this evening before the Emperor.«

So then they all set out for the wood where the nightingale used to sing; half the Court joined in the quest. As they were going along, a cow began to moo. »Ah, there she is!« said the courtiers. »What remarkable strength in such a small creature! Yes, it's certainly not the first time we've heard her.«

»No, but that's a cow mooing,« said the little kitchen-maid. »We've still got a long way to go.«

Then some frogs started croaking in the pond. »Delightful!« said the Emperor's chaplain. »Now I can hear her: just like little church-bells.«

»No, those are frogs,« said the little kitchen-maid. »But I expect we shall soon hear her now.« And then the nightingale began to sing.

»There she is!« said the little girl. »Listen, listen! There she is, up there« – and she pointed to a little grey bird up in the branches.

»Is it possible?« said the gentleman-in-waiting. »Why, I never pictured her like that. How ordinary she looks! I expect she's off colour through having so many distinguished visitors.«

»Little nightingale,« called out the small kitchen-maid quite boldly, »our gracious Emperor would like you to sing to him.«

»With the greatest of pleasure,« said the nightingale, and at once began to sing most deliciously.

»Just like glass bells,« observed the gentleman-in-waiting. »And look at the way her little throat keeps working. I can't make out why we've never heard her before. She'll make a great hit at Court.«

»Shall I sing once more to the Emperor?« asked the nightingale, for she thought the Emperor was there.

»My excellent little nightingale,« replied the gentleman-in-waiting, »it is my very pleasant duty to summon you to a concert this evening at the palace, where you will enchant His Imperial Majesty with your delightful singing.«

»It sounds best out in the open,« said the nightingale. Still, she went along readily enough on hearing it was the Emperor's wish.

At the palace everything had been polished up, until the china walls and floors glittered in the light of thousands and thousands of gold lamps. The loveliest flowers, hung ready for tinkling, were arranged in the corridors; and there was such a draught from the scurrying to and fro that their bells were all set ringing and you couldn't hear a word that was spoken.

In the middle of the great hall in which the Emperor sat was a golden perch for the nightingale. The entire Court was present; and the little kitchen-maid was allowed to stand behind the door, as she now ranked as a regular palace kitchen-maid. Everyone was dressed in their finest clothes, and they all looked at the little grey bird as the Emperor nodded to her to begin.

And the nightingale sang so beautifully that tears came into the Emperor's eyes and trickled right down his cheeks; and then the nightingale's singing became even lovelier – it went straight to his heart. And the Emperor was so pleased that he said the nightingale should have his gold slipper to wear round her neck; but the nightingale said no thank you, she had been rewarded enough already. »I've seen tears in the Emperor's eyes; that's my richest reward. There's a strange power in an Emperor's tears. Heaven knows, they are reward enough!« And then the nightingale let them hear her lovely voice again.

»Who ever saw such airs and graces!« said the ladies around; and they went and filled their mouths with water so as to gurgle when anyone spoke to them; yes, they thought they could be nightingales too. Even the lackeys and ladies' maids expressed their approval; and that's saying a good deal for they are the most difficult of all to satisfy. There's no doubt whatever, the nightingale made a great hit.

She was now to remain at Court and have her own cage, with leave to go out for two walks in the daytime and one at night. She was given twelve attendants, who each held on tightly to a silk ribbon fastened round her leg. There was absolutely no fun in a walk like that.

The whole city was talking of this remarkable bird, and, when two people met, one of them merely said »night« and the other »gale«, and after that they sighed and quite understood each other. What's more, eleven grocer's children were named after her, but not one of them had a note in its head...

One day a large parcel arrived for the Emperor, with the word »Nightingale« written on the outside.

»I expect this is a new book about our famous bird,« said the Emperor. But it wasn't a book at all; it was a little gadget lying in a box – an artificial nightingale that was supposed to look like the live one but was covered all over with diamonds, rubies and sapphires. You only had to wind it up, and it could sing one of the songs that the real nightingale sang; and all the while its tail went up and down, glittering with silver and gold. Round its neck was a little ribbon, on which was written: »The Emperor of Japan's nightingale is poor beside the Emperor of China's.«

»How delightful!« they all said; and the one who brought the artificial bird was at once given the title of Chief Imperial Nightingale Bringer.

»Now they must both sing at once,« suggested somebody. »What a duet that will be!«

So the two birds had to sing together; but it wasn't a success, because the real nightingale sang in her own way, whereas the artificial bird went by clockwork. »It can't be blamed for that«, said the Master of the Emperor's Music. »It keeps perfect time and follows my own methods exactly.« After that, the artificial bird had to sing by itself. It was just as popular as the real one, and of course it was also much prettier to look at, glittering there like a cluster of brooches and bracelets.

Over and over again it sang its one and only song – thirty-three times without tiring – and the listeners would have liked to hear it all once more, but the Emperor thought that now it was time for the real nightingale to do some singing ... But where ever was she? No one had noticed her fly out of the open window, away to her own green woods.

»Bless my soul, what's the meaning of this?« said the Emperor; and all the courtiers were highly indignant and said what an ungrateful creature the nightingale was. »Still, we've got the better one,« they added; and then the artificial bird was obliged to sing once more. That was the thirty-fourth time they were hearing the same song; but they didn't quite know it even yet, for it was so difficult. And the Master of Music gave the bird extraordinary praise; in fact, he declared that it was better than the real nightingale, not merely because of its outward appearance and all the wonderful diamonds, but also for the work inside.

»You see, ladies and gentlemen and, above all, Your Imperial Majesty, with the real nightingale there's no telling what's going to happen. But with the artificial bird everything is fixed beforehand. Such-and-such will be heard and no other.One can account for it all: one can open it up and show the human mind at work, the position of the cylinders, how they go round, and the way in which one thing follows from another!«

Everyone said that they quite agreed, and the Master of Music got permission to show the bird to the public on the following Sunday. »They must also hear it sing,« said the Emperor. And hear it they did. They were as delighted as if they had drunk themselves merry on tea – and that's so like the Chinese! They all said »Oh!« and held up one finger – the finger we call »lick-pot« – and nodded their heads. But the poor fisherman who had heard the real nightingale said: »It don't sound so bad – quite like the bird – and yet there's something kind o' missing.«

The real nightingale was sent into exile – banished from land and realm. The artificial bird had its place on a silk cushion close to the Emperor's bed; all the presents it had been given, gold and precious stones, lay round about, and it was promoted to be Chief Imperial Bedside Minstrel of the First Class on the Left; for the Emperor considered the side on which the heart lies to be the more distinguished, and even an Emperor has his heart on the left. The Master of Music wrote a book in twenty-five volumes about the mechanical bird; it was very long and learned, full of the most difficult Chinese words, and everyone pretended they had read it and understood it, or else of course they would have been thought stupid and got punched in the stomach.

Well, this went on for a whole year, until the Emperor, his Court and all the other Chinese knew by heart every little gurgle in the throat of the artificial songbird; but for that very reason they came to like it all the better. They could join in the singing themselves, and they did. The street-boys sang »zee-zee-zee, kloo-kloo-klook!« and the Emperor sang it, too! It really was tremendous fun.

But one evening, just as the artificial bird was in full song and the Emperor lay listening in bed, something went »snap!« inside the bird. Then there was a »whirrrr«; the wheels all went whizzing round...and the music stopped.

The Emperor jumped quickly out of bed and sent for the doctor, but what could he do? Then they brought along the watchmaker, and after a great deal of talk and poking about he got the bird to work after a fashion; but he said that it mustn't be used too often, as the bearings were almost worn out and it was impossible to get fresh parts that would fit in properly with the music. This was a sad disappointment. Once a year only was the artificial bird allowed to sing, and even that was something of a strain; but on these occasions the Master of Music made a little speech full of difficult words, saying that the bird was just as good as ever – and so of course it was just as good as ever.

Five years had now gone by and presently the whole country was filled with sorrow, for really in their hearts they were all fond of their Emperor; but now he was ill and not likely to live, it was said. A new Emperor had already been chosen, and people stood out in the street and asked the gentleman-in-waiting how their Emperor was. »P!« he replied and shook his head.

Cold and pale lay the Emperor in his magnificent great bed. The whole Court believed him to be dead, and each of them hastened to pay their respects to the new Emperor. The valets ran out to gossip about it, and the palace housemaids had a large tea-party. Everywhere, in all the rooms and corridors, heavy cloth had been laid down in order to deaden the sound of footsteps; the whole palace was as still as still could be.

But the Emperor wasn't dead yet. Stiff and pale he lay in the magnificent bed with its long velvet curtains and heavy gold tassels; through an open window high up on the wall the moon was shining down on the Emperor and the artificial bird.

The poor Emperor could scarcely breathe; it was just as if something was sitting on his chest. He opened his eyes, and then he saw it was Death that sat on his chest and had put on his gold crown and was holding the Emperor's gold sword in one hand and his splendid banner in the other. All round the bed, from the folds in the great velvet curtains, strange faces were peering, some of them hideous, others wonderfully gentle and kind.

They were the Emperor's good and evil deeds, gazing down on him now that Death was sitting on his heart.

»Do you remember that?« they whispered, one after the other. »Do you remember that?« And they told him so much that the sweat stood out on his forehead.

»I never realized that,« said the Emperor. »Music, music! Sound the great Chinese drum,« he cried, »to save me from hearing what they say!«

But still they went on, and Death kept nodding like a Chinese at every word they whispered.

»Music! music!« shrieked the Emperor. »You wonderful little golden bird, sing, I implore you, sing! I've given you gold and precious stones, I've hung my own gold slipper round your neck – sing, I implore you, sing!«

But the bird was silent; there was no one to wind it up, and it couldn't sing without that. But Death went on staring at the Emperor with his great hollow eyes, and everything was so still, so terribly still.

All at once, close to the window, came a burst of most beautiful singing. It was the little live nightingale, perched in a tree outside. She had heard of her Emperor's distress and had therefore come to sing him consolation and hope; and, as she sang, the shapes grew fainter and fainter, the blood in the Emperor's weak limbs ran faster and faster, and Death himself listened and said, »Go on, little nightingale, go on!«

»Yes, if you'll give me the fine gold sword ... if you'll give me the splendid banner... if you'll give me the Emperor's crown!«

And Death gave up each treasure for a song, and still the nightingale went on singing. She sang of the quiet churchyard where the white roses bloom, where the elder-tree smells so sweet, and where the fresh grass is watered with the tears of those who are left behind. Then Death began to long for his garden and floated like a cold white mist out of the window.

»Thank you, thank you!« said the Emperor. »You heavenly little bird, now I know who you are! I banished you from land and realm – and yet you have sung those evil visions away from my bed, you have lifted Death from my heart. How can I ever repay you?«

»You have done already,« said the nightingale. »The first time I sang I brought tears to your eyes – I shall never forget that. Those are the jewels that rejoice a singer's heart ... But sleep now and get well and strong again! I will sing to you.«

And the nightingale sang, and the Emperor fell into a sweet sleep – such a peaceful refreshing sleep. When he awoke, restored once more to health, the sun was shining in through the windows. None of his servants had come back yet, for they thought he was dead; but the nightingale was still singing outside.

»You must never leave me again,« said the Emperor. »You shall only sing when you want to, and the artificial bird – I shall break it into a thousand pieces.«

»No, don't do that,« said the nightingale. »It's done what it could; don't part with it yet. I can't make my home in the palace, but let me come when I feel that I want to; then I'll sit of an evening on this branch by the window, and my singing can make you both gay and thoughtful. I shall sing of those that are happy, and of those that suffer; I shall sing of the good and the evil that are here lurking about you. Your little song-bird must fly round to distant homes – to the poor fisherman and the humble peasant – to those who are far from you and your Court. I love your heart better than your crown ... and yet there's a breath of something holy about the crown... I shall come, I shall sing to you; yet there's one thing you must promise me.«

»Whatever you ask!« answered the Emperor, standing there in the imperial robes that he had himself put on and holding the heavy gold sword to his heart.

»One thing only I ask of you. Let no one know that you have a little bird who tells you everything; that will be best.« And then the nightingale flew away.

The servants came in to look after their dead Emperor. Yes, there they stood, and the Emperor said, »Good morning!«

The Top and the Ball

A top and a ball were in a drawer together with some other toys, and then one day the top said to the ball: »Look here, we live together in the same drawer – shall we become engaged?« But the ball, who was made of morocco leather and fancied herself quite as much as any smart young lady, wouldn't even answer such a ridiculous question.

Next day the little boy whom the toys belonged to came and painted the top red and yellow all over and hammered a brass nail into the middle of it. The top was really a fine sight, as it went spinning round and round.

»Look at me!« said the top to the ball »What do you say now? Don't you think after all we might be engaged? We go so splendidly together: you bounce and I dance. There couldn't be a happier couple than us two.«

»Oh, you think that, do you?« answered the ball. »You don't seem to realize that my father and mother were morocco slippers and that I have a cork inside me.«

»Ah, but I'm made of mahogany,« said the top. »Why, the mayor turned me himself on his own lathe, and he was so pleased about it.«

»Am I really expected to believe that?« asked the ball.

»May I never be whipped again, if I'm not telling you the truth!« answered the top.

»You give a very fine account of yourself,« said the ball. »But I really must say no. You see, I'm what you might call half-engaged to a swallow.

Every time I go up in the air, he pops his head out of the nest and says: »Will you? Will you?« I've already said to myself that I will, and that's as good as a half-engagement. But I promise never to forget you.«

»A lot of good that'll be!« replied the top; and they said no more to each other.

Next day the ball was taken out into the garden. The top watched how she flew high up into the air, just like a bird, until she went clean out of sight. But she came back again each time and, whether from longing or because she had a cork inside her, this was always followed by a high bounce as soon as she touched the ground. The ninth time the ball went up, she never came back; the little boy looked and looked, but she had vanished.

»Ah, I could tell him where she is,« said the top with a sigh. »She's in the swallow's nest and has married the swallow.«

The more the top thought it all over, the more he lost his heart to the ball. The mere fact that he couldn't have her made him love her more than ever; the strange thing was that she should have accepted anyone else.

And the top went on dancing and spinning round, but all the time he was thinking about the ball, who grew more and more beautiful in his imagination. In this way several years went by, till gradually it became nothing more than an old love-affair...

But, although the top was no longer young, suddenly one day he found himself painted all over with gold. Never had he looked so handsome; he was now a gold top, and he whirled and whirled until he hummed. Gosh! It was something like! Then all at once he jumped too high – and disappeared. They looked and looked, even down in the basement, but he was not to be found.

Wherever had he got to?

He had jumped into the dustbin among all sorts of cabbage-stalks, sweepings and rubbish that had come down from the gutter on the roof.

»Here's a nice place for me to come to!« said the top. »My gold paint will soon go off and – did you ever see such riff-raff as I've got around me!« And then he peeped sideways at a long skinny-looking cabbage-stalk and a curious round object that looked like an old apple... But it wasn't an apple at all, it was an old ball that had been lying up in the gutter on the roof for several years and become quite sodden.

»Thank goodness, here's someone at last of one's own class that one can talk to,« said the ball, with a glance at the gilded top, »Actually I'm made of morocco leather, stitched by gentlewomen, and I've got a cork inside me, but nobody would ever think so to look at me. I was just going to marry a swallow, when I landed up in the gutter; and there I've been for five years growing more and more sodden. That's a long time, believe me, for a young lady.«

But the top didn't say a word. His thoughts went back to his old sweetheart, and the longer he listened the more certain he became that this was her.

Presently the maidservant came to clear out the dustbin. »Well, I never! Here's the gold top!« she said. Back in the house the top came in for lots of attention, but nothing was said about the ball, and the top never spoke again of his old love. Love is, of course, bound to fade away, when your sweetheart has spent five years growing sodden in a gutter; you can't be expected to know her again, if you meet her in a dustbin.

The Ugly Duckling

Summertime! How lovely it was out in the country, with the wheat standing yellow, the oats green, and the hay all stacked down in the grassy meadows! And there went the stork on his long red legs, chattering away in Egyptian, for he had learnt that language from his mother. The fields and meadows had large woods all around, and in the middle of the woods there were deep lakes.

Yes, it certainly was lovely out in the country. Bathed in sunshine stood an old manor-house with a deep moat round it, and growing out of the wall down by the water were huge dock-leaves; the biggest of them were so tall that little children could stand upright underneath. The place was as tangled and twisty as the densest forest, and here it was that a duck was sitting on her nest. It was time for her to hatch out her little ducklings, but it was such a long job that she was beginning to lose patience. She hardly ever had a visitor; the other ducks thought more of swimming about in the moat than of coming and sitting under a dock-leaf just for the sake of a quack with her.

At last the eggs cracked open one after the other – »peep! peep!« – and all the yolks had come to life and were sticking out their heads.

»Quack, quack!« said the mother duck, and then the little ones scuttled out as quickly as they could, prying all round under the green leaves; and she let them do this as much as they liked, because green is so good for the eyes.

»Oh, how big the world is!« said the ducklings. And they certainly had much more room now than when they were lying in the egg.

»Do you suppose this is the whole world!« said their mother. »Why, it goes a long way past the other side of the garden, right into the parson's field; but I've never been as far as that. Well, you're all out now, I hope« – and she got up from her nest – »no, not all; the largest egg is still here. How ever long will it be? I can't bother about it much more.« And she went on sitting again.

»Well, how's it going?« asked an old duck who came to pay a call.

»There's just this one egg that's taking such a time,« said the sitting duck. »It simply won't break. But just look at the others – the loveliest ducklings I've ever seen. They all take after their father – the wretch! Why doesn't he come and see me?«

»Let's have a look at the egg which won't crack,« said the old duck. »I'll bet it's a turkey's egg. That's how I was bamboozled once. The little ones gave me no end of trouble, for they were afraid of the water – fancy that! – I just couldn't get them to go in. I quacked and clacked, but it was no good. Let's have a look at the egg... Ay, that's a turkey's egg, depend upon it! Let it be and teach the others to swim.«

»I think I'll sit just a little while yet,« said the duck. »I've been sitting so long that it won't hurt to sit a little longer.«

»Please yourself!« said the old duck, and away she waddled.

At last the big egg cracked. There was a »peep! peep!« from the young one as he tumbled out, looking so large and ugly. The duck glanced at him and said: »My! what a huge great duckling that is! None of the others look a bit like that. Still, it's never a turkey-chick, I'll be bound ... Well, we shall soon find out. He shall go into the water, if I have to kick him in myself!«

The next day the weather was gloriously fine, with sun shining on all the green dock-leaves. The mother duck with her whole family came down to the moat. Splash! into the water she jumped. »Quack, quack!« she said, and one after another the ducklings plomped in after her. The water closed over their heads, but they were up again in a moment and floated along so beautifully. Their legs worked of their own accord, and now the whole lot were in the water – even the ugly grey duckling joined in the swimming.

»It's no turkey, that's certain«, said the duck. »Look how beautifully he uses his legs and how straight he holds himself. He's my own little one all right, and he's quite handsome, when you really come to look at him. quack, quack! Now, come along with me and let me show you the world and introduce you all to the barnyard, but mind and keep close to me, so that nobody steps on you; and keep a sharp look-out for the cat.«

Then they made their way into the duckyard. There was a fearful noise going on, for there were two families fighting for an eel's head, and af- ter all it was the cat that got it.

»You see! That's the way of the world,« said the mother duck and licked her bill, for she too had fancied the eel's head. »Now then, where are your legs?« she said, »Look slippy and make a nice bow to the old duck over there. She's the most genteel of all these; she has Spanish blood, that's why she's so plump. And do you see that crimson rag she wears on one leg? It's extremely fine; it's the highest distinction any duck can win. It's as good as saying that there is no thought of getting rid of her; man and beast are to take notice! Look alive, and don't turn your toes in! A well-bred duckling turns its toes out, like father and mother ... That's it. Now make a bow and say 'quack'!«

They all obeyed; but the other ducks round about looked at them and said out loud: »There! Now we've got to have that rabble as well – as if there weren't enough of us already! Ugh! What a sight that duckling is! We can't possibly put up with him« – and one duck immediately flew at him and bit him in the neck.

»Leave him alone,« said the mother. »He's doing no one any harm.«

»Yes, but he's so gawky and peculiar,« said the one that had pecked him, »so he'll have to be squashed.«

»What pretty children you have, my dear!« said the old duck with the rag on her leg. »All of them but one, who doesn't seem right. I only wish you could make him all over again.«

»No question of that, my lady,« said the ducklings' mother. »He's not pretty, but he's so good-tempered and he can swim just as well as the others – I daresay even a bit better. I fancy his looks will improve as he grows up, or maybe in time he'll grow down a little. He lay too long in the egg – that's why he isn't quite the right shape.« And then she plucked his neck for him and smoothed out his feathers. »Anyhow, he's a drake, and so it doesn't matter so much,« she added. »I feel sure he'll turn out pretty strong and be able to manage all right«.

»The other ducklings are charming,« said the old duck. »Make yourselves at home, my dears, and if you should find such a thing as an eel's head you may bring it to me.«

And so they made themselves at home.

But the poor duckling who was the last out of the egg and looked so ugly got pecked and jostled and teased by ducks and hens alike. »The great gawk!« they all clucked. And the turkey, who was born with spurs and therefore thought himself an emperor, puffed up his feathers like a ship under full sail and went straight at him, and then he gobble-gobbled till he was quite red in the face. The poor duckling didn't know where to turn; he was terribly upset over being so ugly and the laughing-stock of the whole barnyard.

That's how it was the first day, and afterwards things grew worse and worse. The poor duckling got chivied about by all of them; even his own brothers and sisters treated him badly, and they kept saying: »If only the cat would get you, you ridiculous great guy!« And the mother herself wished he were far away. The ducks nipped him, the hens pecked him, and the maid who had to feed the poultry let fly at him with her foot.

After that, he ran away and fluttered over the hedge, and the little birds in the bushes grew frightened and flew into the air. »That's because I'm so ugly,« thought the duckling and closed his eyes – and yet managed to get away. Eventually he came out to the great marsh where the wild-ducks lived and lay there all night, utterly tired and dispirited.

In the morning the wild-ducks flew up and looked at their new companion. »What ever are you?« they asked, and the duckling turned in every direction and bowed as well as he could.

»What a scarecrow you are!« said the wild-ducks, »but that won't matter to us, as long as you don't marry into our family.« Poor thing! He wasn't dreaming of getting married; all he wanted was to be allowed to stay quietly among the rushes and drink a little marsh-water. After he had been there for two whole days, two wild-geese came along – or rather two wild-ganders, for they were both males. It was not long since they were hatched; that's why they were so perky.

»Look here, my lad!« they began. »You are so ugly that we quite like you. Will you come in with us and migrate? Not far off, in another marsh, are some very nice young wild-geese, none of them married, who can quack beautifully. Here's a chance for you to make a hit, ugly as you are.«

»Bang! bang!« suddenly echoed above them, and both the ganders fell down dead in the rushes, and the water became red with blood. »Bang! bang!« sounded once more, and flocks of wild-geese flew up from the rushes, so that immediately fresh shots rang out. A big shoot was on. The party lay ready all round the marsh; some even sat up in the trees on the branches that stretched right out over the rushes. Clouds of blue smoke drifted in among the dark trees and hung far over the water. Splashing through the mud came the gun-dogs, bending back reeds and rushes this way and that. It was terrifying for the poor duckling, who was just turning his head round to bury it under his wing when he suddenly found close beside him a fearsome great dog with lolling tongue and grim, glittering eyes. It lowered its muzzle right down to the duckling, bared its sharp teeth and – splash! it went off again without touching him.

The duckling gave a sigh of relief. »Thank goodness, I'm so ugly that even the dog doesn't fancy the taste of me.« And he lay there quite still, while the shot pattered on the reeds and crack after crack was heard from the guns.

It was late in the day before everything was quiet again, but the poor duckling didn't dare to get up yet;, he waited several hours longer before he took a look round and then made off from the marsh as fast as he could go. Over field and meadow he scuttled, but there was such a wind that he found it difficult to get along.

Towards evening he came up to a poor little farm-cottage; it was so broken-down that it hardly knew which way to fall, and so it remained standing. The wind whizzed so fiercely round the duckling that he had to sit on his tail so as not to be blown over. The wind grew worse and worse. Then he noticed that the door had come off one of its hinges and hung so much on the slant that he could slip into the house through the crack. And that's just what he did.

There was an old woman living here with her cat and her hen. The cat, whom she called Sonny, could arch its back and purr; it could even give out sparks, if you stroked its fur the wrong way. The hen had such short little legs that it was called Chickabiddy Shortlegs; it was a very good layer, and the woman loved it like her own child.

Next morning they at once noticed the strange duckling, and the cat started to purr and the hen to cluck. »Why, what's up?« said the woman, looking round. But her sight wasn't very good, and she took the duckling for a fat duck that had lost its way. »My! What a find!« she said. »I shall be able to have duck's eggs – as long as it isn't a drake! We must give it a trial.«

And so the duckling was taken on trial for three weeks; but there was no sign of an egg. Now, the cat was master in the house and the hen was mistress, and they always used to say »We and the world,« because they fancied that they made up half the world – what's more, much the superior half of it. The duckling thought there might be two opinions about that, but the hen wouldn't hear of it.

»Can you lay eggs?« she asked.

»No.«

»Well, then, hold your tongue, will you!«

And the cat asked: »Can you arch your back or purr or give out sparks?«

»No.«

»Well, then, your opinion's not wanted, when sensible people are talking.«

And the duckling sat in the corner, quite out of spirits. Then suddenly he remembered the fresh air and the sunshine, and he got such a curious longing to swim in the water that – he couldn't help it – he had to tell the hen.

»What's the matter with you?« she asked. »You haven't anything to do - that's why you get these fancies. They'd soon go, if only you'd lay eggs or else purr.«

»But it's so lovely to swim in the water«, said the duckling; »so lovely to duck your head in it and dive down to the bottom.«

»Most enjoyable, I'm sure,« said the hen.

»You must have gone crazy. Ask the cat about it – I've never met any one as clever as he is – ask him if he's fond of swimming or diving! I say nothing of myself. Ask our old mistress, the wisest woman in the world! Do you suppose that she's keen on swimming and diving?«

»You don't understand me,« said the duckling.

»Well, if we don't understand you, I should like to know who would. Surely you'll never try and make out you are wiser than the cat and the mistress – not to mention myself. Don't be silly, child! Give thanks to your Maker for all the kindness you have met with. Haven't you come to a nice warm room, where you have company that can teach you something? But you're just a stupid, and there's no fun in having you here. You may take my word for it – if I say unpleasant things to you, it's all for your good; that's just how you can tell which are your real friends. Only see that you lay eggs and learn how to purr or give out sparks!«

»I think I'll go out into the wide world,« said the duckling.

»Yes, do,« said the hen.

And so the duckling went off. He swam in the water; he dived down;

but none of them would have anything to do with him because of his ugliness.

Autumn now set in. The leaves in the wood turned yellow and brown, the wind seized them and whirled them about, while the sky above had a frosty look. The clouds hung heavy with hail and snow, and the raven who perched on the fence kept squawking »ow! ow!« – he felt so cold. The very thought of it gave you the shivers. Yes, the poor duckling was certainly having a bad time.

One evening, when there was a lovely sunset, a whole flock of large handsome birds appeared out of the bushes. The duckling had never seen such beautiful birds, all glittering white with long graceful necks. They were swans. They gave the most extraordinary cry, spread out their magnificent long wings and flew from this cold country away to warmer lands and open lakes.

They mounted high, high up into the air, and the ugly little duckling felt so strange as he watched them. He turned round and round in the water like a wheel and craned his neck in their direction, letting out a cry so shrill and strange that it quite scared even himself. Ah! he could never forget those beautiful, fortunate birds; and directly they were lost to sight he dived right down to the bottom and, when he came up again, he was almost beside himself. He had no idea what the birds were called, nor where they were flying to, and yet they were dearer to him than any he had ever known; he didn't envy them in the least – how could he ever dream of such loveliness for himself? He would be quite satisfied, if only the ducks would just put up with him, poor gawky-looking creature!

What a cold winter it was! The duckling had to keep swimming about in the water to prevent it freezing right up. But every night the pool he was swimming in grew smaller and smaller; then the ice froze so hard that you could hear it creaking. The duckling had to keep his feet moving all the time to prevent the water from closing up. At last he grew faint with exhaustion and lay quite still and finally froze fast in the ice.

Early next morning he was seen by a peasant who went out and broke the ice with his wooden clog and carried the duckling home to his wife. And there they revived him.

The children wanted to play with him, but the duckling was afraid they meant mischief and fluttered in panic right up into the milkbowl, so that the milk slopped over into the room. The woman screamed out and clapped her hands in the air, and then he flew into the butter-tub, and from there down into the flour-bin, and out of it again. Dear, dear, he did look an object! The woman screamed at him and hit at him with the tongs, and the children tumbled over each other trying to catch him – how they laughed and shouted!... It was a good thing the door was open; the duckling darted out into the bushes and sank down, dazed, in the new-fallen snow.

But it would be far too dismal to describe all the want and misery the

duckling had to go through during that hard winter ... He was sheltering among the reeds on the marsh, when the sun began to get warm again and the larks to sing; beautiful spring had arrived.

Then all at once he tried his wings; the whirr of them was louder than before, and they carried him swiftly away. Almost before he realized it, he found himself in a big garden with apple-trees in blossom and sweet-smelling lilac that dangled from long green boughs right over the winding stream. Oh, it was so lovely here in all the freshness of spring! And straight ahead, out of the thicket, came three beautiful white swans, ruffling their feathers and floating so lightly on the water. The duckling recognized the splendid creatures and was overcome with a strange feeling of melancholy.

»I will fly across to them, those royal birds! They will peck me to death for daring, ugly as I am, to go near them. Never mind! Better to be killed by them than be nipped by the ducks, pecked by the hens, kicked by the girl who minds the poultry, and suffer hardship in winter.« And he flew out on to the water and swam towards the beautiful swans. As they caught sight of him, they darted with ruffled feathers to meet him. »Yes, kill me, kill me!« cried the poor creature and bowed his head to the water awaiting death. But what did he see there in the clear stream? It was a reflection of himself that he saw in front of him, but no longer a clumsy greyish bird, ugly and unattractive – no, he was himself a swan!

It doesn't matter about being born in a duckyard, as long as you are hatched from a swan's egg.

He felt positively glad at having gone through so much hardship and want; it helped him to appreciate all the happiness and beauty that were there to welcome him ... And the three great swans swam round and round and stroked him with their beaks.

Some little children came into the garden and threw bread and grain into the water, and the smallest one called out: »There's a new swan!«

and the other children joined in with shouts of delight: »Yes, there's a new swan!« And they clapped their hands and danced about and ran to fetch father and mother. Bits of bread and cake were thrown into the water, and everyone said. »The new one is the prettiest – so young and handsome!« And the old swans bowed before him.

This made him feel quite shy, and he tucked his head away under his wing – he himself hardly knew why. He was too, too happy, but not a bit proud, for a good heart is never proud. He thought of how he had been despised and persecuted, and now he heard everybody saying that he was the loveliest of all lovely birds. And the lilacs bowed their branches to him right down to the water, and the sunshine felt so warm and kindly. Then he ruffled his feathers, raised his slender neck and rejoiced from his heart: »I never dreamed of so much happiness, when I was the ugly duckling.«

The Red Shoes

There was once a little girl, very delicate and pretty, and yet so poor that in summer she always had to go barefooted and in winter she had to wear big wooden clogs which chafed her insteps most horribly, until they were quite red.

In the middle of the village lived a shoemaker's widow, who had some strips of old red cloth, and out of these she did her best to sew a little pair of shoes. They were rather clumsy-looking shoes, but the old widow meant well; they were for the little girl, whose name was Karen. As it happened, she got the red shoes and put them on for the first time on the very day that her mother was buried. Of course they weren't exactly the right shoes for a funeral, but they were the only ones she had; and so she wore them on her bare feet, as she followed the humble straw coffin.

Just then a large old-looking carriage drove up with a large old-looking lady inside it. She caught sight of the little girl and felt sorry for her. So she said to the parson: »Look here, if you let me have the little girl, I'll take care of her.«

Karen thought this was all because of the red shoes, but the old lady said they were hideous and had them burnt; Karen herself was given nice new clothes and was taught to read and sew. People said how pretty she was, but the looking-glass said to her: »You are more than pretty, you are lovely.«

On one occasion the Queen was passing through the country with her little daughter, who was a Princess. People flocked around the castle, and Karen was there too; and the little Princess showed herself at one of the windows. She was wearing a beautiful white dress; no train nor golden crown, but lovely red morocco shoes – far, far prettier than the ones the shoemaker's widow had made for little Karen. No, there was really nothing in the world like red shoes.

But now Karen was old enough to be confirmed. She was given new clothes, and she was also to have new shoes. The best shoemaker in town took the measurement of her feet in his own private room, where there were big glass cabinets with elegant shoes and shiny boots. They made a brave shoe, but the old lady's sight was far from good, and so it gave her no pleasure. Among the shoes was a red pair just like the ones the Princess had been wearing – oh, they were pretty! The shoemaker explained that they had been made for an earl's daughter but didn't quite fit. »That must be patent leather from the way they shine,« said the old lady.

»Yes, don't they shine!« said Karen; and as they were a good fit, the shoes were bought. But the old lady didn't realize that they were red, for she would never have allowed Karen to go to Confirmation in red shoes. And yet that's just what happened.

Everybody stared at her feet and, as she walked up the aisle to the chancel, she felt that even the old pictures over the tombs, those portraits of the clergy and their wives in stiff ruffs and long black garments, were fastening their eyes on the red shoes. It was these that filled her thoughts, when the priest laid his hand on her head and spoke of holy baptism, of the covenant with God, and of her duty now to become a fully-fledged Christian. And the organ played so solemnly, and the children sang so beautifully, and the old choirmaster sang, too; but Karen thought of nothing but her red shoes.

By the afternoon, sure enough, the old lady had heard from everybody about the shoes being red, and she said how shocking it was; they were quite out of place and in future, when Karen went to church, she must always wear black shoes, however old they were.

Next Sunday there was Communion, and Karen looked at the black shoes, and she looked at the red ones... And then she looked at the red ones again – and put the red ones on.

It was a beautiful sunny day. Karen and the old lady took the path through the cornfield, where it was a bit dusty. At the churchdoor stood an old soldier with a crutch and a funny long beard which was more red than white – in fact, it really was red. He made a deep bow to the old lady and asked if he might dust her shoes. And when Karen also put out her foot, »My! what lovely dancingshoes!« said the soldier. »Stay on tight when you dance!« and he gave the soles a tap with his hand.

The old lady gave the soldier something for himself and went with Karen into the church. The whole congregation stared at Karen's red shoes, and so did all the portraits; and when Karen knelt before the altar and put the gold chalice to her lips, she thought of nothing but the red shoes – it seemed as if they were floating in front of her. She forgot to sing the hymns, and she forgot to say the prayers.

Presently everyone came out of church, and the old lady stepped into her carriage. As Karen raised her foot to get in after her, the old soldier, who was standing close by, said: »My! what lovely dancing-shoes!« Karen couldn't resist – she had to dance a few steps and, once she had started, her feet went on dancing just as though the shoes had some power over them. She danced round the corner of the church – she couldn't stop; the coachman had to run after her and pick her up and carry her back into the carriage. But still her feet went on dancing and gave the kind old lady some dreadful kicks. At last they got the shoes off, and her legs kept still.

When they came home, the shoes were put away in a cupboard, but Karen still kept taking a peep at them. By and by the old lady fell ill; it was said she would never get better. She had to be nursed and cared for, and nobody was more suited for this than Karen. But a big ball was being given in the town, and Karen was invited. She looked at the old lady, who after all couldn't live long, and she looked at the red shoes. She couldn't see there would be any harm. She put on the red shoes, she had a perfect right to do that ... But then she went to the ball and began to dance.

But when she wanted to go to the right, the shoes went dancing off to the left; and when she wanted to go up the room, the shoes went dancing down the room - down the stairs through the street and out by the town-gate. Dance she did and dance she must, away into the dark forest.

Up among the trees she saw something shining. It looked like a face, and so she thought it was the moon; but it was the old soldier with the red beard, sitting and nodding and saying: »My! what lovely dancing-shoes!«

This made her frightened, and she tried to kick off the red shoes, but they still stuck on tight. She tore off her stockings, but the shoes had grown fast to her feet, and so dance she did and dance she must, over field and furrow, in rain and sun, by night and day; but the night-time was the worst.

She danced into the open churchyard, but the dead there didn't dance; they had something better to do. She wanted to sit down by the poor man's grave, where the bitter tansy grew; but peace and quiet were not for her and, when she danced towards the open church-door, she found an angel there in long white robes and with wings reaching from his shoulders to the ground. His face was stern and solemn, and in his hand he held a sword with broad shining blade.

»Dance you shall,« said the angel, »dance in your red shoes until you are cold and pale, until your skin shrivels up like a skeleton's! Dance you shall from door to door, and at all the houses where the children are vain and proud you shall knock till they hear you and are frightened. You shall dance, you shall dance...!«

»Mercy! Mercy!« cried Karen. But she never heard the angel's answer, for the shoes whirled her away through the gate and the field, along highway and byway, dancing, dancing, all the time.

One morning she danced past a door she knew well. From inside came the sound of a hymn; then out came a coffin all covered with flowers. She realized then that the old lady was dead, and she felt that now she was deserted by everyone, as well as cursed by the angel of God.

Dance she did and dance she must, dance on in the dark night ... The shoes whirled her away over thorns and stubble, until she was scratched and bleeding. She danced across the heath up to a lonely little house. She knew that the executioner lived here, and she rapped the window-pane with her knuckles and said: »Please come out! I can't come in, because I'm dancing.«

»Do you mean to say you don't know who I am? I cut off wicked people's heads – my goodness, how my axe is quivering!«

»Please don't cut off my head!« said Karen, »for then I can't show that I'm sorry for my sins. Cut off my feet with the red shoes.«

Then she confessed all her sins, and the executioner cut off her feet with the red shoes. But the shoes went dancing with the little feet across the fields into the depths of the forest. And he made her wooden feet and crutches; he taught her a hymn – the Psalm for Sinners – and she kissed the hand that had wielded the axe and went her way across the heath.

»Surely by now I must have done penance for the red shoes,« she said. »I'll go to church and let everyone see me.« And she did; she went quickly towards the church-door but, when she reached it, there were the red shoes dancing in front of her, and she grew frightened and turned back.

All the next week she was miserable and did nothing but cry, but when Sunday came round she said to herself: »Dear me, I really feel I've been through enough. Surely I'm just as good as many of those that sit so perkily there in church.« And she plucked up her courage and started off, but she got no further than the gate, when she saw the red shoes dancing in front of her, and she grew frightened and turned back and repented deeply of her sins.

Next she made her way to the parsonage and asked to be taken in there as a servant; she would work so hard and do her very best. She never gave a thought to the wages, only that she might have a roof over her head and be with kind people.

The parson's wife felt sorry for her and took her into her service and found her hard-working and sensible. In the evenings Karen sat and listened in silence, while the parson read aloud from the Bible. All the little ones were very fond of her but, when there was talk of dress and finery and of being as pretty as a picture, she would shake her head.

The following Sunday they all went to church, and they asked her to go with them; but with tears in her eyes she looked sadly at her crutches and, when the others went off to hear the word of God, she went alone to her tiny room, where there was just enough space for a bed and a chair, and here she sat devoutly reading her prayerbook. As she did so, the wind brought the sound of the organ to her from the church, and her eyes filled with tears as she lifted up her face, exclaiming: »Help me, O God«!

Then the sun came out so brightly, and straight in front of her stood the same angel in white robes that she had seen that night at the church-door. But instead of the sharp sword he was holding a beautiful green bough that was covered with roses; and he touched the ceiling with it so that it arched itself higher, and where he touched it there shone a golden star. And he touched the walls so that they grew wider; and she saw the organ which was still playing, she saw the old pictures of the clergy and their wives, and the congregation sitting in the carved pews and singing from their hymn-books... You see, the church itself had come to the poor girl in her narrow little room – or was it she who had come to the church? She was sitting in the pew with all the others from the parsonage and, when they had finished the hymn and looked up from their books, they nodded to her and said: »It was right you should come, Karen.« »It was God's mercy!« she answered.

And the organ pealed forth and the young voices of the choir sounded so soft and pure. The bright warm sunshine streamed in through the church-window to the place where Karen was sitting. Her heart was so full of sunshine and peace and joy that at last it broke, and her soul flew on the sunbeams to heaven, where there was no one to ask about the red shoes.

The Little Match-Seller

It was terribly cold. Snow was falling and soon it would be quite dark; for it was the last day in the year - New Year's Eve. Along the street, in that same cold and dark, went a poor little girl in bare feet - well, yes, it's true, she had slippers on when she left home; but what was the good of that? They were great big slippers which her mother used to wear, so you can imagine the size of them; and they both came off when the little girl scurried across the road just as two carts went whizzing by at a fearful rate. One slipper was not to be found, and a boy ran off with the other, saying it would do for a cradle one day when he had children of his own.

So there was the little girl walking along in her bare feet that were simply blue with cold. In an old apron she was carrying a whole lot of matches, and she had one bunch of them in her hand. She hadn't sold anything all day, and no one had given her a single penny. Poor mite, she looked so downcast as she trudged along hungry and shivering. The snowflakes settled on her long flaxen hair, which hung in pretty curls over her shoulder; but you may be sure she wasn't thinking about her looks. Lights were shining in every window, and out into the street came the lovely smell of roast goose. You see, it was New Year's Eve; that's what she was thinking about.

Over in a little corner between two houses - one of them jutted out rather more into the street than the other - there she crouched and huddled with her legs tucked under her; but she only got colder and colder. She didn't dare to go home, for she hadn't sold a match nor earned a single penny. Her father would beat her, and besides it was so cold at home. They had only the bare roof over their heads and the wind whistled through that although the worst cracks had been stopped up with rags and straw. Her hands were really quite numb with cold. Ah, but a little match – that would be a comfort. If only she dared pull one out of the bunch, just one, strike it on the wall and warm her fingers! She pulled one out ... ritch!... how it spirted and blazed! Such a clear warm flame, like a little candle, as she put her hand round it – yes, and what a curious light it was! The little girl fancied she was sitting in front of a big iron stove with shiny brass knobs and brass facings, with such a warm friendly fire burning.. why, whatever was that? She was just stretching out her toes, so as to warm them too, when – out went the flame, and the stove vanished. There she sat with a little stub of burnt-out match in her hand.

She struck another one. It burned up so brightly, and where the gleam fell on the wall this became transparent like gauze. She could see right into the room, where the table was laid with a glittering white cloth and with delicate china; and there, steaming deliciously, was the roast goose stuffed with prunes and apples. Then, what was even finer, the goose jumped off the dish and waddled along the floor with the carving knife and fork in its back. Right up to the poor little girl it came... but then the match went out, and nothing could be seen but the massive cold wall.

She lighted another match. Now she was sitting under the loveliest Christmas tree; it was even bigger and prettier than the one she had seen through the glass-door at the rich merchant's at Christmas. Hundreds of candles were burning on the green branches, and gay-coloured prints, like the ones they hang in the shop-windows, looked down at her. The little girl reached up both her hands ... then the match went out; all the Christmas candles rose higher and higher, until now she could see they were the shining stars. One of them rushed down the sky with a long fiery streak.

»That's somebody dying,« said the little girl, for her dead Grannie, who was the only one who had been kind to her, had told her that a falling star shows that a soul is going up to God.

She struck yet another match on the wall. It gave a glow all around, and there in the midst of it stood her old grandmother, looking so very

bright and gentle and loving. »Oh, Grannie«, cried the little girl, »do take me with you! I know you'll disappear as soon as the match goes out – just as the warm stove did, and the lovely roast goose, and the wonderful great Christmas-tree«. And she quickly struck the rest of the matches in the bunch, for she did so want to keep her Grannie there. And the matches flared up so gloriously that it became brighter than broad daylight. Never had Grannie looked so tall and beautiful. She took the little girl into her arms, and together they flew in joy and splendour, up, up, to where there was no cold, no hunger, no fear. They were with God.

But in the cold early morning huddled between the two houses, sat the little girl with rosy cheeks and a smile on her lips, frozen to death on the last night of the old year. The New Year dawned on the little dead body leaning there with the matches, one lot of them nearly all used up. »She was trying to get warm,« people said. Nobody knew what lovely things she had seen and in what glory she had gone with her old Grannie to the happiness of the New Year.

Simple Simon

(a nursery tale retold)

Away in the country, in an old manorhouse, lived an old squire. He had two sons who were so clever that – well, the fact is they were too clever by half. They made up their minds to go and propose to the King's daughter; and they had a perfect right to do this, because she had announced that she would marry the man who she thought was best able to speak up for himself.

The two sons now spent a week in preparation. A week was all they were allowed; but it was quite long enough, for they had had a good education, and that is such a help. One of them knew the whole Latin dictionary off by heart, and also the local newspaper for the last three years, both backwards and forwards. The other son had learnt up all the by-laws of the city companies and the things every alderman is supposed to know; he thought this would help him to talk politics with the Princess; and, besides, he knew how to embroider braces, he was so very clever with his fingers.

»I shall win the Princess!« cried both of them; and so their father gave them each a beautiful horse. The brother who had learnt off the dictionary and the newspapers got a coal-black horse; and the one who knew all about aldermen and could do embroidery got a milk-white horse; and then they smeared the corners of their mouths with cod-liver oil, so that the words would come out pat. All the servants were down in the courtyard to see them mount their horses, when just at that moment up came the third brother; for there were three of them, though nobody ever took count of the third, because he wasn't a scholar like the other two. They called him Simple Simon.

»Where are you two off to in that get up?« he asked.

»We're going to Court, to talk our way into favour with the Princess. Haven't you heard the proclamation that's been read out all over the country?« And then they told him all about it.

»Gosh! I mustn't miss this!« said Simple Simon. But his brothers laughed at him and rode away.

»Dad, let me have a horse!« cried Simple Simon. »I do so feel like getting married. If she'll have me, she'll have me; and if she won't , then I'll marry her all the same.«

»What nonsense!« said the father. »I've no horse for you. Why, you never open your mouth. But look at your brothers – they are splendid fellows.«

»If I can't have a horse,« said the boy, »then I'll ride the billy-goat. It's my own, and it'll carry me all right, I know.« Then he got astride the billy-goat, dug his heels into its sides and dashed off down the road. Phew! What a rate they went! »Look out! Here we come!« yelled Simple Simon, and his cries went echoing after him.

But his brothers rode on ahead in complete silence. They never said a word, because they had to turn over in their minds all the clever remarks they were going to make. It had to be most cunningly worked out, I can tell you.

»Tally-ho!« shouted Simple Simon, »here we are! Look what I found on the road,« and he showed them a dead crow he had picked up.

»You simpleton!« they said. »What are you going to do with that?«

»I shall give it to the Princess.«

»Yes, do!« they answered, laughing as they rode on.

»Tally-ho! Here we are! Now look what I've found. You don't find that on the road every day.«

The brothers turned round again to see what it was. »You simpleton!« they said. »Why, that's an old clog with the vamp missing. Is the Princess to have that as well?«

»Yes, of course,« said Simple Simon; and his brothers only laughed at him and rode on till they were a long way ahead.

»Tally-ho! Here we are!« shouted Simon. »My word! This is getting better and better. Tally-ho! This is grand!«

»What have you found this time?« asked the brothers.

»Oh, it's too good for anything,« said Simple Simon. »Won't she be pleased, the Princess!«

»Ugh!« said the brothers. »Why, it's mud straight out of the ditch.«

»Yes, that's just what it is,« said Simple Simon, »and the very finest sort, too; it slips right through your fingers.« And he filled his pocket with the mud.

But his two brothers rode on as hard as they could go, and the result

was that they drew up at the city gate a whole hour ahead of him and found the suitors being given numbers in the order of their arrival. They were made to stand in rows, six in each file, and so close together that they couldn't move their arms. This was just as well, for otherwise they might have stabbed each other in the back, just because one was in front of the other.

The rest of the inhabitants all crowded round the castle, right up against the windows, so as to watch the Princess receiving her suitors; but as soon as ever one of them came into her presence, he was completely tongue-tied. »No good!« the Princess kept saying. »Skedaddle!«

Now it was the turn of the brother who knew the dictionary by heart. But he had clean forgotten it while he was standing in the queue; and the floor creaked under him, and the ceiling was all covered with mirrors, so that he saw himself standing on his head. At the window stood three clerks and an alderman, who all wrote down every word that was spoken, so that it could go straight into the newspaper and be sold for a penny at the street-corner. It was dreadful; and what's more, they had made up such a fire that the stove was red-hot.

»It's very warm in here,« said the suitor.

»That's because my father's roasting cockerels to-day,« said the Princess.

»O-o-oh!« was all he could say, as he stood there. He hadn't expected a remark like that, and he was hoping to say something witty. »O-o-oh!«

»No good!« said the Princess. »Skedaddle!« – and away he had to go. After that the second brother came in.

»It's dreadfully hot in here,« he said.

»Yes, we're roasting cockerels for dinner,« said the Princess.

126

»I b-beg your – b-beg your – « he stuttered; and the clerks all wrote down »I b-beg your – b-beg your – «

»No good!« said the Princess. »Skedaddle!«

Now it was Simple Simon's turn. He came trotting in on the billygoat, right into the palace-room. »Why, it's as hot as blazes in here!« he said.

»That's because I'm roasting cockerels,« said the Princess.

»Oh, I say, that's lucky,« said Simple Simon. »So I suppose I can have a crow roasted, can't I!«

»Of course you can, quite easily,« said the Princess; »but have you got anything to roast it in, for I've neither pot nor pan.«

»But I have,« said Simon. »Here's a cooker with a tin handle!« And he produced the old clog and popped the crow straight into it.

»It will make quite a meal,« said the Princess. »But what shall we do for gravy?«

»I've got that in my pocket,« said Simon. »I've enough and to spare.« And he tipped a little mud out of his pocket.

»I do like that!« said the Princess. »You know how to answer; you can speak up for yourself, and you're the one I'm going to marry! But do you realize that every word we've been saying has been written down and will be in the papers to-morrow? Look there by the window – three clerks and an old alderman; and the alderman is the worst, because he doesn't understand a thing.« Of course she said this just to frighten him. And the clerks all guffawed and made a great blot of ink on the floor.

»So these are the gentry?« said Simon. »Well, here's one for the alderman!« And he turned out his pocket and let him have the mud full in the face.

»Well done!« cried the Princess. »I could never have done that, but I'll soon learn.« So in the end Simple Simon became King with a wife of his own and a crown and a throne. And all this comes straight out of the alderman's newspaper; so it may not be perfectly true!

The Fir Tree

Out in the wood was a fir tree, such a pretty little fir tree. It had a good place to grow in and all the air and sunshine it wanted, while all around it were numbers of bigger comrades, both firs and pines. But the little fir tree was in such a passionate hurry to grow. It paid no heed to the warmth of the sun or the sweetness of the air, and it took no notice of the village children who went chattering along when they were out after strawberries or raspberries; sometimes they came there with a whole jugful or had got strawberries threaded on a straw, and then they sat down by the little tree and said, »Oh, what a dear little tree!« That was not at all the kind of thing the tree wanted to hear.

The next year it had shot up a good deal, and the year after that its girth had grown even bigger; for, with a fir tree, you can always tell how old it is by the number of rings it has.

»Oh, if only I were a tall tree like the others,« sighed the little fir. »Then I'd be able to spread out my branches all round me and see out over the wide world with my top. The birds would come and nest in my branches and, whenever it was windy, I'd be able to nod just as grandly as the others.«

It took no pleasure in the sunshine or the birds or the pink clouds that, morning and evening, went sailing overhead.

When winter came and the snow lay sparkling white all around, then a hare would often come bounding along and jump right over the little tree - oh, how annoying that was! ... But two winters passed and by the third winter the tree had grown so tall that the hare had to run round it. Yes, grow, grow, become tall and old - that was much the finest thing in the world, thought the tree.

In the autumn the woodcutters always came and felled some of the tallest trees. That used to happen every year; and the young fir, which was now quite a sizable tree, trembled at the sight, for the splendid great trees would crack and crash to the ground; their branches were lopped off, and they looked all naked and spindly - they were hardly recognisable - and then they were loaded on to waggons and carted away by horses out of the wood.

Where were they off to? What was in store for them?

In the spring, when the swallow and the stork arrived, the tree asked them, »Do you know where they've gone - where they've been taken to? Have you seen anything of them?«

The swallows knew nothing, but the stork looked thoughtful and replied with a nod, »Yes, I believe I know. I came across a lot of new ships, as I flew here from Egypt; they had splendid masts - I daresay it was them - I could smell the fir, and they asked to be remembered to you. Oh, how straight they stand!«

»How I do wish that I were big enough to fly across the sea! And, as a matter of fact, what sort of a thing is this sea? What does it look like?«

»That would take far too long to explain,« said the stork and went his way.

»Rejoice in your youth,« said the sunbeams; »rejoice in your lusty growth, and in the young life that is in you.« And the wind kissed the tree, and the dew wept tears over it, but this meant nothing to the fir tree.

As Christmas drew near, quite young trees were cut down, trees that often were nothing like so big or so old as our fir tree, which knew no peace and was always longing to get away. These young trees - and they were just the very handsomest ones - always kept their branches; they were laid on waggons and carted away by horses out of the wood.

»Where are they off to?« asked the fir tree. »They are no bigger than I am; there was even one that was much smaller. Why did they all keep their branches? Where are they going?«

»We know, we know!« twittered the sparrows. »We've been peeping in at the windows down in the town; we know where they're going. All the glory and splendour you can imagine awaits them. We looked in through the window-panes and saw how the trees were planted in the middle of a cosy room and decorated with the loveliest things: gilded apples, honey cakes, toys and hundreds of candles.«

»And then?« asked the fir tree, quivering in every branch. »And then? What happens then?«

»Well, we didn't see any more. But it was magnificent.«

»I wonder if it will be my fate to go that dazzling road,« cried the tree in delight. »It's even better than crossing the ocean. How I'm longing for Christmas! I'm now just as tall and spreading as the others who were taken away last year. Oh, if only I were already on the waggon - if only I were in the cosy room amidst all that glory and splendour! And then? yes, there must be something still better, still more beautiful in store for me – or why should they decorate me like that? – something much greater, and much more splendid. But what? Oh, the' labouring and longing I go through! I don't know myself what's the matter with me.«

»Rejoice in me,« said the air and the sunlight; »rejoice in your lusty youth out here in the open.«

But the fir tree did nothing of the kind. It went on growing and growing; there it was, winter and summer, always green - dark green. People who saw it remarked, »That's a pretty tree«; and at Christmas time it was the first to be felled. The axe cut deep through pit and marrow, and the tree fell to the earth with a sigh, faint with pain, with no more thoughts of any happines; it was so sad at parting from its home, from the place where it had grown up. For it knew that never again would it see those dear old friends, the little bushes and flowers that grew around – yes, and perhaps not even the birds. There was nothing pleasant about such a parting.

The tree didn't come to itself till it was being unloaded in the yard with the other trees and it heard a man say, »That one's a beauty - that's the one we'll have«

Now came two lackeys in full fig and carried the fir tree into a splendid great room. There were portraits all round on the walls, and by the big tile fireplace stood huge Chinese vases with lions on their lids. There were rocking-chairs, silk-covered sofas, large tables piled with picture-books and toys worth hundreds of pounds - at least, so said the children. And the fir tree was propped up in a great firkin barrel filled with sand, though no one could see it was a barrel because it was draped round with green baize and was standing on a gay-coloured carpet. How the tree trembled! Whatever was going to happen? Servants and young ladies alike were soon busy decorating it. On the branches they hung the little nets that had been cut out of coloured paper, each net being filled with sweets; gilded apples and walnuts hung down as if they were growing there, and over a hundred red, blue and white candles were fastened to the branches. Dolls that looked just like living people - such as the tree had never seen before- hovered among the greenery, while right up at the very top they had put a great star of gold tinsel; it was magnificent – you never saw anything like it.

»Tonight«, they all said, »tonight it's going to sparkle - you see!«

»Oh, if only tonight were here!« thought the tree. »If only the candles were already lighted! What happens then, I wonder? Do trees come from the wood to look at me? Will the sparrows fly to the window-panes? Shall I take root here and keep my decorations winter and summer?«

Well, well, - a nice lot the fir tree knew! But it had got barkache from sheer longing, and barkache is just as bad for a tree as headache is for the rest of us.

At last the candles were lighted – what a blaze, what magnificence! It made the tree tremble in every branch, until one of the candles set fire to the greenery – didn't that smart!

»Oh dear!« cried the young ladies and quickly put out the fire. It was so afraid of losing any of its finery, and it felt quite dazed by all that magnificence ... Then suddenly both folding doors flew open, and a flock of children came tearing in, as if they were going to upset the whole tree. The older people followed soberly behind; the little ones stood quite silent – but only for a moment – then they made the air ring with their shouts of delight. They danced round the tree, and one present after another was pulled off it.

»Whatever are they doing?« thought the tree. »What's going to happen?« The candles burned right down to their branches and, as they did so, they were put out, and the children were allowed to plunder the tree. They rushed in at it, till it creaked in every branch; if it hadn't been fastened to the ceiling by the top and the gold star, it would have tumbled right over.

The children danced round with their splendid toys, and nobody looked at the tree except the old nurse, who went peering among the branches - though this was only to see if there wasn't some fig or apple that had been overlooked.

»A story – tell us a story!« cried the children, dragging a little fat man over towards the tree. He sat down right under it, »for then we are in the greenwood,« he said, »and it will be so good for the tree to listen with you. But I'll only tell one story. Would you like the one about *Hickory-Dickory* or the one about *Humpty-Dumpty, who fell downstairs and yet came to the throne and married the Princess?*«

»*Hickory-Dickory*«, cried some; »*Humpty-Dumpty,*« cried others. There was such yelling and shouting; only the fir tree was quite silent and thought »Shan't I be in it as well? Isn't there anything for me to do?« But of course, it *had* been in it – done just what it had to do.

The little fat man told them the story of *Humpty-Dumpty, who fell downstairs and yet came to the throne and married the Princess.* And the children clapped their hands and called out, »Tell us another story! One more!« They wanted to have *Hickory-Dickory* as well, but they only got the one about *Humpty-Dumpty.* The fir tree stood there in silent thought: never had the birds out in the wood told a story like that. »Humpty-Dumpty fell downstairs and yet married the Princess – well, well, that's how they go on in the great world!« thought the fir tree, and felt it must all be true, because the story-teller was such a nice man. »Well, who knows? Maybe I too shall fall downstairs and marry a Princess.« And it looked forward to being decked out again next day with candles and toys, tinsel and fruit.

»I shan't tremble tomorrov,« it thought. »I mean to enjoy my magnificence to the full. Tomorrow I shall again hear the story about Humpty-Dumpty and perhaps the one about Hickory-Dickory as well.« And the tree stood the whole night in silent thought.

The next morning in came manservant and maid.

»Now all the doings will begin again,« thought the tree. Instead, they hauled it out of the room, up the stairs and into the attic, where they stowed it away in a dark corner out of the daylight. »What's the meaning of this?« wondered the tree. »What is there for me to do here? What am I to listen to?« And it leaned up against the wall and stood there thinking and thinking ... It had plenty of time for that, because days and nights went by. No one came up there and when at last somebody did come it was to put some big boxes away in the corner; the tree was completely hidden – you might have thought it was utterly forgotten.

»It's winter by now outside,« thought the tree. »The ground will be hard and covered with snow, people wouldn't be able to plant me; so I expect I shall have to shelter here till the spring. How considerate! How kind people are! ... If only it weren't so dark and so terribly lonely in here! Not even a little hare ... It was so jolly out in the wood, when the snow was lying and the hare went bounding past; yes, even when it jumped right over me, though I didn't like it at the time. Up here it's too lonely for words.«

»Pee-pee!« squeaked a little mouse just then, creeping out on the floor; and another one followed it. They sniffed at the fir tree and slipped in and out of its branches. »It's horribly cold,« said the little mice, »though this is actually a splendid place to be in, don't you think, old fir tree?«

»I'm not a bit old,« answered the fir tree. »There are lots of people who are much older than I am.«

»Where do you hail from?« asked the mice, »and what do you know?« (They were being dreadfully inquisitive). »Do tell us about the loveliest place on earth. Have you ever been there?Have you been in the larder, where there are cheeses on the shelves and hams hanging from the ceiling – where you can dance on tallow candles and you go in thin and come out fat?«

»No. I don't know the larder,« said the tree, »but I know the wood, where the sun shines and the birds sing«; and then it told all about the days when it was young. The little mice had never heard anything like it before, and they listened closely and said, »Why, what a lot you've seen! How happy you must have been!«

»I?« said the fir tree and pondered over what it had just been saying, »yes, they were really very pleasant times.« But then it went on to tell them about Christmas Eve, when it had been tricked out with cakes and candles.

»Ooh!« said the little mice, »you *have* been a happy old fir tree.«

»I'm not a bit old,« repeated the tree; »I've only this winter come from the wood. I'm just in my prime; my growth is only being checked for a while.«

»What lovely stories you tell!« said the little mice; and they came back the following night with four more little mice who wanted to hear the tree tell stories, and the more it told the better it remembered everything itself, thinking, »Those were really rather jolly times. But they may come again, they may come again. Humpty-Dumpty fell downstairs and yet won the Princess; perhaps I too may win a Princess.« And then the fir tree suddenly remembered such a sweet little birch tree growing out in the wood; that, for the fir free, would be a real beautiful Princess.

»Who is Humpty-Dumpty?« asked the little mice. Then the fir tree told them the whole fairy tale; it could remember every word; and the little mice were ready to jump up to the top of the tree for sheer enjoyment. The night after, many more mice turned up and, on the Sunday, even two rats. But these declared that the tale was not at all amusing, which disappointed the little mice because now they didn't think so much of it either.

»Is that the only story you know?« asked the rats.

»Only that one,« replied the tree. »I heard it on the happiest evening of my life, but I never realised then how happy I was.«

»It's a fearfully dull story. Don't you know any about pork and tallow candles? One about the larder?«

»No,« said the tree.

»Well, then, thank you for nothing« answered the rats and went home again.

In the end, the little mice kept away as well, and the tree said with a sigh, »It really was rather nice with them sitting round me, those eager little mice, listening to what I told them. Now that's over too ... though I shall remember to enjoy myself, when I'm taken out once more.«

But when would that happen? Well, it happened one morning when people came up and rummaged about the attic. The boxes were being moved, and the tree was dragged out. They certainly dumped it rather hard on to the floor, but one of the men at once pulled it along towards the stairs where there was daylight.

»Life's beginning again for me!« thought the tree. It could feel the fresh air, the first sunbeams - and now it was out in the courtyard. Everything happened so quickly that the tree quite forgot to look at itself, there was so much to see all around. The yard gave on to a garden where everything was in bloom. The roses smelt so sweet and fresh as they hung over the little trellis, the lime trees were blossoming, and the swallows flew around saying, »Kvirra—virra-veet, my husband's arrived!« But it wasn't the fir tree they were thinking of.

»This is the life for me!« it cried out joyfully, spreading out its branches. Alas! they were all withered and yellow, and the tree lay in a corner among weeds and nettles. The gold-paper star was still in its place at the top and glittered away in the bright sunshine.

Playing in the courtyard itself were a few of the merry children who at Christmas time had danced round the tree and were so pleased with it. One of the smallest ran up and tore off the gold star.

»Look what I've found still there on that nasty old Christmas tree!« he said, trampling on the branches so that they crackled under his boots.

And the tree looked at the fresh beauty of the flowers in the garden, and then at itself, and it wished it had stayed in that dark corner up in the attic. It thought of the fresh days of its youth in the wood, of that merry Christmas Eve, and of the little mice who had listened with such delight to the story of Humpty-Dumpty.

»All over!« said the poor tree, »if only I had been happy while I could! All over!«

And the man came and chopped up the tree into small pieces, till there was quite a heap. It made a fine blaze under the big copper; and the tree groaned so loudly that every groan was like a little shot going off. This made the children who were playing run in and sit down before the fire; and as they looked into it they shouted »bang!« - but at every pop (which was a deep groan) the tree thought of a summer's day in the wood, or of a winter's night out there when the stars were shining; it thought of Christmas Eve and of *Humpty-Dumpty*, the only fairy tale it had ever heard and was able to tell ... And by this time the tree was burnt right up.

The boys were playing in the yard, and the smallest of them had on his chest the gold star which had crowned the tree on its happiest evening. That was all over now, and it was all over with the tree, and so it is with the story. That's what happens at last to every story – all over, all over!

The Shepherdess and the Chimney-Sweep

Have you ever seen a real old-fashioned cupboard, its wood quite black with age and carved all over with twirls and twisting foliage? There was one just like that in a certain sitting-room. It had been left by a great-grandmother and was carved from top to bottom with roses and tulips and the quaintest flourishes, and in among were little stags poking out their heads that were covered with antlers. But, carved on the middle of the cupboard, was the complete figure of a man; he really did look comic. And his grin was comic, too – you couldn't call it a laugh – and he had billygoat legs, little horns on his forehead and a long beard. The children who lived there always called him »Major-and-Minor-General-Company-Sergeant Billygoatlegs, because it was a difficult name to say, and there aren't many who get that rank. What a job it must have been to carve him out! Well, anyhow, there he was; and all the time he kept looking at the table under the looking-glass, for there stood a lovely little china shepherdess. She had gilt shoes, a frock that was charmingly caught up with a red rose, and a gold hat and shepherd's crook; she was delicious. Close beside her was a little chimney-sweep, as black as coal, though he too was made of china. He was just as trim and tidy as anyone else, for he really only pretended to be a chimney-sweep; the man who made him could just as well have made him a Prince, for that matter.

There he stood, looking so smart with his ladder and with cheeks as pink and white as a girl's. That was really a mistake; better if he'd been just a little bit sooty. He was standing quite close to the shepherdess; they had both been placed where they were and, because of that, they had become engaged. They certainly suited each other: they were both young, both made of the same china, and both equally brittle.

Near them, three times their size, was another figure – an old China-man who could nod. He too was made of porcelain, and he said he was the little shepherdess's grandfather, though he couldn't prove it. Still, he claimed to be her guardian; and so, when Major-and-Minor-General-Company-Sergeant Billygoatlegs had asked for the hand of the little shepherdess, the old Chinaman nodded his consent.

»There's a husband for you,« he said; »a husband I'm almost sure is made of mahogany. He will make you Mrs. Major-and-Minor-General-Company-Sergeant Billygoatlegs. That cupboard of his is full of silver, to say nothing of what he has stowed away secretly.«

»I won't go into that dark cupboard,« said the little shepherdess. »I've heard that he's got eleven porcelain wives in there already.«

»Then you can be the twelfth,« said the Chinaman. »Tonight, as soon as ever the old cupboard starts creaking, you two shall be married – as sure as I'm a Chinese.«And then with another nod he went off to sleep.

But the little shepherdess was in tears and looked at her darling sweet-heart, the porcelain chimney-sweep. »I've something to ask you,« she said. »Will you come with me out into the wide world? We can't possibly stay here.«

»I'll do whatever you like,« said the chimney-sweep. »Let's go at once; I feel sure I can earn enough at my job to support you.«

»How I wish we were safely down from this table!« she said. »I shan't be happy till we're out in the wide world.«

He did his best to console her, and he showed her how to put her little foot on the carved ledges and the gilded tracery that went winding round the leg of the table; and he also used his ladder to help her, and there they were at last on the floor. But when they looked across at the old cup-board, there was such a to-do. All the carved stags were poking out their heads and pricking up their antlers and twisting their necks. Major-and-Minor-General-Company-Sergeant Billygoatlegs jumped right up and shouted across to the old Chinaman, »Look! They're running away, they're running away!«

That gave them a bit of a scare, and they quickly popped into the drawer under the window-seat. They found three or four packs of cards in there, one of them complete, and a little toy-theatre that had been put together after a fashion. They were doing a play, and all the Queens – hearts and diamonds, clubs and spades – sat in the front row fanning themselves with their tulips, while behind them stood all the Knaves showing that they had heads both top and bottom, as they do on cards. The play was about a couple who weren't allowed to get married, and it made the shepherdess cry, because that was her story all over again.

»I can't bear it,« she said. »I must get out of this drawer.« But when they reached the floor and looked up at the table, the old Cinaman had woken up; his whole body was swaying to and fro, for, you see, the lower part of him was all one piece.

»Here comes the old Chinaman!« shrieked the little shepherdess, and she was in such a way that she sank down on her porcelain knees.

»I've got an idea,« said the chimney-sweep. »Let's crawl down into the big pot-pourri jar over there in the corner; we can lie there on roses and lavender and throw salt in his eyes when he comes.«

»That wouldn't be any good,« she said. »Besides, I know the old China-man and the pot-pourri jar used to be engaged; and there's always a little tenderness left over, once people have been like that to each other. No, there's nothing for it but to go out into the wide world.«

»Are you really as brave as that – to come out with me into the wide world?« asked the chimney-sweep. »Do you realize how huge it is, and that we can never come back here again?«

»I do,« she answered.

Then the chimney-sweep looked her full in the face and said, »My way lies through the chimney. Are you really as brave as that – to crawl with me through the stove, past firebricks and flue, till we come out into the chimney? Once we're there, I know what I'm doing. We shall climb so high that they can't get at us, and right at the very top there's a hole leading out into the wide vorld.«

And he led her up to the door of the stove.

»It does look black, « she said; but she went with him all the same, past firebricks and flue, and where it was pitch-dark.

»Now we're in the chimney, « he said, »and, look, there is the loveliest star shining overhead!«

Yes, it was a real star in the sky, shining straight down to them, just as though it wanted to show them the way. And they crawled and crept – it was a horrible climb – up and up. But he kept lifting and helping and holding her, pointing out the best places for her to put her little china feet. And at last they got right up to the top of the chimney and sat down on the edge, for they were tired out, and no wonder.

There was the sky with all its stars over-head, and the town with all its roofs below them. They could see round in every direction, far out into the world. The poor shepherdess had never imagined it was like that; she laid her little head on the chimney-sweep's shoulder and cried and cried till the gold ran from her sash.

»This is too much!« she said. »I can't bear it – the world's far too big. If only I were back on the little table under the looking-glass! I shall never be happy until I'm there again. I've come with you into the wide world; now I want you to take me home again, if you love me at all.«

The chimney-sweep tried every argument. He reminded her of the old Chinaman and of Major-and-Minor-General-Company-Sergeant Billy-goatlegs; but she sobbed so bitterly and kept kissing her little chimney-sweep, so that at last he had to give way to her, wrong as it was.

Then with great difficulty they crawled down the chimney again, crept through the flue and the firebricks – it wasn't at all nice – and there they stood in the dark stove, lurking behind the door so as to find out what was going on in the room. There wasn't a sound. They peeped out .. goodnesss gracious! there in the middle of the floor lay the old China-man. In trying to run after them he had fallen off the table and was lying there smashed into three fragments. The whole of his back had come off in a single piece, and his head had bowled away into a corner. Major-and-Minor-General-Company-Sergeant Billygoatlegs stood where he had always stood, in deep thought.

»How dreadful!« cried the litle shepherdess. »Old Grandpa's broken, and it's all our fault. I shall never get over it.« And she wrung her tiny hands.

»He can still be riveted,« said the chimney-sweep. »He can quite well be riveted. Now, don't get so worked up. When they've glued his back for him and given him a nice rivet in the neck, he'll be as good as new again and able to say all sorts of nasty things to us.«

»Do you think so?« she said – and then they clambered up on to the table where they had been standing before.

»Well, here we are back where we started,« said the chimney-sweep. »We might have saved ourselves all that trouble.«

»I do wish we had old Grandpa safely riveted,« said the shepherdess. »Do you think it'll be very expensive?«

He was mended all right. The family had his back glued, and he was given a nice rivet in the neck. He was as good as new – but he couldn't nod.

»You *have* become high and mighty since you got broken,« said Major-and-Minor-General-Company-Sergeant Billygoatlegs. »Yet I can't see that it's anything to be so proud of. Well– am I to have her, or am I not?«

It was touching to see how the chimney-sweep and the little shepherdess looked at the old Chinaman; they were so afraid he might nod. But he couldn't do that, and he didn't like to have to explain to a stranger that he had a rivet in his neck for good and all. So the porcelain couple stayed together; and they blessed Grandfather's rivet and went on loving each other until at last they got broken.

The Travelling Companion

Poor John was very sad, for his father was terribly ill and was going to die. There wasn't anyone there in the little room except those two. The lamp on the table was burning low, and it was quite late in the evening.

»You've been a good son, John,« said the sick father; »God will be sure to help you on in the world.« And with a solemn, kindly look at his son he drew a deep breath and died; you might have thought he was asleep. John burst into tears. Now he was left without a soul in the world – neither father, mother, sister nor brother. Poor John! He knelt down by the bed and, with many salt tears, kissed his dead father's hand, till at last his eyes closed and he fell asleep with his head against the hard bedpost.

As he slept he had a curious dream, in which he saw the sun and moon bowing before him; and he saw his father alive and well again and heard him laugh just as he always used to laugh when he was really pleased. A beautiful girl, with a gold crown on her fine flowing hair, held out her hand to John, and his father said, »Look what a bride you have won! She is the loveliest in the world.« Then he woke up, and all this beauty had vanished. His father lay dead and cold in his bed; not a soul was with them. Poor John!

The following week the dead man was buried. John walked directly behind the coffin; he had seen the last of the kind father who had been so fond of him. He heard them throw earth on the coffin ... now he could see the last corner of it ... but with the next spadeful of earth that too had gone. Then he felt as if his heart would break, so great was his grief. Round about him they were singing a hymn, a very beautiful hymn, and the tears came into John's eyes. It did him good to cry and soothed his sorrow. The sun shone deliciously on the green trees, as if to tell him, »You mustn't be so sad, John; look at the lovely blue sky. Your father is up there now, praying the good God that all may go well with you.«

»I will always be good,« said John, »then I shall go and join my father in heaven. What joy it will be to see each other again – what a lot I shall have to tell him! And he too will have so much to show me and will explain to me all the beautiful things up there just as he used to do on earth. How happy we shall be!«

John imagined it all so clearly that it made him smile through the tears that were still running down his cheeks. The little birds sat up in the chestnut trees twittering their pleasure – »tweet, tweet!« – in spite of their being at a funeral; but then they knew that the dead man was now in heaven, and had wings that were much larger and prettier than theirs, and was happy now because he had been a good man here on earth. This was what the birds were so pleased about. John noticed how they left the green trees and flew far away into the world, and it made him long to fly away with them. But first he sawed a big wooden cross to put over his father's grave, and when he carried it there in the evening he found the grave strewn with sand and flowers; this had been done by other people out of affection for his dear dead father.

Early next morning John packed up his little bundle, and in his belt he stowed away the whole of his inheritance, amounting to five pounds and some odd silver; with this he meant to wander out into the world. But first he made his way to the churchyard up to his father's grave. There he said the Lord's Prayer, adding »Goodbye, father dear! I promise to be a good man, so you may safely pray the good God that all may go well with me.«

As John went through the fields, the flowers all looked so fresh and lovely in the warm sunshine, and they nodded in the breeze as if to say, »Welcome here in the open – isn't it delightful?« But John turned his head for a last look at the old church where he was christened as a baby and where he had been to church every Sunday with his father and sung hymns. Then, high up in one of the openings of the tower, he caught sight of the church goblin standing there in his little red pointed cap. With bent arm he was shading his face to prevent the sun from dazzling him. John waved goodbye to him and the little goblin waved back with his red cap, laid his hand on his heart and blew him many kisses, to show how he wished him good luck and a happy journey.

Thinking of all the beauty that awaited him in the wonderful great world, John trudged on and on, further than he had ever been before, through streets he had never seen and among people he had never met; he was far away now, surrounded by strangers.

The first night he had to make his bed on a haystack in the field; there was nowhere else to sleep. Still, he found it perfectly comfortable – a king couldn't have fared better. The field, the brook, the haystack and the blue sky overhead – all these made up a perfectly lovely bedroom. The green grass sprinkled with little red and white flowers was the carpet, the elder-bushes and the wild roses were like bunches of flowers, while for wash-basin he had the whole brook to himself with its clear fresh water where the rushes courtesied to him – good evening (they said) and good morning! The moon was a huge nightlight, set high under the blue ceiling, with no danger of it setting light to the curtains. John could sleep quite peacefully, and he did too – didn't wake up again till the sun had risen and all the little birds round about were singing, »Good morning! Good morning! Are you still in bed?«

The bells were ringing for church; it was Sunday, and people were going to hear the parson preach. John went with them, sang a hymn and listened to Gods's word. He felt just as if he were in his own church, where he had been christened and had sung hymns with his father.

Out in the churchyard were a great many graves, with the grass growing very long on some of them. This made John think of his father's grave which would also get to look like these, now that he was unable to weed it and keep it tidy. So he got down and plucked away the grass, set up the wooden crosses that had fallen down, and took the wreaths that the wind had blown away from the graves and put them back in their place thinking, »Perhaps someone will do the same for my father's grave, now that I can't do it myself.«

Outside the gate of the churchyard stood an old beggar leaning on his crutch. John gave him the silver coins that he had and walked on, pleased and happy, into the wide world.

Towards evening a terrible storm blew up. John hastened to find shelter, but it very soon became pitch dark. At last he managed to reach a small church standing all by itself at the top of a slope. Fortunately the door was ajar, and he slipped indside, meaning to stay here till the storm was over.

»I'll sit down here in a corner,« he said. »I'm tired out and can do with a bit of a rest.« So he sat down and with folded hands said his prayers, and before he knew it he was asleep and dreaming, while the lightning and thunder went on outside.

When he awoke, it was the middle of the night; but the storm had passed over, and the moon was shining in on him through the windows. In the middle of the church stood an open coffin with a dead man in it, waiting to be buried. John wasn't a bit afraid, for he had a good conscience and he knew that the dead can do no harm to anyone; it is the wicked living who do harm. Just such a wicked living pair were standing close to the dead man who had been placed here in the church before burial; they meant to do harm to him – not to leave him lying in his coffin, but to throw him outside the church door, poor dead man.

»Why do you want to do that?« asked John. »It's a wicked shame. For Christ's sake, let him sleep.«

142

»Rubbish!« said the two villains. »He has cheated us. He owed us money which he couldn't pay; and now he's gone and died, so we shan't get a penny. That's why we mean to have our revenge; he shall lie like a dog outside the church door.«

»I've not got more than five pounds,« said John. »That's the whole of my inheritance, but you are welcome to it all if you will honestly promise me to leave this poor dead man in peace. I shall manage to get along without the money. I'm lusty of limb, and God will never desert me.«

»Very well,« said the ugly ruffians, »If that's how it is – if you will settle his debt, why, no, we won't hurt him, we promise you.« And then with a loud coarse laugh at his simplicity, they took the money that John paid them and went their way. But John set the dead body to rights again in the coffin, crossed its hands and said goodbye, and after that went on contentedly through the big wood.

All around, wherever the moonlight could pierce the trees, he saw charming little elves frisking merrily about, quite unconcerned, knowing as they did that he was a good innocent creature; it is only bad people who are not allowed a peep at the elves. Some of them weren't any bigger than your finger and had their long yellow hair caught up with combs of gold. They were swinging in couples on the big dewdrops that lay on the leaves and the tall grass; now and then a dewdrop would roll off, so that they tumbled down among the long blades of grass amid shouts of laughter from the other tiny creatures. It was enormous fun. Some of them sang, and John at once recognized numbers of pretty songs he had learnt as a little boy. From one hedge to another big mottled spiders in silver crowns were busy spinning long suspensionbridges and palaces that, with the delicate dew on them, looked like glittering glass in the clear moonlight. All this went on till the moment of sunrise. The little elves then crept into the buds of flowers, and the wind bore upon their bridges and palaces till they were swept away into the air like great cobwebs.

John had just come out of the wood when he heard a deep voice behind him: »Hi, there, my friend, where are you off to?«

»Out into the wide world,« said John. »I've no father or mother. I'm a lad without a penny to bless me; but God will help me, I feel sure.«

»Out into the wide world – that's what I want to do, « said the stranger. »Shall we two join up?«

»All right,« said John, and so they went off together. They soon became great friends, for they were good-hearted fellows both of them. But John couldn't help noticing that the stranger was far more knowledgeable than he was; he had been almost all over the world, and he had something to say on every imaginable subject.

The sun was already high when they sat down under a big tree to eat their breakfast. At that moment an old woman came along – oh, she was ever so old, bent quite double, leaning on a crutch, and on her back she carried a bundle of firewood she had gathered in the wood. Her apron was pinned up and, sticking out of it, John saw three large faggots of bracken and willow twigs. As she came up to them, her foot slipped, and she fell down with a loud scream. Poor old thing, she had broken her leg.

John at once suggested she should be carried to her home, but the stranger opened his knapsack and, taking out a jar, he said that here was an ointment that could heal her leg straight away, so that she could walk home by herself just as though she had never broken her leg. But in return for this she must give him the three faggots she had in her apron.

»That's a high price you're asking,« said the old woman with a queer sort of nod. She didn't at all want to part with her faggots, but on the other hand it wasn't very nice to be left there with a broken leg. So she gave him the faggots, and directly he rubbed the leg with the ointment, sure enough, the old crone was able to get up and to walk far better than before. Yes, the ointment could do all that – but then it wasn't the kind that you buy at the chemist's.

»What do you mean to do with these faggots?« John now asked his travelling companion.

»They are three handsome bouquets,« he said. »I've taken a fancy to them – I'm a rum sort of cove, you know.«

After that, they walked on a good way.

»I say! There's a thunderstorm coming up.« said John, pointing ahead; »look how black those clouds are.«

»Those aren't clouds,« said the Travelling Companion, »those are mountains–glorious great mountains, where you can come up into the pure air high above the clouds, It's splendid there, I can tell you. By tomorrow we ought to be as far as that out in the world.«

It was further off than it looked; they took a whole day before they got to the mountains, where the dark woods grew right up against the sky and there were rocks as big as a town. It was certainly going to be a stiff climb before they got right across, so John and the Travelling Companion turned into an inn to have a good rest and collect strength for the journey next day.

Down in the big taproom of the inn a great many people had come together, for there was a man with a puppet-show. He had just set up his little theatre, and people were sitting round to watch the play. Right in front was a fat old butcher who had taken the very best seat, and beside him sat his great bulldog – ugh, how fierce it looked! – and was all eyes, like everyone else.

Presently the play began. It was a fine play, with a king and a queen sitting on the loveliest throne with gold crowns on their heads and long trains to their robes, for they could well afford them. The most charming wooden puppets with glass eyes and big moustaches stood at every door, opening and shutting them to let fresh air into the room. It really was a delightful play and not in the least sad; but just as the queen stood up and crossed the floor, then – heaven knows what was the bulldog's idea, but as the fat butcher hadn't got hold of it, it made a leap right on to the stage and seized the queen by her slender waist so that it went »crack!« It was simply ghastly.

The poor fellow who was doing the whole performance was terrified and very much upset about his queen, who was the prettiest puppet he owned; and now this disgusting bulldog had bitten off her head. But when they had all gone away, the stranger said – the man, that is, who had come with John – that, never mind, he could put her right; and he pulled out his jar and smeared the puppet with the same ointment he had used for healing the old woman when she broke her leg. As soon as the ointment was rubbed in, the puppet at once became whole again – in fact, she could even move all her limbs of her own accord. There was no need to pull the string; the puppet was like a living person, except for not being able to talk. The proprietor of the little puppet-show was utterly delighted: no more need for him to hold on to the puppet, now that she could dance by herself. None of the others could do that.

Later on when it was night and all the inn-people had gone to bed, someone was heard sighing so deeply and continuously that they all got up to see who it could be. The man who had done the play went down to his little theatre, as it was from there that the sighing came. All the wooden puppets were lying higgledy-piggledy, king, guards and all, and these it was who were sighing so piteously and staring with great glass eyes; for they did so long for some ointment like the Queen's, so that they too could manage to move of their own accord. The queen went right down on her knees and held up her beautiful gold crown, imploring: »Take this, take this, if only my husband and my Court may be rubbed with your ointment!« At that, the poor proprietor of the theatre and all the puppets couldn't help bursting into tears, for he felt so sorry for them. He at once promised the Travelling Companion to pay over to him all the takings of his play next evening, if only he would rub the ointment on four or five of his best puppets. But the Travelling Companion said that all he asked for was the great sword which the other was wearing; and when he was given it he rubbed six of the puppets, who immediately began to dance. And they did it so charmingly that all the maids - the real live girls who were looking on - proceeded to join in. The coachman danced with the cook, the waiter with the chambermaid; and all the guests danced too, and the shovel and the poker, though these two fell over directly they began to hop ... Yes, it was a very merry night!

Next morning John and his Travelling Companion took leave of them all and made their way up the mountains and through the vast pine forests. They climbed so high that at last the church towers far below them looked like little red berries down among all that green, and they could see tremendous distances, miles and miles away, where they had never been in their lives. Never before had John seen so much of the earth's beauty all at once. The sun shone warmly from the clear blue sky, and he heard the huntsmen blowing their horns in among the hills. It was all so beautiful that tears of joy came into his eyes and he couldn't help exclaiming, »O dear kind God, I could kiss you for being so good to us all and giving us so much beauty in the world.«

The Travelling Companion, too, stood with hands clasped, looking out over town and forest in the warm sunshine. At that moment a strangely beautiful sound could be heard above them, and looking up they saw a large white swan hovering in the air. It was very lovely, and it sang as they had never heard a bird sing before. But it grew weaker and weaker, till with bowed head it slowly sank at their feet, where it lay dead, the lovely creature.

»Two such splendid wings,« said the Travelling Companion »wings as white and large as these, are worth money. I'll take them with me. Now do you see why I got myself a sword« – and with a single stroke he cut off both wings from the dead swan, for he meant to keep them.

They now travelled on for miles and miles across the mountains, till at last they saw in front of them a large city with more than a hundred towers glittering like silver in the sunshine. In the middle of the town was a magnificent marble palace with red-gold roofs, where the King lived.

John and his Travelling Companion decided not to go straight into the city, but put up at an inn outside, where they could make themselves tidy; for they wanted to look their best when they went through the streets. The inn-keeper told them that the King was an excellent man who never did harm to a soul, but that his daughter - goodness gracious! there was a bad Princess if you like! Beautiful enough – oh, yes, no one could be as pretty and charming as her; but what good was that? She was a bad wicked witch, through whom numbers of handsome princes had lost their lives. Anyone – be he prince or beggar, it made no odds – anyone could pay court to her. All he had to do was to guess three things she asked him. If he could do that she would marry him and he would become King over the whole land when her father died. But if he failed to guess the three things, then she had him hanged or beheaded. Yes, the beautiful Princess was as bad and wicked as that. Her father, the old King, was very sad about it all; but he couldn't forbid her to be so wicked, because he had once said that he would never have anything whatever to do with her suitors; she could do just as she liked. Whenever a prince came with the idea of guessing so as to win her, he always guessed wrong and was therefore hanged or beheaded. And yet they had warned him beforehand; he needn't have wooed the Princess at all. The old King was so upset by all this sorrow and misery that he spent one whole day every year on his knees praying, with all his soldiers, that the Princess might turn over a new leaf; but she hadn't the slightest intention of doing that. The old dames who went in for brandy coloured it deep black before they drank it - that was their way of mourning - and more could hardly be expected of them.

»What a hateful Princess!« said John. »She really ought to be whipped, it would do her good. If I were the old King, I'd thrash her till she bled like a pig.«

At that moment they heard sounds of cheering outside. The Princess was passing, and she was really so lovely that everyone forgot how wicked she was – that's why they cheered. She was attended by twelve charming young women, all in white silk, carrying yellow tulips and riding on coal-black horses. The Princess herself had a snow-white horse decked with diamonds and rubies; her habit was of pure gold, and the whip in her hand shone like a sunbeam. The gold crown on her head seemed to be set with little stars from the sky above, and her cloak was made of hundreds of pretty butterfly wings. And yet she herself was far more beautiful than anything she wore.

When John caught sight of her, the blood in his face flushed crimson, and he could scarcely utter a word; for the Princess looked exactly like

147

the beautiful girl in the gold crown whom he had dreamt about the night his father died. He thought her so pretty that he couldn't help falling in love with her. Of course, it wasn't true (he told himself) that she could be a wicked witch who had people hanged or beheaded if they couldn't guess what she asked them. »Well, anybody may propose to her, even the humblest beggar, so up to the palace I mean to go. I just can't stay away.«

Everyone warned him against doing that; he would certainly meet the same fate as all the others. The Travelling Companion also advised him not to go, but John felt sure it would be all right. He brushed his shoes and his clothes, washed face and hands, combed his fine yellow hair, and then walked all by himself into the town and up to the palace.

»Come in!« cried the old King, as John knocked at the door. John opened it, and the old King came out to meet him in his dressing-gown and embroidered slippers. He was wearing his gold crown, while he held the sceptre in one hand and the gold orb in the other. »Just a moment!« he exclaimed, and he popped the orb under his left arm so as to be able to shake hands with John. But directly he heard that John was a suitor, he began to cry so hard that he dropped both sceptre and orb on the floor and had to wipe away his tears with his dressing-gown ... Poor old King!

»No, no, don't do it!« said the King. »You'll only come to a bad end, like the rest of them. Just come and look for yourself« – and he took John out into the Princess's pleasure garden, which was a ghastly sight. Dangling from every tree were three or four princes who had proposed to the Princess but made wrong guesses to what she asked them. Their bones rattled at every gust of wind, so that the little birds were much too frightened ever to come into the garden! The flowers were all tied up to human bones, and the flower-pots were filled with grinning skulls. A fine garden it was for a Princess!

»There you are!« said the old King. »You'll meet the same fate as all these others; you'd much better keep away. You're making me very unhappy; I take it so much to heart.«

John kissed the good King's hand and told him all would be well, because he was so in love with the beautiful Princess.

Just then the Princess herself with all her ladies came riding into the courtyard of the palace, so they went out and said good-day to her. She was most charming as she held out her hand to John, and he fell more in love with her than ever – she couldn't possibly be the bad wicked witch people all made her out to be ... They went upstairs, and the young pages served them with jam-tarts and ginger-nuts, but the old King was so upset he couldn't eat a thing, and anyhow the gingernuts were too hard for him.

It was now settled that John should come to the palace again the next morning, when the judges and the whole council would be assembled to hear how he got through the business of guessing. If he did well, then he would still have to come twice more, though there was never anyone yet who had guessed right the first time; they all had to be put to death.

John wasn't a bit anxious about how he would get on. He was in high feather, with thoughts only for the lovely Princess. He was confident that the good God would help him when the time came, but in what way he had no idea and refused to worry about. He went dancing down the road on his way back to the inn where the Travelling Companion was waiting for him.

John couldn't say enough in praise of the Princess, how charming she had been to him and how beautiful she was. He was already longing for the next day to come, when he was to go to the palace and try his luck at the guessing.

But the Travelling Companion shook his head and was full of misgiving. »I'm so fond of you,« he said; »we might have stayed together for a long time yet, and now I have got to lose you already. You poor dear John, I really feel more like crying; but I won't spoil your happiness on what may well be our last evening together. Let's be cheerful, let's be merry. Plenty of chance for me to shed tears tomorrow when you're gone.«

Everybody in the town had at once heard of the arrival of a fresh suitor for the hand of the Princess, and there was general sorrow. The playhouse was closed, the women who sold sweets tied black crape on to their sugarpigs, King and clergy were praying in church; all were in great distress, because they knew that John could not get on any better than the rest of the suitors had done.

Late in the evening the Travelling Companion lifted him very gently off his chair and laid him on the bed. Then when it was pitch dark, he took the two big wings he had cut off the swan and fastened them on to his shoulders. The largest of the faggots he had got from the old woman who broke her leg, this he stuck into his pocket; then, he opened the window and flew straight across the city to the palace, where he sat down in a corner under the window leading into the Princess's bedroom.

The whole town was quiet and still; then the clock struck a quarter to twelve. The window opened, and the Princess, in a big white cloak and with long black wings, flew out across the city till she came to a high mountain. But the Travelling Companion, making himself invisible so that she could see absolutely nothing of him, flew after her and switched her with his faggot till she was positively bleeding wherever he struck. Phew! how they rushed through the air. The wind filled her cloak so that it spread out all round like a great sail, and the moon shone right through it.

»Goodness, how it's hailing!« cried the Princess, every time he switched her – and it served her right. At last she reached the mountain and knocked to be let in. There was a roll like tunder, as the mountain opened, and the Princess went in along with the Travelling Companion; but she didn't notice him, because he was invisible. They passed through a long wide corridor where the walls glistened strangely; there were hundreds and hundreds of glowing spiders that ran up and down the wall and shone like fire. And now they entered a great hall built of gold and silver; red and blue flowers as large as sunflowers gleamed from the walls, but the flowers couldn't be picked because their stalks were horrible poisonous snakes and the petals were flames that darted out of their mouths. The ceiling was entirely covered with shining glow-worms and sky-blue bats that flapped their wings in the most extraordinary way. In the middle of the floor was a throne supported by four horse skeletons with a harness of red fire-spiders. The throne itself was of milkwhite glass and the seat-cushions were little black mice who bit each other's tails. Above it was a canopy of pink cobweb picked out with the sweetest little green flies that gleamed like precious stones.

On the throne sat an old ogre, with a crown on his ugly head and a sceptre in his hand. He kissed the Princess on her forehead and got her to sit beside him on his gorgeous throne and after that the music began. Great black grasshoppers played on Jews'-harps, and the owl – for want of a drum – beat his own stomach. It was a funny concert. Little black goblins, with will-o-the-wisps in their caps, danced about the hall. The Travelling Companion, invisible to everyone, had taken his stand immediately behind the throne, where he could hear and see everything. The courtiers, who now in their turn came in, were very handsome and distinguished-looking, but anyone with eyes in his head soon saw through it all. They were nothing but broomhandles with cabbage-heads to them, that the ogre had bewitched into life and given embroidered robes. Well, it didn't anyhow make any difference; they were only used for show.

After there had been some dancing the Princess told the ogre that she had got a fresh suitor, and so she wanted to know what she should be thinking about when the time came for her to question him on his arrival next day at the palace.

»Oh, well«, said the ogre, »I'll tell you what. You must choose something very simple, because he'll never think of that. Think of one of your shoes – he'll never guess that. Then have his head chopped off; but don't forget, when you come here again tomorrow, to bring me his eyes, for I want to eat them.«

The Princess made a deep curtsey and promised not to forget the eyes. The ogre now opened his mountain and she flew back home. But the Travelling Companion went with her and lashed her so hard with the faggot that she moaned bitterly at the violence of the hailstorm and made all possible haste to get back again through the window into her bedroom. Meanwhile, the Travelling Companion flew back to the inn where John was still asleep, took off his wings, and he too lay down on the bed; for he was tired out, and no wonder.

Early next morning John awoke and the Travelling Companion got up too and said that last night he had had a most curious dream about the Princess and her shoe; and he told John that, because of this, he really must ask whether it wasn't her shoe she was thinking about. For, you see, this was what the Travelling Companion had overheard from the ogre in the mountain – though he didn't mean to say anything to John about that, but only to tell him to ask whether it wasn't her shoe she had been thinking about.

»One thing's just as good as another for me to ask,« said John. »It may be that what you dreamt is perfectly right, for I still hold to my belief that God will help me. All the same, I'd better say goodbye to you because, if I guess wrong, I shall never see you again.«

Then they kissed each other, and John went into the city and up to the palace. The whole hall was crammed with people. The judges sat in their armchairs with eiderdown quilts to pillow their heads, for they had a great deal to think about. The old King stood drying his eyes with a white handkerchief. Now the Princess walked in, looking much prettier even than yesterday, with friendly greetings to everyone; but to John she gave her hand and said, »Good morning, my dear!«

And now came the moment for John to guess what she had been thinking about. Goodness, what a kind look she gave him! But directly she heard him utter the one word »shoe«, she turned as white as a sheet and trembled all over; but what was the good of that – he had guessed right!

Bless my soul, how pleased the old King was! He turned a somersault – you never saw such a beauty! – and everybody clapped both for him and for John, because he had guessed right at the first time of asking.

The Travelling Companion, too, was delighted when he heard how well it had all gone off; but John folded his hands in thanks to the good God who no doubt would help him again the other two times. Already the next day he would have to make a second guess.

That evening passed just as it did the day before. Once John was asleep, the Travelling Companion flew after the Princess out to the mountain and flogged her even harder than last time, for he had now brought two faggots. Nobody saw him, and he could hear everything. The Princess was going to think about her glove, and he passed this on to John as if he had heard it in a dream. So of course John guessed right again, and there was tremendous joy at the palace. The whole Court turned somersaults, just as they had seen the King do the first time – though the Princess lay sulking on the sofa and wouldn't open her mouth. All now depended on whether John could guess right the third time. If he did, then of course he would marry the lovely Princess and would succeed to the throne when the old King died. If he guessed wrong, he would lose his life and the ogre would gobble up his beautiful blue eyes.

The night before, John went early to bed, said his prayers and was soon sleeping peacefully. But the Travelling Companion fastened the wings on his back, buckled the sword to his side and, taking all three faggots with him, flew off to the palace.

The night was pitch dark, and there was such a gale that it blew the tiles off the houses, while the trees in the garden with the dangling skeletons were swaying like rushes in the wind. The lightning flashed continuously, and the thunder rolled as if in a single peal that went on all night. Suddenly the window opened, and the Princess flew out. She was as pale as death, though she only laughed at the fearful weather which she thought wasn't wild enough. Her white cloak billowed in the wind like the great sail of a ship, but the Travelling Companion gave her such a whipping with his three faggots that her blood dripped down to the earth and at last she could scarcely fly any further. However, she got to the mountain in the end.

»What hail, and what a storm!« she exclaimed. »I've never known such weather.«

»Yes, one can have too much of a good thing,« said the ogre. Then she told him how John had gone and guessed right a second time; if he did this tomorrow, he would have won and she could never come to the mountain again, never be able to practise her magic arts any more. She was utterly downcast at the thought.

»This time he shan't guess,« said the ogre »Trust me to find something he has never thought of – or he must be a greater magician than I am. But now let us be merry!« And he took the Princess by both hands and went dancing round together with all the little goblins and will-o'-the-wisps in the room. The red spiders hopped just as merrily up and down the wall; you might have thought that the fire-blossoms were sending out sparks. The owl beat his drum, the crickets chirped and the dusky grass-hoppers played their Jews'-harps. There was such a ball!

But now they had been dancing long enough, and it was time for the Princess to be going home, or else she might be missed at the palace. The ogre said he thought he would go with her, so that at any rate they might be that much longer together.

Then away they flew through the dreadful gale, and the Travelling Companion wore out his three faggots on their backs; never had the ogre been out in such a hailstorm. Outside the palace he said goodbye to the Princess, at the same time whispering to her, »Think of my head!« But the Travelling Companion overheard him and, at the very moment the Princess was slipping through the window into her bedroom and the ogre was turning for home, he caught him by his long black beard and, before the ogre knew what was happening, he whipped out the sword and sliced off his loathsome ogre-head at the shoulders. He threw the body into the sea to the fishes, but the head he merely dipped in the water and then tied it up in his silk handkerchief; he took it back with him to the inn and after that lay down to sleep.

Next morning he gave John the handkerchief, but told him not to undo it until the Princess asked what it was she had been thinking about.

There were so many people in the great hall at the palace that they were squeezed up against each other like radishes tied in a bundle. The Council were sitting in their chairs with the soft pillows, and the old King was wearing new robes with his gold crown and sceptre freshly polished. It made a most charming picture; but the Princess was deathly pale and had on a jet-black dress, as though she were going to a funeral.

»What have I been thinking about?« she asked John; and immediately he undid the handkerchief and was himself quite horrified when he saw the hideous ogre-head. A shudder ran through the whole assembly, for it was a ghastly sight. But the Princess sat like a stone image and couldn't utter a word. At length she got up and gave John her hand, for of course he had guessed right. She paid no heed to anyone, but with a deep sigh she said, »You are now my lord and master; we will have the wedding tonight.«

»Splendid!« cried the old King. »That's the way to do it!« The people all cheered, the Guards' band paraded through the streets, the church bells rang, and the women who sold sweets took the black crape off their sugarpigs, for now they were all happy. Three oxen, roasted whole and stuffed with ducks and chickens, were put in the middle of the market-place; anyone could come and help himself. The most delicious wine gushed from the fountains and, if you bought a twopenny twist from the baker, you got half-a-dozen large buns thrown in – buns with currants in, too.

At night the whole town was lit up, and the soldiers fired off cannon, and the small boys fired off caps, and there was eating and drinking and toasting and frolicking at the palace, where all the good-looking ladies and gentlemen of fashion danced with each other, and from far away you could hear them singing:

»Here is many a maiden fair -
how they long to twirl and sway!
Pipe and tabor wait them there ...
Pretty maiden, do not stay;
dance and stamp until you wear,
falderal, your shoes away!«

But the Princess, you know, was still a witch and not in the least in love with John. The Travelling Companion had not forgotten this, and so he gave John three feathers from the swan's wings and a little phial with some drops in, telling him to have a large tub of water placed beside the bridal bed. When the Princess was about to get into bed, he was to give her a little push so that she fell into the water; there he was to duck her three times after first throwing the feathers and the drops into it. This would free her from the magic spell she was under, and she would love him with all her heart.

John did everything the Travelling Companion had advised him. The Princess gave a loud scream as he ducked her under the water and floundered about in his hands in the form of a large jet-black swan with fiery eyes. When she came to the surface a second time, the swan was white except for a single black ring round her neck. John prayed earnestly to God, and then he doused the bird a third time; instantly she was transformed into the most lovely Princess. She was even lovelier than before and thanked him with tears in her beautiful eyes for having broken the spell that bound her.

The old King arrived next morning with all his Court, and congratulations poured in all day. Last of all came the Travelling Companion, with his stick in his hand and his knapsack on his back. John kissed him affectionately and told him he mustn't go away, but must stay with him there, for he was the cause of all John's happiness. But the Travelling

Companion shook his head and said very gently and kindly, »No, my time is up. I have merely paid my debt. Do you remember the dead man those ruffians wanted to harm? You gave them all you possessed, so that he might have peace in his grave. I am that dead man.« The next moment he was gone.

The wedding lasted a whole month. John and the Princess loved each other dearly, and the old King lived long and happily and allowed their little ones to ride-a-cock-horse on his knee and play with his sceptre. And John became King over the whole country.

The Angel

»Whenever a good child dies, an angel of God comes down to earth,
takes the dead child in its arms, spreads out its great white wings, and
flies away over all the places the child has loved. It gathers, too, a whole
armful of flowers to be carried up to heaven, where they may bloom still
more beautifully than on earth. The good God presses all flowers to his
heart; but to the flower he loves best he gives a kiss, and then the flower
gets a voice and can join in the glorious songs of praise.«

There - that was all told by an angel of God as it carried a dead child
up to heaven, and the child listened as in a dream. They passed over the
places where the little one had played at home, and they went through
gardens full of beautiful flowers.

»Which ones do you think we should take with us and plant in heaven?« asked the angel.

And they came to a lovely slender rose tree, but a wanton hand had
broken the stem, so that the branches, with all their half-opened buds,
hung drooping and withered around it.

»Poor little tree!« said the child. »Take that, then it can bloom when
we come up to God.«

So the angel took the rose tree and gave the child a kiss, and the little
one opened his eyes. They picked some of the fine showy flowers, but
they also took with them the despised marigold and the wild pansy.

»Now we've got flowers,« said the child and the angel nodded; but
they did not yet fly up to God. It was night, and everything was still.
They stayed in the city; they hovered about in one of the narrowest streets,
where there were great piles of straw, ashes and lumber of every kind; for

people had been moving house. There were plates lying in fragments, bits of plaster, old hats and rags - everything that was no longer fit to be seen.

And there among all this junk the angel pointed down to some bits of a flower-pot and to a lump of earth that had fallen out of it and was being held together by the roots of a large wildflower that was dead and done with and had therefore been thrown out into the street.

»We must take that with us,« said the angel. »I will tell you why, as we go along.«

And as they flew on the angel explained. »Down there in that narrow street, below in the basement, lived a poor sick boy. Ever since he was quite small, he had always had to keep his bed, though when he was at his best he managed to go on crutches up and down the little room once or twice - that was the most he could do. For a few days in summertime the sun shone for half an hour right into the front room of the basement, and when the poor boy sat there in the warm sunshine and saw the red blood through his delicate fingers as he held them up before his eyes, then he felt that, yes, today he had been out-of-doors.

»He only knew the woods in their lovely green at springtime by the neighbour's son bringing him the first spray from the beech tree. This he would hold over his head, dreaming he was there among the beeches where the sun shone and the birds sang.

»One spring day the neighbour's son brought him wildflowers, and among these there happened to be one with a root to it; and so this was planted in a flower-pot and placed in the window close to the bed. And the flower was happily planted, for it flourished and sent out new shoots and blossomed every year. It became a wonderful garden for the sick boy, his one treasure on this earth. He watered it and tended it and saw that it got every ray of sun, right up to the last ray that stole in through the low window. And the flower itself spread into his dreams; for him it blossomed, scattered its perfume, and gladdened the eye; to the flower he turned in death, when God called him.

»For a year now he has been in heaven; for a year the flower has stood forgotten in the window and has withered, so that when they moved they threw it out among the sweepings in the street. And that's the flower, the poor dead flower, we have added to our nosegay, because that flower has given more happiness than the grandest bloom in the Queen's garden.«

»But where did you get to know all this?« asked the child that the angel was carrying up to heaven.

»Why, you see,« answered the angel, »I was myself the little sick boy who went on crutches. So of course I know my flower.«

And the child opened his eyes wide and looked into the radiant face of the angel; and at that moment they reached the joy and happiness of God's heaven. God pressed the dead child to his heart, and the child was given wings like the other angel and flew with him hand in hand. And God pressed all the flowers to his heart, but the poor dead wildflower he kissed, and it was given a voice, so that it sang with all the angels hovering around God – some quite near, others in wide circles beyond, further and further away in the infinite distance, but all equally happy. Yes, great and small, they were all singing: the dear good child and the poor wildflower from the scrap-heap, that had been lying withered among the lumber of moving in the dark narrow street.

The Buckwheat

As you go by a field of buckwheat after a thunderstorm, you will often notice that the buckwheat has been scorched quite black. It's just as though a flame had passed over it, and then the farmer says, »It's got that from the lightning.« But how has it happened? I will tell you what the sparrow told me, and the sparrow heard it from an old willow tree that stood — and is still standing – by the side of a field of buckwheat. It's quite a venerable great willow, but wrinkled and aged, with a crack down the middle – and grass and brambles growing out of the crack! The tree leans forward, and the branches hang right down to the ground like long green hair.

In all the fields round about there was corn growing, rye and barley and oats – yes, the lovely oats that has the appearance, when it's ripe, of a whole string of little yellow canaries on a bough. The corn was a wonderful sight; and the heavier the crop, the deeper it stooped in meek humility.

But there was also a field of buckwheat; it was just in front of the old willow. The buckwheat didn't stoop, like the other corn; it held itself up proudly and stiffly.

»I must be just as rich as the grain,« it said, »and I'm much better-looking. My blossoms are beautiful, like apple-blossoms; it's quite a pleasure to look upon me and mine. Do you know anyone finer, my dear willow?«

The willow tree nodded his head as if to say, « You may be sure I do!« But the buckwheat was simply bursting with pride and said, »The stupid tree! He's so old that his stomach has grass growing on it.«

And now a terrible storm blew up. All the flowers in the field folded their leaves or bent their delicate heads while the storm passed over them. But the buckwheat stood up straight in its pride.

»Stoop down like us!« cried the flowers.

»No need whatever for me to!« answered the buckwheat.

»Stoop down like us!« cried the corn. »Here comes the angel of the storm in full flight. He has wings that reach from the clouds right down to the earth; he will strike straight over you, before you can cry for mercy.«

»Very well, but I refuse to stoop,« said the buckwheat.

»Shut up your blossoms and bend down your leaves!« said the old willow. »Don't look up at the lightning, when the cloud bursts; even mankind daren't do that, for in the lightning one may see into God's heaven. But even man can be blinded by the sight of that; what ever would happen to us plants, if we dared so much - we who are far inferior?«

»Far inferior?« said the buckwheat. »Well now, I'm going to look into God's heaven «; and in arrogance and pride it did. The lightning was so fierce that the whole earth seemed to be wrapped in flame.

When the storm had passed away, there in the pure still air stood flowers and corn, all refreshed by the rain; but the buckwheat had been scorched coal-black by the lightning. It was now a dead useless weed on the field.

And the old willow stirred his branches in the wind, and big drops of water fell from his green leaves, just as though the tree were crying. And the sparrows asked, »What are you crying for? It's so lovely here. Look how the sun is shining, how the clouds are sailing by. Can't you smell the perfume of flowers and bushes? Why should you cry, dear willow?«

Then the willow tree told them about the buckwheat's pride and arrogance – and punishment, for that always follows. I, who tell the tale, I heard it from the sparrows. It was they who told it me, one evening when I begged them for a story.

The Bronze Pig

In the city of Florence, not far from the Piazza del Granduca, runs a little cross-street called, I believe, Porta Rossa. There, in front of a kind of vegetable market, stands the quaint figure of a pig cunningly wrought in bronze. Clear fresh water ripples from the mouth of the animal, which has now become blackish green with age. Only the snout is shiny, as if it had been smoothed and polished – as indeed it has been, by the hundreds of children and beggars who take hold of it with their hands and put their mouths to the pig's mouth to drink. It's a perfect picture to see the shapely beast being hugged by some handsome half-naked boy, as he puts his young lips to its snout. Anyone who comes to Florence can easily discover the spot; he has only to ask the first beggar he sees for the bronze pig, and he'll find it at once.

It was a late winter's evening. There was snow lying on the hills, but there was a moon; and moonlight in Italy gives as much light as a gloomy winter's day with us in the North; in fact, it's better, because the air is brisk and cheerful, whereas in the North the cold leaden grey overhead weighs us down to the ground – that cold damp ground that shall one day weigh down on our coffins.

Over in the garden of the Grand Duke's palace, under a roof of pines, where thousands of roses bloom in winter, a little ragged boy had been sitting all day – a boy who might have stood for a picture of Italy herself, smiling and fair and yet suffering. He was hungry and thirsty. No one had given him a thing; and when it grew dark and the garden had to be shut, the attendant drove him out. For a long time he stayed dreaming on the bridge across the Arno, watching the stars twinkle in the water between him and the splendid marble bridge, Della Trinita.

He made his way to the bronze pig, half knelt down, and threw his arms round its neck. Then he put his young lips to the glossy snout and drank great gulps of the cool water. Near by were some lettuce leaves on the ground, and a few chestnuts; these did for his supper. There wasn't a soul in the street – he was all by himself – so he climbed on to the back of the bronze pig, leaned forward till his curly head was resting against the pig's and, before he knew what was happening, he was fast asleep.

It was midnight. The bronze pig stirred and the boy heard it say quite distinctly. »Now then, my lad, hold on tight, I'm going to trot!« And away it trotted with the boy on its back; it was no end of a ride... First, they came to the Piazza del Granduca, where the bronze horse with the figure of the Grand Duke astride it neighed loudly; the various colours in the coat-of-arms on the old town hall shone like transparent pictures; Michael Angelo's David was brandishing his sling. There was a strange life going on. The bronze groups showing Perseus and the rape of the Sabines were only too lifelike, as they stood there; a cry of panic from the women echoed across the great empty square.

At the Uffizi palace, in the arcade where the noble families meet for the Lent carnival, the bronze pig halted.

»Hold tight,« said the animal, »Hold tight! Now we're going up the steps.« The little boy never said a word - half trembling, half thrilled.

They entered a long gallery that he knew well; he had been there before. The walls were covered with gorgeous paintings; here stood statues and busts, each as perfectly lighted as if it were daytime. But finest of all was when the door to one of the rooms at the side swung open ... No, the boy had not forgotten how wonderful this was; but, that night, everything was seen in its fairest lustre.

Here was the nude statue of a beautiful woman, as lovely as only nature or the greatest master of his art could shape her. She was moving her graceful limbs, dolphins leapt at her feet, immortality shone from her eyes. The world calls her the Venus de Medici. All round her was a glitter of marble figures, for which the life of the spirit had passed into the stone: nude statues of fine-looking men, one of them sharpening his sword – the Grinder, he was called – and another group composed of the Wrestling Gladiators. The sword was being sharpened, the wrestlers were grappling, for the goddess of beauty.

The boy was quite dazzled by all this magnificence. The walls were aglow with colour, and everything he saw was life and movement. There were two Venuses to be seen - these pictured the wordly Venus, full-bosomed and ardent, as Titian had clasped her to his heart. It was remarkable to see them. The two women were beautiful. They stretched their lovely unveiled limbs on the soft cushions; their bosoms heaved and their heads moved, so that their rich locks hung down over the curving shoulders, while their dark eyes spoke out the glowing thoughts within.

Yet of all these pictures not one dared to come right out of its frame. The goddess of beauty herself, the gladiators and the grinder, stayed in their places, rapt at the radiant glory of the Madonna, Jesus and St. John. The holy pictures were pictures no longer; they were the Holy Ones themselves.

What splendour and beauty from room to room! And the boy saw it all, for the bronze pig went step by step through the whole magnificent pageant. One marvel ousted the other from his mind; a single picture only fixed itself firmly in his thoughts, and that one chiefly because of the happy-looking children to be seen there; once, in the daytime, the boy had nodded to them.

No doubt, many people pass by this picture without thinking, and yet there's a wealth of poetry in it. It shows Christ going down to the underworld; but it's not the damned that are seen around him – no, it's the heathen. The Florentine, Angiolo Bronzino, did this painting. Most beautiful is the certainty in the children's faces that they are going to heaven; two little ones are already embracing, and one small child is stretching out his hand to another below him and pointing to himself as if to say, »I'm going to heaven!«All the older folk are standing uncertain, hoping or bending humbly in prayer before the Lord Jesus.

The boy looked at this picture longer than at any other; the bronze pig stood still before it. A gentle sigh was heard. Did it come from the picture or from the creature's breast? The boy waved his hand to the smiling children ... and then the pig trotted off with him, away through the open entrance.

»Thank you – God bless you – you lovely pig!« said the little boy, patting its back as it went bumpety-bump down the steps with him.

»Same to you, my boy!« said the bronze pig. »I've helped you and you've helped me, because only with an innocent child on my back can I collect enough strength to run. And, look, I may even venture into the light coming from the lamp in front of the image of the Virgin. I can take you wherever you like, except inside the church. But from outside, when you are with me, I can see in through the open door. Don't get off my back! If you do that, I shall lie as dead as you see me lying by daytime in the Porta Rossa.«

»I won't leave you, my dear piggy,« said the boy; and away they went tearing through the streets of Florence out to the square before the church of the Holy Cross. The great double-door flew open, and the candles on the altar shone through the church out on to the deserted square.

A curious radiance came from a monument in the left aisle; hundreds of stars that were never still formed a kind of halo around it. Above the grave was a fine coat-of-arms – a red ladder on a blue field – that seemed to glow like fire. It was the grave of Galileo. The monument is quite simple, but the red ladder on a blue field is a device full of meaning; it might have belonged to Art itself, whose path leads on and up a glowing ladder – to heaven. All the prophets of the mind are taken up into heaven as the prophet Elijah was.

In the right aisle of the church every figure on the rich tombs seemed to have come to life. Here stood Michael Angelo, there Dante with the laurel wreath on his brow, Alfieri, Machiavelli; here, side by side, repose these famous men who are the pride of Italy. It's a glorious church, far finer than Florence's marble cathedral, though not so large.

There seemed to be a movement in the marble clothing of the statues; these mighty figures seemed to hold their heads still higher, as they looked through the darkness, amid music and singing, up towards the glittering colours of the altar, where surpliced choirboys swung their golden censers, and the heavy fumes of incense came pouring from the church into the open square.

The little boy stretched out his hand towards all this glitter – and at that moment the bronze pig bolted from the spot. The boy had to hold on very tight; the wind whizzed past his ears. He heard the church door creak on its hinges as it closed, but all at once he seemed to lose consciousness; he felt an icy chill – and opened his eyes.

It was morning. He found himself half slipping off the back of the bronze pig, which was standing where it always stood in the Porta Rossa.

The boy was filled with fear at the thought of the woman he called mother, who had sent him out yesterday and told him to get money. He had none – and he was hungry and thirsty. Once more he put his arms round the neck of the bronze pig, kissed its snout and then, with a last nod to it, wandered off into one of the narrowest streets which was only just wide enough for a donkey and its load. A great iron-studded door was standing ajar; he went in here and climbed a stone staircase with dirty walls and a greasy rope for banisters, till he came to an open balcony hung with rags. From here a stairway led down into the courtyard, which had a well with strong wires that could be drawn up to every floor of the house; the water-buckets swung there side by side, while the pulley squeaked and a bucket would sway about in the air until the water slopped over into the yard. Another dilapidated flight of steps led up again. Two sailors – Russians they were – came lurching cheerily down and nearly knocked the poor boy over; they were just coming from their nightly bout of drinking, and with them was a woman, no longer young, yet vigorous, with thick dark hair. »How much have you brought back?« she asked the boy.

»Don't be angry!« he pleaded. »I didn't get anything – nothing at all.« And he caught hold of his mother's dress, as if to kiss it. They went into their room. I will not describe it – beyond saying that there was one of those handled jars there for holding fire; they call it a 'marito'. She picked this up and warmed her fingers, and then jabbing the boy with her elbow she said, »Nonsense, of course you've got some money!«

The child was crying. She let out at him with her foot, and he wept aloud. »Will you stop it, or I'll break your squalling head for you!« And she brandished the fire-pot she had in her hand, while the boy dived to the ground with a scream of terror. Then a neighbour stepped in at the door; she, too, had her 'marito' with her. »Felicita! What ever are you doing to the child?«

»The child's mine,« answered Felicita. »I can murder him if I want to – and you too, Gianina!« And she swung her fire-pot. The other put up her own to parry the blow, and the two pots clashed together, so that the fragments, embers and ashes went flying all over the room ... But the boy, in a flash, was out of the door, across the yard, and clean away from the house. The poor child ran and ran, till at last he was quite out of breath. He halted at the church of the Holy Cross, whose great doors had opened for him last night, and went in. The whole church was lighted up. He knelt down at the first tomb on the right – it was Michael Angelo's – and presently he sobbed out aloud. People came and went; mass was being said, and no one took any notice of him. Only an elderly citizen paused and looked at him – and then went away like the others.

Hunger and thirst tormented the boy, till he felt quite faint and ill. He crept into a corner between the wall and the marble monument and went to sleep. It was getting on towards evening when he was woken by some-one giving him a nudge; he started up, and there was the same elderly citizen standing in front of him.

»Are you ill? Where do you live? Have you been here all day?« – these were some of the many questions the boy had to answer. The old man took him along to a small house in one of the side-streets near by; it was a glover's workshop. They stepped inside and found the man's wife busily sewing. A little white poodle, clipped so short that the pink skin could be seen, hopped on to the table and jumped up at the little boy. »Innocent souls make friends at once,« said the woman and patted both dog and boy. The kindly pair gave him something to eat and drink, and they said he might stay the night with them – tomorrow old Giuseppe would speak to his mother. He was given a simple little bed, though for him, who so often had to sleep on a hard stone floor, it was a royal couch. He slept soundly and dreamt of the glorious pictures and the bronze pig.

Next morning old Giuseppe went out, and the poor child wasn't at all pleased, because he felt that this going out meant that he would be taken back to his mother; that made him cry, and he kissed the lively little dog, and the woman gave them both a friendly nod.

And what was the news that old Giuseppe brought back? He had a lot to tell his wife, and she nodded and stroked the boy's cheek. »He's a very nice child,« she said. »What a splendid glover he'll make, like you! And his fingers – they're so supple and artistic. Madonna clearly meant him to be a glover.«

So the boy stayed there in the house, and the wife herself taught him to sew. He ate well, he slept well, he grew playful, and he began teasing Bellisima, as the little poodle was called. When he did that, the wife shook her fist and scolded him angrily, which touched the boy's heart, and he went and sat thoughtfully in his little room. This faced on to the street and was used for drying skins; the windows had stout iron bars in front. He couldn't sleep; he had the bronze pig on his mind, and suddenly he heard outside, »Pit-pat, pit-pat!« Yes, that must be the pig! He ran to the window, but there was nothing to be seen; it had already gone by.

»Help the gentleman to carry his paintbox,« said the glover's wife next morning to the boy, as the young painter from next door came toiling along himself with this and a large roll of canvas. The boy took the box and followed the painter. They made their way to the picture gallery and went up the same steps that he knew so well from the night when he rode on the bronze pig. He remenbered the statues and pictures, the lovely marble Venus, and the ones that stood living in colour; and once more he saw the Mother of God, Jesus and St. John.

Now they halted before Bronzino's painting in which Christ is going down to the underworld and the children around him are smiling in their sweet confidence of heaven. The poor boy smiled, too; for here was his heaven ...

»Well, now go home!« the painter said to him, when he had already been standing there so long that the man had put up his easel.

»May I see you paint?« said the boy. »May I see how you get the picture over on to this white sheet?«

»I'm not going to paint yet,« answered the man. He took out his crayon; there was a quick movement of his hand, while he measured the great picture with his eye; then, although it was only a thin line that you saw, yet there stood the figure of Christ poised as in the painted picture.

»But now be off, will you!« said the painter; and the boy wandered silently home, seated himself up on the table – and learnt to sew gloves. Yet all day long his thoughts were in the picture gallery, and this caused him to prick his fingers and do his work clumsily. But there was no more teasing of Bellissima. When evening came and the streetdoor happened to be open, he slipped outside. It was cold, but starlight and beautifully clear. He wandered off through the quietened streets and was soon standing in front of the bronze pig which he stooped and kissed on its shiny snout. Then, sitting on its back, »You dear piggy«, he said, »How I have longed for you! We must go for a ride tonight.«

The bronze pig never stirred, and the spring water went on gushing from its mouth. As the boy sat there astride the pig, he felt a tug at his clothes. He looked down, and there was Bellissima, little naked close-cropped Bellissima. The dog had slipped out of the house and gone along with him without his noticing. Bellissima started barking as if to say, »Don't you see I've come - what are you sitting there for?« A fiery dragon could hardly have frightened the boy more than the little dog in a place like this. Bellissima out in the street and 'undressed' (as the old mother put it) – whatever would come of it? The dog never went out in winter without a little sheepskin coat, which had been specially made for her. It could be fastened round her neck to a red collar with bells and a bow to it and also tied under her body. The dog looked almost like a little fawn when she was allowed to go trotting out with her mistress in wintertime. And now Bellissima had come along, without her coat – what would come of it? All the boy's fancies had disappeared; however, he kissed the bronze pig and picked up Bellissima in his arms and, as the dog was shivering with cold, he ran along as fast as he could.

»What's that you're running off with?« cried two policemen he came across. Bellissima barked at them. »Where did you steal that pretty dog?« they asked, and took her away from him.

»Oh, give her back!« wailed the boy.

»If you didn't steal her, then you can tell them at home that the dog may be fetched from the police station.« And they told him where this was and went off with Bellissima.

What a terrible thing to happen! The boy didn't know whether to jump into the river or to go home and confess everything; they'd be sure to kill him, he felt. »But I'm quite ready to be killed. Then I shall die and go to heaven.« And he went home – chiefly, in order to be killed.

The door was shut, and he couldn't reach the knocker. There was no one about in the street, but he found a loose stone and with that he banged at the door. »Who is it?« came a cry from inside.

»It's me!« he answered. »Bellissima's lost. Open the door and kill me!«

There was a fearful to-do, especially from the mistress, about the poor poodle. Her eyes went straight to the wall, where the dog's coat was supposed to hang ... and there it was.

»Bellissima at the police station!« she bawled out. »You wicked child! How did you tempt her out? She'll die of cold, poor delicate creature, among those rough policemen.«

Father had to go off at once... and the woman kept wailing, while the boy was in tears. Everybody in the house rushed in, the painter among them; he took the boy on his knee and questioned him thoroughly. Bit by bit he got the whole story out of him - about the bronze pig and the picture gallery. It wasn't easy to make it all out; but the painter consoled the boy and spoke up for him to the woman, though she wasn't pacified till the old man came in with Bellissima, who had been with the policemen. Then there was joy all round, and the painter patted the poor lad's shoulder and gave him a handful of pictures.

Oh, they were splendid things - such comical heads - but, best of all, there was a lifelike drawing of the bronze pig itself. Nothing could be finer! A few strokes, and there it was on paper with the house and all sketched in at the back.

»Goodness! To be able to draw and paint - why, you could bring the whole world to your own home!«

The first moment he had to himself the following day, the boy seized a pencil and on the back of one of the pictures he tried to copy the drawing of the bronze pig - and he managed it. A bit crooked perhaps, rather up and down, one leg thick and another thin; still, you could make it out, and the boy himself was delighted with it. The only thing was - he couldn't help noticing - that the pencil wouldn't go quite as straight as it should; but the next day there was another drawing of the bronze pig beside the first, and that was a hundred times better. The third one he drew was so good that everybody could see what it was.

But the glove-making made slow progress, and so did the errands in town; for he had now learnt from the bronze pig that any picture can be put on paper, and the city of Florence is a complete album of pictures - all you have to do is to turn over the pages. In the Piazza della Trinita there is a slender column and at the top of it stands the goddess of Justice, blindfold, and holding her scales. She was soon put on paper, and it was the glover's small boy who had put her there. The collection of pictures got bigger and bigger, but so far there was no living thing in any of them. Then one day Bellissima came frisking around him. »Stand still!« he cried out to her, »then you'll make a lovely picture and be put in with my other ones.« But Bellissima wouldn't stand still, so she had to be tied up. She was tied up by her head and tail; but she barked and wriggled, and the string had to be tightened. Then the mistress came in.

»You wicked boy! My poor little dog!« was all she could splutter; and she pushed the boy away, yes, kicked him with her foot, and turned him out of the house - the wicked child, the ungrateful wretch! And tearfully she kissed her little half-strangled Bellissima.

Just at that moment the young painter came up the stairs – and this is where the story takes a turn ...

In the year 1834 there was an exhibition at the Academy of Art in Florence. Two paintings that were hung side by side attracted a great many spectators. The smaller painting showed a merry little boy, who sat drawing. His model was a small white curiously cropped poodle, but the creature wouldn't stand still and was therefore tied up, head and tail, with string. It was all so true to life that it was bound to appeal to everybody. The painter was said to be a young Florentine, who had been found in the street as a child and brought up by an old glover. He had taught himself to draw, and his talent had been discovered by a now famous painter just as the boy was on the point of being turned out of the house because he had tied up his mistress's darling - the little poodle - and used it for a model.

The glover's boy had become a splendid painter, as was shown by this picture and, even more, by the larger one that hung beside it. In this there was only one figure – a handsome ragged boy, asleep in the street, leaning up against the bronze pig in the Porta Rossa. Everyone who saw the painting knew the spot. The child's arm was resting on the pig's head. As the boy slept, the lamp before the image of the Madonna threw a warm, telling light on the lovely pale features of the child. It was a wonderful painting. It had a large gilt frame, at the corner of which hung a laurel wreath; but twined among the green leaves was a black ribbon, with a long piece of crape drooping down from it.

The young artist had just died.

The Darning Needle

There was once a darning needle who was really so fine that she fancied she was a sewing needle.

»Now, do mind what you're about,« said the darning needle to the fingers who picked her up. »Don't drop me! If I fall on the floor, I might never be found again, I'm so fine.«

»Oh, come, come!«said the fingers. »Not as fine as that« – and squeezed her round the waist.

»Look, here I come with my retinue,« said the darning needle, trailing a long thread after her; but it hadn't any knot. The fingers guided the needle straight to the cook's slipper; the leather upper was split and had now got to be repaired. »Work like this – what a come-down!« said the darning needle. »I shall never get through. I shall break, I shall break« – and break she did. »There, I told you so,« said the darning needle. »I'm too fine.«

Now she was no good at all, thought the fingers; but, all the same, they couldn't let go of her. The cook dropped some sealing-wax on her and stuck her in the front of the scarf round her neck. »Look, now I'm a brooch,« said the darning needle. »I was certain I should make my way in time. One who is something will always go far.« And she laughed inside her, for you can never tell from the outside whether a darning needle is laughing. There she sat, as proudly as if she were driving in her carriage and looking all about her.

»May I venture to inquire whether you are made of gold?« she asked a pin sitting next to her. »I admire your looks – with a head of your own, too, though it's rather small. You must try and make it grow, for we can't all be waxed on one end.« With that, the darning needle drew herself up so proudly that she fell off the scarf into the wash-tub, just as the cook was rinsing it out.

»Now we're off on our travels,« said the darning needle. »I only hope I don't get lost.« But she did.

»I'm too fine for this world,« she said as she sat in the gutter. »Still, my conscience is clear, and that's always a comfort. And the darning needle held herself straight and kept up her spirits.

All sorts of things went floating over her - sticks, straws, bits of newspaper. »Look at the way they go sailing along,« said the darning needle. »Little do they realize what is at the bottom of it all: I am at the bottom - here I sit! ... Look, there goes a stick that thinks of nothing in the world but a 'stick', and that's what he is. There goes a straw - see how he twists and turns! Don't think so much about yourself, or you'll bump into the kerb ... There goes a bit of newspaper - the news in it is all forgotten, and yet it still spreads itself... I stay patient and quiet. I know what I am, and I shan't change.«

One day there was something near by shining so beautifully that the darning needle thought it was a diamond; but it proved to be a bit of broken bottle, and as it was so bright the darning needle spoke to it and introduced herself as a brooch. »You're a diamond, aren't you?« »Well, yes – something of the sort,« was the answer. And so they each thought the other to be worth a great deal, and they chatted together about how stuck-up everybody was.

»You see, I have lived in a box belonging to a young lady,« said the darning needle; »and that young lady was a cook. She had five fingers on each hand, but I never knew anything like the conceit of those five fingers. They had nothing to do but to hold me - to take me out of the box and put me back again.«

»Did they glitter at all?« asked the bit of broken bottle.

»Glitter!« replied the darning needle. »No, they swaggered! They were five brothers, all fingers by birth. They stood up straight beside each other, though their heights were all different. First, at the end of the row, came *Tom Thumb*, who was short and fat; his place being outside the others, he had only one joint in his back and could only bow once, but he used to explain that if ever he were cut off a man's hand that man would never be taken for war service. Next came *Lick-Pot*, who found his way into sweet and sour alike, pointed at the sun and moon, and was the one who pressed on the pen when they wrote. *Longshank* looked over the others' heads. *Goldbrand* wore a gold ring round his middle, and little *Peer Playboy* did nothing at all and was proud of it. It was all swagger, nothing but swagger; and that's why I went into the wash-tub.«

»And here we sit and glitter,« said the bit of glass. Just then a lot more water came down the gutter, till it overflowed and carried the bit of glass away with it.

»There, now he has had a step up,« said the darning needle. »I'll stay where I am – I'm too fine to move – but that's something I'm proud of; it deserves respect.« So she sat there stiffly and thought her own thoughts.

»I'm so fine that, really, I might almost have been born of a sunbeam. I believe, too, that the sun regularly looks for me under the water. Oh, I'm so fine that my own mother can't discover me; if I had my old eye, which broke, I really believe I should cry - though of course I couldn't do that; one doesn't cry.«

One day some street boys were fishing about in the gutter, where they came across old nails, ha'pennies and things of that sort. It was a messy occupation, but it was just what they enjoyed.

»Ow!« cried one of them – he had pricked himself on the darning needle. »I say, what a beast of a thing!«

»I'm not a beast, or a thing; I'm a young lady,« said the darning needle. But nobody heard her. The sealing-wax had come off, and she had turned black. But black is so slimming, and so she fancied herself finer than ever.

»Here comes an eggshell on the water,« cried the boys; and then they stuck the darning needle into the shell.

»A white background – and me in black!« said the darning needle. »How becoming! Well, now they can see me ... I do hope I shan't be seasick, for then I should break.« Well, she wasn't seasick, and she didn't break.

»A steel stomach is just the thing to prevent seasickness and also a reminder that one's a bit above the common herd. I've quite recovered. The finer you are, the more you can put up with.«

»Crunch!« went the eggshell, as a cart ran over it. »Ooh! what a squeeze!« said the darning needle. »Now I *am* seasick – I'm breaking!« But she didn't break, in spite of being run over by the cart. She was lying at full length – and there she may as well stay.

The High Jumpers

The flea, the grasshopper and the skipjack* once wanted to see which of them could jump the highest. So they invited the whole world, and anyone else who liked, to come and watch the sport. They were three first-class jumpers; you could see that as they came into the room together.

»Now, the one that jumps highest shall have my daughter,« said the King; »for it seems so shabby that these gentlemen should have nothing to jump for.«

The first to make his bow was the flea. He really had perfect manners, with greetings for everyone; he had of course gentle blood in his veins and was accustomed to mix only with mankind, and that does make such a difference.

Next came the grasshopper, who it's true was a good deal stouter than the flea and yet by no means lacking in polish; he was wearing his native green uniform. This gentleman, moreover, said that he came of a very old family in Egypt and that here at home he was held in high esteem; he had been brought straight from the fields and put into a house of cards, three storeys high, built of nothing but court-cards with their picture sides facing inwards, and with doors and windows that were cut out of the waist of the Queen of Hearts. »I can sing so well,« he told them, »that sixteen native crickets, who've been chirping ever since they were small and yet never been given a house of cards, have become so nettled at hearing me that they've grown even thinner than they were to begin with.«

In this way each one of them, both the flea and the grasshopper, gave a

---

* A skipjack is a toy made from the merrythought of a goose or duck. With the aid of an elastic fastened to one end of a peg which is stuck into a lump of cobbler's wax fixed under the wish-bone, it can be made to leap into the air.

full account of himself and why he felt that he had every right to marry a princess.

The skipjack said nothing, but it was reckoned that he thought the more; and the Court dog had only to sniff at him to be able to answer for the skipjack's coming of a good family. The old alderman, who had been decorated three times for holding his tongue, declared that he was certain the skipjack was endowed with second sight: you could tell from his back whether it was going to be a mild or a hard winter, and that's a thing you can't even tell from the back of the man who writes the almanac.

»Well, for the moment I shan't say a thing,« said the old King. »I'll just bide my time, as it were, and keep my thoughts to myself.«

Now the jumping had to begin. The flea jumped so high that no one could see him, and so they protested that he hadn't jumped at all, and that was a mean trick.

The grasshopper only jumped half as high, but he jumped straight into the King's face, and the King said it was disgusting.

The skipjack stood still for some time hesitating, till at last people began to think that he couldn't jump at all.

»I hope he isn't unwell,« said the Court dog, and it took another sniff at him ... flip! went the skipjack with a little sidelong jump right into the Princess's lap as she sat on her low gold stool.

Then the King declared, »The highest jump is the jump up to my daughter – that's a very subtle thing to do. But a good headpiece is wanted for an idea like that, and the skipjack has shown that he has a good headpiece. He has strength of mind.«

And so he won the Princess.

»All the same, I jumped the highest,« said the flea. »What does it matter, though? Let her take that goose-fellow by all means, with his peg and his cobbler's wax. Anyhow, my jump was the highest. The trouble is that in this world it's size that counts, to make sure of being seen.«

And, with that, the flea went abroad on foreign service, where he is said to have been killed.

The grasshopper went and sat in a ditch, pondering on the way of the world, and he too remarked, »Yes, size is the thing, size is the thing!« And then he sang his own mournful little song, and that's where this story comes from. But even though it's been printed, it's not absolutely certain that it's true.

The Wild Swans

Far, far away, where the swans fly to when we are having winter, lived a King who had eleven sons and one daughter, Elise. The eleven brothers – they were Princes – went to school with stars on their breasts and swords at their sides. They wrote on gold slates with diamond pencils, and they were just as good at learning their lessons off by heart as at reading them from the book; you could tell at once they were Princes. Their sister Elise sat on a little plate-glass stool with a picture-book that had cost half the kingdom. Yes, those children had all they wanted, but that wasn't to go on for ever.

Their father, who reigned over the whole country, married a wicked Queen who was not at all nice to the poor children – they noticed it the very first day. There was a great set-out for the wedding all over the Castle, and so the children were left to play »visitors«. But instead of them getting their usual fill of cakes and roast apples, the Queen only gave them sand in a teacup and told them they could just pretend it was something.

A week later she sent the little sister, Elise, out into the country to be boarded with some farm-people, and it wasn't long before she put so many ideas into the King's head about the poor Princes that he ended by never giving them a thought.

»Fly out into the world and look after yourselves,« said the wicked Queen. »Fly in the form of big birds without voices.« But all the same she couldn't harm them as much as she would have liked to; they were turned into eleven beautiful wild swans. With a strange cry they flew out of the castle windows away over the park and the woods.

It was still early morning when they passed the spot where their sister Elise lay sleeping in the farm-house. They hovered above her roof, twisted their long necks and beat their wings; but no one heard them or saw them. They had to fly off again, high up into the clouds, far out into the wide world. At last they came to a big dark wood that stretched right down to the shore.

Poor little Elise was left in the farm-house to play with a green leaf; she had nothing else to play with. She pricked a hole in the leaf and peeped up at the sun through it and this made her think she could see the bright eyes of her brothers, and whenever the warm rays of the sun shone on her cheeks it reminded her of all their kisses.

One day passed just like another. When the wind blew through the big rose bushes in front of the house, it whispered to the roses, »Can anyone be prettier than you?« And the roses nodded their heads – »Yes, Elise is.« And when the old wife sat on Sundays at the door reading her hymn-book, the wind used to turn over the pages and say to the book, »Can anyone be more devout than you?« »Yes, Elise is,« answered the hymn-book. And that was perfectly true, what the roses and the hymn-book said.

When she was fifteen, she had to go back home; and when the Queen saw how pretty she was, it made her angry and full of hatred. She would have liked to turn her into a wild swan like her brothers, but she didn't dare to straight away because the King wanted to see his daughter.

Early in the morning the Queen went to the bathroom, which was built of marble and decked out with soft cushions and the most beautiful rugs; and she took three toads, kissed them, and said to the first one, »Sit on Elise's head when she gets into the bath, so that she becomes as lazy as you.« To the second one the Queen said, »Sit on her forehead, so that she may become as ugly as you and her father won't know her.« »And you,« she whispered to the third toad, »keep close to her heart and give her wicked thoughts to torture her.« Then she put the toads into the clear water, which at once turned a greenish colour, and she called Elise, undressed her and made her go into the water. As she plunged in, one toad hopped into her hair, another on to her forehead, and the third on to her breast; but Elise didn't seem to notice anything. Directly she stood up, there were three poppies floating on the water. If the creatures hadn't been poisonous and kissed by the witch, they would have been turned into red roses; though, mind you, they did change into flowers, just from resting on her head and at her heart. She was too innocent and good for witchcraft to have any power over her.

When the wicked Queen saw this, she rubbed walnut-juice into her till she was quite dark-brown; she smeared her pretty face with a nasty smelly ointment, and let her beautiful hair get all matted. You would never have known it was the pretty Elise.

So when her father saw her, he was horrified and said that this wasn't his daughter. Nor could anyone else recognize her; no one could but the watch-dog and the swallows, and they were small fry whose opinion went for nothing.

Poor Elise cried, and her thoughts turned to her eleven brothers who had all disappeared. Sadly she crept out of the Castle and walked all day across field and fen till she came to the big wood. She had no idea where to make for, but she felt so glum and missed her brothers terribly. They, too, no doubt, like herself, were roving about somewhere; she would look for them and find them.

She had not been long in the wood when night fell. She had wandered far away from any road or path; and now she lay down on the soft moss, said her evening prayer, and rested her head on a tree-stump. The air was very soft and still, and all around in the grass and on the moss were ever so many glow-worms shining like green fire. When she gently touched one of the boughs with her hand, the gleaming insects fell about her like shooting stars.

All night she dreamt about her brothers; they were playing together as children again, writing on gold slates with diamond pencils, and looking at the lovely picture-book that had cost half a kingdom – though on the slate they no longer wrote simply noughts and crosses. No, they wrote down the bold deeds they had accomplished, all they had been through and had seen. And in the picturebook everything was alive; the birds sang, people came out of the book and talked to Elise and her brothers. But when she turned the page they at once jumped in again , so as not to make a muddle of the pictures.

When she woke up, the sun was already high; in fact, she couldn't really see it because the tall trees spread out their branches so thickly overhead – though the golden sunbeams played through them like fluttering gauze. There was a fresh smell of greenery, and the birds almost came and perched on her shoulders. She heard the plashing of water; there were a number of large springs that all flowed into a pond with a fine sandy bottom to it. And although there were thick bushes growing round it, there was one place where the stags had rooted out a great opening; and here Elise made her way down to the water, which was so clear that if the wind hadn't stirred the boughs and bushes she might have thought they were painted on the bottom of the pond – so sharply was every leaf reflected there, whether it had the sun shining through it or hung completely in the shade.

The moment she saw the reflection of her own face she was horrified, it was so brown and hideous; but when she dipped her hand in the water and rubbed eyes and forehead, the white skin shone out again. After that, she took off her clothes and waded out into the fresh water; nowhere in the world could there have been found a lovelier royal child than she was.

When she was dressed again and had plaited her long hair, she went to the bubbling spring, drank from her cupped hands, and then wandered further on into the wood without really knowing where she was going. She thought of her brothers, and of the good God who would certainly not forget her; it was he who made the wild apples grow food for the hungry, he who now showed her just such a tree, its branches weighed down with fruit. Here she ate her dinner, put props under the branches, and then walked on into the darkest portion of the wood. There all was so still that she could hear her own footsteps, hear every little withered leaf that was crumpled in her path. Not a bird was to be seen, not a ray of sun could pierce the dense foliage of the trees; the tall trunks stood so near to each other that, when she looked ahead, it was as though she were shut in by a whole lattice-work of timber, set close together. Oh, here was loneliness as she had never known it before.

The night grew very dark; not a single little glow-worm gave out its light from the moss. Sadly she lay down to sleep. Then it seemed to her that the branches overhead were parted and that God looked down on her with gentle eyes and that little angels were peeping out over his head and under his arms. When she woke up in the morning, she wasn't sure whether she had dreamt it or whether it really happened.

She had only gone a short way when she met an old woman with berries in her basket; the old woman gave her a few. Elise asked if she hadn't seen eleven princes riding through the wood. »No,« said the old woman, »but yesterday I saw eleven swans with gold crowns on their heads swimming down the river near here.« And she took Elise a little further till they reached a slope. At the foot of this wound a stream; the trees on its banks stretched their long leafy boughs across to each other, and where their natural growth was not enough for them to meet, there they had wrenched their roots out of the earth and leaned across the water with their branches intertwined.

Elise said good-bye to the old woman and walked along the river till she came where it flowed out by the great open shore. The whole glorious ocean lay there before the young girl's eyes; but not a sail nor a boat of any kind was to be seen – how ever was she to get any further? She looked at the countless pebbles lying there on the beach, all of them round from the grinding of water. Glass, iron, stones – everything that was washed up had been shaped by the water, although this was far softer than her delicate hand. »It never tires of rolling, and in this way it can smooth down what is hard. I will be just as tireless. Thank you for your lesson, you clear rolling waves. One day - my heart tells me - you will carry me to my dear brothers.«

On the washed-up seaweed lay eleven white swan-feathers, which she collected into a bunch. They had drops of water on them – whether from dew or from tears, one could not say. It was lonely on the shore, but she didn't mind that, for the sea was continually changing. Yes, in a few hours it might change more than the freshwater lakes did in a whole year.

If a large black cloud appeared, it was as though the sea would say, »I, too, can look dark and threatening«; and then the wind got up and the waves showed the white of their eyes. But if the clouds shone pink and the wind was lulled, then the sea was like a rose-leaf; sometimes it was green, sometimes white. Yet, however quietly it rested, there was always a gentle movement along the shore; softly the water rose and fell, like the breast of a sleeping child.

As the sun was about to set, Elise saw eleven wild swans with gold crowns on their heads flying towards the land; they hovered in the air, one behind the other, looking like a long white ribbon. Elise clambered up the slope and hid behind a bush, while the swans came and settled near her flapping their great white wings.

Directly the sun had sunk below the horizon, the swans' feathers suddenly fell away from them, and there stood eleven handsome princes, Elise's brothers. She uttered a loud cry; for although they had changed a lot, she knew it was them – felt that it must be them, sprang into their arms and called them by their names. And they were overjoyed when they saw and recognized their little sister, who had grown so tall and beautiful. They laughed and cried, and between them soon came to understand how wicked their stepmother had been to them all.

»As long as the sun's in the sky,« said the eldest, »we brothers fly as wild swans; but when the sun goes down, we get back our human shape. So we always have to be careful at sunset to have ground under our feet; for, you see, if we were then flying up in the clouds we should, as human beings, crash to our death down below. We don't live here. There's a country beyond the sea that's just as beautiful as this, but it's a long way there; we have to cross the great ocean, and there's no island on our way where we might pass the night – nothing but a lonely little rock sticking up in the middle of it all, just big enough for us to rest on side by side. If the sea gets up, then the spray dashes high above us; but, all the same, we thank God for that little rock. There we can pass the night in our human shape, or else we could never visit our dear mother country; for we need two of the longest days of the year for our flight. Only once a year are we allowed to visit our own home; eleven days are all we may stay, flying over this great wood, from which we can see the castle where we were born and where our father lives and can also see the high tower of the church where Mother is buried ... Here we feel a kinship with trees and bushes; here the wild horses gallop over the plain as we saw them in our childhood; here the carcoal-burner sings the old songs we danced to as children; here is the land of our fathers, the place we feel drawn to, and here we have found you, our darling sister. For two days longer we may stay here, but then we must fly away across the sea to a glorious country, and yet it is not our own. How can we take you with us? We have neither ship nor boat.«

»If only I could set you free!« she exclaimed. And they talked together nearly all night, with only two or three hours' sleep.

Elise was woken up by the sound of swans' wings whirring overhead. Her brothers were again transformed and were flying round in large circles; in the end they disappeared altogether – though one of them, the youngest, stayed behind. The swan laid its head in her lap, and she stroked its white wings; they kept with each other all day. Towards evening the others came back and, as the sun went down, there they stood in human form.

»Tomorrow we fly away and dare not come back for a whole year, but we couldn't possibly leave you like this. Have you the courage to come with us? My arm is strong enough to carry you through the wood; then surely, between us, our wings must be strong enough to fly with you across the sea.«

»Yes, take me with you,« said Elise.

They spent the whole of that night making a net from the supple bark of the willow and the sturdy rushes, till it was really strong. Elise lay down on this and, as soon as the sun appeared and the brothers were changed into wild swans, they seized the net in their beaks and flew up high into the clouds with their dear sister, who was still asleep. The rays of the sun fell straight on her face, and so one of the swans flew above her head to shade her with its outstretched wings.

They were a long way from land when Elise woke up. She thought she was still dreaming, so strange did it seem to her to be carried through the air, high up over the sea. Beside her was a bough full of delicious ripe berries and a bunch of tasty roots, which the youngest of her brothers had gathered and put there for her. She gave him a grateful smile, for she knew that he was the one flying just above her head and shading her with his outstretched wings.

They were so high up that the first ship they saw below them looked like a white seagull floating on the water. Behind them was a great cloud – a huge mountain of a cloud – and against this Elise could see the shadow of herself and of the eleven swans, looking enormous as they flew there. Never before had she seen such a splendid picture; but as the sun rose higher and the cloud was left further behind them, the shadowy picture disappeared.

All day long the swans went whizzing through the air like arrows, and yet not so fast as before because now they had their sister to carry. A storm got up, and night was approaching. Elise was terrified to see the sun going down, and still there was no sign of the lonely rock in the ocean. She fancied the swans were quickening the beat of their wings. Oh, dear! It was her fault that they were not getting on fast enough. The moment the sun had set, they would be turned into human beings, crash into the sea and be drowned. Then she prayed to God from the bottom of her heart; but still she could see nothing of the rock. Black clouds came up, violent squalls heralded a gale; the clouds loomed in one threatening billowing mass like lead, as they surged along, with flash after flash of lightning.

Now the sun had sunk to the very edge of the ocean, and Elise's heart trembled. Then, all at once, the swans darted downwards – so quickly that she thought she was falling – but the next moment they were gliding smoothly again. The sun was half below the horizon. Then for the first time she caught sight of the little rock underneath her; it looked no bigger than a seal sticking up its head out of the water. The sun was sinking fast; now it was as small as a star. And then her foot touched solid ground, the sun went out like the last spark of a bit of burning paper, and there were her brothers standing arm in arm around her – though there was only just room for them and for her and no more. The sea dashed against the rock and drenched them like a shower of rain; the sky was one continual glimmer of flame with peal after peal of rolling thunder; but the brothers and their sister held each other's hands and sang a hymn, which they found was a comfort and gave them courage.

The air at dawn was pure and still. As soon as the sun rose, the swans flew off with Elise from the islet. There was still a strong sea running; and, as they gained height, the white foam on the dark-green sea looked to them like millions of swans swimming on the water.

When the sun got up higher, Elise saw in front of her, half floating in the air, a mountainous country with masses of ice glittering on the rocky slopes and in the middle of it all a·palace that seemed to stretch for miles, with rows and rows of bold colonnades one above another, while down below were woods of waving palm trees and gorgeous flowers as large as mill–wheels. She asked whether that was the country they were making for, but the swans shook their heads, for what she saw was the lovely everchanging cloud-palace of the fairy Morgana; they would never dare to take a mortal in there. Elise stared across at it; then mountains, woods and palace all melted away and in their place were a score of stately churches, all just like each other, with high towers and pointed windows. She fancied she heard the sound of an organ, but it was the sea she could hear. By this time she was quite close to the churches, and then they were changed into an entire fleet sailing along beneath her. She looked down... and it was nothing but a sea-mist scudding across the water. Yes, it was an everchanging scene that was spread before her; and at last she sighted the real country she was bound for. The beautiful blue mountains rose in front of her. Long before the sun went down, she was sitting on the mountain side before a large cave that was overgrown with delicate green creepers; they looked like embroidered curtains.

»Now let's see what you dream about here tonight,« said the youngest brother, as he showed her where she was to sleep.

»If only I could dream how to set you all free!« she answered. And her mind could think of nothing else, and she prayed most earnestly to God to help her; yes, even in her sleep she went on praying. And it seemed to her that she flew high up through the air to Morgana's cloud-palace and that the fairy came to welcome her, looking so beautiful and dazzling – and yet so like the old woman who gave her berries in the wood and told her about the swans with the gold crowns on their heads.

»Your brothers can be set free,« said the fairy. »But have you enough courage and endurance? It's true the sea is softer than your delicate hands, and yet it can alter the shape of hard stones. But the sea doesn't feel the pain your fingers will feel; it has no heart, and will not suffer the fear and agony you must endure. Do you see this stinging nettle I've got in my hand? There are lots of this kind growing round the cave where you sleep. Only these nettles and the ones that come up on the graves in the churchyard are any use – remember that. They are the ones you must gather, though they will blister your skin. Crush the nettles with your feet, and you will be able to get flax. With this you must weave and hem eleven shirts of mail with long sleeves. Throw these over the eleven wild

swans, and the spell will be broken. But one thing you must bear well in mind – that from the moment you start work, and all the time till it's finished, even if it takes years, you must never speak. The first word you utter will stab your brothers to the heart like a murderous dagger. Their lives will depend on your tongue. Whatever you do, remember this!«

So saying she touched Elise's hand with the nettle; it burnt like fire and woke her up. There was broad daylight, and close to where she had been sleeping lay a nettle like the one she had seen in her dream. She knelt down in thanks to God, and then she went out of the cave to begin her work ... With her delicate hands she took hold of the horrid nettles, which seared her like fire and burnt great blisters on her hands and arms. But she would readily put up with this, if only she could set her dear brothers free. She crushed every nettle with her bare feet, and then wove the green flax with it.

After sunset her brothers came to her and were dismayed to find her so silent. They thought it was some fresh piece of witchcraft of the wicked stepmother's; but when they saw Elise's hands, they realized what she was doing for their sake, and the youngest brother burst out crying; and wherever his tears fell her pain stopped and the burning blisters disappeared.

She spent the whole night working, for she could not rest till she had freed her beloved brothers. All the next day, while the swans were gone off, she sat there by herself, and yet never had the time flown so quickly. One shirt of mail was done already, and she was just beginning on the second.

Suddenly a hunting horn rang out among the hills. Elise grew very frightened. Nearer and nearer came the sound; she could hear the baying of hounds. In terror she made for the cave, tied into a bundle the nettles she had gathered and hackled, and sat down on it.

Just then a big hound came bounding out of the bushes, and then another, and yet another. They kept barking loudly and running to and fro. In a very short time the whole hunt was there outside the cave; handsomest of them all was the King of the land. He came forward to Elise; never had he seen a more beautiful girl.

»How came you here, you lovely child?« he asked. Elise shook her head, for she didn't dare to speak; the deliverance – the very lives of her brothers were at stake. And she hid her hands under her apron, so that the King shouldn't see how she had to suffer.

»Come with me,« he said. »This is no place for you. If you are as good as you are beautiful, I will dress you in silk and velvet, put a gold crown on your head, and you shall make your home in my richest palace« – and then he lifted her on to his horse. She cried and wrung her hands, but the King said, »I want you to be happy, that's all. One day you will thank me.« Then away he rode through the mountains, holding her in front of him on his horse, and the hunt came galloping after.

As the sun went down, there lay the magnificent capital with its churches and domes ahead of them; and the King took her into his palace, where great fountains were playing in the lofty marble halls and where walls and ceiling were gay with splendid paintings. But she had no eyes for any of this – hers were filled with tears and sorrow. She resigned herself to letting the women dress her in royal clothes, plait pearls in her hair and draw elegant gloves over her blistered fingers.

As she stood there in all that splendour, her beauty was so dazzling that the courtiers bowed still deeper before her, and the King chose her to be his bride – although the Archbishop shook his head and whispered that this pretty creature from the woods was a witch, he felt certain, who had blinded their eyes and turned the King's head.

But the King wouldn't hear of it. He ordered the music to play, the rarest dishes to be brought in, and the loveliest girls to dance for her; she was taken, too, through sweet-scented gardens into the grandest rooms. But still no smile played about her lips or from her eyes; sorrow, it seemed, was all she could ever be heir to. And now the King showed the way to a little room near by, where she was to sleep. It was decked out with costly green hangings, so that it looked very like the cave that she came from. On the floor lay the bundle of flax she had spun from the nettles, and from the ceiling hung the shirt of mail she had already finished. One of the huntsmen had brought all this along with him as a curiosity.

»Here you can dream that you're back in your old home,« said the King. »Here is the work you were busy with. Now, with all your splendour around you, it may amuse you to call those days to mind.«

When Elise saw these things that were so dear to her heart, a smile played about her lips and the blood came back to her cheeks at the thought of being able to save her brothers. She kissed the King's hand, and he pressed her to his heart and had the church bells to announce the wedding. The lovely dumb girl from the woods was to be Queen of the land.

But then the Archbishop whispered wicked words into the King's ear – though they didn't reach his heart, for the wedding was to take place. The Archbishop himself had to set the crown on her head, and out of sheer spite he pressed the narrow circlet down over her forehead, so that it hurt her; and yet a heavier ring lay round her heart – sorrow for her brothers – and she never noticed the bodily pain. Her mouth was dumb, for a single word would have meant the death of her brothers; but in her eyes there lay a deep affection for the noble handsome King who did everything to make her happy. Every day she grew more and more fond of him. If only she dared confide in him – tell him of her suffering! But no, dumb she must remain, dumb to the end of her task. And so she used to slip away from him at night, make her way into the little private room that was fitted out like the cave, and there she wove one shirt after another; but just as she was beginning on the seventh, she ran out of flax.

She knew that the right nettles were growing in the churchyard, but she must gather them herself. How was she to get there?

»Oh, what is the pain in my fingers compared with this agony in my heart!« she thought. »I must risk it. God will not forget me.« Then, as fearful of heart as though she were on some wicked errand, she stole down into the garden in the dear moonlight, went through the long avenues out into the empty streets till she came to the churchyard. There she saw, sitting on one of the largest gravestones, a group of frightful-looking witches called Lamias. They were taking off their rags as if they meant to bathe, and then they clawed with their long skinny fingers in the newmade graves, dragged out the corpses and ate their flesh. Elise had to pass close by them, and they fastened their horrible eyes on her; but she said a prayer, gathered the stinging nettles and carried them back to the palace.

Only one person had seen her – the Archbishop. He was still up, while the others were asleep; so, after all, he was right in what he suspected –

everything was not as it should be with the Queen. She was a witch, and that was how she had taken in the King and all his people.

When the King came to confession, he told him what he had seen and what he feared; and as the cruel words came from his lips, the carved images of the saints shook their heads as if to say, »It isn't true; Elise is innocent!« But the Archbishop explained it in quite another way and made out that the saints were witnessing against her and that they shook their heads at her being so wicked. At that, two great tears ran down the King's cheeks, and his heart misgave him as he went back home. At night he pretended to be asleep, though he got no peaceful slumber, for he noticed how Elise used to steal out of bed, doing this regularly every night; and each time he went quietly after her and saw her disappear into her little private room.

Day by day his looks grew darker. Elise noticed this but couldn't make out why it was. It frightened her; and how heavy was her heart when she thought of her brothers! Her salt tears ran down on the royal purple velvet and lay there like sparkling diamonds, and everyone who saw the rich splendour of her robes wished they were Queen. Meanwhile Elise had all but ended her task; only one more shirt was to be made. But now there was no flax left, and not a single nettle. So once again – only this time would be the last – she must go and gather a few handfuls in the churchyard. She was terrified at the thought of this lonely journey and of the horrible Lamias, but her will was as firm as her trust in God.

Off she went, but the King and the Archbishop followed after. They saw her disappear through the iron gates into the churchyard and, as they came up to it, there were the Lamias sitting on the gravestone just as Elise had seen them. The King turned away, for he fancied he saw her among them - her whose head that very evening had rested against his heart.

»Let the people judge her,« he said. And the people condemned her to be burnt at the stake. She was led away from the splendid royal halls to a dark damp cell, where the wind whistled in through the barred window. In place of velvet and silk they gave her the bundle of nettles she had gathered; she could lay her head on that. The coarse itching shirts of mail she had woven would do for a blanket to cover her ... But they couldn't have given her anything more precious. She set to work again, with a prayer to her God. The street boys outside sang jeering songs about her; not a soul had a kind word to comfort her.

Then, towards evening, close to the grating, she heard the whir of a swan's wings. It was the youngest of the brothers who had found his sister. She sobbed aloud with joy although she knew that the coming night might well be the last she had to live. Still, for all that, her task was nearly done and her brothers were with her.

The Archbishop came in to be with her during her last hour – he had promised the King to do that - but Elise shook her head and made signs for him to go. That night she must finish her task, or else everything would have been wasted – all the pain, the tears and the sleepless nights. The Archbishop went off saying the cruellest things about her; but poor Elise knew she was innocent and went on with her work.

Little mice scampered about the floor, dragging the nettles to her feet to give some help, and a thrush perched on a window bar and sang all night as cheerfully as he could, to keep up her spirits.

It was still only twilight; the sun would not rise for another hour. And there stood the eleven brothers at the palace gate, demanding to be taken to the King. But this couldn't be done (was the answer they got) for it was still night, the King was asleep and mustn't be disturbed. They begged, they threatened, the guard was turned out, and finally the King himself appeared and asked what it was all about. But at that moment the sun rose, and there were no brothers to be seen - though away over the place flew eleven white swans.

And now the whole populace came pouring out of the city gate, eager to see the witch burnt. A poor broken-down horse pulled the cart in which she sat. She had been given a smock made of coarse sacking; her beautiful long hair hung loose about her shapely head, her cheeks were pale as death, and her lips moved slightly as her fingers kept weaving the green flax. Even on the road to her death she would not give up the work she had begun. The ten shirts of mail lay at her feet; and now she was doing the eleventh, while the mob jeered at her.

»Look at the witch - the way she's mumbling! No hymn-book for her, no, it's her loathsome black magic she has got there. Take it away from her, tear it into a thousand pieces!«

And they all crowded in on her to tear up what she had made. But eleven white swans came flying down and perched around her on the cart, flapping their great wings till the crowd gave way in panic.

»A sign from heaven! She must be innocent!« many of them whispered, though they didn't dare to say it aloud.

The executioner then seized her by the hand – but she quickly threw the eleven shirts over the swans and, lo and behold, there stood eleven handsome princes! But the youngest had a swan's wing instead of one arm, for his shirt had a sleeve missing, which she hadn't had time to finish.

»Now I may speak,« she said. »I am innocent.«

And the people, seeing what had happened, bowed down to her as to a saint; but Elise herself, after all the strain and fear and suffering she had been through, sank back lifeless into the arms of her brothers.

»Yes, innocent she is,« cried the eldest brother. And then he told them all that had happened; and, while he was speaking, a perfume as of a million roses spread around, because every faggot from the stake had taken root and put out branches, and a high sweetsmelling hedge stood there with crimson roses. Right at the top was a single flower of the purest white, glittering like a star. This the King broke off and laid on Elise's breast, and she awoke with peace and happiness in her heart.

And the church bells all rang out of their own accord, and huge flocks of birds came flying in. The bridal procession back to the palace – no King had ever seen the like of it before.

A Good Temper

From my father I have inherited the best possible thing – a good temper. And who was my father? Well, but that has nothing to do with temper. He was lively and vigorous and plump; his person, outwardly and inwardly, was at complete variance with his profession. And what was his profession, his place in society? Well, if it were to be written down and printed right at the beginning of a book, then it's likely that a good many people, when they read it, would put the book aside and say »It strikes me as horrible; that kind of thing doesn't appeal to me at all.« And yet my father was neither horsebutcher nor hangman – on the contrary, his job often placed him ahead of the very worthiest men in the town and he was there quite properly, quite in his own right. He had to go first – before the bishop, before princes of the blood – yes, always in the foremost place, for he drove a hearse!

There, now it's out. And I must say that, when you saw my father sitting up there on the box of death's omnibus, wearing the long trailing black cloak, with the crape-bordered three-cornered hat on his head, and when too you saw his face looking for all the world like a sketch one draws of the sun round and laughing, then all thought of sorrow and the grave became impossible. His face seemed to say: »It makes no odds; it'll be much better than we imagine.«

So, you see, it's from him that I get my good temper and the habit of regular visits to the churchyard; and these can be very enjoyable, as long as you go there in a good temper. Well, and then there's another thing: I take in the local paper, just as he used to do.

I'm not so young as I was – I have no wife, children or library – but, as I said, I take in the local paper and find that sufficient. It's the best paper for me, and so it was for my father. It's extremely useful and contains all a man requires to know: for instance, who is preaching in the churches, and who is preaching in the latest books; where to find a house, servants, clothes and food; who is selling off, and who is going off himself. And then you come across so much charity, and so much innocent verse that couldn't offend anyone; matrimonial advertisements; appointments kept and unkept ... all is simple and natural. One can perfectly well live happily – and get buried – by taking in the local paper. And in that way you will have such a lovely lot of paper by the end of your life that you will have a nice soft bed to lie on, unless you prefer wood shavings.

The local paper and the churchyard have always been my two most stimulating forms of exercise, my two happiest hunting-grounds for a good temper.

Now, anyone can dip into the local paper; but come with me to the churchyard. Let us go there, when the sun is shining and the trees are green; let us walk between the graves. Each of these is like a closed book with the back uppermost; you can read the title telling us what the book contains (and yet telling us nothing), though *I* know – know it from my father and from my own observation. I have it in my grave-book, and that's a book I have made for my own profit and enjoyment. They are all in there, and a certain number of others as well ... And now here we are at the churchyard.

Behind this white-painted railing, where there once was a rose-tree – it's gone now, but a sprig of evergreen from the next grave reaches its green fingers across to it in order to make a bit of show – there lies a most unhappy man; and yet, when he was alive, he was what is called well off, with an easy competency and something to spare, but he took everything – well, art, at any rate – much too seriously. An evening spent at the theatre in the hope of whole-hearted enjoyment, would be completely ruined for him if the stage mechanic merely put too strong a light on each cheek of the moon, or if the flies hung in front of the wings instead of behind, or if a palm tree was shown growing on the island of Amager, a cactus in the Tyrol, or beech trees in the far north of Norway. What does it matter? Who bothers about such things? After all, it's only play-acting, and it's meant to give pleasure ... Then he used to find that the audience applauded too much – or applauded too little. »This wood's too damp,« he used to say, »it'll never catch light this evening.« And then he would look round to see what sort of people were laughing at the wrong time, in places where they shouldn't and that annoyed him. He couldn't endure it, and it made him unhappy; and now he's in his grave.

Here lies a very fortunate man – that is to say, a very distinguished man of high birth, and it was lucky for him that he was, for otherwise he would never have come to anything. But nature orders all these things so wisely that it's pleasure to think about it. His coat was embroidered back and front, and he took his place in a drawing-room just like some rare pearl-embroidered bell-pull which always has a good stout cord behind it to do the job. He, too, had a good stout cord behind him, a deputy who did the job and still does it behind just such an embroidered bell-pull. Yes, you see, everything is so wisely ordered that it's easy enough to be good-tempered.

Here lies – dear me, it's really very sad – here lies a man who for sixty-seven years had been making up his mind to say something smart. His one object in life was to get hold of a witty idea, and finally he really did – he felt positive of that – and he was so delighted that he died of it, died of delight at having thought of it. But nobody was the better, for nobody heard what it was. I can well imagine that this witty idea won't leave him a moment's peace in the grave, for suppose it was something witty that had to be said at lunchtime to be really effective, and that as a good ghost he can only (according to common belief) issue forth at midnight, then his smart sally will come at the wrong time; nobody will laugh, and he can take his witty idea back with him into the grave. A sad, sad grave, to be sure.

Here lies a dame who was terribly stingy. When she was alive, she used to get up in the night and mew, so that the neighbours should think she kept a cat. Yes, she was as stingy as that!

Here lies a young lady of good family. At a party she always *would* sing, her contribution being an Italian song that began: »I have no voice to tell thee ...« which was the truest thing she ever said.

Here is a damsel of another kind. When the heart's canary begins to twitter, the ears of commonsense are stopped. The fair damsel – there she stood in her halo of matrimony. It's an everyday story, but that's a nice way of putting it. Let the dead rest!

Here lies a widow woman, who had melody in her mouth and gall in her heart. She went prowling round among neighbouring families in search of their faults, just as in olden days *Nosey Parker's Weekly* used to go round looking for a street-lamp that wasn't alight.

Here is a family vault. All the members of this family seemed to be united in the belief that, if everybody (newspapers and all) said »it was such-and-such« and yet their little son came home from school and said »this is how I heard it«, then his way was the only right way, because he was one of the family. And it's a fact that, if the family cock happened to crow at midnight, then of course it must be morning, even though the watchman and all the town clocks declared it to be midnight.

The great Goethe ends his *Faust* by saying that it »may be continued.« So, too, may our ramble about this churchyard. I often come out here. If some friend of mine, or even one who is not a friend, makes things too difficult for me, I come here and hunt out a grassy spot and dedicate it to the man or woman I want to get buried; and then I bury them at once – they lie there dead and powerless, until they return as new and better people. I write an account of their life and ways as seen by me, into my grave-book. That's how everybody ought to go about it – not get annoyed when someone treats them too badly, but bury him straight away. Keep cheerful and stick to the local paper for this is written by the people – though often inspired by someone else.

When the time comes for me and my life's history to go to the binders, then put this inscription on my grave: »A good temper.« There's my story in a nutshell.

The Shadow

In the hot countries, my word! how the sun scorches you. People become quite brown, like mahogany, and in the very hottest countries they get burnt into negroes. But now we are only going to hear about a learned man who had come straight from a cold climate to a hot one, where he seemed to think he could trot about just as if he were at home. Well, he soon broke himself of that habit. During the day-time he and all sensible people had to stay in their houses with doors and shutters closed. It looked as though the whole house was asleep or nobody at home. To make things worse, the narrow street with the tall houses where he was staying had been built in such a way that from morning till evening it lay in the full blaze of the sun – it was really more than one could stand. The learned man from the cold country – a young, clever man – he felt as if he were in a sweltering oven; it told on him so much that he got quite thin. Even his shadow began to shrink, for the sun affected that as well, and it grew much less than it was at home. These two didn't properly revive until the sun had gone down.

It was really a most amusing sight. As soon as the lamp was brought into the room the shadow stretched itself all along the wall, right up to the ceiling; it was obliged to stretch in order to get its strength back. The learned man went out on to the balcony to have his stretch and, as the stars came out in the clear delicious air, he felt he was coming to life again. On all the balconies in the street – and in the hot countries every window has a balcony – people were coming out, for you must have air, even if you are used to being mahogany. Both above, and below, it grew quite lively. Shoemakers, tailors and all moved out into the street; tables and chairs were brought out, and candles lit – hundreds of them. One gave a speech, and another a song; people strolled about, carriages rolled by, donkeys went tinkling past – ting-a-ling-a-ling – from the bells they were wearing. There were funerals and hymn-singing, street-boys letting off crackers, and bell-ringing from the churches – yes, there was plenty going on down there in the street. Only in the house directly opposite the house of the learned stranger was there no sign or sound of life. And yet someone must be living there because there were flowers on the balcony, growing so beautifully in the hot sun, and they couldn't do that without being watered; so someone must be watering them – there must be people in the house. Besides, towards evening the door over there was opened, but the interior was dark – at any rate, in the front room – though from further inside came the sound of music. The learned stranger thought the music wonderful; but this may have been merely his imagination, because except for the sun itself, he found everything wonderful down there in the hot countries. His landlord said that he didn't know who had taken the house opposite; nobody was ever to be seen and, as for the music, he found it too tiresome for anything. »It's just as though someone were sitting and practising a piece he couldn't get on with – always the same piece. 'I *will* get it right!' he keeps saying; but he won't, however long he practises.«

One night the stranger woke up; he was sleeping with his balcony door open. The curtain in front of it was blown a little to one side, and a curious blaze of light seemed to come from the opposite neighbour's balcony. All the flowers shone like flames in the loveliest colours, and there amidst the flowers stood a graceful slender girl; she too seemed to glitter, and the sight of her quite dazzled his eyes. But then he opened them very wide indeed and he had only just woken up. He leapt from his bed, crept behind the curtain ... but the girl was gone, the glitter was gone, and the flowers had lost their shining splendour, though they stood up as straight as ever. The door was ajar, and from a far corner of the room came the sound of music so soft and enchanting that it could easily make you give way to romantic thoughts. It was, though, a sort of magic – who ever could be living there? Where was the proper way in? The whole ground floor was given up to shops; people couldn't possibly keep on running in and out of these.

The stranger was sitting one evening out on his balcony with a light burning in the room behind him; and so, quite naturally, his shadow appeared over on his neighbour's wall. Yes, there it was, immediately opposite among the flowers on the balcony; and when the stranger moved, then the shadow moved, which is a way that shadows have.

»I believe my shadow is the only living thing to be seen over there,« said the learned man. »Look how nicely it sits among the flowers. The door is standing half-open – what a chance for the shadow to pop inside, have a look round and then come and tell me what it has seen! Now then, make yourself useful!« he said in fun. »Kindly step inside ... Well, aren't you going?« And he gave the shadow a nod, and the shadow nodded back. »That's right, go along – but mind you come back.« The stranger stood up, and the shadow over on the neighbour's balcony did the same. And the stranger turned round, and so did the shadow. Anyone watching carefully could have seen quite well that the shadow went in at the half-open balcony door at the very moment that the stranger went into his room and dropped the long curtain behind him.

Next morning the learned man went out to drink his coffee and read the papers. »Hullo!« he exclaimed, as he walked out into the sunshine, »Why, where's my shadow? Then it really did go off last night and never came back. What a fearful nuisance!«

He was very annoyed, not so much because the shadow had disappeared, but because he knew there was a story, well-known to everybody at home in the cold countries, about a man without a shadow; and if he went back now and told them his own story, they would be sure to say that he was just an imitator, and that was the last thing he wanted. So he made up his mind to say nothing about it, and that was very sensible of him.

When evening came, he went out on to his balcony once more. He had the light put in just the right place behind him, knowing that a shadow always likes to have its master as a screen; but he couldn't get it to come out. He made himself long, he made himself short – there was no shadow, not a sign of it. He coughed, »Ahem! Ahem!« but that was no good.

It was very annoying but after all everything grows so fast in the hot countries, and a week later he noticed to his great delight that he had got a new shadow growing out from his feet whenever he walked in the sun; the roots must still have been there. In another three weeks he found himself with quite a respectable shadow which, as he made his way home to the northern countries, grew more and more on the journey till at last it was twice as big and heavy as he wanted. So the learned man went home and wrote books about what is true and good and beautiful in the world; and days and years went by – yes, many years.

Then one evening he was sitting in his room, and there came a gentle knock at the door. »Come in,« he called out; but no one entered. So he went and opened the door, and there in front of him was a – well, really such an astonishingly thin person that he made him feel quite uncomfortable. However, the visitor was very smartly dressed – he was no doubt a man of some distinction.

»Whom have I the honour of addressing?« asked the learned man.

»Yes, I thought you wouldn't recognize me,« said the distinguished -looking stranger. »I've now such a body of my own that I've positively got flesh - and clothes too. You never expected to see me as prosperous as this, did you? Don't you know your old shadow? No, of course you never thought I should turn up again. One way and another I am now extremely well off; if I want to purchase my freedom, I can do it.« And he rattled a great bunch of valuable seals that were hanging from his watch, and ran his hand along the thick gold chain he was wearing round his neck. Phew! The way his fingers all sparkled with diamond rings - all perfectly genuine too!

»Upon my soul, you take my breath away,« said the learned man. »What on earth does it all mean?«

»Well, it *is* rather out of the ordinary,« said the Shadow. »But then, you see, you yourself are not ordinary either; and I, ever since I was a little toddler, have trod in your footsteps – you know that well enough. As soon as you felt I was able to make my own way in the world, off I went alone. I've done extremely well for myself; and yet I was seized with a kind of longing to see you just once again before you die – for die you must, one day. I also felt I'd like to revisit this part of the world; for you know, one's always so fond of the country one comes from. I realize that you've got hold of a new shadow – do I owe you, or it, anything? If so, please tell me.«

»Well, I never! Is it really you?« cried the learned man. »Now, that *is* extraordinary! I never imagined one's old shadow could turn up again as a human being.«

»Tell me what I owe you,« said the Shadow. »I don't like the idea of being in any sort of debt to you.«

»How can you speak like that?« said the learned man. »What's this debt you're babbling about? You owe me nothing. I am utterly delighted at your good fortune. Sit down, old friend, and do let me hear how it all happened and what you saw at our neighbour's across the street, down there in the middle of the hot countries.«

»Very well, I'll tell you,« said the Shadow, sitting down. »But, in that case, promise me that, wherever you may meet me here in this town, you will never tell anyone that I have been your shadow. I'm thinking of getting married, for I have ample means to support a family.«

»Don't let that worry you,« said the learned man. »I shan't tell a soul who you really are. There's my hand on it. I promise you; and a man's as good as his word.«

»And so is a shadow,« said the Shadow, expressing it the only way possible.

It was, when you come to think of it, quite astonishing how much of a human being the Shadow had become. He was dressed all in black, made of the finest broadcloth, with patent leather boots and a hat that folded up into a matter of crown and brim - to say nothing of the seals, gold chain and diamond rings already mentioned. Yes, there's no doubt about it, the Shadow was got up very smartly, and this it was that made him such a perfect man.

»Well, now you shall hear the whole story,« said the Shadow, stamping his patent leather boots down on the sleeve of the learned man's new shadow which lay there at his feet like a poodle. He may have done this out of pride, or possibly because he hoped to make it stick to his own feet. The shadow that was lying there kept perfectly still, not wishing to miss anything; above all, it wanted to find out how one could break away like that and earn the right to be one's own master.

»Whom do you think I found living over there in the neighbour's house?« said the Shadow. »The fairest of the fair – Poetry! I was there for three weeks, and it meant as much as living for three thousand years and reading all that man has imagined and written down. Believe me, that is so. I have seen everything and I know everything.«

»Poetry!« cried the learned man. »Yes, yes, in the large towns she often lives like a hermit. Poetry! Yes, I caught a glimpse of her for one short second, but my eyes were full of sleep. She stood on the balcony, glittering as the Northern Lights glitter. Go on, my good fellow; go on! You were on the balcony, you went in at the door, and then – ?«

»Then I found myself in the antechamber,« said the Shadow. »The room you have always been looking across at is the antechamber. There was no lamp or candle there, but only a sort of twilight. You could see a long row of different-sized rooms, so brightly lit that I should have been quite blinded if I had gone right into Poetry's inner room. But I was careful, I took my time – as indeed one should.«

»Yes, you slowcoach, but what did you see after that?« asked the learned man.

»I saw everything, and you shall hear all about it; but – mind you, I'm not being in any way stuck up – but, now that I'm independent and so well-informed, to say nothing of my good standing and excellent connections, I should be much obliged if you would address me with rather more respect.«

»Oh, I beg your pardon,« replied the learned man. »It's sheer force of habit that I can't get rid of. You are perfectly right, sir, and I will bear this in mind. But now please tell me about all that you saw.«

»Yes, all,« said the Shadow; »for I saw everything and I know everything.«

»What did the inner rooms look like?« asked the learned man. »Was it like being in the green forest? Or in some holy church? Were the halls like the starlit sky when one is standing on the mountain heights?«

»Everything was there,« said the Shadow. »But I didn't go right inside; I stayed in the twilight of that front room, and it was an especially good place to be, for I saw everything and I know everything. I have been in the antechamber of the court of Poetry.«

»Yes, but what did you see, sir? Were all the gods of antiquity striding through those great halls? Were the heroes of old doing battle there? Were the darling children at play, and did they tell you their dreams?«

»I was there, I repeat, and you must understand that I saw everything there was to see. Had you come across, you would not have become a man; but I did. And I also learnt to know my innermost nature, as I received it at birth, my relationship to Poetry. No, when I was with you, I never gave it a thought; but at sunrise and at sunset, you remember, I always grew remarkably large – in the moonlight I stood out almost plainer than yourself. In those days I didn't understand my own nature; in the antechamber it dawned upon me – I was a man ... When I came away, I was changed, ripened, but by then you had left the hot countries. As a man, I was ashamed to go about as I did; I was in need of boots, clothes, all that human varnish by which man can be recognized. I took refuge – I can safely tell you this, because you won't put it in a book – I took refuge under the skirt of a woman selling cakes and hid there; the woman had no notion how much she was concealing. Not until night-time did I venture out. I ran about the streets in the moonlight. I stretched myself right up the wall – that tickles your back so delightfully. Up and down I ran, peeping in at the highest windows, into rooms on the ground floor and rooms under the roof. I peeped where no one else can peep and saw what no others saw – what nobody should see! When all's said and done, it's a low-down world we live in. I would never be a man, if it weren't generally considered to be worth while. I saw the most inconceivable things happening among women, men, parents and their own dear darling children. I saw,« added the Shadow, »what none are supposed to know, but what all are dying to know – trouble in the house next door ... If I had a newspaper, it would have had plenty of readers! But I used to write direct to the person in question, and there was panic wherever I went. They were terribly afraid of me – and, oh! so fond of me. The professors made me a professor, the tailors gave me new clothes; I was well provided for. The master of the mint made me coins, and the women said I was handsome. And that's how I became the man I am. Well, now I'll say goodbye. Here's my card. I live on the sunny side of the street and am always at home in rainy weather.« And the Shadow took his leave.

»How extraordinary!« said the learned man.

Time passed, and the Shadow turned up again.

»How are things going?« he asked.

»Ah, well,« sighed the learned man, »I write about the true and the good and the beautiful, but no one bothers his head about that sort of thing. It makes me quite desperate, for it means so much to me.«

»It wouldn't worry me,« said the Shadow. »I'm getting fat – which is just what one should try to be. I'm afraid you don't understand the world, and you're getting ill. You should travel. I'm going abroad this summer; won't you come with me? I should so like a travelling companion. Come with me, as my shadow! It will be a great pleasure to have you with me, and I'll pay your expenses.

»Surely that's going a bit far,« said the learned man.

»It depends how you take it,« said the Shadow. »It'll do you a world of good to travel. If you will be my shadow, you shall have everything on the trip for nothing.«

»That really is the limit!« said the learned man.

»Well, that's what we have come to nowadays, and there's no going back on it,« and with that the Shadow went away.

Things went badly for the learned man. He was dogged by care and sorrow, and his ideas about the true and the good and the beautiful were to most people about as attractive as roses to a cow. He ended by falling quite ill.

»Why, to look at, you're no more than a shadow,« they told him; and this made him shudder, for it set him thinking.

»You must go and take the waters somewhere,« said the Shadow, who came to see him one day. »That's the only thing. You shall come with me for the sake of old times. I'll pay your expenses, and you can write an account of our travels and kind of keep me amused on the journey. I want to go to a watering-place; my beard isn't growing as it should – that too is an ailment – and one can't do without a beard. Now, be sensible and say you'll come; and of course we'll travel as friends.«

And away they went. But now the Shadow was master, and the master shadow; always together, driving, riding, walking; side by side, or one in front and one behind, according to the position of the sun. The Shadow always knew how to hold on to the master's place, whereas the learned man never gave the matter a thought; he was extremely good-natured, gentle and friendly. One day he said to the Shadow: »Seeing that we now travel together as equals like this and that we also grew up from childhood together, oughtn't we to pledge ourselves in a toast of friendship? It would be so much more sociable.«

»I dare say,« said the Shadow, who was now the real master. »It all sounds very frank, and I'm sure that you mean well; I too mean well and will be just as frank. As a learned man, you know of course how queer nature is. Some people can't bear the feel of grey paper; it upsets them. Others go all goosey if you scrape a nail against a pane of glass. That's just how I feel when you talk to me in the familiar tone of an equal. It's as though I were being thrust back into my first humble position with you. Of course, it's not pride – it's only what I feel. So, although I can't allow you to be familiar with me, I am quite willing to meet you half-way and myself to be familiar with you.«

And, from then on the Shadow treated his former master as an inferior.

»It really is a bit steep,« thought the learned man,»that I have to call him 'Sir', while he can call me what he likes.« Still, he had to put up with it.

In due course they came to a watering-place, where there were many visitors and among them a beautiful princess, who suffered from the complaint of over-sharp sight, and this was most disturbing.

She noticed at once that the newcomer was utterly different from all the others. »They say he's here to make his beard grow, but I know the real reason: he can't throw a shadow.«

Her curiosity was aroused, and so she lost no time in having a stroll and a talk with the foreign gentleman. Being a princess, she didn't need to stand on ceremony, and so she said straight out, »Your trouble is that you can't throw a shadow.«

»Your Royal Highness must be very much better,« said the Shadow. »I know that the complaint you suffer from is that you see far too clearly, but it must have gone - you are cured. The fact is, I have a most unusual shadow. Haven't you noticed the person who is always with me? Other people have an ordinary shadow, but I am no lover of the ordinary. A gentleman gives his lackey for a livery finer cloth than he uses himself; and that's why I have had my shadow tricked out as a human being. Yes, look, I've even given *him* a shadow. It was very expensive, but I like having something that nobody else has got.«

»Heavens!« thought the Princess. »Have I really been cured? This spa is the finest in existence. Water nowadays has astonishing properties. But I won't go away; the place is beginning to amuse me. I like this foreigner immensely. I do hope his beard won't grow, because then he would be off at once.«

In the great ballroom that evening the Princess danced with the Shadow. She was light enough, but he was still lighter; never had she known a partner like that. She told him the country she came from; he knew it and had been there while she was away; he had peeped in at the windows on every floor and seen all sorts of things through them, so that he was able to answer the Princess and let fall little hints that quite astonished her. He must be the wisest man in the world, she thought, so great was her respect for what he knew. Then they danced together again, and she fell in love - which to the Shadow was obvious enough, for she could very nearly see right through him. And after that they had another dance, and she was on the point of telling him - but she kept her head. She remembered her country and her kingdom and all the people she had to rule over. »He's a wise man,« she told herself; »that's a good thing. And he dances beautifully; that's also good. But I wonder how deep his knowledge goes; that is just as important. He must be thoroughly tested.« So she gradually began to put to him the most difficult questions, which she herself couldn't have answered; and a curious look came into the Shadow's face.

»You can't answer that!« cried the Princess.

»I learnt that in the nursery« said the Shadow. »I believe even my shadow over there by the door can answer that.«

»Your shadow!« said the Princess. »That would be very remarkable.«

»Well, I won't say for certain that he can,« said the Shadow, »but I should imagine so. He has now been with me so many years, listening to me all the time - I should imagine he can. But may I draw your Royal

Highness's attention to one thing: he takes such pride in passing for a human being that, to get him into the right mood (which he has to be, if he is to answer well), he must be treated exactly the same as a human being.«

»I do like that,« said the Princess.

So then she went up to the learned man by the door and chatted with him about the sun and the moon and about people, both inside and out, and his answers were wonderfully shrewd and sound.

»What a man this must be, when his mere shadow is as wise as that!« she thought. »And what a blessing it would be for my people and kingdom, if I chose him as a husband! I'll do it.«

And they soon came to an understanding, the Princess and the Shadow. But no one must hear of it until she was back in her own kingdom. »No one, not even my shadow,« said the Shadow; and he had his own reasons for saying that. At last they reached the country over which the Princess ruled, when she was at home.

»Listen, my friend,« said the Shadow to the learned man. »I've now become as happy and powerful as a man can be. Now I should like to do something special for you. You are to live continually with me at the Castle, drive out with me in the royal carriage and have ten thousand pounds a year. But you must let everybody call you 'Shadow'; you mustn't ever say you have been a man; and once a year, when I sit in the sun on the balcony to show myself to the people, you must lie at my feet in the way that a shadow does. Let me tell you - I am marrying the Princess; the wedding is to take place this evening.«

»Goodness gracious!« said the learned man, »what could be worse than that? No, I won't, I won't do it. We'd be swindling the whole country, Princess and all. I'll tell them everything – that I am the man and you are the shadow, and that you are only dressed up.«

»Nobody will believe you,« said the Shadow. »Be sensible, or I'll call the guard.«

»I'm going straight to the Princess,« said the learned man. »But I'm going first,« said the Shadow, »and you're going to prison.« And go he did, for the sentries obeyed the one they knew the Princess wanted to marry.

»You are trembling,« said the Princess, as the Shadow came up to her. »Has anything happened? You mustn't get ill to-night, just when we are to have our wedding.«

»I have been through the most horrible experience possible,« said the Shadow. »Just fancy - of course, a poor shadow-brain like that can't stand much - fancy! my shadow has gone mad. He thinks that he's a man and that I - just imagine - am his shadow!«

»How terrible!« exclaimed the Princess. »He's safely shut up, I hope?«

»Yes, yes. I'm afraid he'll never recover.«

»Poor shadow!« said the Princess. »How unfortunate for him! It would be a real kindness to relieve him of the scrap of life that is left him. And now I come to think it over properly, I believe that's what has got to be done – put him quietly out of the way.«

»It does seem hard,« said the Shadow, »for he was a faithful servant.« And he produced a kind of sigh.

»You have a noble character,« said the Princess.

At night the whole town was illuminated. Guns went off – boom! Soldiers presented arms. It was no end of a wedding. The Princess and the Shadow came out on to the balcony to show themselves and to get one more round of cheering – hooray!

The learned man heard nothing of all this, for he had already been put to death.

It's Absolutely True!

I t's a terrible affair!« said a hen - speaking, too, in quite another part of the town from where it all happened. »It's a terrible affair about that chicken-house. I daren't sleep alone tonight. It's a good thing there are so many of us roosting together.« And then she told them her story, which made the other hens' feathers stand on end and even set the cock's comb drooping. It's absolutely true!

But let's begin at the beginning. It was in a chicken-house at the other end of the town. The sun went down, and the hens flew up. One of them was a white short-legged bird, who regularly laid her eggs and was altogether a most respectable hen. When she got to her perch she preened herself with her beak, and a little feather came out and went fluttering down. »So much for that one!« she said. »The more I preen, the lovelier I shall grow, no doubt!« Of course it was only said in fun, because she was the fun-maker among the hens, though in other ways (as you've just heard) most respectable. After that, she went off to sleep.

All about was quite dark; hen sat with hen, but the one next to her was still awake. She had heard, and had not heard - as you must often do in this world, if you are to live in peace and quiet. And yet she couldn't help saying to the hen perched on the other side of her, »Did you hear that? I give no names, but there is a hen who means to pluck out her feathers for the sake of her looks. If I were a cock, I'd simply despise her.«

Now directly above the hens sat the owl, with her owl husband and her owl children. They had sharp ears in that family; they could hear every word their hen neighbour said; and they rolled their eyes, and the owl mother fanned herself with her wings. »Don't take any notice – but of course you heard what she said, didn't you? I heard it with my own ears, and they're going to hear a lot before *they* drop off. One of the hens has so far forgotten what is fit and proper for a hen that she's calmly plucking out all her feathers in full view of the cock.«

»*Prenez garde aux enfants!*« said the father owl. »Not in the children's hearing!«

»But I must tell the owl over the way; she's so highly respected in our set.« And away flew the mother.

»Tu-whit,tu-who!« they both hooted, and it carried right down to the doves in the dovecot across the yard. »Have you heard, have you heard? To-who! There's a hen that's plucked out all her feathers for the sake of the cock. She'll freeze to death, if she isn't dead already, tu-who!«

»Where, ooh, where?« cooed the doves.

»In the yard opposite. I as good as saw it with my own eyes. Really the story's almost too improper to repeat; but it's absolutely true.«

»Tr-rue, tr-rue, every wor-rd!« said the doves; and they cooed down to their hen-run, »There's a hen, some say there are *two*, who have plucked out all their feathers so as to look different from the others and to attract the attention of the cock. It's a risky thing to do; suppose they catch cold and die of fever ... Yes, they're dead – *two* of them.«

Then the cock joined in: »Wake up, wake up!« he crowed, and flew up on to the wooden fence. His eyes were still sleepy, but he crowed away all the same; »Three hens have died of love for a cock; they had plucked out all their feathers. It's a horrible story – I don't want it – pass it on!« »Pass it on!« squeaked the bats; and the hens clucked and the cocks crowed, »Pass it on, pass it on!« And so the story flew from one hen-house to another, till at last it came back to the place where it had really started.

»There are five hens« - that's how it ran - »who have all plucked out their feathers to show which of them had got thinnest for love of the cock. Then they pecked at each other till the blood came and they all fell down dead, to the shame and disgrace of their family and the serious loss of their owner.«

The hen that had lost the one loose little feather didn't of course recognize her own story and, as she was a respectable hen, she said, »How I despise those hens! - though there are plenty more just like them. That's not the kind of thing to be hushed up, and I shall do my best to get the story into the papers, so that it may go all over the country. It'll serve those hens right, and their family too.«

And into the papers it came - all there in print - and it's absolutely true: *»One little feather can easily become five hens!«*

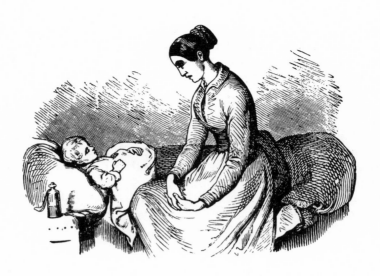

The Story of a Mother

A mother was sitting by the bed of her little child, and she was in great
grief because she was afraid it was going to die. The child was terribly
pale, the little eyes had closed, and its breathing was very soft and low –
though now and then it gave a deep breath like a sigh, and the mother
looked still more sadly at the poor little soul.

Then there was a knock at the door, and a poor old man came in
wrapped in a kind of large horse-cloth. You see, that keeps you warm,
and he needed it badly, because it was the middle of winter and everything out-of-doors was covered with ice and snow, and there was a biting
wind.

And as the old man was trembling with cold and the little child had
gone off to sleep for a moment, the mother went and put a small mug of
beer on the stove to warm it up for him. The old man sat there gently
rocking, and the mother sat down on a chair close beside him. Her sick
child was breathing heavily as she looked at it, and she took its hand.

»You don't think I shall lose him, do you?« she said. »Surely God
won't take him away from me.«

And the old man – it was Death himself – he nodded so strangely that it
could just as well have meant yes as no. And the mother looked down in
her lap and the tears ran down her cheeks ... Her head became so heavy –
for three days and nights she hadn't closed her eyes – that now she fell
asleep, though only for an instant; then she started up trembling with
cold. »What's happened?« she said, looking in every direction. But the

old man was gone, and her little child was gone, he had taken it with him; and over in the corner the old clock whirred and whirred, the great leaden bob fell, bump! on to the floor, and the clock stopped. But the poor mother rushed out of the house calling for her child.

There, out in the snow, sat a woman in long black clothes, who said, »Death has been in your room; I saw him hurry away with your little child. He goes faster than the wind, and he never brings back what he has taken away.«

»Only tell me which way he went,« said the mother. »Tell me the way, and I shall find him.«

»I know the way,« said the woman in black; »but, first, before I tell you, you must sing me all the songs you have sung to your child. I know them well, and I love them. I am Night, and I saw your tears as you sang them.«

»I will sing them all, all,« said the mother; »but don't stop me from catching him up – from finding my child.«

But Night sat still and said nothing. Then the mother wrung her hands and sang and cried; and there were many songs, but even more tears. After that, Night said to her, »Go to the right, into that dark forest of firs; that is the path I saw Death take with your little child.« Deep inside the forest she came to where the paths crossed, and she did not know which one to take. A bramble bush was growing there, which had neither leaf nor blossom for it was mid-winter and the twigs were all frosted over. »Did you see Death go past with my little child?« »Yes, I did,« replied the bramble, »but I won't tell you which way he went unless you will first warm me at your breast. I'm freezing to death; I shall soon be nothing but ice.«

And the mother pressed the bramble so tightly to her bosom, to make it really warm, that the thorns pierced her flesh and she shed great drops of blood. But the bramble shot out fresh green leaves and blossoms in the cold winter's night – such was the warmth from a sorrowing mother's heart. Then the bramble bush told her the right way to go.

Next she came to a big lake, where there was neither ship nor boat to carry her across. The lake was not frozen enough to bear her, nor was it thawed or shallow enough for her to wade through; and yet cross it she must, if she would find her child. So she lay down to try and drink up the lake, and nobody on earth could do that, though the grief-stricken mother was hoping all the same for a miracle.

»No, that will never do,« said the lake. »Let us two see if we can't come to an agreement. I collect pearls, and your eyes are the two clearest I have ever seen. If you will weep them out for me, I will carry you across to the great green house where Death lives and looks after flowers and trees; each of them is a human life.«

»Oh, I will give anything to come to my child,« said the mother, already worn out with weeping. And she wept still more, and her eyes sank to the bottom of the lake and became two precious pearls. But the lake lifted her up as if she was in a swing, and she felt herself whirled across to the further shore where there was an extraordinary house with a frontage that ran for miles and miles. You couldn't tell whether it was a mountain with woods and caves, or whether it was a regular building – though the poor mother couldn't see it because, you remember, she had wept her eyes out.

»Where shall I find Death, who went off with my little child?« she asked.

»He hasn't come yet,« said the old woman who looked after the graves and the huge greenhouse of Death. »But how did you find your way here, and who helped you?«

»God has helped me,« she said. »He is merciful, and you will be merciful too. Where shall I find my little child?«

»Well, but I don't know it,« said the woman, »and you of course can't see. Many flowers and trees have faded to-night; Death will soon be here to transplant them. You know, every human being has his tree of life or his flower, each one according to his nature; they look just like other plants, but they have hearts that beat. A child's heart can also beat. Bear that in mind; perhaps you will be able to recognize your own child's heart-beat. But what will you give me for telling you what to do next?«

»I have nothing left to give,« answered the poor mother. »But I will go to the ends of the earth for you.«

»That's no good to me,« said the woman. »But you can give me your long black hair. You know yourself how lovely it is, and I like it very much. You shall have my white hair instead; it's better than nothing.«

»If that's all you ask for,« she said, »then I'll gladly let you have it.« And she gave her beautiful black hair and received the old woman's snow-white hair in exchange.

And then they went into Death's huge greenhouse, where flowers and trees grew strangely together. There stood delicate hyacinths under bell-glass, and big lusty peonies. There grew water-plants, some quite fresh, others rather sickly, with water-snakes sprawling over them and black crayfish nipping their stalks. There stood lovely palm-trees, oaks and sycamores; and there, too, was parsley and flowering thyme. Every tree and flower had a name of its own; each was a human life that was still being lived, in China, in Greenland, all over the world. There were big trees in small pots, cramped so terribly that they were ready to burst their pots; and often, too, there was a common little flower growing in rich soil, nursed and cared for, with moss round it. But the sorrowing mother bent down over all the tiniest plants and listened to the human heart-beats inside them till, among millions of them, she recognized that of her own child.

»There it is!« she cried and stretched out her hands over a little blue crocus that stood there weakly and drooping.

»Don't touch it!« said the old woman. »But stand here, and when Death comes – I am expecting him any moment now – don't let him pull up the plant; no, you just threaten to do that to the other flowers, and this will frighten him, for he must answer to God for them. None may be pulled up without God's permission.«

Suddenly there was a rush of ice-cold air through the place, and the blind mother could tell that Death had come.

»How were you able to find your way?« asked Death. »How could you get here more quickly than I did?«

»I am a mother,« she said.

And Death stretched out his long fingers towards the delicate little flower. But she kept her hands tightly round it – tightly and yet anxiously for fear she might touch one of its petals. Then Death breathed on her hands, and she felt that this was colder than the icecold wind, and her hands dropped limply away.

»You see, you can do nothing against me,« said Death. »But God can,« she answered. »I only do what God wills,« said Death. »I am his gardener. I take all his flowers and trees and plant them out in the great garden of Paradise in the unknown land – though how they will grow there and what it is like there, I may not tell you.«

»Give me back my child!« pleaded the mother in tears. Suddenly she clutched two beautiful flowers near by, one in each hand, and cried out to Death: »I'll pull up all your flowers, for I'm desperate.«

»Don't you touch them!« said Death. »You say you are so unhappy, and now you are ready to make another mother equally unhappy.«

»Another mother!« cried the poor woman and immediately let go of both flowers.

»There, you can have your eyes back,« said Death. »I fished them up out of the lake; they were shining so brightly. I didn't know they were yours. Take them back, they are now clearer than ever. Then look down into the deep well over there, and I will tell you the names of the two flowers you wanted to pull up. You will see their whole future, their whole human existence, you will see what you were just going to disturb and destroy.«

She looked down into the well; and it was a joy to see how one flower became a blessing to the world - to see how much pleasure and happiness was spread around. And she saw the life of the other, full of sorrow and want and fear and wretchedness.

»Both are the will of God,« said Death.

»Which of them is the flower of misery and which the flower of happiness?« she asked. »I may not tell you that,« replied Death, »but this you shall hear: one of those two flowers belonged to your own child – it was your own child's destiny you saw, your own child's future.«

Then the mother shrieked in terror: »Which of them was my child? Tell me that. Save the little innocent, save my child from all that wretchedness! Rather take him away, take him into God's kingdom! Forget about my tears – my pleading – all that I have said and done!«

»I don't understand you,« said Death. »Do you want your child back or shall I carry him you know not where?«

The mother wrung her hands, fell on her knees and prayed to God: »Don't listen to me when I pray contrary to thy will – thou knowest best. Don't listen to me!« And she buried her head in her lap.

And Death went away with her child into the unknown land.

The Garden of Eden

There was once a King's son. Nobody had so many fine books as he
had. He could read for himself about all that had ever happened in the
world and see it set out in beautiful pictures. He could learn, too, about
peoples and countries; and yet where the Garden of Eden was to be found,
there wasn't a word about that; and, as it happened, this was the very
thing he was always wondering.

When he was still quite small but was going to begin school, his
grandmother had told him that every flower in the Garden of Eden was a
lovely cake and their stamens full of the most delicious wine. One flower
would have history on it, another geography or your tables. You only
had to eat cake to know your home-work; and the more you ate, the more
history, geography and tables you got to know.

He believed it all at the time; but as he grew bigger, learnt more and
became so much cleverer, he realized that there must be very different
delights in the Garden of Eden.

»Why, why, did Eve pick from the Tree of Knowledge? Why did Adam
eat of the forbidden fruit? If it had been me, it would never have happened – and sin would never have come into the world.«

That is what he said at the time, and he still said it when he was
seventeen. The Garden of Eden quite filled his thoughts.

One day he went into the woods. He went all alone, for there was
nothing he liked better. Night was falling, and the clouds came up so
that it rained as if the whole sky were a sluice that had opened its flood-

gates. It was as dark as it would be at night in the deepest well. At one moment he slipped in the wet grass, at another he tripped up on the bare stones that jutted out from the rocky ground. Everything was dripping wet; the poor Prince hadn't a dry stitch left on him. He was obliged to crawl across large blocks of stone where the water was oozing out of the overgrown moss. He was very nearly fainting when all at once he heard a strange roaring sound, and he saw in front of him a large lighted cave. Blazing in the middle of it was a fire big enough to roast a deer, and that's just what was happening. A magnificent stag, antlers and all, was slowly turning on a spit between two felled branches of fir. An oldish-looking woman, tall and burly, as though she were a man dressed up, sat by the fire throwing on one bit of fuel after another.

»Come along,« she said, »come right up to the fire and dry your clothes.«

»There's a fearful draught in here,« said the Prince, as he sat down on the floor.

»It'll be still worse when my sons come back,« answered the woman. »This is the Cave of the Winds you have come to. My sons are the Earth's four Winds. Do you follow me?«

»Where are your sons?« asked the Prince.

»Well, you know, foolish questions are often hard to answer,« said the woman. »My sons are out on their own, playing tennis with the clouds in the great hall up there« – and she pointed up above her head.

»Oh, I see,« said the Prince. »The fact is, your sharp way of talking isn't a bit like the gentle way of the women I usually meet.«

»Well, I expect they have nothing else to do. I have to be sharp, if I'm to keep my boys in order. Still, I can manage it, headstrong as they are. Do you see those four sacks hanging on the wall? My sons are just as afraid of them as you were of the switch behind the mirror. You see, I can double the boys up, and then into the bag they go – and no nonsense about it. There they stay and don't come trapesing out until I think fit. But, look, there is one of them.«

It was the North Wind who brought an icy chill with him; great hailstones pattered on the floor and snowflakes drifted around. He was wearing bearskin trousers and jacket, a sealskin hood came well down over his ears, long icicles hung from his beard, and there were hailstones rolling down one after another from his coat-collar.

»Don't go straight up to the fire,« said the Prince. »Your face and hands might easily get frost-bitten.«

»Frost!« said the North Wind with a loud guffaw. »Frost! Nothing I like better! What sort of a spindle-shanks are you, anyway? What brings you into the Cave of the Winds?«

»He's my guest,« said the old woman, »and if you're not satisfied with that explanation, you can come into the sack ... There! now you know what to expect.«

That was the way to treat him, and the North Wind now told them where he came from and where he had been for nearly a month past. »I come from the Polar Sea,« he said; »I've been on Behring Island with the Russian walrus hunters. I sat sleeping at the helm, as they sailed away from the North Cape. Now and then I woke up for a while and found the stormy petrel flying round my legs. He's a comic bird. He gives one smart flap with his wings and then keeps them outstretched and motionless, and that gives him all the speed he wants.«

»Yes, but don't make such a long story of it!« said the mother of the Winds. »And so then you came to Behring Island?«

»It's a wonderful place. There's a dancing-floor as flat as a plate, with moss and half-thawed snow, sharp stones and skeletons of walruses and polar bears, looking as they lay there like giants' arms and legs, all mouldy and green. You'd think the sun had never shone on them. I breathed a bit on the fog so as to get a glimpse of the hut. It was a house built from the wreckage and covered with walrus-skins, the fleshy side outwards, red and green all over. On the roof a live polar bear sat growling. I went down to the shore to have a look at the bird's-nests and at the unfledged young ones gaping and screaming. I blew down into their thousand throats and taught them to shut their mouths. Lower down the walruses were tumbling about like living entrails or enormous maggots with pig's heads and teeth a yard long.«

»You describe it all very well, my son« said the mother. »It makes my mouth water to listen to you.«

»After that came the fishing. The harpoon was plunged in the heart of the walrus, so that the steaming blood spirted up like a fountain over the ice. Then I too had my own little game to think about. I started to blow and made my sailing ships, the tall rock-like icebergs, nip and crush the boats – phew! How the people whimpered and shrieked, but I shrieked louder. The dead whale carcases, the chests and the tackle all had to be dumped on the ice. I shook snowflakes over them and let them drift south with their catch in their trapped vessels, to taste salt water. They'll never come back to Behring Island.«

»Then you've done harm,« said the mother of the Winds.

»Others could tell of the good I have done,« he replied. »But here comes my brother from the West. He's my favourite brother, with a tang of the sea and a wonderful freshness about him.«

»Is that the little Zephyr?« asked the Prince.

»Yes, that's Zephyr right enough,« said the old woman. »But he's not so little, after all. In the old days he was a good-looking boy, but that's all past and gone now.«

He looked like a savage, but he was wearing a sort of padded helmet to protect his head. In his hand he held a mahogany club cut from the mahogany woods of America. He couldn't do with less than that.

»Where have you been?« his mother asked.

»In the forest wildernesses,« he said, »where the thorny creepers make a fence between every tree, where the water snake lies in the grassy swamp, and mankind seems unnecessary.«

»What did you do there?«

»I looked at the deep river, I saw how it plunged down from the rocks and turned to spray, flying up to the clouds to carry the rainbow. I saw the wild buffalo swimming in the river, though the stream forced him along with it and he drifted with a flock of wild duck that flew into the air as they reached the rapids. The buffalo had to go down them; I enjoyed that, and I started such a gale that old, old trees went sailing and were dashed to smithereens.«

»And didn't you do anything else?« asked his mother.

»I turned somersaults on the prairie, I patted the wild horses and shook down coconuts. Bless you, yes – I've plenty to tell, though one shouldn't say all that one knows. Of course, you know that perfectly well, old lady« – and he gave his mother such a hearty kiss that she nearly toppled over backwards. He really was a boisterous lad.

Next came the South Wind wearing a turban and a flying Bedouin cloak. »It's mighty cold in here,« he said, throwing logs on the fire. »Easy to tell that the North Wind got home first.«

»It's hot enough in here to roast a polar-bear,« said the North Wind.

»You're a polar bear yourself,« answered the South Wind.

»Do you two want to go into the sack?« threatened the old woman. »Sit down on that stone and tell us where you've been.«

»In Africa, mother,« he replied. »I was out lion-hunting with the Hottentots in the land of the Kaffirs. What grass there is, growing there on the plain, green as an olive! The gnu antelope was prancing about, and the ostrich ran races with me though I'm quicker on my pins, mind you. I found my way to the desert with its yellow sand that looks like the bottom of the sea. I came across a caravan. They killed their last camel to get water to drink but they didn't get much. There was a scorching sun overhead, and a blistering sand underfoot. There was no limit to the far-flung desert. I romped about in the fine loose sand and whirled it up into great pillars – it was no end of a go! You should have seen how forlorn the dromedary stood, and the way the merchant drew his caftan over his head. He flung himself down before me as if before Allah, his God. Now they are buried, with a pyramid of sand heaped above them all. One day, when I blow it away, the sun will bleach their bones, and travellers will be able to see that man was here in days gone by; otherwise they could never believe it in the desert.«

»So you've only done harm,« said the mother. »Into the sack with you!« and, before the South Wind knew what was happening, she had him by the waist and into the sack. He rolled over on the floor, but she squatted on top and so then he had to lie still.

»That's a lively lot of boys you have,« said the Prince.

»Yes, you may well call them that,« she replied, »and I know how to manage them. Here we have the fourth.«

It was the East Wind; he was dressed like a Chinese.

»Oh, so that's where you come from,« said the mother. »I thought you were in the Garden of Eden.«

»I don't fly to it till tomorrow,« said the East Wind. »It will be just a hundred years tomorrow since I was there. I've just come from China, where I danced round the Porcelain Tower and made all the bells ring. Down in the street the officials were being flogged; bamboo canes were being broken across their shoulders. And they were men of high rank, too, from the first to the ninth class. They kept crying out, 'Thank you very much, my fatherly benefactor'; but they didn't mean it. And I set the bells ringing and sang, *tsing, tsang, tsu.*«

»You are always up to mischief,« said the old mother. »It's a good thing you are going to the Garden of Eden tomorrow; that always tends to improve you. Drink deep from the fountain of wisdom, and bring a little bottle home, full, for me.«

»Right - I will,« said the East Wind. »But why have you put my brother from the South into the sack? Let him out! I want him to tell me about the Phoenix bird. The Princess in the Garden of Eden always wants to hear about that bird, when I pay her a visit every hundred years. Do be a nice kind mother and open the sack, and you shall have two pocketfuls of fresh green tea straight from the spot where I picked it.«

»Well, well, for the sake of the tea and because you're my pet child, I'll open the sack.« As she did so, the South Wind crawled out, but he looked rather sheepish that the foreign Prince should have seen it.

»Here's a palm leaf for you to give the Princess,« said the South Wind. »This leaf was given me by the old Phoenix bird, the only one left in the world. With his beak he has scratched on it the account of his whole life, the hundred years he has been living. Now she can read it for herself. I saw how the Phoenix bird himself set fire to his nest and sat till he was burnt right up, like a Hindu's wife. How the dry twigs did crackle ... and the smoke and the perfume there was! Finally, everything went up in flames; the old Phoenix bird turned to ashes, while his egg lay red-hot in the fire - and then burst open with a loud bang and the young one flew out. Now he is Regent over all the birds and the only Phoenix bird left on earth. He has bitten a hole in the palm leaf I gave you; that's his way of sending greetings to the Princess.«

»Now let's have something to eat,« said the mother of the Winds. And with that, they all sat down to have some of the roasted stag; and the Prince sat beside the East Wind, and in that way they soon became great friends.

»I say,« said the Prince, »just tell me, will you - who, exactly, is this Princess there's so much talk about? And where is the Garden of Eden?«

»Ho, ho!« said the East Wind, »if that's where you want to go, why, then come and fly with me tomorrow. But, all the same, I feel bound to tell you that no mortal man has been there since the time of Adam and Eve. Of course, you know all about them from your Bible.«

»Yes, yes,« said the Prince.

»That time they were driven out from the Garden of Eden, it sank down into the earth, though it kept its warm sunshine, its soft air and all its glorious beauty. There lies the home of the Queen of the Fairies; there too, is the Island of the Blest, where death never comes and it's so wonderful to be. Get on my back tomorrow, and I'll take you with me. I'm pretty sure it can be managed. But you mustn't chatter any more now; I want to go to sleep.« And after that they all of them went to sleep.

Early next morning the Prince woke up and was a good deal puzzled to find that he was already high above the clouds. He was sitting on the back of the East Wind, who certainly had a firm hold on him. They were so high in the air that woods and fields, rivers and lakes, looked to be there on a large coloured map.

»Good morning!« said the East Wind. »You might just as well sleep on a little longer, for there isn't much to look at on the flat country below us. Unless you want to count the churches! They stand out like specks of chalk on the green board down there.« They were fields and meadows that he called the green board.

»It was rude of me not to say goodbye to your mother and your brothers,« said the Prince.

»You can't be blamed when you're asleep,« said the East Wind and flew on faster than ever. You could hear it in the forest tree-tops, as they passed over them, rustling all the leaves and branches; you could hear it on the sea and on the lakes, for, wherever they flew, the waves dashed higher and the big ships curtsied low in the water like floating swans.

Towards evening, as it grew dark, the large towns were a cheerful sight with the lights burning down there in one place and another. It was just as it is when you set light to a bit of paper and see numbers of little sparks like so many children coming out of school. And the Prince clapped his hands, but the East Wind told him to stop that and hold on tight or he might easily fall down and get caught on a church steeple.

The eagle from the dark woods flew nimbly enough, but the East Wind was nimbler still. The Cossack on his little horse coursed away over the plains, but the Prince's coursing was of another kind.

»There, now you can see the Himalayas,« said the East Wind; »they are the highest mountains in Asia. We should soon come to the Garden of Eden now.« Then they turned more south, and presently there was a perfume of flowers and spices. Figs and pomegranates were growing wild, and the vine too grew wild with blue and purple grapes. Here both alighted and stretched themselves in the soft grass where the flowers nodded to the Wind as if to say, »Welcome back!«

»Is this the Garden of Eden?« asked the Prince.

»Bless you, no!« replied the East Wind. »But we shall soon be there now. Do you see that wall of rock over there and the big cave where the grape-vines are hanging like huge green curtains? We've got to go in through there. Wrap your cloak round you, because here we have the scorching sun while a single pace off it is icy cold. A bird brushing past the cave has one wing out here in hot summer and the other inside there in cold winter.«

»So this is the way to the Garden of Eden?« asked the Prince.

Now they entered the cave. Phew! How icy cold it was – but it didn't last long. The East Wind spread out his wings, and they shone like the brightest fire. Goodness! What caves these were! The great blocks of stone from which the water dripped down hung above them in the strangest shapes. At one moment the caves were so narrow that they had to creep on all fours, at another as lofty and wide as in the open air. They looked like mortuary chapels with silent organ pipes and banners of stone.

»We seem to be taking the path of death to the Garden of Eden,« said the Prince. But the East Wind never answered a word. He merely pointed ahead, where the loveliest blue light was shining straight at them. The stone blocks overhead turned more and more to a mist, which finally showed as clearly as a white cloud in the moonlight. Now they found themselves in a wonderful soft air, as though breathed from roses in the valley.

And there, too, flowed a river, clear as the air itself, with fishes like silver and gold. Purple eels, shooting out blue sparks at every wriggle, were frisking down there in the water; and the broad leaves of the water-lily had the colours of the rainbow, while the flower itself burned with an orange flame, fed by the water like a lamp kept alight by the oil. A solid bridge of marble – yet as cunningly devised as though it were worked in filigree and glass bugles – led across the water to the Island of the Blest, where the Garden of Eden lay blossoming.

The East Wind took the Prince in his arms and carried him across. There he heard flowers and foliage singing the loveliest songs from his childhood, but in swelling tones more beautiful than any human voice can sing them.

Were those palm trees or gigantic water plants growing there? Never had the Prince seen trees so tall and full of sap. There in long festoons hung the most astonishing creepers, such as are only to be found in gold and colour on the margins of old missals or twining about the initial letters. There was the strangest assembly of birds, flowers and twisting tendrils. In the grass close by stood a flock of peacocks spreading out their gorgeous tails. Yes, surely that's what they were ... but no, when the Prince touched them he found that they weren't animals but plants; they were huge dock leaves, that shone here with all the splendour of a pea-cock's tail. Lions and tigers, nimble as cats, went bounding through the greenwood with its scents of olive-blossom, and they were tame lions and tame tigers. Wild wood-pigeons, gleaming like the finest pearls, flapped their wings against the lion's mane, while antelopes, usually so timid, stood nodding their heads, as though they too would like to join in the frolic.

Now came the Fairy of the Garden of Eden . Her dress shone like the sun, and her face was as gentle and kind as a happy mother's whose child has made her glad. She was young and pretty, and with her were beauti-ful girls, each with a glittering star in her hair.

The East Wind handed her the leaf with the Phoenix bird's writing on it, and the Fairy's eyes sparkled with joy. She took the Prince by the hand and led him into her castle, where the colour of the walls was like the petal of the finest tulip when held up against the sun. The ceiling, too, was one enormous radiant flower, and the more you looked up at it the deeper its cup seemed to be. The Prince stepped to the window and glanced through one of its panes. There he saw the Tree of Knowledge with the serpent, and Adam and Eve standing close by. »Haven't they been driven out?« he asked; and with a smile the Fairy explained to him that time, like that, had burned its picture upon every pane, not in the customary way – no, there was life in it, leaves were stirring on the trees, people came and went, just as things do in a reflection. Then he glanced through another pane, and there he saw Jacob's dream, with the ladder going right up to heaven and the angels hovering up and down on their great wings. Yes, all that had ever happened in the world lived and moved in those panes; time alone could have burned such cunning pictures into the glass.

The Fairy smiled and led him into a geat lofty hall. Here the walls seemed to be made of transparent pictures, with each face more beautiful than the other. There were millions of them, whose happy laughter and singing flowed together into a single melody. The ones highest up were so tiny that they looked smaller than the smallest rosebud when it's a mere speck in a drawing. And there in the middle of the hall stood a big tree with hanging branches heavy with fruit. Golden apples, large and small, hung like oranges among the green leaves. This was the Tree of Knowledge, of whose fruit Adam and Eve had eaten. From every leaf there dripped a glittering red dewdrop; it was as though the tree wept tears of blood.

»Now let us get into the boat,« said the Fairy. »There we will enjoy some refreshment out on the rolling wave. The boat swings at her moorings, while every country in the world will pass before us.« And it was astonishing to see how the whole coast moved. First came the towering snow-clad Alps with clouds and dark fir trees; the horn sounded deep and wistful, and the shepherd was yodelling in the valley. Then the banana trees bent their long drooping branches over the boat; coal-black swans swam on the water, and the strangest animals and flowers were to be seen on the shore: it was Australia, the fifth continent of the world, that glided past with its Blue Mountains in the distance. They heard the priests chanting, and they watched the savages dancing to tomtoms and trumpets of bone. The Pyramids of Egypt jutting up into the clouds, overturned pillars and sphinxes half buried in the sand, went sailing by. The Northern Lights flared over the glaciers of the north – a display of fireworks that none could equal. The Prince was enchanted; and he naturally saw a hundred times more than we have just described. »May I stay here for good?« he asked.

»That depends on yourself,« replied the Fairy. »As long as you don't, like Adam, allow yourself to be tempted to do what is forbidden, you may certainly remain.«

»I shall not touch the apples on the Tree of Knowledge,« said the Prince. »After all, there are thousands of fruits here as fine as they are.«

»Test yourself, and if you are not strong enough, then go with the East Wind who brought you; he is just flying back and won't come here again for a hundred years. That's a time that in this place you will find goes by like a hundred hours, though it's a long enough time for temptation and sin. Every evening, as I leave you I must cry out to you, Come with me! I must beckon to you with my hand, but stay where you are. Don't come, because if you do your longing will increase at every step; you will come to the hall where the Tree of Knowledge grows; I shall be asleep under its drooping fragrant branches; I must smile as you bend over me, but if you kiss my mouth Eden will sink deep into the earth and be lost to you for ever. The keen wind of the desert will whistle around you, the cold rain will drip from your hair. Sorrow and tribulation will be your lot.«

»I'll stay here,« said the Prince; and the East Wind kissed his forehead and said, »Be strong, and we shall meet again here in a hundred years. Goodbye! Goodbye!« – and the East Wind spread out his great wings. They flashed like summer lightning at harvest-time or the Northern Lights in the depth of winter. »Goodbye! Goodbye!« was echoed from flowers and trees. Storks and pelicans flew in a line like fluttering ribbons and kept him company to the boundary of the Garden.

»Now our dances will begin,« said the Fairy. »At the end, when I dance with you, as the sun goes down you will see me beckon to you; you will hear me cry out, Come with me! But don't do it. I must repeat that every evening for a hundred years. Every time that moment is past, you will gain more strength, till at last you never give it a thought. Tonight is the first time – now I have warned you.«

And the Fairy led him into a great hall of transparent white lilies; the yellow filaments of every flower made a little gold harp, which gave out the sound of strings and flute. The loveliest girls, slender and graceful, clad in billowy gauze that revealed the beauty of their limbs, swayed in the dance and sang of the sweets of living and how that they would never die and the Garden of Eden would bloom for ever.

And the sun went down, and the whole sky became a sheet of gold, which gave the lilies a tinge of the loveliest rose. And the Prince drank of the foaming wine handed him by the girls, and he felt a happiness he had never known before. He saw how the far end of the hall opened ... There stood the Tree of Knowledge in a shining splendour that dazzled his eyes. The singing that came from it was soft and beautiful like the voice of his mother, and it was as though she sang to him, »My child, my darling child!«

Then the Fairy beckoned and called to him so tenderly, »Come with me! Come with me!« that he rushed over to her and quite forgot his promise – forgot it the very first evening – as she beckoned and smiled. The perfume, the fragrant perfume all around, grew stronger, the melody of the harps far lovelier; and the millions of smiling heads in the hall, where the Tree was growing, seemed to nod and sing, »Man should know everything. Man is the lord of the earth.« And they were no longer tears of blood that fell from the leaves of the Tree of Knowledge – they were stars, red and sparkling, it seemed to him. »Come with me! Come with me!« echoed the quivering notes, and at every step the Prince's cheeks burned hotter, his blood ran faster. »I must!« he said. »There's no sin in that – cannot possibly be. Why not follow beauty and joy? I only want to see her asleep. It will be none the worse, as long as I don't kiss her; and I shan't do that. I am strong, with a firm will.«

And the Fairy threw off her glittering robe, bent back the branches, and a moment later was hidden among them. »Not yet have I sinned« said the Prince, »nor will I« – and he drew aside the branches. There she lay, already asleep, beautiful as only the Fairy in the Garden of Eden can be. She smiled in her dreams, and as he bent over her he saw the tears trembling between her eyelashes.

»Is it for me you weep?« he whispered. »O loveliest of women, do not weep! Now at last I have learnt to know the happiness of Eden. It streams through my blood, through my thoughts; in my mortal limbs I can feel angelic power and immortal life. Doom me to eternal night – one moment like this is wealth enough.« He kissed the tear from her eye, his mouth touched hers...

Then there came a crash of thunder louder and more terrible than had ever been heard. Everything fell in ruin: the beautiful Fairy, the blossoming Eden, sank, sank down deep – the Prince saw it sink into black night, until it gleamed far away like a shining star. The chill of death ran through his limbs; he closed his eyes and lay long as if dead.

A cold rain fell on his face, a keen wind blew about his head, as his senses came back to him. »What have I done?« he sighed. »I have sinned like Adam – sinned so that Paradise has sunk deep down below.« And as he opened his eyes, he saw the star once more in the far distance, the star that shone like the sunken Paradise. It was the morning star in the sky.

He rose up – and found himself in the great forest near to the Cave of the Winds, and the mother of the Winds was sitting beside him. She looked angry and lifted up her arm.

»The very first evening!« she said. »I thought as much. Well, if you were my boy, you should go straight into the sack.«

»He shall go there in time,« said Death, who was a sturdy old man carrying a scythe and with great black wings. »He shall be laid in a coffin, but not now. I'll just make a note of him and let him rove the world a little longer and atone for his sins and grow better; I shall come one day. Just when he least expects, I shall have him into the black coffin, put it on my head and fly up towards the star. There, too, the Garden of Eden is in flower, and if he is kind and good he shall be allowed to go in; but if his thoughts are evil and his heart still full of sin, he will sink with the coffin deeper than Eden sank, and I shall only fetch him back every thousand years, either to sink deeper still or to remain on the star - that glittering star up there.«

The Happy Family

The biggest green leaf in this country, depend upon it, is a burdock leaf. Hold it in front of your tummy, and it would do for an apron; put in over your head in the rain, and it's almost as good as an umbrella – it's a tremendous size. A burdock never grows by itself; where there's one growing, there are lots more. It's a lovely sight, and all that loveliness is food for snails. The big white snails that fine folk in the old days used to have stewed into a fricassee, muttering »Yum, yum, how delicious!« as they ate it – for they really did love the taste of it – these snails lived on burdock leaves, and that's how the burdocks came to be sown.

Well, there was an old manor-house where they had given up eating snails; these had quite died out, but the burdocks hadn't died out. They grew and grew all over the paths and flower-beds, till they were quite out of hand; there was an absolute forest of burdocks. Here and there stood an apple tree or a plum tree; otherwise you'd never have guessed it was a garden. The whole place was covered with burdocks – and in the middle of them lived the last two snails, both extremely old.

They didn't themselves know how old they were, but they could well remember that there had once been many more of them; that they belonged to a family coming from foreign parts, and that it was for them and theirs that the whole forest had been planted. They had never been outside it, though they realized that something else existed in the world called *The Manor*, where you got boiled and then turned black and were laid out on a silver dish; but what happened after that nobody knew. They couldn't anyhow imagine what it felt like to be boiled and to lie on a silver dish, but it must be delightful and very much the correct thing.

Neither the cockchafer nor the toad nor the earthworm, when questioned, could reply; none of them had ever been boiled or laid on a silver dish.

The old white snails were the finest folk imaginable – they knew that. The forest existed entirely for them, and the Manor existed for them to be boiled and laid on a silver dish.

They were now living quite happily all by themselves, and as they had no children they had adopted a little common snail that they brought up as their own. But the little creature wouldn't grow, being just a common snail. And yet the old folk, especially Mother – Mother Snail – fancied she could see that he was getting on; and she asked Father Snail, supposing he couldn't see this, to feel the little shell; and he felt it and came to the conclusion that Mother was right.

Then one day there was a heavy shower of rain. »Listen to the rub-a-dub-a-dub on the burdock leaves!« said Father Snail.

»Yes, and some of the drops are coming through,« answered Mother Snail. »Why, they're running right down the stalk. My, what a drenching we shall get! I'm so glad of our good houses and of our little one's too. I really think more has been done for us than for any others. Anyone can see that we are the cream of creation. We have houses from birth, and the burdock forest was sown for our benefit. I should like to know how far it goes and what there is outside it.«

»There's nothing outside it,« said Father Snail. »Nowhere can there be a better home than ours, and I have nothing more to wish for.«

»Oh, but I have,« said Mother Snail. »I should like to go to the Manor and be boiled and laid on a silver dish. That's what happened to all our ancestors; I'm sure there must be something extra special about it.«

»The Manor-house may have fallen into ruins by now,« said Father Snail, »or be overgrown with burdocks, so that the people can't get out. Anyhow, there's no need for haste; you're always in such a fearful hurry, and our little one is beginning to take after you. Why, he's actually been crawling up that stalk for three days; it makes me dizzy to look at him.«

»Now then, no scolding!« said Mother Snail. »He crawls along so coolly, I'm sure he will be a great joy to us; and after all what else have we old folk to live for? But have you thought about this – where we are to find a wife for him? Don't you think that somewhere deep in the burdock forest there might be someone of our sort?«

»Well, I've no doubt there are plenty of blacks snails,« said the old father, »black ones without a house of their own; but that would be such a come-down, and they do think such a lot of themselves. No, but we might commission the ants to see to it. They go trotting to and fro as if they had something to do; surely they would know of a wife for our little snail.«

»Yes, of course, we know the most beautiful one you could think of,« cried the ants, »though there might be difficulties, as she's a queen.«

»That wouldn't matter,« said the old snail. »But has she a house of her own?«

»She has a palace,« replied the ants, »the most beautiful ant palace with seven hundred corridors.«

»Thank you!« said Mother Snail. »Our son's not going into an ant-hill. If that's the best you can do we'll commission the white gnats instead; they fly all over the place, rain or shine, and they know the burdock forest inside and out.«

»We've got a wife for him,« cried the gnats. »A hundred yards off, perched on a gooseberry bush, is a little snail with a house of her own. She lives all by herself and is quite old enough to get married. It's only a hundred yards away.«

»All right,« said Father Snail. »But let her come to him. He's got a burdock forest, and she's only got a bush.«

So the gnats went and fetched the little lady snail. It took her a week to arrive, but of course that was the great thing about it – she was clearly one of the right sort.

Then came the wedding. Six glow-worms did their best with lighting; otherwise, the whole thing went off quietly, for the two old snails didn't care for feasting and jollification. But Mother Snail made a charming speech – Father was too overcome to manage that – and then they handed over the whole of the burdock forest to the young couple and repeated what they had always said – that it was the best place in the world and, if they lived honest upright lives and multiplied, they and their children would one day go the manor-house and be boiled black and laid on a silver dish.

When the speech was over, the old snails crawled into their houses and never came out again; they went to sleep. The two young ones took charge of the forest and raised a large offspring. But they were never boiled or laid on a silver dish, so they came to the conclusion that the Manor must have fallen into ruins and that everybody in the world had died out; and as no one contradicted them, it must have been true. The rain beat down for them on the burdock leaves – rub-a-dub-a-dub – and the sun shone for them to give colour to the burdock forest, and they were very happy! The whole family were happy – yes, they really were.

The Drop of Water

I suppose you know what a magnifying glass is – a sort of round eye-glass that makes everything a hundred times bigger than it is? If you take it and hold it in front of you and look at a drop of water out of the pond, you can see any number of strange-looking creatures that you would otherwise never see in the water; yet, sure enough, there they are. It looks rather like a plateful of shrimps hopping about among each other; and they are so ferocious that they tear off each other's arms and legs, buttocks and thighs – though, in spite of that, they are quite pleased and cheerful in their own way.

Now there was once an old man whom everybody called Creepy-Crawly, because that was his name. He always would have the best of everything and, if other means failed, then he got what he wanted by magic.

Well, one day he sat holding his magnifying glass in front of him and looking at a drop of water that came from a puddle in the ditch. Goodness, what a lot of creeping and crawling there was! Hundreds of little creatures were all hopping around and tugging at each other and eating each other.

»Really it's quite repulsive,« said old Creepy-Crawly. »Can't they be made to live in peace and quiet and to mind their own business?« And he puzzled and puzzled, but it all came to nothing, and so he was forced to use magic. »I must colour them to make them stand out more clearly,« he said; and he poured the merest drop of red wine into the drop of water.

227

But it was witch's blood, the very finest kind at twopence a drop. Then all those weird little creatures turned pink all over; they might have been a whole townful of naked savages.

»What have you got there?« asked another old magician who hadn't got a name – and that was just what made him so distinguished.

»Well, if you can guess what it is,« said Creepy-Crawly, »I'll make you a present of it. But it isn't easy to find out, if you don't know.«

And the magician who hadn't got a name took a peep through the magnifying glass. It looked exactly like a whole town where everybody was running about without anything on. It was horrible; but still more horrible was the sight of people pushing and elbowing each other, wrestling and wrangling, snapping and snarling. Those at the bottom should be on top, and those at the top should be down at the bottom. »Look there! His leg is longer than mine. Pooh! Away with it! And here's a chap with a little pimple behind his ear; a harmless little pimple, but it hurts him, and it shall hurt him still more.« And they slashed at it and pulled him about, and then they ate him for the sake of the little pimple. Another was sitting there as still as any maiden might, wanting nothing but peace and quiet; but the maiden had to come forward and be pulled and tugged, till finally they ate her right up!

»That's extremely funny,« said the magician.

»Yes, but what do you make of it all?« asked Creepy-Crawly. »Have you any idea what it is?«

»It's plain enough,« said the other. »It must be Copenhagen or some other big city, for they're all alike. A big city, anyway.«

»It's ditch-water,« said Creepy-Crawly.

The Shirt Collar

There was once a swell gentleman whose entire kit consisted of a bootjack and a comb – though he had the neatest shirt collar you ever saw, and it's about this collar that our story is to be.

The collar was now old enough to think of getting married, and it so happened that in the wash he came across a garter.

»My word!« said the collar. »Never have I seen anyone so slender and refined, so delicate and pretty. May I ask your name?«

»No, I won't tell you,« replied the garter.

»Where do you live?« asked the collar.

But the garter was very shy and thought it was an odd question to have to answer.

»I should think you are a girdle,« continued the collar, »a sort of understrap. Yes, I can see you are both useful and ornamental, my dear.«

»You're not to speak to me,« said the garter. »I can't see that I have given you the slightest excuse.«

»Oh, yes, you have. When anyone's as pretty as you,« said the collar, »that's excuse enough.«

»Don't come so near,« said the garter. »You look so very masculine.«

»Well, I am, I'm no end of a swell,« said the collar; »I've got a bootjack and a comb« – which of course wasn't true, for they belonged to his master. He was just showing off.

»Don't come so near; I'm not used to it,« said the garter.

»Little prude!« snorted the collar and was taken out of the wash-tub, starched, hung over a chair in the sun and then laid along the ironing-board, where he was given a hot iron.

»Madam,« said the collar,« »dear widow lady, I'm getting so hot, I shall soon be quite another person; I'm losing all my creases. Ugh! You're burning a hole in me – oh, will you marry me?«

»You rag!« said the iron, going disdainfully over the collar; for she fancied she was a steam-engine meant to draw trucks on the railway.

»You rag!« she repeated.

The collar was a bit frayed at the edges, and so the big scissors came along to trim them. »My!« said the collar, »you must be a leader of the ballet. How you can do the splits! I've never seen anything so charming; nobody can touch you at it.«

»I know,« said the scissors.

»You deserve to be a countess,« said the collar. »All I have is an elegant master, a bootjack and a comb. If only I had an earldom!«

»Can the creature be proposing to me?« said the scissors, highly indignant. And she gave him such a violent jag that he had to be thrown away.

»I shall have to propose to the comb, that's all,« said the collar. »It's remarkable how you still have all your teeth, my dear. Have you never thought of marrying?«

»Why, yes,« answered the comb. »Surely you've heard that I'm engaged to the bootjack?«

»Engaged,« sighed the collar. Now there was no one left to propose to, and so he came to despise the whole idea.

A long time passed, till at length the collar found himself in a bag at the paper-mill; there was a large party of rags, the fashionables in one group and the common herd in another – just as it should be. They all had a great deal to say, but nobody so much as the collar; he was a terrible one to brag.

»When I think of all the love-affairs I've had!« he said. »I never got a moment's peace. I was no end of a swell in those days, very stiff and starchy, with a bootjack and a comb that I never used. You should have seen me then – seen me all ready for a party. Never shall I forget my first love; she was a girdle – so refined and delicate and pretty – she threw herself into a wash-tub for my sake ... And then there was a widow lady, who was glowing with passion, but I kept her waiting till she turned black. There was the *première danseuse* from the ballet; she gave me the gash I've still got – she wanted to eat me! My own comb was gone on me,

and she lost all her teeth from being crossed in love. Yes, I've been through a lot of that sort of thing, but I am sorriest of all for the garter – I beg her pardon – the girdle, who jumped into the wash-tub. I have so much on my conscience; it's high time I changed into white paper.«

And that's what happened. All the rags were turned into white paper; but the collar became this very bit of white paper we have before us, on which the story has been printed. It was all because he boasted so terribly afterwards of what had never actually occurred. And this is worth bearing in mind, so that *we* don't behave like that; for, after all, we never can be quite certain that we too mayn't find ourselves one day in the rag-bag and be turned into white paper and have the whole story of our life printed on us, even the most private happenings, so that we ourselves have to run around blabbing it out, like the collar.

The Flax

The flax was in full bloom. It had the loveliest blue flowers, as soft as the wings on a moth, and even more delicate. The sun shone down on the flax and the rain-cloud watered it; and this was just as good for the flax as it is for little children to be washed and then have a kiss from mother. They are much nicer after that, aren't they? And so, too, was the flax.

»They say that I hold myself remarkably well,« said the flax, »and that I'm growing lovely and long – they'll get a fine piece of linen from me. My word, how lucky I am! I must be the very luckiest of the lot. I'm so well off – I shall go far. How the sun does cheer me up, and how I do enjoy the freshness of the rain! Yes, I'm wonderfully lucky. I'm the very luckiest of them all.«

»Well, well,« said the hedge-stakes. »You don't know the world, but we do. We've got knots in us.« And they creaked out miserably:

»Snip, snap, snorum,
basselorum,
the song is over.«

»No, it isn't!« said the flax. »The sun will shine tomorrow; the rain is so refreshing. I can hear myself growing; I can feel that I'm flowering. Yes, I'm the luckiest of them all.«

But one day people came and seized the flax by its top and plucked it up, root and all – it did hurt. Then it was laid in water as though it was to be drowned, and after that it was put over the fire as if it was to be cooked. It was terrible.

»One can't always be on velvet,« said the flax; »things have to be tried out before you can know them.«

All the same things were as bad as could be. The flax was bruised and broken, scutched and hackled, and goodness knows what else besides. It was put on the spinning-wheel, where it whirred and purred – it was impossible to collect your thoughts.

»I've been amazingly lucky,« thought the flax in the midst of its pain. »One must be thankful for the good one has enjoyed. Thankful, ay, thankful« – and it was still saying this when it came on the loom – and then it was turned into a splendid great piece of linen. The whole flax, every single bit that was growing on it, was turned into the one piece.

»Oh, but this is quite wonderful – I could never have believed it. Yes, yes, fortune is certainly on my side. A lot they knew about it, those hedge-stakes, with their

»Snip, snap snorum,
basselorum!«

The song is by no means over. Why, it's only just beginning. How wonderful! True, I've had a hard time, but I've got something to show for it: I'm the luckiest of them all. I'm so strong and so smooth, so white and so tall. It's something very different to just being a plant, even if one has a flower. As a plant, there's no one to look after you, and you only get watered when it rains. Now I have someone to wait on me. The maid turns me round every morning, and the water-jug gives me a shower-bath every evening. Why, even the parson's wife has made a speech about me, saying I was the best bit of linen in the parish. I cannot be better off than I am.«

And now the linen was brought into the house and came under the scissors. What clipping and cutting and pricking with needles – my word, there was! It was no fun at all. But the linen was made into twelve pairs of – things which are seldom mentioned, but must be worn by everyone; yes, a whole dozen of them.

»There now, look at that! At last I've come to something. So that's what I was marked out for. Oh, dear, it's too wonderful. Now I'll be some use in the world, and that's as it should be, that's enjoyment of the right kind. We've been turned into twelve garments; and yet we are all one and the same, we are a dozen. What marvellous luck!«

Years passed – and at last they could hold together no longer.

»Some day there's got to be an end,« said each of them. »I should like to have held out a little longer, but it's no good asking the impossible.« And then they were torn into rags and remnants; they imagined they were clean done with, for they were combed and crushed and boiled and goodness knows what – and there they were, turned into the most delicate white paper!

»Why, this *is* a surprise – a most delightful surprise,« said the paper. »Now I'm finer than ever, now I shall be written on. There's no end to

what they can write. It really is astonishing luck.« And the most delightful stories were written on it, stories that people read, good stories of the
right kind that made men wiser and better. The words given to the paper
were a blessing to many.

»This is more than ever I dreamed of, when I was a little blue flower in
the field. How could I imagine that I should one day bring joy and
knowledge to mankind. I still can't understand it. And yet, look! it has
actually come to pass. Heaven knows I myself have done nothing but
what in a small way I was forced to do in order to exist. And yet I am
borne on like this from one joy and honour to another. Every time I think
»the song is over,« it simply passes on to something much higher and
better. I'm sure to be sent travelling now, sent right round the world, so
that all mankind may read me. That's the most likely thing to happen.
Previously, I had blue flowers; now, in place of those flowers, I have the
most wonderful thoughts. I am the luckiest of all!«

But the paper didn't go travelling. It was sent to the printer; and all
that was written on it was set up in type for a book;, in fact, for hundreds
and hundreds of books, because in that way many more people could get
benefit and joy from it than if the single paper it was written on had gone
chasing round the world and got worn out by the time it was half-way.

»Yes,« thought the paper with writing on it. »This, after all, is much
the nicest way – one that never occurred to me. I shall stay at home and be
respected like an old grandfather. It was on me that they wrote, into me
that the words flowed straight from the pen. I stay here, while the books
go chasing around. Now there is a real chance to get something done.
Oh, how pleased, how lucky I am!«

The paper was then tied up in a bundle and laid on a shelf. »Repose is
sweet, when your work is done,« said the paper. »It's very right that we
should take ourselves in hand, and think seriously about what is in us.
It's only now that I really understand what is in me. 'Know thyself' – that
is the real step forward. What will happen next, I wonder? A going
forward of some kind – always going forward!«

One day all the paper was put in the fireplace to be burnt, for it
mustn't be sold to the grocer for wrapping up butter and sifted sugar.
And all the children in the house stood round to see it flare up; they
wanted to see the ashes give out all those red sparks that seemed to turn
away and go out, one after another, so quickly; those are the children
running out of school, and the last spark of all is the schoolmaster.
Sometimes you think he must have gone already; but there he comes, a
bit after all the others.

All the paper lay in a bundle, on the fire. Ooh! how it went flaring up!
»Ooh!« it sighed, and the next moment it was a sheet of flame. It blazed
higher into the air than ever the flax had been able to lift its little blue
flower, and shone brighter than ever the white linen had been able to

shine; all the letters written on it turned quite red in an instant, and all the words and thoughts went up in a blaze.

»Now I'm going right up into the sun,« was the cry from the flame; and it was as though a thousand voices all said it at once, and the flame shot up through the chimney right out at the top ... And, more delicate even than the flame, quite invisible to the human eye, there hovered tiny little beings, just as many as there had been blossoms on the flax. They were even lighter than the flame from which they had come, and when it went out and all that was left of the paper was the dusky ash, they danced away over it once more and wherever they touched it you could see their footprints; they were the red sparks: »The children ran out of school, and last of all came the schoolmaster«. It was great fun to look at, and the children of the house stood singing over the dead ashes –

»Snip, snap, snorum,

basselorum,

the song is over.«

But the little invisible beings each of them said: »No, no, the song is never over. That's what is so lovely about the whole thing. I know this, and that's why I'm the luckiest of them all.«

But the children couldn't follow that, nor even hear it, and they were not meant to either; for children mustn't know everything.

Heartbreak

The story we are bringing in here is really a story in two parts. The first part might just as well be left out; the only thing is, it makes a good foundation – and that's such a help.

We were staying at a manor-house in the country, and it chanced that the master and mistress went away for the day. While they were gone, there came a good woman from the neighbouring market-town. She had brought her pug-dog with her, and she had come, she said, in the hope of getting some shares taken in her tannery. She had brought her prospectus with her, and we advised her to put it in an envelope and to write on the outside the address of the owner of the house: »Inspector-General Sir – –« and so on.

She took our advice, picked up a pen and then paused, asking us to repeat the address slowly. This we did, and she began writing; but in the middle of spelling out »Inspector-General« she got stuck and, with a sigh, remarked, »I am but a woman.« She had put her pug-dog down on the floor while she wrote, and now he began growling. After all, he had gone with her for enjoyment and for the sake of his health, and in a case like this they had no business to put him on the floor. He was a snub-nosed, podgy little pug.

»He won't bite,« said his mistress. »he has got no teeth. He's just like one of the family, very faithful and very grumpy – though he has been teased into *that* by my grandchildren, who play at 'weddings' and insist on his being a bridesmaid; poor old chap, he finds that so exhausting.«

236

Then she handed in her prospectus and picked up the pug again ... Well, there's the first part of the story, which might just as well have been left out.

The pug died – that's Part II.

It was about a week later. We drove to the market-town and put up at the inn. Our windows faced the back, where the yard was divided in two by a wooden fence. On one side hung skins and hides, both raw and tanned; here was all the wherewithal for a tannery, and it belonged to the widow. The pug-dog had died that morning and been buried here in the yard. The widow's grandchildren - that's to say, the tanner-widow's, for the pug had not been married –were patting the grave firm; and it was a splendid grave, which must have been a pleasure to lie in.

The grave was edged round with broken bits of pottery and strewn with sand; at the head they had placed half a beer-bottle, with the neck upwards; and there was nothing allegorical about that.

The children danced round the grave, and the eldest boy, a shrewd little fellow of seven, suggested there should be a special exhibition of the pug's grave for all those living in their street. The charge for admission should be a trouser-button – that was something every boy would have and could also pay for the little girls with. The proposal was carried unanimously.

So all the children from their street, and from the back-lane as well, came along and paid their buttons. There were lots of them who had to get on with only one brace that afternoon; never mind, they had seen the pug-dog's grave, and it was well worth the expense.

But outside the tan-yard, right against the gate, was a little ragged girl, standing so gracefully there, with the prettiest curls and delightfully clear blue eyes. She didn't say a word, and she didn't cry, but every time the gate opened she looked as far in as she could. She hadn't a button - she knew that - and so she was left standing sadly outside, standing there till

the others had all had their look at the grave and had gone away. Then at last she sat down, held her little brown hands before her face and burst into tears; she alone had not seen the dog's grave. That was heartbreak, as bitter for her as it may sometimes be for one who is grown up.

We saw it all from above; and, seen from above, this was like so many of the troubles of all of us – why, yes, we can smile at them ... There is the story, and anyone who doesn't understand it had better take shares in the widow's tannery.

The Goblin
at the Grocer's

There was once a student, a proper student, who lived in the attic and didn't own a thing; and there was a grocer, a proper grocer, who lived on the ground floor and owned the whole house. It was the grocer that the little goblin kept in with, for here every Christmas Eve he was given a bowl of cream with a big lump of butter in – the grocer could manage that; and the little goblin stayed in the shop, and that explains a good deal.

One evening the student came into the shop by the back-door to buy some candles and cheese; he hadn't anyone to send, and so he came himself. He got what he required, paid for it and received a »good evening« nod from the grocer and his wife. She was a woman who could do much more than nod – she had a regular gift of the gab – and the student nodded back and then stood there lost in reading from the sheet of newspaper that the cheese had been wrapped up in. It was a page torn out of an old book that never ought to have been torn up like that – an old book full of poetry.

»There is some more of that book,« said the grocer. »I gave an old woman some coffee beans for it. I'll let you have the rest of it for six-pence.«

»Thank you,« said the student. »Let me have it instead of the cheese. I can eat plain bread and butter. It would be a shame for the whole book to be torn to bits. You are a splendid man and a practical man, but you have no more idea of poetry than that tub.«

That was a rude thing to say, especially at the expense of the tub; but the grocer laughed, and the student laughed – after all, it was only said as a kind of joke. But the little goblin was annoyed that anyone should dare to speak like that to a grocer who was his landlord and sold such excellent butter.

At nightfall, when the shop was shut and everyone but the student had gone to bed, the little goblin went in and took away the goodwife's »gab«, which she didn't need while she was asleep, and wherever he gave it to any piece of furniture in the room downstairs this acquired speech and language; it could express its thoughts and feelings quite as well as the goodwife herself. But only one at a time could have it, and that was a blessing, otherwise they would all have been talking at once.

And the little goblin passed the gift of the gab to the tub where the old newspapers were kept. »Is it really true,« he asked, »that you don't know what poetry is?«

»Of course I do,« said the tub. »It's the kind of thing that's to be found at the foot of a newspaper column and that people cut out. I rather think I have more of it in me than the student has; and yet I'm only a humble tub beside the grocer.«

And then this gift of the gab was passed on to the coffee-mill - goodness, what a clatter! – and after that to the till and the buttercask. They all thought the same as the tub, and what the majority are agreed upon must be respected.

»Now for the student!« – and the little goblin crept softly up the backstairs to the attic where the student's room was. There was a light inside, and the little goblin peeped through the keyhole and saw the student reading the tattered book from the shop. But how bright it was in there! Out of the book shone a clear beam that turned into a treetrunk and then into a huge tree which rose high up and spread its branches right out over the student. The leaves were all so fresh and green, and every blossom was the head of a lovely girl, some with dark flashing eyes, others with eyes of the clearest blue. Every fruit was a shining star, and marvellous was the beauty of the songs it sang.

Never had the little goblin imagined – let alone seen or felt – such splendour. And so he stayed standing on tiptoe, peeping and peeping, until the light in the attic died down. No doubt, the student blew out his lamp and got into bed; but, all the same, the little goblin didn't go away, for the sound of the singing was still so soft and lovely, a perfect lullaby for the student as he lay down to rest.

»It's astonishing here,« said the little goblin to himself, »I never expected this. I think I will stay with the student.« And he pondered ...

and pondered sensibly ... and then he sighed: »But the student hasn't any cream or butter.« So he went – yes, he went down again to the grocer's and it was a good thing he did, because the tub had nearly used up the goodwife's gibble-gabble in declaring on one side all it had to say, and now it was just about to roll over and do the same on the other side, when the little goblin came and fetched the »gab« back for the grocer's wife. Still, the whole shop, from the till to the firewood, took their cue ever after from the tub; and so completely did it win their respect and confidence that, when the grocer afterwards read out theatre and art criticisms from his newspaper, they all thought that these came from the tub.

But now the little goblin could no longer sit quietly listening to all that wisdom and understanding downstairs. No, as soon as ever a light glimmered from the room in the attic, its beams were like powerful cables dragging him up there; and he had to be off and take a peep through the keyhole. There a sense of grandeur surged around him, such as we feel by the rolling sea when God passes over it in the gale, and he burst into tears. He had no idea himself why he wept, but somehow the tears that he shed were tears of happiness. How wonderful it must be to sit with the student under that tree! But that could never be – he was glad to stand at the keyhole. He was still here on the chilly landing when the autumn wind blew down from the trap-door in the ceiling, so cold, so cold. Yet the little fellow did not feel this until the light went out in the room under the roof, and the songs died away before the wind. Then – oh! how he shivered, and he crept down again to his snug corner, where it was so wonderfully cosy ... Later on came the Christmas bowl of cream with a big lump of butter - yes, yes, now the *grocer* was the one!

But in the middle of the night the little goblin was woken up by a fearful hubbub outside, where people were thumping on the shutters. The watchman was blowing his whistle; there was a big outbreak of fire; the whole street seemed to be ablaze. Was it this house on fire or the neighbour's? Where was it? How terrible! The grocer's wife got so flurried that she took off her gold ear-rings and put them in her pocket, so as at any rate to save something. The grocer dashed after his bonds, and the maid after the silk mantilla she had managed to buy for herself. Each one wanted to save his most precious belonging, and so did the little goblin. He was up the stairs at a bound and into the room of the student, who was standing quite calmly at the open window looking out at the fire over at the opposite neighbour's. The little goblin snatched up the wonderful book from the table, popped it into his red cap and held on to it with both hands. The dearest treasure of the house was saved! Then away he bolted, out on to the roof, right up on to the chimney, where he sat lit up by the burning house over the way and with both hands clutching his red cap that held the treasure. Now he knew where his heart lay and whom he really belonged to. But as the fire was just then put out and he could think calmly – well, then: »I'll divide myself between them,« he said. »I can't give up the grocer altogether, because of the cream and the butter.«

That was quite like a human being. We, too, have to go to the grocer for the cream and the butter.

In a Thousand Years' Time

(written in 1853)

It's a fact – a thousand years from now people will cross the ocean through the air on wings of steam! America's young settlers will visit old Europe. They will come over to see our monuments and our vanishing cities, just as we in our day go touring among the crumbling splendours of Southern Asia. A thousand years from now they will come.

The Thames, the Danube, the Rhine will still be rolling on; Mont Blanc still standing with snowy cap; the Aurora Borealis still glittering over the countries of the North. But age upon age will be dust, rows of momentary potentates forgotten, like those who already slumber in the funeral mound where the prosperous corn-merchant, on whose land it lies, has made himself a seat for gazing out over his waving cornfields.

»To Europe!« is the cry from the young sons of America. »To the land of our fathers, the wonderful land of memories and dreams – Europe!«

The airship comes. It is crowded with passengers, for the crossing is quicker than by sea. The electro-magnetic cable under the ocean has already telegraphed how many the air caravan is bringing. Now Europe

is in sight – it is the coast of Ireland – but the passengers are still asleep; they are not to be woken up till they are over England. There they will set foot on European soil in the land of Shakespeare, as it is called by men of intellect; the land of politics, of machinery, it is called by others. There is a stop here for a whole day, so generous of its time is this busy generation toward great England and Scotland.

On goes the journey through the Channel Tunnel to France, the country of Charlemagne and Napoleon. Molière's name crops up; the scholars speak of a classical and romantic school of distant antiquity; heroes, poets and scientists are acclaimed of whom our age knows nothing, but who will yet be born in that crater of Europe called Paris.

The air-steamer flies over the country from which Columbus set out, where Cortez was born, and where Calderon sang his dramas in surging verse. Beautiful dark-eyed women still live in the flowering valleys, and the Cid and the Alhambra are celebrated in ancient song.

Through the air, again, across the sea to Italy, where ancient eternal Rome once stood; it has been wiped out! The Campagna is a wilderness, and of St. Peter's only a solitary bit of wall is to be seen, and there are doubts whether even this can be genuine.

Then to Greece, so as to sleep a night at the sumptuous hotel on the top of Olympus and show that they have been there. Their next goal will be the Bosporus to get a few hour's rest and to see the place where Byzantium stood. Poor fishermen now spread their nets where legend tells of the garden of the harem in the days of the Turks.

Remains of great cities by the swirling Danube, cities our age never knew, will be passed in their flight, although here and there in places rich in memories yet to be created – which time will bring forth – here and there the air-caravan will come down and then take off once more.

Down there lies Germany once encircled by a dense network of railways and canals – the country where Luther spoke and Goethe sang, where Mozart in his day held the sceptre of music. Great names will have won lustre in science and art, names unknown to us now. One day spent in Germany, and another in the North to see the native lands of Ørsted and Linnaeus and to see Norway, home of the old-time heroes and the young Norwegians. Iceland is taken on the journey back; Geyser boils no longer, Hecla is extinct; but, as an everlasting monument to the sagas, that rocky island still stands firm in the foaming sea.

»There's a lot to look at in Europe,« says one young American, »and we've done it in a week. Yes, it's quite possible, as the great traveller (he mentions a name of that era) has shown in his famous book *How to see Europe in a week.*«

'She Was No Good'

The mayor was standing at his open window. There he was in his shirt-sleeves, with a breast-pin in his shirt-frill, and he had just given himself a wonderfully clean shave, though he had managed to cut himself slightly; however, he had stuck a bit of newspaper over the place.

»Hullo, young 'un!« he called out.

The »young 'un« was none other than the washerwoman's son, who happened to be passing and respectfully took off his cap; the peak of this had been bent so as to go easily into the boy's pocket. There, in his shabby but clean, neatly-mended clothes and his heavy clogs, the boy stood as respectfully as if he were in the presence of the King himself.

»You're a good lad,« said the mayor, »with good manners. I suppose your mother's rinsing clothes, down by the river and you've got to take her that stuff you have in your pocket. It's dreadful about your mother. How much have you got?«

»A pint,« answered the boy in a low, timid voice.

»And she had just the same this morning, eh?« the man went on.

»No, it was yesterday,« said the boy.

»Two pints make a quart. She's no good. It's so sad with that class of people. Tell your mother she ought to be ashamed of herself. And mind *you* don't become a drunkard – though I expect you will ... Poor child! ....
Run along.«

And the boy went. He still kept his cap in his hand, and the wind blew through his yellow hair until it stood up in long tufts. He turned out of the street into the lane that led down to the river, where his mother was standing out in the water at her washing bench and beating the heavy linen with her washing-bat. There was a current running, for the sluices were open; the sheets were caught by the millstream and looked like carrying the bench away; yes, the washerwoman had to hold on tight.

»I was nearly done for,« she said. »It's a good thing you've come, for my strength was beginning to fail me, and I needed some help. It's cold in this water; I've been standing here for six hours. Got something for me?«

The boy produced the bottle, and the mother put it to her lips and took a good pull.

»Ah, that's what I wanted – how it warms me up! It's as good as a hot meal, and it doesn't cost so much. Take a drink, my son – you look so pale, you must be shivering in those thin things; after all, it is autumn. Huh! the water's cold. I hope I'm not going to be ill. But no, that shan't happen. Let me have a drop more – and you, too, but only a sip; you mustn't get into the way of it, my poor penniless child.«

Then she climbed on to the little jetty where the boy stood, and stepped ashore. The water was dripping from the rush-matting she had wrapped round her middle and was oozing from her skirt.

»I toil and slave till the blood's ready to spurt out of my finger-nails; but it makes no odds, as long as I can bring you up respectably, my boy.«

Just then a rather older woman came up, a poor-looking creature, lame in one leg and with a great big lock of false hair hanging over one eye which was meant to be hidden by the curl, but it only made her blind eye more noticeable. She was a friend of the washerwoman's; »Lame Maren with the curl« the neighbours called her.

»Poor thing! How you do toil and slave out in that cold water! You must be dying for a drop of something to warm you, and yet people make such a fuss about the little nip you take.« And, with that, the washer-woman was given the whole story of what the mayor said to her boy; for Maren had overheard it all, and she was vexed that he should speak like that to a child about its own mother and about the little nip she allowed herself, especially when his Worship was just giving an elaborate dinner with lashings of wine – »tasty wines and strong wines, rather more than's good for many of 'em, but they don't call that drinking! They're all right, but you're no good!«

»So he's been talking to you, child,« said the washerwoman, and her lips trembled as she spoke. »You have a mother who's no good! Well, maybe he's right, but he shouldn't say so to her child. Still, I've had to put up with a lot from that house.«

»You were in service, weren't you, at their house when the mayor's father and mother were alive? But that's a long time ago. Bushels of salt have been eaten since then, so we may well be thirsty.« And Maren laughed. »There's a big dinner this evening at the mayor's; it ought to have been put off, but it was too late – the food had all been cooked. I heard about it from the footman. A letter arrived an hour ago to say that the younger brother in Copenhagen is dead.«

»Dead!« exclaimed the washerwoman, turning deathly pale.

»Come, come!« said the other. »Do you take it so much to heart? Well, of course you knew him from being in service at their house.«

»Is he dead? He was the best, the kindest, of men. God doesn't get many like him« – and the tears ran down her cheeks ... »Good gracious! How my head swims! All because I drank off that bottle – it was too much for me. Oh, I do feel ill.« And she steadied herself against the fence.

»Goodness, you *are* poorly, my dear,« said Maren. »But we shall see, it may pass off ... Why, you're downright ill – I'd better get you back home.«

»But there's my washing –«

»I'll see after that. Now take my arm. The boy can stay here and mind the things for the present; then I'll come and wash the rest – there isn't much to do now.«

And the washerwoman's feet tottered under her.

»I've been standing too long in the water. I've had neither bite nor sup since early morning. I feel feverish all over. O merciful God, help me home! My poor child!« And she burst into tears.

The boy cried too, and soon he was sitting alone on the river-bank beside the wet linen. The two women slowly went up the lane – the washerwoman still tottering – round into the street, past the mayor's house, and just outside it she collapsed on the pavement. A crowd collected.

Lame Maren rushed into the house for help. The mayor and his guests peeped out of the windows.

»It's the washerwoman,« he said. »She's had a drop too much; she's no good. It's a pity for that goodlooking boy of hers. I quite like the child, but the mother's no good.«

After a while she was brought round again and helped back to her humble dwelling, where she was put to bed. Honest Maren set to and mixed her a mugful of warm beer with butter and sugar – no medicine like it, according to Maren – and then off she went to the river and did some feeble but wellmeant rinsing; she really only drew the wet linen ashore and laid it in a basket.

In the evening she sat with the washerwoman in her humble room. She had managed to get the patient a few potatoes and a fine fat piece of ham from the mayor's cook, but this only made a good supper for Maren and the boy. The sick woman was contented with the smell, which she said was so nourishing.

Then the boy went to bed – the same bed in which his mother lay – but he slept crosswise at her feet, with an old piece of carpeting over him made up of blue and red strips that had been sewn together.

And now the washerwoman felt a little better; the warm beer had strengthened her, and the smell of the fine food had done her good.

»Thanks, kind soul that you are!« she said to Maren. »I'll tell you the whole story as soon as the boy's asleep. I believe he is already – what a dear good child he looks, there with his eyes closed. He little knows what his mother has been through. Heaven preserve him from that!...

»I was in service with the mayor's parents – his father was a Councillor – and it happened that their youngest son, who had just left school, came home. In those days I was young and flighty – but respectable, I swear to God,« said the washerwoman. »The young student was wonderfully gay and cheerful; every drop of blood in him was honest and good; there wasn't a better creature on earth. He was a son of the house, whereas I was only a maid, but we became lovers – in all chastity and honour. There's nothing wrong in a kiss between two that really love each other. And he told his mother about it, for to him she was like a God on earth – she was so wise and kind and lovable ... Before he went away, he placed his gold ring on my finger; and as soon as he had left, my mistress called me to her. She stood and spoke to me as solemnly, and yet as gently, as the Lord himself might have done; she showed me clearly in spirit and in truth the difference between him and me. 'At present he only sees how pretty you are but prettiness will fade. You haven't had the education that he has; you won't be equal in things of the mind; there is what stands in the way. I respect the poor (she went on); with God they may take a higher place than many that are rich; yet on earth we must be careful to keep on the right track as we drive ahead, or else the carriage will upset – and you two will upset. I know that a worthy man, an artisan, Erik the glover has asked you to marry him; he is a widower without children and is well off. Now think it over.'

Every word she spoke cut me to the quick; but my mistress was right in what she said, though it wrung my heart and weighed me down. I kissed her hand and wept bitter tears – even more so, when I came to my room and flung myself on my bed. It was a sad night that followed; heaven knows how I suffered and wrestled with myself! Then on the Sunday I went to the Lord's table to pray for guidance. It was like an act of Providence: as I came out of church, I met Erik the glover. And now there was no longer any doubt in my mind. We were suited to each other in position and outlook; in fact, he was even well-to-do, and so I went straight up to him, took his hand and said, 'Do you still feel the same about me?' 'Yes', he replied, 'now and always!' 'Will you marry a girl who honours and respects you, but doesn't love you – though that might come?' 'It will come!' he said, and at that we joined hands. I went back to my mistress. I still carried at my breast the gold ring that her son had given me. I couldn't put it on my finger by day, but only every night when I went to bed. I kissed the ring till my lips were bleeding, and then I gave it to my mistress and told her our banns were to be published in church next week, for me and the glover. Then my mistress took me in her arms and kissed me. She didn't say I was 'no good', though I daresay I was better in those days; but then I knew little as yet of the world and its hardships. After that came the wedding at Candlemas; and the first year passed off well. We had a journeyman and an apprentice, and you, Maren, looked after us.«

»Ah, you were a wonderful mistress,« said Maren. »Never shall I forget how kind you and your husband were.«

»Yes, it was during our good year that you were with us. We were still without a child. The young student I saw nothing of ... Yes, I did see him once, but he didn't see me. He came to his mother's funeral. I saw him standing at the grave, so pale and sorrowful – but that was for his mother. When later the father died, he was abroad and didn't come back, nor has he ever been back since. He never got married, I know. I think he became a lawyer. He forgot me completely and, if he had seen me, he wouldn't have known me again – I look so ugly now. And a good thing, too!«

She went on to speak of her heavy days of trial – how misfortune seemed to come hurtling over them. They had five hundred dollars of their own and, as there was a house in the street to be bought for two hundred and it would pay to have it pulled down and build a new one, they bought the house. Mason and carpenter got out an estimate showing that it would cost over a thousand more. Erik had enough credit and got a loan of money from Copenhagen; but the master of the ship that was to bring it them lost his ship and the money as well.

»It was just then that I gave birth to my dear boy who is sleeping here ... His dad fell ill of a painful lingering disease; for nine months I had to dress him and undress him. Our affairs went from bad to worse; we kept on borrowing. Everything had to be sold, and then my husband died ... I've toiled and slaved and striven for the sake of the child, washing steps, washing linen coarse or fine; but I wasn't meant to be better off, such is the will of God. Still, he'll soon give me my release, I expect, and provide for the boy.«

Then she fell asleep.

As the morning wore on, she felt much better – strong enough, she thought, to go back to her work. But she had no sooner gone out into the cold water than she was seized with trembling and faintness. Convulsively she clutched out in front of her, took a step up and then fell. Her head came down on dry land, but her feet were out in the river; her wooden clogs which she had worn to stand in – each with a wisp of straw in it – floated down the stream. Maren found her here, when she arrived with coffee.

At home a message had just come from the mayor that she was to come to him at once, for he had something to tell her. It was too late. A barber surgeon was sent for to bleed her; but the washerwoman was dead.

»She has drunk herself to death,« said the mayor.

With the letter that brought him news of his brother's death was a copy of the will. This included a bequest of 600 dollars to the glover's widow who at one time was in service with his parents. The money was to be paid out to her and her child in larger or smaller sums, as might seem best.

»There was some sort of foolish nonsense between her and my brother,« said the mayor. »It's a good thing she's out of the way. Now the boy can have the lot. I'll put him with respectable people and he may turn out a good workman« ... And heaven's blessing fell on these words.

The mayor sent for the boy, promised to look after him, and told him what a good thing it was his mother was gone – she was no good.

They bore her to the churchyard, to the poor people's burial-ground. Maren planted a little rose tree on the grave, and the boy stood beside it.

»My darling Mother!« he said with eyes full of tears. »Is it true about her being 'no good'?«

»No, she *was* good!« said the old servant, looking upward. »I've known it for years, and more than ever since last night. I tell you, she was good – and God in his heaven knows it too, however much the world may say, 'She was no good'.«

The Bottle-Neck

In a little crooked street, tucked away among several poor dwellings, stood a tall narrow half-timbered house that was everywhere sagging and out of line. There were poor people living in it, and it looked poorest up in the attic, where, hanging in the sunshine outside the little window, was an old dented birdcage without even a proper drinking-glass; all it had for the water was a bottle-neck, turned upside down, with a cork in underneath. An old spinster was standing at the open window; she had just trimmed the cage with chickweed, and a small linnet was hopping from perch to perch, singing for all it was worth.

»Ay, it's all very well for you to sing«, said the bottle-neck - well, it didn't say it quite as we should say it, for a bottle-neck can't talk; but it thought like that inside itself; just as we sometimes talk to ourselves. »Yes, it's all very well for you to sing, you that have sound limbs. You should try what it's like to lose all the lower part of you, like me, with nothing left but neck and mouth, and that with a cork in it; you wouldn't sing then! Still, I must say, it's nice to see someone enjoying himself. I've got no reason to sing and, anyhow, I can't sing. I could once, when I was a whole bottle and used to be rubbed with a cork; they called me a perfect lark, a great lark! And then, when I was out in the woods with the furrier's family and his daughter got engaged - yes, I remember it all as if it was yesterday. I've had a lot of adventures, when I come to think of it. I've been through fire and water, I've been down into the black earth, I've been higher up than most; and now here I am hanging outside the birdcage in air and sunshine. Perhaps you might care to hear my story, though I'm not going to tell it aloud because I can't.«

And then the bottle-neck - talking to itself or thinking to itself - began its story, which was certainly a remarkable one. And the little bird sang its cheerful song, while down in the street people walked and drove, each thinking about his own affairs - or about nothing at all. But the bottle-neck was thinking hard.

It remembered the blazing furnace in the factory, where it had been blown into existence. It still remembered how hot it had been, how it had looked into the roaring kiln that it first came from and how it longed to jump straight into it again – and yet how it gradually, as it cooled off, felt quite satisfied to be where it was. It stood in a row with a whole regiment of brothers and sisters, all from the same furnace; but some were blown into champagne bottles, others into beer bottles – and that does make a difference! It's true that later on, out in the world, a beer bottle may have the most precious *Lacrymae Christi* inside it, while a champagne bottle may be filled with blacking; still, the shape does show what one was born to: noble is noble, even with blacking inside.

After a while all the bottles were packed up, our flask among them. It never thought at that time of ending as a bottle-neck and of working up to be a bird's drinking-glass, though that's quite a worthy walk of life – one is something, at any rate. It didn't see daylight again until it was unpacked with the other bottles in the wine-merchant's cellar and was rinsed out for the first time; that was a funny sensation. There it lay, empty and uncorked, feeling curiously dull; it missed something, but didn't exactly know what it was it missed. Presently it was filled up with a good vintage wine; it was corked and sealed and labelled »first quality« on the outside. This was like getting »v.g.« in an examination, though the wine really was good and the bottle was good. We are all of us lyric poets when we are young. The bottle was full of songs and sounds of things it knew nothing about – of the green sunny hills where the wine grows, where the gay young girls and the merry young men join in song and kiss – ah, how wonderful to be alive! All this singing went ringing inside the bottle just at it does inside the young poets who, equally, often know nothing about it.

One morning it was sold. The furrier's boy was to fetch a »bottle of the best«, and it was put into the picnic basket together with ham, cheese and sausages; there was delicious butter and the finest bread – all packed but the furrier's daughter herself. She was young and pretty, with laughing brown eyes, and a smile on her lips that said just as much as her eyes. Her hands were so delicate and white, and yet neck and throat were even whiter; you could see at once that she must be one of the prettiest girls in the town, and yet she was still not engaged.

The picnic basket rested on her lap, as the family drove out to the woods. The neck of the bottle stuck out of the corners of the white napkin; there was a red seal on the cork, and it looked straight into the young girl's face. It also looked at the young sailor sitting beside her; they had been friends from childhood. He was the son of a portrait-painter and had lately taken his mate's certificate, passing with distinction, and tomorrow he was to sail with his ship, far away to foreign countries. There had been a lot of talk about this while the packing was going on and, as she listened, there was little enough joy to be seen in the eyes or lips of the furrier's pretty daughter.

The young couple went strolling in the green wood, talking together. What did they talk about? Well, the bottle couldn't hear, being still in the basket. It was a wonderful long time before they took it out, but, when at last they did, delightful things had happened, and their eyes were all smiling; the furrier's daughter was smiling too, but she didn't say much and her cheeks were blushing like two crimson roses.

Father took up the full bottle and the corkscrew ... Yes, it *is* strange, this business of having your cork drawn for the first time. Never since then had the bottle-neck been able to forget that solemn moment; it had uttered a regular »pop!« as the cork flew, and then it gurgled as the wine gushed into the glasses.

»Here's to the happy pair!« cried the father, and each glass was drunk right up, and the young mate kissed his lovely bride.

»Health and happiness!« said the two old people. And the young man filled up the glasses again. »To my safe return and our wedding in a year's time!« he cried; and when their glasses were emptied, he picked up the bottle, and, waving it above them, he said to it, »You have shared in the finest day of my life; you shall never serve another!«

He flung it away high in the air. The last thing the furrier's daughter imagined was that she would ever see it flying again; but she did. It now dropped in among the dense reeds by the little lake in the wood. The bottleneck could still remember so vividly how it lay there pondering. »I gave them wine, and they give me water from a swamp – though I'm sure they mean well.« The two lovers and the delighted old folk were out of sight by now, but it heard them singing and celebrating for some time longer. Then two village boys came along and peeped in among the reeds; they saw the bottle and picked it up. So now it would be cared for.

At the house in the wood, where the two boys had their home, their eldest brother, who was a seaman, had come yesterday to say goodbye, as he was just leaving on a longish voyage. His mother stood there packing one thing and another, which his father was to take into the town that evening when he went to see his son once more before he sailed and to give him a last greeting from them both. A small bottle of medicated brandy had just been packed in, when here came the two boys with a larger, stronger bottle they had found. This would hold more than the small bottle, and the brandy was such splendid stuff for a weak digestion, as it had St. John's wort juice in it. This time the bottle wasn't filled with red wine as it had been before, but with a bitter drink; yet this too may often be good – for the digestion. It was the new bottle, then, not the small one, that was to go along with him ... and so here was our bottle once more on its travels. It was brought on board for Peter Jensen, and this turned out to be the very ship the young mate was sailing in, though he never saw the bottle and wouldn't anyhow have recognized it or have thought, »Why, that's the one out of which we drank to our engagement and my return home«.

It's true, there was no longer any wine in it, but there was something just as good; and whenever Peter Jensen got it out, his messmates always called it »the chemist«; it dispensed good medicine - good, that is for the digestion - and this lasted as long as there was a drop left. Those were pleasant days, and the bottle used to sing when it was rubbed with the cork, so that it got the name of the great lark, »Peter Jensen's Lark.«

A long time had passed, and the bottle now stood empty in a corner when it happened - whether on the outward or homeward voyage, the bottle didn't really know, for it hadn't been ashore - that a gale got up, with great weltering seas, heavy and black, that lifted and flung the vessel about. The mast snapped, a heavy sea stove in a plank, the pumps were no longer working, the night was pitch-dark. The ship sank, but in the last minute the young mate scribbled on a sheet of paper, »In God's name - we are sinking!« He wrote the name of his girl, himself and his ship, put the paper into an empty bottle that was handy, pushed the cork hard in and hurled the bottle out into the raging sea. He had no idea it was the very bottle from which a toast of hope and happiness had been drunk for him and for her; now it was tossing on the wave with a last greeting and with news of his death.

The ship went down, and the crew with her, but the bottle flew on like a bird, for inside it was a heart, a lover's letter. And the sun rose, and the sun set, looking to the bottle just as in its earliest days the red-hot furnace had looked; it longed to fly into it again. It met with calms and more gales, but it struck no rock and was swallowed by no shark. For over a year it drifted about, now to the north, now to the south, as the currents carried it. It was otherwise its own master - but you can get tired even of that.

The paper with writing on it, the young mate's last farewell to his sweetheart, would only cause sorrow, if it came into her hands; but where *were* those hand that had gleamed so white as they spread out the cloth on the fresh green grass in the woods that day of their betrothal? Where was the furrier's daughter? Yes, where was her country, and what was the country that now lay nearest? The bottle didn't know; it drifted and drifted and was at last utterly tired of drifting - it was never intended for this - and yet it went on drifting till at last it came to land, to a foreign land. It couldn't make out a word of what was said; it was no lingo it had ever heard before, and one misses a lot if one doesn't know the language.

The bottle was picked up and examined. The paper was seen inside it, taken out and twisted and turned; but the people didn't understand the writing on it. They realized of course that he bottle must have been thrown overboard and that there was something about it on the paper, but what this might be - that was a mystery. And the paper was put back into the bottle, which was then stood away in a big cupboard in a big room in a big house.

Whenever strangers came, the paper was taken out and twisted and turned, so that at last the writing, which was only in pencil, became more and more difficult to read, and in the end you couldn't even tell that they were letters. The bottle stood another year in the cupboard and was then moved up into the attic, where it got covered with dust and cobwebs. Here it fell to thinking of those better days, when it poured out red wine in the cool woods, and when it went rocking on the waves and had a secret to carry - a letter, a parting sigh.

And now for twenty years it stood up in the attic. It might have stood there longer, if the house hadn't had to be rebuilt. The roof was stripped off, and the bottle was seen and discussed, but it didn't understand the language. You don't learn a language by standing in an attic, even for twenty years. »If I had stayed downstairs«, it thought, »I expect I should have learnt it.«

The bottle was now washed and rinsed - it was about time! It felt quite clean and transparent and even young again in its old age, but the paper it had been carrying was washed out completely - it had vanished.

This time the bottle was filled up with seeds; it had never come across that kind of thing before. It was corked tight and well wrapped up, so that it couldn't see either lamp or candle, let alone sun or moon; and really one should be able to see something when travelling, thought the bottle. Well, it didn't see a thing though it did what was most important - it got away and came to the right place, where it was unpacked.

»What a lot of trouble those foreigners have taken with it!« said some-one, »and after all I daresay it's broken«. But it was not broken. The bottle understood every word they said; it was the same language it had heard at the furnace and at the wine-merchant's and the woods and on board ship - the one real good old language that it could understand. The bottle had come home to its own country and was being welcomed back. From sheer delight it had very nearly jumped out of the hands that held it, and it scarcely noticed that the cork was drawn. The contents of the bottle were shaken out, and it was itself put down in the cellar to be shut away and forgotten. Still, there's no place like home, even in the

cellar. It never thought of wondering how long it had been there – it must have been years, though it was quite comfortable. Then one day people came down and fetched the bottles, our bottle with the rest.

Out in the garden there were great goings on. Flaming lamps hung in festoons, and Chinese lanterns glowed like great transparent tulips. It was such a lovely evening too, with still, clear weather and the stars shining brightly; the moon was at the new – really you could see the whole round moon like a blue-grey ball edged half-way round with gold. It was a fine sight, for fine eyes.

Down solitary walks there was also some lighting – well, at least enough for anyone to see their way. Bottles had been placed between the hedges, with a candle in each; there, too, was our bottle that one day was to end up as a bottle-neck, a bird's glass. It was delighted beyond measure with all that it saw about it, for it found itself once more in the green-wood, once more joining in gaiety and festival, listening to music and song and to the murmur and buzz of a crowd, especially from that corner of the garden where the lamps were ablaze and the Chinese lanterns flaunting their colours. It's true that it was standing in an out-of-the-way path, but it was just this which gave food for thought: here was the bottle carrying its candle, standing at this spot for use and enjoyment, and that's as it should be. At such a moment twenty years in an attic are forgotten – and it is well to forget.

Close to the bottle passed a solitary couple arm in arm, just like that other couple long ago in the wood, the young mate and the furrier's daughter; the bottle felt as if it was living that all over again. Guests were strolling in the garden, and there were others who came to look at them and the decorations, and among these was an old spinster without relatives, but not without friends. She was thinking just the same as the bottle. She was thinking of the green wood and of a couple of young lovers who had meant much to her; she had had a share in all that – a half share. It had been her happiest hour, and that's something one never forgets, however old a maid one becomes. But she didn't recognize the bottle, and the bottle didn't recognize her; that's how we pass each other by in the world ... till we meet again, as these two did, for here they were together in the same town.

The bottle was brought from the garden to the wine-merchant's and once more filled with wine and sold to the aeronaut who was to go up in his balloon the following Sunday. There was a great crowd of people to see this, a military band, and all sorts of preparations. The bottle looked on from a basket, where it lay next to a live rabbit which was very nervous because it knew it was to be taken up with the balloon in order to come down by parachute. The bottle knew nothing about up or down; it saw how the balloon kept bellying out bigger and bigger, and when it couldn't get any bigger it began to rise higher and higher and to get very unsteady. Then the ropes that held it were cut, and away it floated with aeronaut, basket, bottle and rabbit; the band played, and everyone shouted, »Hurrah!«

»This is a rum way to travel – up in the air«, thought the bottle. »It's a new kind of sailing. There's not much danger of a collision up here!«

Thousands of people followed the balloon with their eyes, and so did the old spinster. She stood at her open attic window, where the cage was hanging with the little linnet, which at that time had no water-glass, but had to do with a cup. In the window itself stood a myrtle in a pot and this had been moved a bit to one side, so as not to be knocked down as the old spinster leaned out to look. She saw the aeronaut quite clearly in the balloon, and how he dropped the rabbit by parachute, and after that drank everybody's health, and then threw the bottle high into the air. Never did she dream that this was the very bottle she had once seen flying through the air for her and her friend that glorious day in the green wood, when they were very young.

The bottle had no time for dreaming; it was all so unexpected to find itself suddenly at the highest point of its career. Roofs and steeples lay far below, people all looked so tiny.

And now it was falling, falling, and at a very different speed to the rabbit's. The bottle turned somersaults in the air – it felt so young and reckless. It was half-full of wine, though not for long. What a voyage! The sun shone on the bottle, everyone kept their eyes on it, the balloon was already vanishing in the distance, and in a moment the bottle had vanished too. It fell on a roof and was broken; but the bits had such a lot of way on that they couldn't stop, but went bouncing and rolling till they came right down in the yard and lay there in still smaller pieces. Only the neck of the bottle held out, and that was cut off as cleanly as if had been done with a diamond.

»That'd do fine for a bird-glass,« said the man in the basement. But he himself had neither bird nor cage, and it would be too much to expect him to buy these just because he had found a bottle-neck that would do for a bird-glass. The old spinster in the attic might like to have it; and so the bottle-neck went up to her, had a cork put in it, and what before was on top now came down below – as often happens when there are changes. Then it was given some clean water and was hung in front of the cage of the little bird that sang for all it was worth.

»Ay, it's all very well for you to sing«, was what the bottle-neck said; and it really was remarkable to think, it had been in the balloon. That was all that was known about it. Now it hung there as a bird's drinking-glass and could listen to the rumbling and tumbling of the street below – listen, too, to the old spinster talking in her room. She happened to have a visitor, an old lady friend, and they were talking together, not about the bottle-neck, but about the myrtle in the window.

»No, you certainly mustn't throw away two dollars on a bridal bouquet for your daughter«, said the old spinster. »You shall have a lovely one from me, full of blooms. Do you see how beautifully the tree stands? Well, you know, it's a cutting from the myrtle you gave me the day after I got engaged – the tree I myself was to get my bridal bouquet from, when the year was up; but that day never came. The eyes closed that were to have brought me happiness and joy through life. Sweetly he sleeps, dear soul, at the bottom of the sea ... The tree grew old, but I grew still older; and, as the tree began to droop, I took the last new shoot and put it in the ground, and now it has grown to ever such a big tree and is at last quite fine enough for a wedding, to make a bridal bouquet for your daughter.«

There were tears in the old maid's eyes. She spoke about the friend of her youth, of their betrothal in the wood. She thought of the toast they had drunk, and she thought of the first kiss ... but she didn't say it aloud, being an old maid now. She had so many memories, but she never dreamed that just outside her window was yet another memory from those days – the neck of the bottle that said »pop!« when the cork went bursting off at the toast. But neither did the bottle-neck know her again, as it wasn't listening to the story she was telling – partly because it only thought of itself.

The Money-Pig

There were such a lot of toys in the children's playroom. On the top of the wardrobe stood the money-box; it was made of earthenware in the shape of a pig, with a slit in its back, of course; and the slit had been enlarged with a knife so that even half-crowns could go in – and two *had* gone in, besides a good many coppers. The money-pig was crammed so full that it couldn't rattle any longer, and a money-pig can't rise higher than that. There it was, up on the shelf, looking down on everything in the room; it knew well enough that with what it had got in its stomach it could buy up the whole place. That's what we call having self-assurance.

The others thought so, too, though they didn't actually say so. The chest-of-drawers had a drawer half-open, with a big doll sticking up that was rather old and had a rivet in its neck; it peeped out and said, »Now let's play 'men and women,' that's always rather fun.« And then there was such a set-out; even the pictures turned their faces to the wall (for they knew they had backs as well), but it wasn't because they minded.

It was the middle of the night; the moon shone through the window and gave free lighting to the room. Now the game was to begin; everyone had been invited, even the pram, which really belonged to the rougher toys. »Each one has his points,« said the pram. »We can't all be gentlefolk. Someone must do the work, as the saying is.«

The money-pig was the only one to receive a written invitation; they were afraid he was too high up to be able to hear an invitation by word of mouth. Nor did he answer whether he was coming; in fact he didn't come. If he was to join in, it must be from his own place; they could arrange that, and they did.

The little toy theatre was immediately put up in such a way that he could see right into it. They meant to begin with a play, and after that there was to be tea and discussion; but they began with this straight away. The rocking-horse spoke about training and bloodstock, the pram about railways and steampower – you see, in each case it was something in their own line which they could talk about. The clock spoke on politic-tic-tics; it knew what the time was, though they said it was never right. The malacca cane stood up and swaggered about his ferrule and silver knob, for he was tipped both top and bottom. On the sofa lay two embroidered cushions, pretty and feather-brained. And now the play could begin.

They all sat and looked on and were requested to smack, crack and rattle to show their enjoyment. However, the riding-whip said that he never cracked for the elderly, but only for young people not yet engaged. »I crack for everybody,« said the cracker. »Well, there's one place where one *has* to be,« thought the spittoon – these were the kind of thoughts that came to everyone as they watched the play. The piece wasn't up to much, but it was well acted. All the players turned their painted side towards the audience; they were only meant to be seen on one side, not on the other. They all acted splendidly – right in front of the stage, as their wires were too long, but that only made them easier to see. The riveted doll was so thrilled that her rivet came out, and the money-pig was (in his

own way) so thrilled that he made up his mind to do something for one of the players – to put him in his will as the one to have a public funeral with him, when the time came.

They honestly enjoyed it all so much that they gave up the idea of tea and went on with the discussion. That's what they called playing 'men and women'; but there was no malice in it, for it was only play. And each one thought of himself and of what the money-pig might be thinking; and the money-pig thought further ahead, for he was thinking of his will and his funeral – and when could that be? It always comes before it's expected ...

Crash! Down fell the money-pig from the wardrobe; there he lay on the floor in bits and pieces, while the coins went dancing and hopping around. The small ones rolled, the big ones bowled, especially one of the half-crowns that was so eager to see the world. And see the world it did – so did they all - while the broken bits of the money-pig found their way to the dustbin. But the next day there on the wardrobe stood a new earthenware money-pig. Not a penny was in it as yet, and so this one couldn't rattle either; it was like the other in that. Anyhow, it had made a beginning – and with that we will make an end.

Five Peas from One Pod

There were five peas in a pod; they were green, and so they thought the whole world must be green – and that was right enough. The pod grew and the peas grew, fitting themselves into the available houseroom; they were all in a row. The sun shone outside, warming the pod right through, and the rain washed it clear. It was in a nice cosy spot, light by day and dark by night, just as it should be, and the peas grew larger and more and more thoughtful as they sat there, for of course they had to do something.

»Have I got to stay here for ever?« they said in turn. »I only hope I shan't get hard from sitting here so long. I've a sort of idea there is something outside; it's just a feeling I have.«

Weeks passed. The peas turned yellow and the pod turned yellow. »The whole world's turning yellow,« they said, and they had a perfect right to say it.

All at once they felt a tug at the pod; it was broken off by somebody's hand and then found itself down in a coat-pocket among several other full pods. »Now we shall soon be opened,« they said – and waited for it to happen.

»I wonder which of us will get on best,« said the smallest pea. »Well, anyhow, we'll soon know.«

»What is to be will be,« said the biggest one.

»Pop!« The pod split open, and all five peas came rolling out into the bright sunshine. They lay in a child's hand; a little boy was clutching them, and he said they were just the very peas for his pea-shooter; and straight away one of the peas was put into the shooter and fired off.

»Now I'm flying out into the wide world; catch me if you can!« – and he was gone.

»I«, said the second, »I shall make straight for the sun; that's a proper pod and will suit me down to the ground.« And away he went. »We'll take it easy wherever we come,« said the other two; »but anyhow we'll go rolling ahead!« And so they first had a roll on the floor before they came into the peashooter, but they came there in the end. »We'll get on best!« they cried.

»What is to be will be,« said the last pea and was shot into the air. He flew up to the old board under the attic window, right bang into a crack where there was some moss and soft earth, and the moss covered him up. There he lay hidden, though not hidden from God.

»What is to be will be,« he repeated.

Inside, in the little attic, lived a poor woman who went out daily to clean stoves – even to saw up firewood and do heavy jobs, for she was strong and hardworking – but she was still as poor as ever. At home, in the little attic, lay her half grown-up only daughter, who was terribly thin and delicate. For a whole year she had to keep her bed, unable (it seemed) either to live or die.

»She'll go and join her little sister«, said the woman. »I had the two of them, and it was hard enough for me to look after them both; but then the Lord went shares with me and took one to himself. I should so like to keep the one I have left, but it looks as if he doesn't want the children to be parted and she must go up to her little sister.«

However, the sick girl stayed on. She lay patient and quiet all the long day, while her mother was out earning some money.

It was springtime, and early one morning, just as the mother was going off to work, the sun shone beautifully through the little window on to the floor, and the sick girl glanced down at the lowest pane of glass.

»Why, whatever is that bit of green peeping out there by the window? It keeps swaying in the wind.«

Her mother went and opened the window a little way. »Well, I never!« she said. »I do believe it's a little pea-plant that has pushed up with its green leaves. How ever did it find its way into this crack? There, now you've got a little garden to look at.«

So the sick-bed was moved nearer to the window, where the girl could see the sprouting pea, and the mother went off to work ...

»Mother, I feel I'm getting better,« said the young girl in the evening. »The sun has been shining in on me so warmly today. The little pea is getting on so splendidly that I believe I shall get on splendidly, too, and soon be up and out in the sun«.

»I only hope you may,« said the mother, though she hadn't much faith in its happening; still, she found a little stick for the green shoot which had given her child such happy hopes of life and put it up to save the shoot from being broken by the wind. She lashed a strong piece of string to the windowsill and to the upper part of the windowframe, so that the pea's tendril might have something to cling to as it climbed up; and, sure enough, it did. You could see, from day to day, how it grew.

»Why, goodness me, it's going to flower!« said the woman one morning; and now she too began to hope and believe that her dear sick daughter would recover. It struck her that the child had lately been talking more cheerfully; the last few mornings she had sat up in bed looking with sparkling eyes at her little pea-garden of a single pea. The week after, the invalid for the first time was up for over an hour. She sat completely happy in the warm sunshine; outside the open window stood a pink pea-flower in full bloom. The young girl bent her head and softly kissed the delicate petals. That day was like a festival.

»It was God himself who planted it and made it thrive to bring hope and joy to you, my darling child, and to me as well,« said the happy mother and smiled at the flower as though it were an angel from heaven.

Well, and now what about the other peas? The one that flew out into the wide world crying »Catch me if you can!« landed in the gutter on the roof and finished up in a pigeon's crop, where he lay like Jonah in the whale. The two lazy ones took the same line; they were also eaten up by pigeons, so after all they made themselves useful. But the fourth pea – the one that wanted to fly up into the sun – this one rolled into the streetgutter and lay there for weeks on end in the dirty water, where he swelled up like anything.

»I'm getting wonderfully fat,« said the pea. »I shall go on till I burst, and I doubt if any pea can do better than that, or ever has done. I'm the most remarkable of the five out of our pod.«

And the gutter agreed with him.

But the young girl at the attic window stood there with shining eyes and the glow of health on her cheeks. And she folded her delicate hands over the pea-blossom and gave thanks to God for it.

»My pea's the best,« said the gutter.

Ib and Little Christina

Not far from the river Guden, in the forest of Silkeborg, is a long hill that looms up like a great rampart; it's known as »The Ridge«. At the foot of this, to the west, there stood – and still stands – a small farm where the soil is so poor that the sand glistens through the scanty crops of rye and barley. It all happened a good many years ago now. The people who lived there cultivated their little holding and also kept three sheep, one pig and two oxen; in fact, they made quite a good living by just taking things as they came. Why, yes, they could even have afforded to keep a couple of horses; but like the rest of the farmers in those parts, they used to say, »A horse eats itself up« – it eats as much as it earns. In the summer Jeppe Jens cultivated his parcel of land, while in the winter he was a good hand at making wooden shoes. And, besides, he had a man to help him, who knew how to cut out clogs that were strong, light and well-shaped. They also made spoons and ladles; and this brought in money. No one could have said that the Jeppe Jenses were badly off.

Their only child, a little boy of seven called Ib, used to sit and look on; he would cut a stick – and sometimes he would cut his finger. But one day he cut out two bits of wood so that they looked like little wooden clogs; these, he said, were to be given to little Christina, the lighterman's small daughter. She was as graceful and delicate as a child of gentle birth. If her clothes had been cut as finely as she had been born and bred, no one would have supposed that she came from a turf-house on Seis Heath. That was where her father lived; he was a widower, who made a living by carrying logs on his barge from the forest down to the eel-traps at Silkeborg, and sometimes even further to Randers. He had no one to look after the little girl, Christina, who was a year younger than Ib, and so she was nearly always with her father on the barge or else among the heather and cranberry bushes. When he had to go as far as Randers, then it was that little Christina went across to Jeppe Jens's.

Ib and little Christina got on very well together in every way. They grubbed and rummaged, they crawled and they ran; and one day the two of them ventured, quite by themselves, almost to the very top of the Ridge and some distance into the forest, where they found some snipe's eggs; that was a marvellous event.

Ib had never yet been over to Seis Heath, never sailed on the barge through the lakes along the river Guden, but now he was going to; he had been invited by the lighterman, and on the previous evening he went home with him.

Early next morning the two children sat on the top of the logs that were piled up high on the barge and ate bread and raspberries. The lighterman and his mate poled the barge ahead – they had the stream with them – swiftly down the river, which joined up the lakes and seemed itself to be shut in by woods and rushes; and yet there was always a way through, however much the old trees leaned forward over the water and the oaks stretched out their naked branches as if rolling up their sleeves to show their rugged bare arms. Old alder trees, that the stream had loosened from the bank, clung by their roots to the bottom and looked like little wooded islands; water lilies rocked gently on the river. It was a glorious trip for them ... And then they came at last to the eel-traps, where the water went roaring over the weir; that was a great sight for Ib and Christina.

In those days there wasn't yet any factory or town in that district, only the old farmyard, and they hadn't much livestock. The water roaring over the weir and the cry of the wild duck were then the liveliest sounds to be heard in Silkeborg ... When the logs were unloaded, Christina's father bought himself a whole bunch of eels and a young slaughtered pig, which were all put together in a basket in the stern of the barge. The homeward voyage was now against the stream, but the wind was at their backs and, when they hoisted sail, it was as good as having two horses to tow them.

As soon as they had brought the barge so far upstream that it lay alongside the forest where the mate would now only have a short way to go home, he and Christina's father landed, at the same time telling the children to keep quiet and mind what they did. However, they didn't do this for long; they felt they must take a peep down in the basket where the eels and the young pig were kept, and then they had to try the weight of the pig and hold it in their hands; and, as both wanted to hold it, they ended by letting it drop into the water, where it drifted away with the stream. It was a terrible thing to happen.

Ib jumped ashore and ran a little way, and then Christina came after him. »Take me with you!« she cried; and very soon they were deep in the thicket, out of sight of both barge and river. They ran a little further, and then Christina fell down and cried, and Ib picked her up.

»Keep close by me,« he said, »the house is over there« – but it wasn't.

They walked and walked, over dead leaves and withered fallen branches
that crackled under their feet. At one moment they heard a piercing cry ...
They stood still and listened. Then came the scream of an eagle – it was a
horrible scream – they were utterly terrified. But ahead of them, in the
thick of the forest, they found the most delicious bilberries growing –
masses and masses of them. This was far too tempting for them not to
stay, and so they stayed and ate till their lips and cheeks were quite blue.
Again there was a cry.

»We shall get whipped because of the pig,« said Christina.

»Let's go back to our house,« said Ib; »It's here in the wood«. So they
went on, till they came to a road; but this wasn't the way home. It was
getting dark, and they were frightened. The wonderful stillness all about
them was broken by hideous screeching from the great horned owl and by
cries of birds that were strange to them. At last they got lost in a copse;

Christina began to cry, and so did Ib; and after they had been crying some time. they lay down on a pile of leaves and fell asleep.

The sun was already high when the two children woke up. They felt cold; but, on a mound near by, the sun was shining down through the trees – they would be able to warm themselves up there, and Ib thought it might even be possible to see his own home. But they were a long way off from that, in quite a different part of the forest. They clambered up to the top of the mound, which went sloping down to a clear transparent lake; here they saw fish in shoals, lit up by the rays of the sun. They had never expected to see this; and close by was a large bush full of nuts, seven to a bunch sometimes. They picked them and cracked them and ate the delicious kernels, which were just getting ripe and firm ... And then came another surprise, a frightening one. Out of the thicket stepped a tall oldish woman; her face was quite brown, her hair was shiny black, and the white of her eyes flashed like a blackamoor's. She had a bundle on her back and a knotted stick in her hand; she was a gipsy. The children didn't at first understand what she said; but she pulled out three large nuts from her pocket and told them that, tucked away inside each one of them, were the most wonderful things; they were wishing-nuts.

Ib took a good look at her. She seemed so friendly that he plucked up courage and asked if he might have those nuts. The woman gave them to him and picked herself a whole pocketful from the hazel bush. Ib and Christina gazed in astonishment at the three wishing-nuts.

»Is there one with a waggon and horses in it?« asked Ib.

»There's a golden coach with golden horses,« said the woman.

»Then give me that one,« said little Christina, and Ib gave it to her; and the woman tied up the nut in the little girl's handkerchief.

»Has this one got inside it a pretty little scarf like the one Christina wears?« asked Ib.

»It has ten scarves,« said the woman, »and smart dresses, stockings and hat.«

»Then I'd like that one, too,« said Christina, and Ib let her have the second nut as well. The third was a little black nut.

»You must have that one,« said Christina, »that's also a pretty one.«

»What's inside it?« asked Ib.

»The best thing of all for you,« said the gipsy woman.

Ib held the nut tight. The woman promised to put them on their right way home; so along they went, but in exactly the opposite direction to the one they ought to have gone – though the gipsy woman mustn't therefore be accused of wanting to steal children.

In the tangled forest they came across a woodman who knew Ib and helped the two children to get back home, where people were in a state of great alarm about them. They were both forgiven, though they really deserved a good whipping – first, because they had dropped the pig into the water, and then because they had run away.

Christina went back to her home on the Heath, while Ib remained in the little house in the wood. The first thing he did in the evening was to take out the nut which contained »the best thing of all«. He put it between the door and the door-frame, pushed the door to, the nut cracked, but not a sign of kernel was to be seen; the shell was full of a kind of snuff or earth-mould; it was what we should call worm-eaten.

»Yes, I thought as much,« said Ib. »How could there, inside that little nut, be room for 'the best thing of all'? Christina won't get any fine dresses or golden coach out of her two nuts either.«

And winter came on, and then the New Year. Several years went by. Ib was now to be confirmed, and the parson lived a long way off. About that time the lighterman called one day at the house of Ib's parents and told them that little Christina was now to go out and earn her living, and that it was a rare slice of luck for her to be going where she was – into service with such worthy people. Just fancy, she was going to the rich innkeeper's, Herning way, out west. There she was to lend a hand to the man's wife and after that, if she suited and was confirmed there, they would keep her.

So Ib and Christina had to say goodbye to one another. Sweethearts they were called, and she showed him at parting that she still had the two nuts he gave her when they ran away together in the forest and she told him that in her cupboard she treasured up the little wooden clogs which as a boy he had made for her. And so they parted.

Ib was confirmed; but he stayed at home with his mother, for he was now a clever maker of wooden shoes and in summer he looked after the little farm. He was all his mother had for this; Ib's father had died.

Only seldom did they hear anything of Christina, from a postman or some eel-fisherman: she was doing well at the rich innkeeper's and, when she had been confirmed, she wrote to her father and asked to be remembered to Ib and his mother. In the letter she spoke of six new chemises and a beautiful dress that she had been given by her master and mistress. This was certainly good news.

One fine day in the following spring Ib and his mother heard a knock on the door; there stood the lighterman with Christina. She had come over to spend the day; there happened to be the chance of a lift as far as Tem village and back again, so she seized it. She looked beautiful – a regular young lady – and was very well dressed; her clothes were cut just right for her. There she stood in her Sunday best, while Ib was in his old workaday clothes. He couldn't find a word to say. True, he took her hand, held it tight, and felt tremendously happy; but he couldn't get his tongue to work. Little Christina could; she talked and chattered, and she kissed Ib right on the mouth.

»Do you mean to say you didn't know me?« she asked; but even when the two of them were alone and he stood still and held her hand, all he could say was simply this: »You've become a kind o' fine lady, while I'm so awkward and shabby ... Christina, how I have thought about you all this time!«

And they walked arm in arm up on to the Ridge and looked across the river Guden away to Seis Heath with its great clumps of heather. Ib said nothing; and yet, when they parted, it was clear to him that Christina must become his wife. After all, since they were little, they had been called sweethearts; they were, he felt, an engaged couple, even though neither of them had actually said so.

They had only a few more hours together before she must leave again for Tem, from which early next morning she would be driven back to the west. Ib and her father went with her as far as Tem. There was a bright moon and, when they arrived, Ib was still holding Christina's hand, and he couldn't let go of it; his eyes shone, but he said very little, though his heart was in every word he uttered. »If you haven't grown too hard to please,« he said, »and can put up with living at Mother's with me as your husband, then we two'll become man and wife some day ... but of course we can wait awhile yet.«

»Yes, Ib, let's see how it goes,« she said; and she pressed his hand, and he kissed her lips. »I have faith in you, Ib,« said Christina, »and I think I love you. But let me sleep on it.«

And with that they separated. Ib told the lighterman that he and Christina were as good as engaged, and the lighterman felt that that was just how he'd always imagined it. He went back to Ib's home and spent the night there, and after that there was no more talk about the engagement.

A year went by. Two letters passed between Ib and Christina – the words »faithful unto death« were written where he signed his name. One day the lighterman walked in at Ib's. He had heard from Christina, who wished to be remembered to Ib. As to the rest of what he had to say the lighterman was a bit slow about that, but it came to this: Christina was getting on well – only too well – for she was a pretty girl, respected and liked. The innkeeper's son had been home for a holiday; he had a job in some big concern in Copenhagen, in an office. He was very fond of Christina, and she had taken a fancy to him; his parents made no objection. The only thing was, Christina had it very much at heart that Ib was still so devoted to her; and so she felt that she must put the thought of happiness from her, said the lighterman.

At first Ib didn't say a word, but turned as white as a sheet. Then with a shake of his head, he declared, »Christina must not put away the thought of her happiness.«

»Won't you write her a line?« suggested the lighterman.

And Ib did write, though he found it hard to put the words together just as he wanted them, and he kept crossing out and tearing up; but the next morning there was a letter ready for little Christina, and here it is:

»I have read the letter you wrote to your father and see that you are getting on well in every way and may do even better. Ask your heart, Christina, and think well over what you are letting yourself in for if you marry me. What I have got is little enough. Don't think of me, or how it affects me, think of your own good. You are not tied to me by any promise, and if you ever gave me one in your heart, I release you from it. Wishing you all the happiness in the world, dear Christina – God will no doubt bring me consolation.

Ever your loving friend

Ib.«

The letter was sent off, and Christina received it.

About Martinmas her banns were published at the church on the heath as well as in Copenhagen, where her bridegroom was living. With her mistress she travelled across to him there, because his various business duties prevented him from coming so far as Jutland. Christina had arranged to meet her father in the village of Funder, which was the nearest place for him to see her on her journey. There Ib and Christina took leave of each other. Some remark was made about this, but not a word came from Ib. So often nowadays he seemed to be lost in thought, said his old mother. Yes, lost in thought – that was true, for he was often thinking of the three nuts he got as a child from the gipsy woman – and gave two of them to Christina – wishing-nuts they were. With hers (you remember) one of them had a golden coach and horses inside, and the other one had the loveliest clothes. That was just it! All this luxury would now come to Christina over in Royal Copenhagen; she was getting her wish. For Ib there had been nothing but black mould. »The best thing of all« for him, the gipsy had said – yes, and that wish had also been granted. The black earth was the best thing for him. Now he understood properly what the woman had meant; the black earth, the refuge of the grave – there, for him, was the best thing of all.

And years went by – not many, but long, thought Ib. The old couple at the inn passed away, the one soon after the other; their whole fortune, thousands of pounds, came to the son. Well, now Christina could certainly have the golden coach and her lovely clothes.

For two long years after that there was no letter from Christina and, when at last her father got one, the letter was clearly not written by anyone who was well-off or contented. Poor Christina! Neither she nor her husband had known how to go quietly with all that money. »Light come, light go« – there was no blessing in it, for they had never looked for one.

The heather bloomed, and the heather faded. For many winters the snow had drifted over Seis Heath and over the Ridge where Ib had his sheltered home. Then, in the sunshine of spring, as Ib was out ploughing, he turned up (as he thought) a bit of flint-stone, which came up from the ground like a great black shaving; and when he picked it up he saw that it was a piece of metal and that where the plough had sliced into it, it gleamed brightly. It was a heavy great gold bangle from ancient times. An old burial-mound had been levelled here and one of its valuable ornaments discovered. Ib showed it to the parson, who told him how fine it was; and after that he took it to the local magistrate, who sent a report to Copenhagen and advised Ib to take his precious find along there himself.

»My man, you've found the best thing in the earth you could possibly find,« said the magistrate.

»The best thing!« thought Ib. »The best of all for me – and in the earth! So the gipsy woman was right about me, after all, if *that* was the best.«

And Ib sailed with the smack from Aarhus to Royal Copenhagen. For him who had only crossed the Guden, it was like a voyage to the other side of the world. And Ib arrived in Copenhagen.

The value of the gold he had found was paid out to him; it was a large

sum – six hundred dollars. There in the rambling by-streets of great Copenhagen walked Ib from the forest on Seis Heath.

On the very evening before he was to join the master of a ship returning to Aarhus, he lost his way in the streets and took a very different direction to the one he meant. He had come across Knippels Bridge to Christianshavn instead of to the rampart at Vesterport. He was steering westward all right, but not to the place he was bound for. Not a soul was to be seen in the street. Just then a little mite of a girl came out of a poor shabby-looking house; Ib spoke to her about the way he wanted and this startled her; she looked up at him and burst into tears. He asked her what was the matter; she answered something he didn't understand and, as they were both directly under a lamp and the light from it shone straight on her face, a queer feeling came over him; you see, it was the living image of little Christina that he saw in front of him, just as he remembered her from the time when they were children together.

And he went with the little girl into the shabby house, up the narrow worn stairs, till they came to a tiny sloping garret under the roof. The air in the room was heavy and close; no light was burning; over in the corner someone could be heard sighing and breathing with difficulty. Ib struck a match. It was the child's mother who lay there on the squalid bed.

»Is there anything I can help you with?« asked Ib. »The little one fetched me, but I'm a stranger here myself. Isn't there a neighbour or someone I can call?« and he raised the woman's head for her.

It was Christina from Seis Heath.

For years her name hadn't been mentioned at home in Jutland; it would only have disturbed Ib's peace of mind. And the accounts one heard – for rumour proved to be true – weren't any of them good: all that money which her husband had inherited from his parents had made him proud and extravagant; he had given up his regular job, had travelled for six months abroad, had come back and got into debt, and yet done nothing but loaf about. More and more the carriage began to tilt, and at last it overturned. The numerous friends who had made merry at his table said of him that he deserved what he got, for he had lived like a madman. His dead body was found one morning in the canal that runs through the Castle Park.

The mark of death was on Christina. Her youngest child, only a few weeks old – expected in prosperity, born in wretchedness – was already in its grave, and now Christina was so far gone that she lay deserted and dying in a mean garret such as she might have put up with in her younger days, on Seis Heath; but now that she was accustomed to better things, she felt the misery of it. It was her elder child, also a little Christina, who was sharing her poverty and hunger and had brought Ib up to her.

»I'm afraid I'm going to die and leave the poor child all alone,« she sighed. »What on earth is to become of her?« That was all she could manage to get out.

Ib struck another match and found a bit of candle, which brought some light to the wretched room. And now he looked at the little girl and thought of Christina in those far-off days. For Christina's sake he would be kind to this child whom he did not know. The dying woman looked at him, her eyes opened wider and wider ... Did she recognize him? He never knew, never heard her speak another word.

It was in the forest by the River Guden near Seis Heath. The sky was grey, the heather was no longer in flower, and westerly gales were whirling the yellow leaves from the forest out into the river and away over the heath to where the lighterman's turfhouse stood, now inhabited by strangers. But at the foot of the Ridge, well sheltered by tall trees, lay the small farmhouse, whitewashed and painted. Indoors, a peat fire was blazing in the stove; indoors, there was sunshine sparkling in a child's eyes and the spring song of a skylark sounded in the prattle from a child's smiling red lips. All was mirth and merriment, for little Christina was there. She was sitting on Ib's knee; for her, Ib was father and mother, too – her own had vanished as a dream does for both child and grown-up. Ib sat in his snug, trim little house, a well-to-do man; but the little girl's mother lay in a pauper's grave in Royal Copenhagen.

Ib had money put by, they said; gold from the ground. And then, you see, he also had little Christina.

The Storks

On the last house in a village was a stork's nest. There in the nest sat the mother stork with her four young ones all sticking out their little black-beaked heads, for their beaks hadn't yet turned red. A bit further off along the top of the roof stood the father stork, very stiff and straight; he had one leg tucked up under him in order to keep him wide awake while he was on guard. He stood so still you might have thought he was a wooden statue. »I expect it looks fearfully smart for my wife to have a sentry at her nest,« he thought to himself. »People won't of course know that I'm her husband; no doubt, they imagine that I've had orders to stand here. It must look extremely well.« And he continued to stand on one leg.

Down in the street quite a crowd of children were playing, and when they caught sight of the storks one of the cheekiest boys – and presently the whole lot of them – began singing the old rhyme about the storks, though they sang it in the words as he could remember them: –

> »Storkie, Storkie he-bird,
> fly back to your she-bird!
> She's lying snugly in her nest
> with four such lanky young ones.
> The first we'll hang him,
> the second we'll bang him,
> the third we'll burn him,
> the fourth we'll turn him
> topsy-topsy-turvy!«

»Just listen to what those boys are singing!« said the young storks. »They say we're to be hanged and burnt.«

»Don't bother your heads about that,« said the mother stork. »Simply take no notice, then it'll be all right.«

But the boys went on singing and pointing up at the storks. Only one boy – his name was Peter – said that it was a shame to poke fun at animals and refused to join in. And the mother stork comforted her young ones by saying, »Don't worry! Just look how calmly your father is standing there – on one leg too.«

»We're so frightened,« answered the young ones and ducked their heads deep down into the nest.

The next day, when the children again came out to play and saw the storks, they started on their song:

> »The first we'll hang him
> the second we'll bang him ...«

»Shall we really be hanged and banged?« asked the little storks.

»No, of course not,« said the mother. »You are to learn how to fly. I shall put you through it all right. Then we'll go out on to the meadow and call on the frogs. They'll bow to us in the water and sing *ko'ax, ko'ax!* and then we'll eat them up. It'll be great fun.«

»And what then?« asked the young storks.

»There's a meeting of all the storks in the country, and after that the autumn manoeuvres begin. You must be able to fly well by then – that's most important – for those who can't are stabbed to death by the general's beak. So take good care to learn all you can when drilling begins.«

»Then we're going to be banged, all the same, as the boys said we should. There they are – saying it again!«

»Listen to me and not to them,« said the mother stork. »Once the great manoeuvres are over we shall fly off to the warm countries – far, far away across mountain and forest. Egypt is where we fly to, with her three-cornered stone houses that go tapering to a point until they're higher than the clouds. They're called Pyramids and are older than any stork can imagine. There's a river that overflows, so that the land all turns to mud. We can walk about in mud and eat frogs.«

»Ooh!« chorussed the young storks.

»Yes, it's too lovely,« she went on. »You do nothing but eat all day and, while we are so very well off, in this country there isn't a green leaf on the trees; it's so cold here that the clouds freeze to bits and then flutter down like little scraps of white paper.« It was snow she meant, only she didn't know how to explain it more clearly.

»And will those rude boys freeze to bits, too?« asked the young storks.

»No, not to bits, though they get so cold that they nearly do and are obliged to sit indoors twiddling their thumbs in a dingy room. You, on the other hand, can fly about in a foreign country where there are flowers and warm sunshine.«

By now some time had passed, and the young storks had grown so much that they could stand up in the nest and see a long way round them, and the father stork came flying every day with nice frogs, small snakes and all the storky titbits he could lay his beak on. Oh, it was comic to see the tricks he did for them! He would turn his head right back over his tail, and he clacked his beak together as though it was a little rattle; and then he used to tell them stories, which were all about the marsh.

»Now then,« said the mother stork one day, »it's time you learnt to fly.« Then all four storklings had to come out on the top of the roof. Goodness! How they wobbled about! How they balanced themselves with their wings and were on the verge of tumbling over!

»Watch me, will you,« said the mother. »Here's the way to hold your head, this is how to put out your legs – left, right, left, right! That's what'll help you on in the world.« Then she flew a little way; and the young ones did an awkward little jump and – down they came with a wallop, for they were too heavy in the body.

»I don't want to fly,« said one young stork and crept back into the nest. »I shan't bother about going to the warm countries.«

»So you'd rather freeze to death here, would you, in the wintertime? Shall the boys come, then, and hang you and toast you and roast you? All right, I'll call them.«

»No, no,« said the young stork, hopping back on to the roof with the others. By the third day they could manage a little proper flying , and so they fancied that the air was a thing they could sit and rest on. Well, they tried this, but down they flopped – and had to get busy with their wings again. The boys now came down the street singing their song:

»Storkie, Storkie he-bird!«

»Shall we fly down and peck out their eyes for them?« asked the young ones.

»No, don't do that,« said the mother. »Just pay attention to me – that's much more important. One, two, three! and away we fly to the right. One, two, three! to the left now, round the chimney. There, that was splendid. Your last flight was so graceful and correct that you shall all be allowed to come with me to the marsh tomorrow. Several nice stork families will be there with their children. Mind you let me see that mine are the smartest, and that you can strut; that always looks well and makes a good impression.«

»But what about having our revenge on those rude boys?«

»Let them call out what they like. Remember you'll be flying up into the clouds and going to the land of the Pyramids, while they'll have to freeze, without so much as a green leaf or a sweet apple.«

»But we'll have our revenge,« they whispered to one another; and then they had to go on with their drill.

Of all the boys in the street none was worse about singing the mocking-song than the boy who began it. He was quite a little fellow – he can't have been more than six. The young storks quite believed he was a hundred because, you see, he was so much bigger than their mother and father; and what did they know about the age of children and grown-up people? Vengeance should be wreaked in full, they felt, in the boy who first began to mock them and who kept on at it. The young storks were most annoyed and the bigger they grew the less they would put up with it. At last their mother had to promise them that very well, they should get their own back, but she wouldn't agree to anything till their last day there in the country.

»We must wait, you know, and see how you get on in the great manoeuvres. If you make a mess of it on that occasion, the general will run his beak into you, and then of course the boys will have been right after all – in a way, at any rate. So now let's see.«

»Very well, you *shall!*« said the young ones. And then they really got down to it; they practised every day for all they were worth, until their flying was as easy and graceful as possible.

Now autumn arrived. All the storks came flocking together in readiness for flying away to the warm countries during our winter. What a field-day it was! They had to go over town and forest simply to show how well they could fly, for it was a long journey they had ahead of them. Our young storks did their test so gracefully that they easily passed it, with a credit in frogs and snakes. This was a first-class pass, and their frogs and snakes they could eat; and they did, too.

»Now for our revenge!« they said.

»Certainly,« said the mother stork. »I've worked out a plan that'll be the very thing. I know where the pond is in which all the human babies are lying until the stork comes to fetch them away to their parents. The little darlings are asleep dreaming more beautifully than they will ever manage to dream later on. Every parent would like to have a baby like that, and all children want a sister or a brother. Now we'll fly off to the pond and fetch a baby for each of the children who haven't sung that cruel song poking fun at the storks. No baby for the others!«

»But the one who began the singing – that naughty, nasty boy – what shall we do with him?« cried the young storks.

»In the pond lies a little dead baby that has dreamt itself to death. We'll take the boy that one, and he'll cry because we've brought him a dead little brother. But the good boy – you haven't forgotten him, have you? – the one who said it was a shame to poke fun at animals – we'll bring him both a brother and a sister; and as that boy's name is Peter, you shall all be called Peter, too.«

And everything happened as she said. The storks were all called Peter, and they are still called Peter to this day.

The Bell

At the close of day, in the narrow streets of the city, as the sun went down and the clouds shone like gold up between the chimneys, one person after another would often hear a strange sound like the ringing of a church bell. But it was only heard for a moment, as there was such a rumbling of carts and such a lot of shouting; that always disturbs a listener. »There's the evening bell,« people said. »It's for sunset.«

Those who went outside the city, where the houses stood wider apart with gardens and paddocks of their own, had a far finer view of the evening sky and could hear the bell ring much louder. It was as though the sound came from a church in the very depths of the silent, fragrant wood; and people looked in that direction and became quite solemn ...

A long time now passed, and one would say to another, »I wonder if there's a church out there in the wood? There's a strange beauty in the sound of that bell; oughtn't we to make our way out there and go into it all more carefully?« And the rich ones drove, and the poor ones walked, but they all found the road to be curiously long. And when they came to a big clump of willows that were growing on the fringe of the wood, they sat down there and looked up into the long branches and fancied that they were well out in the wilds. A pastry-cook from the city came out and put up his tent, and then another pastry-cook turned up and hung a bell immediately above his tent – a bell that was tarred over to resist rain, but it had no clapper. Then, when the time came for people to go home again, they said how romantic it had been; and that means a good deal, quite apart from their having had tea. Three of them declared that they had made their way into the wood, right to the very end of it, and all the time they could hear the mysterious bell, though it seemed to them just as if the sound came from the city. One man wrote a whole poem about it and said that the bell sounded like a mother's voice to her dear good child; no music was sweeter than the sound of the bell.

The ruler of the country was also told about it, and he promised that whoever could really find out where the sound came from should have the post of »Universal Bell-ringer«, even if it turned out not to be a bell.

Numbers of people now went to the wood in the hope of getting such a good appointment, but there was only one who came home with any kind of explanation. None of them had been far enough into the wood, nor had this man either, but all the same he made out that the bell-sound came from a very big owl in a hollow tree. It was a kind of owl of wisdom that kept knocking its head against the tree; but whether the sound came from the owl's head or from the hollow trunk he couldn't yet say with any certainty. So he was appointed Universal Bell-ringer, and every year he wrote a little essay on the owl, but no one was any wiser than before.

And now it happened to be Confirmation Sunday. The parson had spoken with a fine sincerity. The Confirmation candidates had been deeply moved; for them it was a day of great moment. From being children they suddenly became grown-up; the soul of a child had now, as it were, to pass over into a wiser person. It was beautifully sunny. The boys and girls who had just been confirmed went out of the city, and from the wood came the sound, strangely deep, of the big unknown bell. At once they all felt a desire to go there – all but three of them. Of these, one had to go home to try on her ball-dress, for it was this dress and this ball that were the real reason she had been confirmed this time, otherwise she wouldn't have come. The second was a poor boy who had borrowed his Confirmation suit and his shoes from the landlord's son, and he had to take them back by a certain time. The third said that he never went to places he didn't know unless his parents went with him, and that having always done as he was told he wanted to go on doing so, even after being confirmed. And that's not a thing to jeer at – but that's just what they all did.

Well, and so three of them didn't go, but the others trotted off. The sun shone, the birds sang, and the young people sang too, holding each other's hands; for, you see, they were all still at school and in the sight of heaven were simply boys and girls who had just been confirmed.

But after a while two of the smallest got tired, and so they both went home again. Two little girls sat down and made wreaths; they gave up too. And when the others got as far as the willow trees where the pastry-cook had his tent, they said, »Well, here we are! There isn't really any bell; it's only a sort of idea that people get into their heads.«

At that moment from the depths of the wood came the sound of the bell, so pure and so solemn that four or five made up their minds, after all, to walk a little further into the wood. This grew so thick and so leafy that it was tremendously hard work to make headway. Woodruff and anemones were almost too tall; flowering convolvulus and trailing brambles hung in long festoons from tree to tree, where the nightingale sang and the sunbeams played. Yes, it was all very beautiful, but it was no place for young girls to walk; their dresses would have got torn to shreds. There were large boulders overgrown with moss of various colours, and fresh spring water came trickling out with strange tones that seemed to say »klook-klook«!

»I wonder if that could be the bell,« said one of the boys, lying down to listen. »This is worth going into carefully.« So he stayed behind and let the others go on.

They came to a hut built out of bark and branches with a large crab-apple tree leaning over it as though to empty out the whole of its cornu-copia on the rose-grown roof. The long branches followed the line of the gable, and from this hung a little bell. Could that be the one they had kept on hearing? Yes, they all agreed about that – except one, who said that this bell was too small and delicate to be heard as far away as they had heard it, and that these tones were very different from those that could move the human heart so deeply. The one who spoke was a prince, which made the others say, »A fellow like that always thinks he knows better than other people.«

So they let him go on alone and, as he went his heart was more and more filled with the loneliness of the wood. Yet he could still hear the little bell which the others were so pleased with; and now and then, when the wind was coming from the direction of the pastry-cook's, he could also hear how they were singing over their tea. But the deep notes of the bell sounded louder still, and now it was just as if an organ were playing an accompaniment; the sound came from the left, from the same side as the heart.

Suddenly there was rustling in the bushes, and there before the prince was a little boy in wooden clogs and a jacket so short that you couldn't help seeing what long wrists he had. They both recognized each other; the boy was the one who couldn't join the rest after Confirmation be-cause he had to go and take back his suit and his shoes to the landlord's son. He had done that, and now in his wooden clogs and old clothes he had gone off alone; so loud and deep was the sound of the bell that he felt he really must come out to the wood.

»Well, then, we may as well go along together,« said the prince. But the poor boy in the clogs was very shy and pulled at his short sleeves, saying that he was afraid he wouldn't be able to keep up with the other. Besides, he thought that the bell ought to be looked for on the right, for that was the direction for finding all that was great and glorious.

»Well, in that case we shan't see anything of each other,« said the prince, nodding to the poor boy, who plunged into the darkest, densest

part of the wood, where the thorns tore his humble clothes to shreds and also his face, hands and feet until they were bleeding. The prince likewise got some nasty scratches, but at least he had sunshine to brighten his path; and he's the one we'll go along with now, for he was a bold lad.

»I will and must find the bell,« he said, »even if I have to go to the ends of the earth.«

Horrible-looking monkeys sat up in the trees, baring their teeth as they grinned. »Shall we pelt him?« they chattered. »Shall we pelt him? He's the son of a king.«

But he steadily made his way deeper and deeper into the wood, where the most wonderful flowers were growing. There were star lilies with blood-red filaments, pale-blue tulips that glittered in the wind, and apple trees on which the apples looked exactly like great shining soap bubbles. Just imagine how those trees must have sparkled in the sunlight! Bordering the lovely green meadows, where stag and doe were frisking on the grass, stood magnificent oaks and beeches; and whenever one of the trees had a split in its bark, grass and long creepers were growing out of it. There were also long stretches of woodland with peaceful lakes on which swans were swimming and flapping their wings. The prince often stood still and listened, thinking that it might be from one of these deep lakes that the sound of the bell came up to him; but then he noticed that, sure enough, it wasn't there, but still further in the wood, that the sound of the bell came from.

It was now sunset. The sky shone red as fire, and a deep hush came over the woodland. The boy went down on his knees and sang his evening hymn and said to himself, »I shall never find what I'm looking for. Now the sun is setting and night, dark night, is coming on. Yet perhaps I may have one more glance at the round red sun before it sinks below the horizon. I'll climb up those rocks towering there as high as the tallest trees.«

And, catching hold of tendrils and roots, he clambered up the wet rocks past writhing water snakes and toads that almost seemed to bark at him.

Yet he reached the top before the sun, seen from that height, had completely vanished. Oh, what magnificence! The sea, the glorius ocean, tumbling its long waves on the shore, lay stretched out before him; and the sun stood like a great shining altar in the distance, where sea and sky met and everything was fused in glowing colours. The woodland sang and the ocean sang and his heart sang too. Nature was a great holy cathedral, in which trees and hovering clouds were its columns, flowers and grass its altarcloth of woven velvet, and the vault of heaven its mighty dome. Now the crimson colours faded as the sun went down; but millions of stars were kindled, millions of diamond lamps were lit, and the young prince spread out his arms towards the sky, towards the ocean and wood – and suddenly from the path on the right, in his short sleeves and wooden clogs, came the poor boy who had that day been confirmed. He had got there just as quickly, by his own route. They ran to meet each other, taking each other by the hand there in the great cathedral of nature and poetry. And above them sounded the sacred invisible bell, while blessed spirits hovered about it in joyful praise to God.

Holger the Dane

In Denmark there's an old castle at Elsinore called Kronborg; it juts out into the Sound, where every day the big ships sail past in hundreds, English, Russian and Prussian. They fire a salute to the old castle with their guns – boom! – and the castle guns answer back – boom! That's the guns' way of saying »Good morning« and »Many thanks«. In winter, when the Sound is frozen hard right across to Sweden, no ships can sail there; it's more like a great big road, where the Danish and Swedish flags are flying and Danish and Swedish people say »Good morning« and »Many thanks« to each other, though not with guns. No, they do it with a friendly shaking of hands, and they get white bread and biscuits from each other; for other people's food tastes best. Still, the real gem of it all is old Kronborg; and it's down below this that Holger the Dane sits in the deep dark cellar to which nobody comes. He is clad in iron and steel, with his head resting on his brawny arms; his long beard hangs down over the marble table, into which it has grown fast. There he sits and dreams; but, as he dreams, he sees everything that's going on up here in Denmark. On Christmas Eve an angel of God comes and tells him that what he has dreamt is quite true and that he may go to sleep again, as Denmark is not yet in any real danger. But if ever she is, well, then old Holger the Dane will stand up so that the table will split in two when he wrenches his beard free. Out he will come and strike till his blows resound in every country on earth.

An old grandfather sat telling all this about Holger the Dane to his little grandson, and the boy knew that what granddad said was true. And while the old man sat telling his tale, he was carving a large wooden figure which was supposed to be Holger the Dane and would be placed on the forepart of a ship; for the old grandfather was a woodcarver – or rather, a man who cuts out figureheads after which every ship is to be named. And here he had cut out Holger the Dane, who stood so straight and proud with his long beard, holding his broadsword in one hand but leaning on the coat-of-arms of Denmark with the other.

And the old grandfather told so many stories about remarkable Danish men and women that at last his little grandson felt that now he knew quite as much as Holger the Dane, who after all only dreamt about it; and when the boy went to bed his thoughts were so full of it all that he pressed his chin well down into the bedclothes and felt he had a beard which had grown right into them.

But the old grandfather stayed sitting at his work and carved away at the last part of it, the Danish coat-of-arms. And now he had finished and, as he looked at the whole thing and thought of all he had read and heard and all he had told the boy that evening, he gave a nod and wiped his spectacles and said as he put them on again., »No, I don't suppose Holger the Dane will come in my time, though the boy over in that bed may possibly get to see him and be there when it comes to the pinch.« And the old grandfather nodded again; the more he looked at his Holger the Dane, the more certain he became that it was a good figure he had made. It fairly seemed to glow, and the armour shone like iron and steel; the nine hearts in the Danish arms looked redder and redder, and the lions capered in their golden crowns.

»It's the grandest coat-of-arms in the world,« cried the old man. »The lions stand for strength, and the hearts for gentleness and love.« He looked at the top lion and thought of King Canute, who made great England subject to the Danish throne; he looked at the second lion and thought of Valdemar, who brought all Denmark together and subdued the Wendish lands, and he looked at the third lion and thought of Margaret, who united Denmark, Sweden and Norway. But as he looked at the red hearts, they gleamed more brightly than ever; they turned into flames that moved, and his thoughts followed each one of them.

The first flame led him into a dark narrow cell. There sat a prisoner, a beautiful woman, Christian IV's daughter, Leonora Christina, and the flame settled like a rose on her breast and blossomed together with the heart of her who was the noblest and best of all Danish women.

»Yes,« said the old grandfather, »that's certainly a heart in Denmark's coat-of-arms.«

And his thoughts followed another flame, which led him out to sea where the guns roared and the ships lay shrouded in smoke; and the flame pinned itself like a ribbon on Hvitfeldt's chest, as he blew himself up with his ship to save the fleet.

And a third flame led him to the wretched huts of Greenland, to which the priest Hans Egede brought love by word and deed; the flame was a star on his breast, a heart in the Danish coat-of-arms.

And the old grandfather's thoughts went on ahead of the flickering flame, for they knew where the flame would go. In the peasant-woman's humble parlour Frederick VI stood and chalked his name on the beam; the flame quivered on his breast, quivered in his heart; in the peasant's cottage his heart became a heart on Denmark's shield. And the old grandfather wiped tears from his eyes, for he had known and lived for King Frederick with the silvery hair and honest blue eyes; he folded his hands and looked silently in front of him. Then his son's wife came in and said that it was getting late: now he must have a rest and, anyhow, supper was laid.

»But, I say, that is lovely, what you've done, granddad,« she said. »Holger the Dane and the whole of our old coat-of-arms! Seems as I've seen that face before.«

»No, that you can't have done,« replied the old man. »But I've seen it, and I've tried hard to carve it in wood the way I can remember it. It was that time the English ships lay in the Roads, on our Danish 2nd of April, when we showed we were true Danes. On board the *Denmark,* where I was serving in Captain Bille's squadron, I had a man beside me – it was just as if the cannon-balls were afraid of him! He kept singing old songs in the jolliest way and fired and fought like a superman. I can still remember his face – though where he came from, or where he went afterwards, I never knew; nobody knew. I've often thought it may have been Holger the Dane himself, who had swum down from Kronborg to help us in danger's hour. Well, that was a notion I had, and there stands his likeness.«

The figure threw its great shadow all the way up the wall, even over part of the ceiling; it looked as if it were really Holger the Dane himself standing there behind it, for the shadow moved; but this might also have been because the flame in the candle didn't burn steadily. And his son's wife kissed the old grandfather and led him to the big armchair by the table, and she and her husband – who, you see, was the old man's son and father of the little boy who lay in bed – sat and ate their supper. And the old grandfather spoke about the Danish lions and the Danish hearts, about strength and gentleness; and very clearly he showed how there was another kind of strength besides that of the sword: he pointed to a shelf full of old books, among which were all Holberg's plays – plays that were often read because they were so amusing and you really felt you knew all the characters in them from bygone days.

»There, look – he knew how to carve, too,« said the old grandfather. »He hacked away at the follies and oddities of people for all he was worth.« And the old man nodded across to the looking-glass, where the calendar with a picture of the Round Tower on it was put up, and said, »Tycho Brahe was another who used the sword, not to hack at flesh and bone, but to carve a clearer way up among all the stars in the sky ... And then he, too, whose father's calling was the same as my own, he whom we've seen ourselves with his white hair and broad shoulders, he whose name is known in every country of the world - yes, he was a sculptor; I am only a carver. You see, Holger the Dane can come in many shapes, so that the whole earth may hear of Denmark's strength. So let us drink the health of Bertel Thorvaldsen!«

But the little boy in bed could plainly see old Kronborg castle and the Sound, and the real Holger the Dane sitting far below with his beard grown fast to the marble table and dreaming of all that went on overhead. Holger the Dane was dreaming, too, of the humble little room where the wood-carver sat; he heard everything that was said and nodded in his sleep and said, »That's right, don't forget me, you Danish people! Bear me in mind, and I'll come in the hour of need.«

Off Kronborg the sun was shining in broad daylight, and the wind carried the notes of the huntsman's horn across from our nextdoor neighbours in Sweden. The ships sailed past and fired their salute - boom, boom! - and from Kronborg came the answer - boom, boom! But, however loud the firing, Holger the Dane never woke, because after all it was only »Good morning« and »Many thanks«. There must be a different kind of shooting to make him wake up; but he'll wake all right, for there's stout stuff in Holger the Dane.

The Old House

Standing in our street there used to be an old, old house; it was nearly three hundred years old – you could see that for yourself on the beam, where the date had been cut beside tulips and twining hops. There were whole verses, too, in old-fashioned spelling, and above every window a leering face was carved on the beam. One storey jutted out a good way above the other, and just under the roof was a lead gutter ending in a gargoyle, the rainwater was supposed to run out of its jaws but, as there was a hole in the gutter, it ran instead out of the gargoyle's stomach.

All the other houses in the street were so very new and neat-looking, with large windowpanes and smooth walls; it was quite easy to see that they would have nothing to do with the old house: they probably thought, »how long is this monstrosity to stand here? It's a blot on the street. Look at that bay-window sticking out so much that no one from our windows can see what's going on in that direction. The front steps are as broad as a castle's and as steep as a church tower's. The iron banisters look just like the entrance to an ancient tomb, with brass knobs and all. It's ridiculous.«

There were also new, neat-looking houses on the opposite side of the street, and they thought the same as the others; but at one of their windows sat a little boy with fresh rosy cheeks and bright beaming eyes, who liked the old house much the best, whether by sunlight or moonlight. As he looked across at the wall where the plaster had come off in places, he felt he was discovering all sorts of quaint pictures on it. He could see just what the street looked like before with bay-windows, pointed gables and flights of steps. He could make out soldiers with battle-axes, and gutters that went writhing about like snakes and dragons ... That was a house worth seeing if you like! And over there lived an old gentleman who wore plush breeches and a coat with big brass buttons, and had a wig you could see was a real wig. Every morning an old manservant came in to tidy up for him and go errands; otherwise the old gentleman in the plush breeches was quite alone in the old house. Now and again he came to the window and looked out. Then the little boy nodded to him, and the old gentleman nodded back; and in this way they got to know each other and became friends, without either having spoken a word. But of course that made no difference whatever.

The little boy heard his mother say to his father, »The old gentleman over the way is very well off, but he's terribly lonely.«

The Sunday after, the little boy took and wrapped something up in paper and went downstairs; then, as the man who went errands came past, he said to him, »Will you please take this over to the old gentleman from me? I've got two tin soldiers, and this one's for him, as I know he's so terribly lonely.«

The old servant looked very pleased, gave the boy a nod and took the tin soldier over to the old house. Later on, word came asking whether the little boy would care to come across himself and pay a visit. His parents gave him leave, and so over to the old house he went.

The brass knobs on the handrails of the front steps shone much brighter than usual, almost as if they had been polished up specially for the visit; and the carved trumpeters (for, carved on the door, there were trumpeters standing among tulips) seemed to be blowing their trumpets for all they were worth, till their cheeks looked chubbier than ever. Yes, they blew, »TataranTAra! Little boy com-ing! TataranTAra!« ... and the door opened. The hall was full of old portraits – knights in armour and ladies in silk dresses, the rattle of armour and the rustle of dresses. Then there were some stairs – a long way up and a short way down – and you found yourself on a balcony that was certainly rather rickety, with big holes and long cracks, but with grass and leaves pushing up through all of them; for the whole balcony out there – court and wall, too – was so overgrown with green stuff that it looked like a garden; yet it was only a balcony. Here stood old flowerpots made like faces with donkey's ears, and the flowers in them were sprouting at their own sweet will. One of the pots was crammed to the brim with carnations, or rather with their green shoots which were saying quite plainly, »The air has stroked me, the sun has kissed me and promised me a little flower on Sunday, a little flower on Sunday.«

292

Then they came into a room where the walls were covered with pigskin leather and flowers printed on it in gilt.

»*What's gilded may weather; there's nothing like leather*,« said the walls. He saw highbacked chairs, finely carved, with arms on both sides. »Sit down, sit down!« they said. »Oh, how my joints do crack! I'm afraid I'm getting rheumatics like the old cupboard. Rheumatics in the back – ow!«

And then the little boy came into the room that had the bay-window, where the old gentleman was sitting. »Thank you for the tin soldier, my young friend,« he said. »And thanks for coming over to see me.« »Thanks, thanks!« or »crack, crack!« came from all the bits of furniture; there were such a lot of them that they almost fell over each other in trying to see the little boy.

In the middle of the wall hung the picture of a beautiful lady, with such a young and happy face, but dressed in the old-fashioned way with powdered hair and stiff-looking skirts. No thanks or cracks came from her, but she gazed with her gentle eyes at the little boy, who at once asked the old gentleman, »Where did you get her?«

»Round at the second-hand shop,« said the old gentleman. »They've always got lots of pictures of people that no one knows or bothers about, because they are all in their graves. But I knew her once upon a time, and now she's been dead and gone these fifty years.«

Under the picture, behind glass, was a bunch of faded flowers; they must also have been fifty years old, by the look of them. And the pendulum on the big clock swung to and fro and the hands went round, and the things in the room were all getting older and older, but they didn't notice it.

»They say at home,« said the little boy »that you are so terribly lonely.«

»Oh, well,« he replied, »old memories and all they can bring with them come and visit me, and now you've come too ... I get along very well.«

And then he took down from its shelf a book full of pictures: pictures of great long processions, the most wonderful coaches such as you never see nowadays, soldiers like the knave of clubs, and medieval townsmen with fluttering banners. On their banner the merchant tailors had scissors, held by two lions; and on theirs the cordwainers had a two-headed eagle instead of a boot, because shoemakers like to be able to say about everything, »There you are – that's a pair« ... Yes, it was a glorious picture-book.

Meanwhile, the old gentleman went into another room to fetch sweets and apples and nuts; you really did have a splendid time over at the old house.

»I can't bear it!« said the tin soldier, who was standing on the chest of drawers. »It's so lonely and wretched here. If you're accustomed to family life, it's impossible to settle down here. I can't bear it. The days are so

293

terribly long, and the evenings even longer. It's not a bit the same here as it was over at your house, where your father and mother talked so pleasantly and all you dear children kicked up such a heavenly din. Crums! How lonely the old gentleman is! Do you think he ever gets a kiss? Do you think he ever gets a kind look, or a Christmas tree? He'll never get a thing – except a funeral ... I can't bear it!«

»Why do you make yourself so miserable?« said the little boy. »I find it splendid here; and after all, think of the visits you have from the old memories and all they can bring with them.«

»I daresay. But I don't see them and I don't know them,« said the tin soldier. »I can't bear it.«

»But you must,« said the little boy.

Just then the old gentleman came back with a very jolly face, bringing delicious sweets and apples and nuts; and the little boy thought no more about the tin soldier. Presently he went home as pleased as possible. Days and weeks went by, and there was nodding over to the old house and nodding back from the old house; and, finally, the little boy went across there again.

And the carved trumpeters blew, »TataranTAra! Little boy com-ing! TataranTAra!« From the old portraits came rattling of sword and armour, and rustling of silk dresses; the pigskin spoke from the walls, and the old chairs had rheumatics in the back – ow! It was the first visit all over again; for at the old house, one day or one hour was just like another.

»I can't bear it,« said the tin soldier. »I've been so miserable here that I've cried tears of tin. No, I'd rather go off to the war and lose arms and legs; it would be a change, anyway. I can't bear it. Now I know what it is to have visits from your old memories and whatever they can bring with them. I've had visits from mine and, believe me, they're precious little comfort, in the long run. At last I nearly threw myself off the chest of drawers. I could see you all over in your house as clearly as if you'd been here. There we were again that Sunday morning – you remember, don't you? You children were all standing by the table singing the hymn that you sing every morning. You stood there reverently with folded hands, and your father and mother were loooking just as solemn, when suddenly the door opened and your little sister Mary, who isn't yet two years old and always begins dancing when she hears music or singing of any kind, was brought into the room. Of course, she oughtn't to have been – and there she was, beginning to dance, only she couldn't get hold of the rhythm, because the hymn-notes were so drawn out. First, she stood on one leg, bending her head right forward; and then she stood on the other leg, bending her head right forward; but it wouldn't do. You all kept straight faces; though it must have been pretty difficult; but I couldn't help laughing to myself, and that's how I came to fall off the chest of drawers and get a lump which is still there. Of course it was wrong of me

to laugh ... And now the whole of that goes buzzing round in my head, and all the other things I've been through. I suppose these are the old memories and whatever they can bring with them! ... Do tell me if you still sing on Sundays? Tell me something about your little sister Mary. And how's my old friend, the other tin soldier? Yes, he's the lucky one – I can't bear it.«

»You've been given away,« said the little boy. »You've got to stay here – can't you see that?«

The old gentleman brought along a drawer containing lots of things to look at: a »gloryhole« of treasures, a box of perfumes, old playing-cards larger and more gilded than you'd ever see nowadays. And large drawers were opened, and the piano was opened – it had a landscape painted inside the lid – and it sounded so husky when the old gentleman played it. And then he hummed a little song.

»Yes, she used to sing that,« he said with a nod to the portrait he had bought at the second-hand shop; and the old gentleman's eyes shone brightly.

»I want to fight! I want to fight!« yelled the soldier at the top of his voice, and took a flying leap on to the floor ...

Well, but what ever had become of him? The old gentleman searched, and the little boy searched, but he had gone, gone for good. »Never mind, I shall find him,« said the old gentleman; but he never did. There were too many holes and chinks in the floor. The tin soldier had fallen through one of them, and there he lay in an open grave.

So that day passed, and the little boy went home. The week passed, and several more after it. The windows were frozen right over; the little boy had to keep breathing on it to make a peep-hole for himself over to the old house. There the snow had drifted over all the twiddles and lettering on the front and lay deep over the whole flight of steps, as if nobody was at home. And indeed nobody *was* at home, for the old gentleman was dead.

In the evening a carriage stopped outside, and he was brought down to it in his coffin; he was to be taken away and buried in the country. Now they were driving off, but nobody followed him, for all his friends were dead. The little boy blew a kiss to the coffin as it drove away.

Some days after there was a sale at the old house, and the little boy could see from his window how they took away the old knights and the old ladies, the flower-pots with long ears, the old chairs and the old cupboards – some to one place, some to another. The lady's portrait which had been found at the second-hand shop returned to the second-hand shop and went on hanging there, as nobody knew her any more and nobody wanted the old picture.

In the spring the house itself was pulled down, for it was a monstrosity, people said. From the street you could see right into the room with the pigskin hangings, which were tattered and torn; and the greenstuff about the balcony sprawled in wild confusion round the tottering beams ... And then it was all cleared away.

»Good riddance!« said the neighbouring houses.

A fine new house was built there with large windows and smooth white walls, but in front –really where the old house had stood – a small garden was planted, and a wild vine grew against the neighbour's wall. In front of the garden they put a big iron railing with an iron gate; it looked so grand that people stopped and peeped in. Scores of sparrows were there, clinging to the vine and chattering away like anything to each other – though not about the old house, as they couldn't remember that.

No, so many years had gone by that the little boy had grown up to be a man, and a fine man too, whose parents were proud of him. He had just got married, and he and his dear wife had moved into his house where the garden was. He stood there beside her, while she planted a wild flower she had come across in the fields and found so lovely. She was planting it with her own fingers – ow! what ever was that? She had pricked herself on something sharp that was sticking up out of the soft earth. It was – just imagine! – it was the tin soldier, the very one who got lost up at the old gentleman's and went rumbling and tumbling among timber and rubbish and had ended by lying for years in the ground.

The young wife gave the soldier a wipe, first, with a green leaf and then with her delicate handkerchief – it had such an exquisite perfume; to the tin soldier it was like waking up from a deep sleep.

»Let me have a look at him,« said the young man with a laugh but then he shook his head. »No, it can't possibly be him, though he reminds me of an episode I had with a tin soldier when I was a small boy.« And then he told his wife about the old house and the old gentleman and the tin soldier that he sent across to him because he was so terribly lonely. He told the tale so exactly as it all happened that the young wife's eyes filled with tears as she thought of the old house and the old gentleman.

»But it may quite well be the same tin soldier,« she said. »I shall keep him and remember everything you've told me; but you must show me the old gentleman's grave.«

»Well, but I don't know where it is. Nobody knows; for, you see, all his friends were dead. There was no one to look after it, and of course I was only a small boy then.«

»How terribly lonely he must have been!« she said. »Terribly lonely,« said the tin soldier. »But it's wonderful not to be forgotten.«

»Wonderful!« cried something near by, though no one but the tin soldier saw that it was a piece of the pigskin leather from the wall; it had lost all its gilt and looked like a clod of damp earth. Still, it had a mind of its own and was ready to speak it: *»What's gilded may weather; there's nothing like leather.«*

But the tin soldier wasn't so sure about that.

»There's a Difference«

It was in the month of May; the wind still blew cold. But spring had come, said the bushes and trees and fields and meadows. The country was full of blossom, even in the quickset hedge; and here was spring herself, unfolding her tale. It was a little apple tree that spoke for her, with one bough especially, so fresh and vigorous, loaded up with delicate pink buds that were just going to open. The little tree knew well enough how beautiful it was – for you can have it in the bud as well as in the blood – and so it wasn't surprised when a smart-looking carriage drew up in front of it and the young countess said that this apple bough was the most graceful sight imaginable; it was an emblem of spring at her loveliest. And the bough was broken off, and the young countess held it in her delicate fingers and shaded it with her silk parasol ... Then they drove on to the castle with its lofty great rooms and elegant apartments. Sheer white curtains fluttered at the open windows, and beautiful flowers stood in clear sparkling vases; in one of these (it seemed to be carved out of new-fallen snow) the apple bough was put among fresh bright-green sprays of beech. It looked delicious.

The result was, the bough became very pleased with itself; and that was of course just like a human being.

People of all sorts passed through the rooms and ventured, as far as their standing allowed, to show their admiration; some didn't say a thing, while others said far too much, so that the apple bough came to realize that there's as much difference between people as between plants. »Some are for show and some to provide food; there are also some that aren't wanted at all,« thought the apple bough, and as it had been put

299

close to the open window, with a view of both garden and fields, it had plenty of flowers and plants to look at and think about. There they were, rich and poor; some of them very poor indeed.

»Poor despised weeds!« said the apple bough. »There's a difference here, with a vengeance. How unhappy they must feel – if that sort *can* feel the same as we others can. Yes, there's a difference here, and a difference there *must* be, or we should all be equal.«

And the apple bough looked down with a kind of pity on one sort of flower, especially, that was to be seen all over the fields and ditches. No one made a nosegay of these, they were much too common; you could even find them among the cobbles, shooting up like the coarsest weed, and then they had the horrible name of »the devil's milk pail.«*

»Poor despised plant!« said the apple bough. »You can't help being what you are – being so common and having that ugly name. You see, it's the same with plants as with people: there's got to be a difference.«

»A difference, has there?« said the sunbeam, kissing the apple blossom, but also kissing the yellow dandelion out on the field. All the sunbeam's brothers kissed them, the poor flowers as well as the rich ones.

The apple bough had never given thought to God's boundless love for everything that lives and moves on earth, never given thought to how much that's beautiful and good may lie hidden yet not forgotten ... But that, too, was so like a human being.

The sunbeam, light's own ray, knew better, »You don't see very far, and you don't see very clearly. Where's this despised weed you're so sorry for?«

»It's the dandelion,« said the apple bough. »Never is it made into a nosegay. It gets trodden underfoot; there are too many of them; and, when they run to seed, it flies like little fluffs of wool over the road and sticks to people's clothing. Weeds – that's what they are ... and yet there must also be weeds. I'm only too thankful I'm not one of them, that's all.«

Across the fields came a whole flock of children; the smallest of them was so tiny that it had to be carried by the others. And when it was put down on the grass among the yellow flowers, it chortled with glee, kicked out its little legs, rolled over and over, then plucked only the yellow flowers and in sweet simplicity gave them kisses. The rather bigger children broke off the flowers from their hollow stalks, binding them all together, link by link, until there was a whole chain; first, a chain for the neck, then another for the shoulders, and another for the waist, and another for the bosom, and another for the head. There was a grand array of green links and chains; but the biggest children carefully took the dandelions that had finished flowering – that is, they took the stalk with its fluffy composite seed–crown, that light airy wool-blossom which is a little masterpiece of its own, as if made of the most delicate feathers, snowflakes or swan's-down – they held this to their mouths so as to blow

* In English called 'dandelion'.

the whole thing away with one puff. The boy who could do that would get a new suit of clothes before the year was over – so Granny said.

The despised flower was quite a prophet on this occasion.

»There!« said the sunbeam. »Do you see its beauty? Do you see its power?«

»All very well for children,« said the apple bough.

Then an old woman came out on the field; and with her stumpy knife, though it hadn't any handle, she dug round the root of the flower and pulled it up. Some of the roots she would use to make coffee; other would bring in money, as she was taking them to the chemist for his medicines.

»Still, beauty ranks higher,« said the apple bough. »Only the chosen few can enter the realm of the beautiful. There's a difference between plants, as there is between people.« And then the sunbeam spoke of God's boundless love shown through everything that is created and has life and of its equal distribution in time and eternity.

»Well, that's what *you* think,« said the apple bough.

Then some people came into the room and, with them, the young countess who had found such a nice place for the apple bough in the clear sparkling vase where the sunlight fell. She was carrying a flower or something, hidden in three or four big leaves that were wrapped round it like a paper cornet to prevent any draught or breath of air doing it harm; and it was being carried more carefully than ever the delicate apple bough had been. Very gently the big leaves were now taken away – and there was the soft fluffy seed-crown of the despised yellow dandelion. This was the flower she had picked so carefully and carried so tenderly, in order that not one of the delicate plume-like darts that make up its misty shape and sit so lightly should blow away. Entire and intact she held it, and admired its lovely shape, its airy brilliance, its quite peculiar fabric, its beauty at the very moment of vanishing before the wind.

»Just look how marvellously God has made it!« she said. »I want to paint it alongside the apple blossom. That, of course, we all find so infinitely lovely, but this humble flower has also in another way received just as much from heaven; so different are they, and yet both children in the realm of beauty.«

And the sunbeam kissed the humble flower; it kissed, too, the blossoming apple bough, whose petals appeared to blush.

The Story of the Year

It was late in January, and there was a tremendous blizzard. The snow went driving and swirling along highway and byway. The window-panes were simply plastered with snow, and each time a heap of it crumped down from the roof, people made a wild dash to avoid it. They ran, they rushed, they flew into each other's arms and clutched tight for a moment, just long enough to get a firm foothold. Horses and carriages seemed to have been powdered all over. The footmen stood with their backs to the horses, so as to ride with their backs to the wind. People on foot kept steadily under the lee of a cart that could only get along slowly in the deep snow; and when the gale at last went down and a narrow path was swept along the front of the houses, people still kept stopping when they met, for none of them cared to take the first step by treading out in the deep snow so that the other might slip by. There they stood without saying a word, till at last by a kind of tacit agreement each of them sacrificed one leg and let it plunge into the piled-up snow.

Towards evening it turned to a dead calm. The sky looked as if it had been swept clean and become further off and more transparent. The stars seemed to be brand-new, and some of them very blue and bright – it was freezing hard – the top layer of snow might very well get so firm that by morning it would bear the sparrows. They were hopping about, up and down, where the snow had been shovelled, but there was precious little they could find to eat and they felt the cold terribly.

»Tweet!« said one of them to another. »Is this what they call the New Year? Why, it's worse than the old one, so we might just as well have gone on with that. I'm disappointed, and I've good reasons to be.«

»Yes, and to think that people have been running about with guns to shoot the New Year in!« said a shivering little sparrow. »They battered doors with pots and pans and were quite crazy with joy at the old year having gone. I must say I was pleased, too, for I reckoned that now we should have warmer weather. But not a bit of it! Why, it's freezing harder than ever. These humans have got their calendar all wrong.«

»They have indeed!« said a third sparrow, who was old and had gone grey on top. »They've a thing nowadays they call the Almanack. I suppose it's an invention of their own, and so everything's got to go by it; but it doesn't. When spring arrives, the year begins; that's nature's way, and that's what I go by.«

»But when will spring arrive?« asked the others.

»It'll come when the stork comes, but there's no knowing with him when he'll arrive; and here in the town there isn't a soul who has any idea. They're better informed out in the country. Shall we fly out there and wait? We shall be nearer to spring, I feel sure, out in the country.«

»Ah, that may be all very well,« said one of them, who had been twittering for some time without actually saying anything. »But here in the town I enjoy certain advantages that I'm afraid I might miss out there. Living in a house near by is a human family that's hit upon the sensible idea of fastening against the wall three or four flower-pots with the large opening turned inwards and the bottom facing outwards with a hole cut in it large enough for me to fly in and out. I and my husband have got our nest there, and from there all our young ones have flown out. The human family have of course rigged up the whole thing just for the fun of watching us, or else I don't suppose they'd have done it. They scatter bread-crumbs – also for their own amusement – and that's how we get our food. We are, in a manner of speaking, provided for ... And so I think my husband and I will stay where we are. We're most disappointed – but we'll stay.«

»And we're flying off to the country, to see if there's any sign of spring.« And away they flew.

In the country it was still winter, no doubt about that: the frost was several degrees sharper than in the town. A keen wind was blowing across the snowbound fields. The farmer, wearing his great mittens, sat in his sledge and slapped his arms together to get the cold out of them; and, with the whip lying across his knees, the raw-boned horses galloped until they steamed. The snow crackled, and the sparrows hopped freezing in the wheel tracks; »Tweet! When's the spring coming? What a time it's taking!«

»What a time!« resounded across the fields from the highest bank all covered with snow. It might have been an echo they heard, or it might well have been the voice of the funny-looking old man who sat on the top of the snowdrift in spite of the weather. He was white all over, like a peasant in a white homespun coat, with long white hair, white beard, very pale, and with large bright eyes.

»Who's that old fellow over there?« asked the sparrows.

»I can tell you,« answered an old raven perched on the gate-post, who was condescending enough to admit that we are all little birds in the sight of heaven and therefore entered into conversation with the sparrows and told them who the old fellow was. »He's Winter, the old man from last year. He's not dead, as it says in the Almanack; no, he's a sort of guardian to the little Prince Spring who's now on his way. Depend upon it, Winter's the one that calls the tune. B'rrh! I'll bet you're freezing, you little 'uns.«

»There, isn't that just what I said,« twittered the smallest sparrow. »The Almanack is simply one of man's inventions. It isn't made to follow nature. They should leave that to us, who're born cleverer.«

And a week went by, and nearly another. The forest was black, the frozen lake lay heavy and stiff like lead; the clouds – well, they were hardly clouds, they were damp icy mists clinging to the countryside. The great black crows flew about in silent flocks; everything seemed asleep ... Then a sunbeam went gliding over the lake, and the surface shone like molten tin. The snow lying over the fields and slopes had lost some of its glitter, though the white figure of Winter himself still sat there looking steadily southward; he never noticed that the blanket of snow seemed to be sinking into the earth and that here and there a little grass-green patch of ground was showing, which was soon swarming with sparrows.

»Cheep-cheep! Is this the spring?«

»Spring!« went the echo across field and meadow and through the dark-brown woods, where the moss shone fresh and green on the trunks of trees. And now through the air came flying from the south the first two storks; each of them had a pretty little child on its back, a boy and a girl. The children greeted the earth with a kiss; and wherever they set foot, white flowers sprang up out of the snow. Hand in hand they went up to the old ice-man, Winter, and snuggled right up to him in fresh greeting. At the same moment all three were hidden from view, and the whole countryside with them; everything was shrouded in a thick damp mist, ever so dense and heavy. Presently a light breeze got up; and then the wind came tearing along with tremendous gusts and drove the mist away, and the sun shone warm. Winter himself had vanished, and Spring's sweet children sat on the throne of the year.

»This is what I call New Year,« said the sparrows. »Now we'll surely get back our rights, and something to make up for the hard winter.«

Whichever way the two children turned green buds were shooting from bush and tree, grass grew longer, cornfields a brighter and brighter green. All around her the little girl kept scattering flowers; she had masses of them in her lap, which appeared to be teeming with flowers and always full of them, however busily she kept on scattering; in her eagerness she shook a regular snow of blossom over the apple and peach trees, so that they stood out in all their glory before ever they'd properly got their green leaves.

304

And she clapped her hands, and so did the boy, and then out came birds – goodness knows where from – and they all twittered and sang , »Spring has come!«

It was a lovely sight. And many an old granny came and stood outside her door in the sunshine, gave herself a little shake, and looked at the yellow flowers that were flaunting their colour all over the meadow just as they did when she was young. The world was young again. »It's wonderful out here today,« she said.

The woods were still a brownish green, with bud upon bud, though the woodruff was out in all its freshness and fragrance. Violets were there in abundance; so, too, were anemones, cowslips and oxlips – yes, there was sap and strength in every blade of grass, making it quite a magnificent carpet to sit on; and there sat Spring's young couple, holding each other's hands and singing and smiling and growing more and more.

A soft rain fell down upon them, but they took no notice; raindrops and tears of joy mingled together. Bride and bridegroom kissed each other, and at that instant the wood sprang into leaf. When the sun rose, all the woods were green.

Hand in hand the bridal pair wandered beneath the fresh leafy awning that hung above their heads, where only sunbeams and shadows chequered the colour of the green. A cool fragrance and a maiden purity lay in those delicate leaves. Runnel and brook went rippling between the green velvety rushes over the dappled stones. »Plenty abounds«, all nature proclaimed, »and will abound, for ever and ever.« And the cuckoo called and the lark twittered; it was glorious spring. Yet the willows had woolly gloves over their blossoms; they were being tremendously cautious, and that *is* so tiresome.

So days and weeks went by, and the heat became almost oppressive; waves of warm air passed through the corn, which grew yellower every day. On the forest lakes the North's white lotus spread out its huge green leaves over the surface of the water, and the fish would look for shade underneath them. On the sheltered side of the wood, where the sun beat down on the farmhouse wall and warmed the full-blown roses through and through, while the cherry trees hung full of juicy black, nearly sunbaked berries, there sat Summer's lovely wife whom we saw as a child and as a bride. And she looked up at the gathering clouds as they billowed in dark purple masses like mountains, piling up higher and higher. From three sides they approached; lower and lower, like a sea reversed and turned to stone, they came down towards the forest where everything, as if by enchantment, was hushed to silence. Not a breath of air was stirring, every bird was still; and, while all nature lay solemn and expectant, people in carriages, on horse or on foot went hurrying down roads and path to get to shelter.

Suddenly there was a flash, as if the sun were breaking out – a blinding, blistering flash – and then all was dark again, as a crash went rolling overhead. Rain came down in sheets; there was night – and day; stillness – and uproar. The young reeds in the marsh swayed their brown plumes like a billowy sea, the branches of the trees were hidden in mist, and then once more came darkness and light, silence and uproar ... Grass and corn lay beaten down flat, as though washed away never to rise again. All at once the rain died down to a few drops, the sun came out, and on leaf and blade the raindrops gleamed like pearls; birds began singing, fish leapt up from the brook, midges danced; and out on a rock where the salt seawater had been whipped into foam, sat Summer himself, that sturdy man with lusty limbs and dripping hair; there he was, cooled and strengthened by his bath, sitting in the warm sunshine. All around, nature too was cooled and strengthened, everything grown vigorous, rich and beautiful. It was summertime, warm delicious summertime.

Fresh and sweet was the smell that came from the rich fields of clover. The bees went mumbling through the ruins of a court-house; the bram-

ble twined about the old altar slab that, washed by the rain, glistened in the sunlight; and the queen bee flew there with her swarm and made wax and honey. No one saw them but Summer and his sturdy spouse; it was for them that the altar table was spread with nature's offerings.

And the evening sky glittered like gold – no church has a dome so rich; and the moon shone between evening and morning glow. It was summer-time.

And days and weeks went by. The bright scythes of the harvesters gleamed in the cornfields. The branches of the apple tree bent low with the weight of their red and yellow fruit; the hops smelt delicious, hanging in great clusters; and under the hazel bushes, with their heavy bunches of nuts, sat man and wife, Summer and his graver-looking spouse, taking a rest.

»What abundance!« she cried. »Blessings on every side, everything homely and good; and yet somehow I long for rest – quiet – or whatever the word is ... Why, they're ploughing again already. Men are always after more – and still more ... Look, there are the storks flocking up to follow the plough at a distance; the bird of Egypt that brought us through the air. You remember, don't you, that time we two came as children up here to the North? We brought flowers with us, and lovely sunshine, and green woods, but these have been roughly treated by the wind and are turning brown and dark like the trees in the south – though they don't, like them, bear golden fruit.«

»Are they what you want to see?« said Summer. »Then feast your eyes on this!« And at a wave of his hand the leaves of the forest turned red and gold, and a blaze of colour spread right through the woods; rosebushes were aflame with scarlet hips, elder trees heavy with dark-brown berries, wild chestnuts fell ripe from their dark-green husks, and within the wood was a second flowering of violets.

But the Queen of the Year became still more pale and quiet. »It blows cold,« she said. »The nights are damp and misty. I long for the land of my childhood.«

And she saw the storks, one after the other, flying away and stretched her hands out after them. She looked up at their nests, now empty; and in one there sprouted the long-stalked cornflower and in another the yellow mustard, as if the nest was only there as a fence and protection for them. The sparrows, too, came up to the nest. »Tweet! Where have the family gone off to? Perhaps they can't stand the cold winds and have gone abroad ... Pleasant journey!«

The leaves in the forest turned more and more yellow, and one by one they fell to the ground. The autumn gales came tearing in, for harvest-time was nearly over. The Queen of the Year lay on a pile of yellow leaves and turned her gentle eyes towards a twinkling star, and her husband stood beside her. The leaves were caught up in a whirling gust and, when this died down, she was gone. Only a butterfly, the last of the year, was left fluttering in the cold air.

After that came the wet mists, the icy blast, and the long dark nights. The Monarch of the Year was standing with hair that, unknown to himself, was as white as snow; he thought it was the snowflakes falling from the clouds, for there was a thin layer of snow covering the green fields.

And the church bells were ringing for Christmas.

»There go the birthday bells,« said the Monarch of the Year. »Soon the new King and Queen will be born, and I, like her, shall have rest – rest in that twinkling star.«

And there among the fresh green fir trees, where the snow lay, stood the angel of Christmas and gave his blessing to the young trees that were to go to his feast.

»Joy in the house and under the green branches!« said the year's old monarch; a few weeks had aged him into a hoary patriarch. »My time for rest is drawing near; the young couple. of the coming year will now receive crown and sceptre.«

»And yet the power is yours,« said the angel of Christmas, »power – not

rest: Let the snow lie out there and keep the young seed warm. Learn to see homage paid to another, though still you're a prince; learn to be forgotten, though still you're alive. Your hour of freedom will come, when spring comes.«

»When does spring come?« asked Winter.

»It comes when the stork comes.«

And with his white locks and snowy beard old Winter sat, freezing and bent, yet strong as the winter gale and the power of ice, high on a hillock's snowdrift, gazing away to the south, just as the Winter before had sat and gazed. There was creaking of ice and crunching of snow, skaters went curving on the polished surface of the lakes, and ravens and crows stood out sharply against the white background. Not a breath of wind was stirring; and in the still air Winter clenched his fists, and the ice became fathoms thick between shore and shore.

Then the sparrows came out from the town again and asked, »Who's that old fellow over there?« And the raven was on his gate-post again – or a son of his, it doesn't matter which – and he answered, »That's Winter, the old man from last year. He's not dead, as they make out in the Almanack; he's the guardian of the spring that will soon be here.«

»Soon be here!« said the sparrows. »Then we'll have good days and better treatment. The old way was no good.«

And in silent thought Winter gave a nod to the black leafless forest, where the delicate shape and curve of every tree showed clearly, and in their winter slumber the icy mists sank slowly down from the clouds. The Monarch was dreaming of the days of his youth and his manhood, and by dawn the whole forest was beautiful with hoar-frost. It was Winter's dream of Summer; and the sunshine sprinkled the hoar-frost down from the branches.

»When will spring be here?« asked the sparrows.

»Spring!« came like an echo from the slopes where the snow lay. And the sun shone warmer and warmer, the snow melted, the birds twittered, »Spring is coming!«

Then, flying high through the air, came the first stork; and the second came with him. Each had a beautiful child on its back, as they coasted down on to the open field; they kissed the earth, and they kissed the silent old man. Then, like Moses on the mountain, he was borne away in a cloud-mist and disappeared. The story of the year was over.

»Perfectly right!« said the sparrows. »And very pretty to look at, too; but it's quite different from the Almanack, so it must be wrong.«

Everything in Its Right Place

We must go back more than a hundred years.

Behind the wood beside a large lake was an old manor-house with a deep moat round it full of reeds and bulrushes. Right up against the bridge leading to the entrance-gates stood an old willow leaning out over the reeds.

From the sunken road came the sound of horn and clattering hoofs, which made the young goose-girl bustle to get her geese away from the bridge before the hunt came galloping over. They rode up so quickly that she had to jump in a hurry up on to one of the high coping-stones of the bridge to avoid being ridden down. She was still half a child, slight and delicate, with a charming expression in her face and two clear bright eyes; but the squire took no notice of this. He came dashing along at top speed, took his hunting crop by the other end and in brutal joke lunged right at her chest with the butt end, so that she toppled over backwards.

»Everything in its right place,« he bawled out. »Into the ditch with you!« ... and then he burst into laughter – it was supposed to be so funny – and the others laughed too. The whole party were yelling and bawling, and the hounds all baying; it was a real case of –

»moneyed birds on the bust!«

Goodness knows how much money he still had in those days.

The poor goose-girl put her hand before her as she fell and caught hold of one of the overhanging branches of the willow; with the help of this she managed to keep herself clear of the mud, and as soon as the hunt had all safely passed through the big gates she did her best to clamber up again. But the branch broke off at the top, and the goosegirl would have fallen heavily back into the reeds, if at that very moment a strong hand hadn't seized her from above. It was a travelling pedlar, who had been looking on from a short way off and now hurried to her rescue.

»Everything in its right place!« he said mimicking the squire, as he dragged her up on to the bank. He tried putting the broken branch back where it was when it snapped, but »in its right place« – that won't always work. So he stuck the branch down in the moist earth: »grow if you can and make a good flute for them up at the manor.« It would serve them right (he said to himself) if the squire and his hunting friends were jolly well made to run the gauntlet. And then he went into the manor-house, though not into the private side - he was much too humble for that. No, he went into the servants' hall, and the servants turned over his goods and bargained with him. Meanwhile, from the festive board above them came a hullabaloo that was supposed to be singing; it was the best they could do. There were bursts of laughter and yelping of hounds, and a riot of gorging and tippling; wine and old ale foamed in glass and tankard, and the watch-dogs joined in the feasting. Now and then one of the animals would be kissed by a young nobleman after its nose had first been wiped with the long flap of its ear. The pedlar was called up with his wares, but really only for them to make fun of him. The wine had gone to their heads and the sense gone out. They poured ale into a stocking, so that he might drink with them – come on, quick! Most ingenious, wasn't it. More laughter. Whole herds of cattle, farms, farmers and all, were staked on the throw of a single card and lost.

»Everything in its right place!« cried the pedlar, once he was well away again from Sodom and Gomorra, as he called it. »The open road – that's the place for me; it was no place for me, up at the manor.« And the little goose-girl nodded to him from the gate.

Days and weeks went by, and it turned out that the broken willow branch that the pedlar had stuck in beside the ditch was still keeping fresh and green – why, yes, it was even putting out new shoots. The little goose-girl saw that it must have taken root, and she was immensely pleased. It was her tree, she felt.

But, while this went forward, everything else at the manor fell badly behind, for gambling and guzzling are shaky stilts to stand on.

Before half-a-dozen years had passed, the squire walked out of the house as poor as a beggar; and the manor was bought by a wealthy pedlar, who turned out to be the very man who had been mocked and made a fool of and offered ale in a stocking. But honesty and enterprise, they're bound to prosper, and now the pedlar was lord of the manor. But that was the end of all card-playing there. »That kind of reading is no

good to anyone,« he said, »and I'll tell you what it comes from; the first time the Devil saw the Bible, he wanted to mimic it with a book that was supposed to be like it, and so he invented cards.«

The new squire took a wife, and who should she be but the little goose-girl, who had always been gentle, good and kind; and in her new clothes she looked as fine and handsome as if she had been born a great lady. How did it all happen? Oh, well, that story would take too long, now that we're so busy; anyhow it happened, and the most important is what comes next.

Things went wonderfully well now at the manor; Mother looked after it inside, and Father outside. Blessings were almost rained upon them, for plenty comes where plenty is. The old house was done up and re-painted, the moat was cleaned out and fruit-trees planted. It all looked nice and friendly, and the floors were as smooth and bright as a bread-trencher. On winter evenings the lady of the house sat with her maids in the large hall, spinning wool and linen; and every Sunday evening there was reading aloud from the Bible – what's more, by the Councillor himself; for he was made a Councillor, the pedlar was, though not until he was quite an old man. The children grew up - yes, they had children - and they were all well-educated, though of course they weren't all equally clever; that's the same in every family.

But the willow branch outside the gates had grown into a splendid tree, standing free and unlopped. »That's our family tree,« said the old people, and the tree was to be honoured and respected, they told the children, not forgetting the ones that weren't clever ...

And now a hundred years had gone by.

It was in our own day. The lake had now become a marsh, and the old manor was more or less wiped out. There was an oblong pool of water with some stone-edging beside it; that was all that was left of the deep moat, and here stood a splendid old tree with stooping branches. It was the family tree. There it stood, showing how fine a willow can be when left to itself. It's true, the stem was split down the middle, right from the root up to the crown, and the gales had twisted it a bit out of shape. Nevertheless, it stood; and from every crack and cranny, into which soil had been blown by wind and weather, there sprouted grass and flowers. Especially near the top, where the large boughs branched off, there was a positive little hanging garden of raspberries and chickweed; yes, even a tiny mountain ash had taken root and stood so slender and delicate up there in the middle of the old willow, which was mirrored in the black water when the wind drove the duckweed out into a corner of the pool. A narrow path across the fields led close by the tree.

High up the slope near the woods, with a beautiful view, stood the new manor, large and imposing, with window-panes so clear that you might easily think that there weren't any. The large flight of steps at the front-door looked like an arbour of roses and broad-leaved plants. The lawn was such a lovely green that you might have thought every blade of grass was attended to night and morning. Inside, the rooms were hung with valuable paintings; and there too, covered with silk and velvet, were chairs and sofas that could almost walk on their own legs, tables with shining marble tops, and books with leather bindings and gilt edges ... Yes, they must certainly be rich people who lived here. And they were too - very distinguished - they were the baron and his family.

Place and people were just like each other. These also said, »Everything in its right place«; and therefore all the pictures that had once been the ornament and pride of the old manor were now hanging in the passage leading to the servant's hall. Absolute rubbish, they called them, especially two old portraits: the one showed a man in a pink coat and wig, the other a lady with piled-up powdered hair and a red rose in her hand, but both alike encircled with a wreath of willow sprigs. Both pictures had a number of round holes in them; this was because the little barons always would go and shoot their crossbows at the old couple.

They were paintings of the Councillor and his wife, from whom the whole family were descended.

»But they don't really belong to our family«, one of the little barons would say. »He was a pedlar, and she was a chit of a girl who minded the geese. They weren't like Mum and Dad.« The pictures were just rubbish, and »everything in its right place,« they said; and so great-granny and great-grandad found their way to the passage leading to the servants' hall.

The parson's son was private tutor at the manor. He was out one day with the little barons and their eldest sister, who had just lately been confirmed, and their way led along the path down towards the old willow tree. As they walked, she gathered a bunch of wild flowers – »everything in its right place« – and they made one beautiful whole. At the same time she followed every word that was said, and it pleased her to hear the parson's son speaking about the power of nature and about the great men and women of history. She had a fine healthy disposition, noble in mind and spirit, and a heart filled with love for everything created by God.

Down by the old willow tree they came to a halt. The youngest boy did so want to have a flute cut off for him; he had had one before from other willows, and so the parson's son broke off a branch.

»Oh, don't do that!« cried the young baroness; but already it was done. »You see,« she said, »it's our famous old tree. I'm so fond of it. That's of course why they laugh at me at home, though I don't mind. There's an old story about this tree ...«

And then she told the whole tale of what we have just heard about the tree, the old manor, and about the goose-girl and pedlar who met here and afterwards became founders of the noble family to which the young baroness belonged.

»They refused a title, the honest old souls,« she continued. »Their motto was, 'Everything in its right place', and they felt it wasn't their place to let themselces be given a title for money. It was their son, my grandfather, who was made a baron. He's said to have been a great scholar, highly thought of and popular with the princes and princesses, invited to all their big parties. He's the one that the others at home think most of, but I'm not sure myself; there's something about the first old couple that draws my heart to them. It must have been so snug, so patriarchal, in the old manor, where the mistress sat spinning with her maids and the old master read aloud from the Bible.«

»They must have been fine, sensible people,« said the parson's son; and, with that, they plunged into talk about nobles and commoners and, from the way that the parson's son talked about the position of the nobility, you would hardly have thought that he belonged to the middle class at all.

»It's a great thing,« he said, »to belong to a family that has distinguished itself, to have a sort of spur in your blood urging you on to do good work. It's wonderful to inherit a name that's a card of admission to the leading families. Nobility implies what is noble; it's the gold coin that bears the stamp of its own value. It's the fashion of our time – and of course many poets hold the same view – to regard everything done by the upper classes as wrong and foolish, while among the poor the lower you go down the more they shine. Well, that's not what I think, for that idea is utterly and completely false. Among the upper classes you may come across many moving little incidents. My mother has told me of one, and I could instance several others. She was calling at a good house in town – I think my grandmother had nursed her ladyship as a child. My mother was standing in the room with the aristocratic old husband, when he saw down in the courtyard an old woman hobbling on crutches. She used to come every Sunday and get a few shillings. »Ah, there's the poor old dear,« said the husband. »She finds it so hard to get along.« And before my mother grasped what was happening, he was out of the door and down the steps; he, His 70-year-old Excellency, had himself gone down to the poor woman, to save her the difficult climb after the money she had come for. That's of course only a trifling instance but, like the widow's mite, it rings from the bottom of the heart, from the depth of human nature. In that direction should the poet point, of that should he sing, especially at the present time, for it will do good and make people kinder and more tolerant. But when some bit of a man, just because of this blue blood and a pedigree like an Arab horse, stands whinnying on his hind legs in the street or complaining in the room that 'people from the street have been in here' after a commoner has paid a call, then nobility has begun to go rotten and is no more than a mask of the kind that Thespis originated; a fellow like that is simply a laughing-stock and a target for satire.«

Such was the homily of the parson's son. Rather long perhaps, but at any rate the flute was finished.

There was a big party on at the manor, with many guests from the country and from the capital; ladies dressed with taste – and without taste. The spacious rooms were crowded. Neighbouring parsons stood respectfully clustered in a corner – it looked rather like a funeral. But it was an entertainment, though it hadn't yet got started. There was to be a great concert, and so the little baron had his willow-flute with him, but he couldn't get a note out of it, and neither could his dad, so the flute was no good. There was music and singing of the kind that gives most pleasure to the performers. Delightful, all the same.

»You, too, are an expert?« said a lordling (a true son of his father) to the parson's son. »Can you really play a flute that you've made yourself? This is indeed genius to the fore – worthy to take the seat of honour. Bless you! I keep well abreast of the times – one has to. Now I'm sure you'll sweep us all off our feet with your little instrument«; and he handed him the little flute that had been cut from the willow tree down by the pool. Then at the top of his voice he announced that the tutor was going to oblige them with a solo on the flute.

The idea was simply to make fun of him – that was quite clear – and so the tutor had no wish to play; but they crowded round and pressed him, till at last he took the flute and put it to his lips.

It was a queer sort of flute. It had a note as prolonged as the whistle from a steam engine, only much more piercing. It sounded right over the courtyard, garden and woods, miles out into the country; and with the sound came a blast of wind roaring, »Everything in its right place« – and away flew the baron, as if carried by the wind, out of the manor right bang into the cowman's cottage; and the cowman flew up, not into the drawing-room – he couldn't come there – no, but into the servant's hall among the menservants in their smart livery. The haughty fellows were half paralysed at the idea of such a humble creature daring to sit at table with them.

But in the great hall the young baroness flew up to her rightful place at the head of the table, while the parson's son had the seat beside her. There they sat, the two of them, looking like a newly-married couple. An aged count belonging to the oldest family in the country remained undisturbed in his place of honour; for the flute played fair, as was only right. The witty nobleman, who was the cause of the flute-playing – the one who was a true son of his father – flew head first in among the chickens, and he wasn't the only one.

The flute was heard for miles around, and there were tales of strange happenings. A wealthy merchant and his family, driving in a coach and four, were blown clean out of the coach and couldn't even find a place in the dickey. Two rich farmers, who in our time had grown too big for their own cornfields, were blown down into the ditch. Yes, it was a dangerous flute. Luckily it burst at the first note, and that was a good thing, for then it went back into its pocket: »Everything in its right place.«

Not a word was said next day about what had happened, and that's how we come to talk of »piping down«. Besides, everything was back where it was before, except that the two old pictures of The Pedlar and The Goose-girl were hanging in the great hall, where they had been blown up on to the wall; and, as a genuine art-critic said they had been painted by a master-hand, they were left there and restored; before that, you see, there had been no way of telling their value. How could there be? Now they hung in the place of honour. »Everything in its right place« – and it comes there in the end. Eternity is long, longer than this story.

»Something«

I want to be something,« said the eldest of five brothers. »I want to be of some use in the world. Never mind how humble my job is; as long as what I do is well done, that'll be something. I'll make bricks – people can't do without them – then at least I shall have done something.«

»Something, yes, but far too little,« said the second brother. »Your 'something' will be as good as nothing – just a labourer's job – something a machine can do. No, no, much better be a builder; that would be something – that's what I'll be. That's a real position; then you can join the Masons' Guild, get the rights of a citizen, have your own banner and keep your own inn. Yes, if all goes well, I can have men under me and be called 'master' and my wife become 'mistress'. That'll be something.«

»It's nothing at all,« said the third brother. »It doesn't belong to any of the classes – and a town has lots of classes ranking far higher than a 'master'. You may be a good enough fellow, but as 'master' you're simply one of the so-called lower classes ... No, I know something better than that. I mean to be an architect, to enter the world of art and imagination, to climb high in the realm of intellect. I suppose I shall have to begin from the bottom – yes, to put it quite bluntly, I must begin as a carpenter's apprentice; wear a cap, though I'm used to a top hat; run and fetch beer and brandy for ordinary journeymen; put up with their familiarity, and that is so aggravating. Still, I shall pretend to myself that the whole thing is a masquerade – freedom with a mask on! Tomorrow (that's to say, as soon as I've served my time) I shall go my own way; I shan't care a hang about the others. I shall go to the art-school, learn drawing, win the title of architect. That's something! That's a great deal! I can become 'my Lord' and 'your Honour!', yes, and have a bit tacked on to my name both in front and behind. I'll build and build, as the others did before me. That's always something to bank on ... Well, there's my idea of 'something'«.

»But that 'something' doesn't appeal to me in the slightest,« said the fourth brother. »I'm not following in the wake of anyone. I'm not an imitator; I mean to be a genius, cleverer than the whole lot of you put together. I shall create a new style and put forward the plan for a building, suited to our country's climate and materials, to our nationality, to the development of the present age – and then add an extra floor by my own genius.«

»But suppose the climate and materials aren't good enough,« said the fifth brother, »that'll be a snag, for these two mean a great deal. Nationality, too, can easily get so enlarged that it becomes an affectation. The improvements of the present age may run away with you, as is often the case with youth. It's obvious that none of you will ever really come to anything, however much you think you will. Still, do as you like, I shan't take after you. I'll stand aside and criticize what you do. There's always something wrong in everything; I'll pick that out and run it down – that'll be something!«

And he did, and people said of the fith brother, »Yes, there's certainly something in him. He's got brains, but he doesn't do anything.« Which only showed that he was something.

Well, there's not much to that story, and yet it will go on till the end of the world.

But is that all we are to hear about the five brothers? *That* wasn't anything ... All right, keep listening: it's really no end of a story.

The eldest brother, who made bricks, noticed that, out of every brick as soon as it was finished, there came rolling a little coin. Only a copper coin, it's true; but a number of little copper coins, when put together, turn into a bright half crown, and wherever you knock on the door with that – at the baker's, the butcher's, the tailor's or the whole lot of them – the door flies open and you get whatever you want. There, that's what came from the bricks. Some of them, of course, went to pieces or broke in two, but even these could be used.

Up on the dyke old Mother Margaret, poor woman, wanted so much to run up a little cottage for herself. She was given all the broken bricks, and a few whole ones as well; for the eldest brother had a good heart, even if the only solid proof of this was in the bricks he made. The poor woman put up the house herself. It was cramped for space, one window was lopsided, the door too low, and the thatching might have been better done; but there was good shelter and a distant view over the sea, as it dashed in all its fury against the dyke. The salt spray would spatter the

whole house, still standing there, when he who had made the bricks was dead and gone.

The second brother – well, by this time he could build differently, for, after all, he was trained to it. Once his test piece had been handed in, he packed up his bag and trolled the journeyman's song:

> My youthful feet shall never lag,
> while foreign lands endear me,
> with work to fill my money-bag
> and buoyant soul to cheer me.
> I've pledged the love I left behind:
> not long I'll stay a-roamin'.
> Hurrah! Good workers always find
> a bower to build their home in.

And he did. When he got back to the town and became a 'master', he put up house after house – a whole streetful of houses; and so well that it gave the town quite a name, then the houses built him a little house that was all for himself ... But how could the houses build? Very well, ask them; they won't answer, but there are people who will, and they'll say, »Why, of course, this street built his house for him.« True, it was small, with a clay floor, but when he danced along it with his bride the floor soon got shiny and polished, and from every brick in the wall grew a flower; this was just as good as an expensive wall-paper. It was a delightful house, and they were a happy young couple. The Mason's banner was flying outside, and journeymen and apprentices gave him three cheers: Hurray! Hurray! Hurray! That was certainly something ... And then he died – that was something, too.

Next came the architect, the third brother, the one who had begun by being a carpenter's apprentice, wearing a cap and running errands, but then on leaving the art-school had risen to be a master-builder, 'my Lord' and 'your Honour'. Yes, and even if the houses in the street did build a house for the brother who was a mason, still the street was now named after this one, and the finest house in the street became his. That was something, and he was something – with a long title, too, before and after his name. His children were called gentleman's children, and when he died his widow was a gentleman's widow – that's something! His name was still to be read at the street corner, still to be heard on people's lips – as the name of a street. Yes, indeed, that's something!

Then came the genius, the fourth brother, who wanted to hit upon something new and orginal with an extra floor to it; but this gave way, and he fell down and broke his neck. Still, he had a lovely funeral with banners and band, with flowers in the newspaper and along the cobbled road; and there were three speeches made over his grave, each one longer than the other; and this would have pleased him, because he was very fond of being talked about. A monument was put over his grave, only one storey, but still that's always something.

By this time he was dead, same as the other three brothers; but the last of them, the one who went in for criticism, outlived them all; and that was just as it should be, because in that way he got in the last word – and it was highly important for him to have the last word. Of course, he was the brainy one, they said. And now his hour had come, too; he died and arrived at the gate of heaven. They always arrive there in twos, and here he stood with another soul that also wanted to go in – none other than old Mother Margaret from the house on the dyke.

»I expect it's for the sake of the contrast that I and this miserable creature have to arrive here together,« said the critic. »Well, my good woman, and who may you be? Do you want to get in, too?« he asked.

And the old woman did her best to curtsey; she thought it was St. Peter himself who was speaking. »I'm a poor woman – got no family – old Margaret from the house on the dyke.«

»I see. And what have you done down there, may I ask? Something, I suppose?«

»Something? No, sir, I can't say I have done nothing at all down in that world – nothing as'll open this 'ere gate for me. It'll be a real mercy, if I'm allowed to go in through that door.«

»How did you come to leave that world?« he asked, merely for something to say, for he was tired of having to stand there waiting.

»How I come to leave? Well, I can't hardly say. You see, sir, I was weak and poorly the last few years, and so I didn't feel I could bear to crawl out of bed and go out into the frost and cold. It's been a hard winter, hasn't it? But now I've got over it, I hope. We had a couple of day's dead calm, though 'twas bitter cold – I dessay your Reverence remember. The ice was

frozen over as far out from the shore as you could see. Everybody in the
town was out on the ice, and there was dancing and what I think they
calls skating, with a band playing and folks eating and drinking. The
sound of it all come right into my little room. It was just getting a bit
dark like, and the moon was up, though it wasn't yet shining full. From
my bed I could see through the window right out over the seashore; and
there, in the part where the sky and sea join, there come up a queer white
cloud. I laid there looking at it, looking at the black spot in the middle; it
grew bigger and bigger, and I knew what *that* meant. I'm old and used to
the weather, but it's not often you'll see that sign. I recognized it, and it
give me a shock. Twice afore in my life I've seen the same thing coming,
and I knew with the spring tide there'd be a terrible gale, and then it'd be
all over with them poor people as was drinking and romping and rollick-
ing out there together. The whole town, young and old, was there. Who
was a-going to warn them, if none of 'em saw nor recognized what I did?
I was that frightened and yet more with my wits than I been for I don't

know how long. I come out of bed and across to the window, but I hadn't
the strength to go no further. Still, I got the window open. I could see
people running and jumping about over there on the ice, see the gay-
looking flags, hear the boys cheering and the girls and young men singing; they was having no end of a time ... But higher and higher rose the
white cloud with the black bag in it. I called out at the top of my voice,
but nobody heard me; I was too far away. Soon the storm would burst,
the ice break, and everyone out there go through it without a chance of
being saved. My voice wouldn't carry that far, and I'd never have the
strength to reach 'em myself. If only I could bring 'em ashore somehow!
Then God give me the idea of setting fire to my bed. Better to let the
house burn down than for all them folks to die miserably. So I set it

alight, saw the red flames, and, yes, I managed to get out of the door; but there I laid – 'twas all I could do. The blaze come out after me and out of the window, away over the roof. They saw it from where they was out on the ice, and they all ran as fast as they could to try and save poor me, who they thought was burning to death inside; there wasn't a one who stayed behind. I heard 'em coming, but I also heard a kind of whizzing in the air, and then I heard the thunder rumble like there was big guns firing. The spring tide heaved up the ice, and it broke all to pieces. But they reached the dyke, where the sparks was flying all around me. I brought 'em all safely back; but I suppose I couldn't stand the cold and all that shock, and so I've come up here to the gate of heaven. They tell me that's even opened for a poor creature like me. O'course, I ain't no longer got a house down there on the dyke; still, I know that don't give me the right to come in here.«

Then the gate of heaven opened, and the angel took the old woman in. She dropped a straw outside, one of the straws from her bedding which she had set light to in order to save all those people on the ice; and the straw had turned to pure gold, but a gold that grew and twined into the loveliest tracing.

»There, that's what the old woman brought,« said the angel to the critic. »Now show me what you've brought. I know, of course, that you've not *done* anything – not so much as made a brick. If only you could go back again and bring at least that much. I dare say it wouldn't have been worth anything, if you had made it; still, made with a will, that would always have been something. But you cannot go back, and I can do nothing for you.«

Then the poor soul, the woman from the house on the dyke, pleaded for him. »His brother made and gave me all them bricks and pieces I used for running up my little cottage. That meant a tremendous lot to poor me. Well, now can't all them bits and pieces count as one brick for him? That'd be an act of mercy, and he badly needs one now. This is the home of mercy, ain't it?«

»Your brother, he that you called the least of you,« said the angel, »he whose honest work seemed to you so inferior, now gives you his heavenly mite. You shall not be turned away. You shall be allowed to stand out here and meditate; try and help forward the life you lived below. But you shall not come in until by good work you have done *something*.«

»I could have put that better,« thought the critic, but he didn't say so aloud; and perhaps that was already *something*.

The Snail and the
Rose Tree

Round the garden ran a hedge of hazels, and on the other side of it were fields and meadows with cows and sheep. But in the middle of the garden stood a rose tree in full bloom; and under this was a snail, very self-contained, for he contained himself.

»Wait!« said the snail. »My time will come. I shall do a bit more than grow roses or bear nuts or give milk like cows and sheep.«

»We expect a great deal from you,« said the rose tree. »May I ask when it's to be?«

»I take my time,« said the snail, »but your're always in such a hurry. No, people like to be kept in suspense.«

A year later the snail lay sunning himself in much the same spot under the rose tree, which was putting out buds and blossoming roses, always fresh, always new. And the snail crept half-way out, stretched out his horns and drew them in again. »Everything looks the same as last year,« he said. »Not the slightest progress. The rose tree keeps on with his roses, but that's all that happens.«

Summer passed, autumn was ending, and still the rose tree went on having buds and blooms until the snow came. The weather turned wet and blustering. The rose tree bent towards the earth, the snail crawled into the ground.

Now a new season began; and the roses came out, and so did the snail.

»You're quite an old rose now,« said the snail. »You'll soon have to think about going ... You've given the world all you had in you. How much that was worth is a matter I haven't had time to consider. But it's quite clear that you haven't done a thing for your inner development, or you'd have had very different results to show. How do you account for that? Why, you'll soon be nothing but a stick. Do you see what I'm driving at?«

»You frighten me,« said the rose tree. »I've never given it a thought.«

»No, you never were one to think, were you? Have you ever worked out for yourself why you flowered and how the flowering came to pass – that way and no other?«

»No,« said the rose tree, »I flowered in sheer joy, because I couldn't help it. The sun was so warm, the air so refreshing. I drank in the pure dew and the pouring rain; I breathed, I was alive. There came strength to me from the earth below, strength too from above; I felt a happiness that was always new, always deep, and so I had to be always blossoming. That was my life; it was all I could do.«

»You've had a very easy life,« said the snail.

»Yes, I certainly have. Everything's been done for me,« said the rose tree. »But you've been even luckier. You are one of those thoughtful, highly gifted creatures who mean to astonish the world one day.«

»No, no, not a bit of it,« said the snail. »The world's nothing to me. What have I to do with the world? I have as much as I can manage with myself – and in myself!«

»But shouldn't we all of us give the best we have to others – offer what we can? It's true, I've only given roses; but you, who are yourself so gifted, what have you given to the world? What will you give?«

»What have I given – what shall I give? I spit at the world. What's the good of it? It means nothing to me. Go on, grow your roses – that's all you're good for. Let the hazels bear nuts, let the cows and the sheep give milk; they've each got their public, and I've got mine, inside me. I withdraw into myself, and there I stay. The world's nothing to me.« And with that the snail went into his house and sealed it up.

»What a pity it is!« said the rose tree. »No creeping in for me, however much I try to. I've always got to come out – come out into roses. Their petals drop off and fly away in the wind. Still, I did see one of the roses being put into the housewife's hymn-book; and one of my roses found a place at a pretty girl's breast, and another was kissed with the greatest

delight by the lips of a child. That was a rare blessing – it did me good – something to remember all my life.«

And the rose tree went on blooming in innocence; and the snail still dozed in his house. The world was nothing to him.

And years went by.

The snail had become earth to earth, and the rose tree earth to earth; the keepsake rose in the hymn-book had also vanished ... But in the garden new rose trees were coming out, and new snails were growing up that crept into their houses and spat – the world was nothing to them.

Shall we read the tale again from the beginning? It won't be any different.

The Last Dream of the Old Oak Tree

(A Tale for Christmas)

Up in the wood, at the top of the slope going down to the open shore, stood an old oak tree, such a hoary old oak, just 365 years old – though a long time like that was no more for the tree than so many days would be for us. We are awake in the daytime and sleep at night, and that's when we have our dreams; but the tree is quite different. The tree is awake during three of the seasons, and it isn't till winter that it gets its sleep. Winter is its time for sleeping, winter is its night after the long day that is called spring, summer and autumn.

Many a warm summer's day had a day-fly danced round the top of the tree – lived and hovered and felt happy – and if ever the little creature rested for a moment in quiet contentment on one of the big cool oak-leaves, the tree would remark: »Poor little thing! Just a single day is the whole of your life. How short that is! It's terribly sad.«

»Sad!« the day-fly would answer. »What makes you say that? Why, everything's so wonderfully bright and warm and lovely, and I'm so happy.«

»But only for one day, and then it's all over and done with.«

»Done with!« said the day-fly. »What's done with? Will you be done with, too?«

»No, I shall live for perhaps thousands of your days, and my day is whole seasons long. That's something so long that you simply can't reckon it out.«

»No, because I don't understand you. You may have thousands of my days, but I have thousands of moments to be pleased and happy in. Does all this world's loveliness come to an end, when you die?«

»No,« said the tree. »I expect it goes on longer – far, far longer – than I can imagine.«

»Well, in that case, you and I must have just the same, mustn't we, only we reckon differently.«

And the day-fly danced and swerved in the air, revelled in the delicate working of its wings and their velvety gauze, revelled in the warm air that was filled with perfume from clover in the fields and from wild roses and elder-blossom and honeysuckle that grew on the hedges, not to mention sweet woodruff, cowslip and pennyroyal. So strong was the scent that it made the day-fly feel quite tipsy. The day was long and beautiful, full of joy and happy impressions; and then, as the sun was setting, the little fly would feel pleasantly tired out with all that gaiety. Its wings could not carry it any longer and, ever so gently, it glided down on to a soft swaying blade of grass, nodded its head in the way that it does and fell happily asleep. That was death.

»Poor little day-fly!« said the oak tree. »What a short life that was!«

And every summer day it happened again: the same dance, the same talk, answers and passing away. It happened, one after another, to whole generations of day-flies, and all of them were just as happy and cheerful. The oak tree stood there awake all through its morning of spring, its noonday of summer and its evening of autumn. Now its time for sleeping – its night – was drawing near; winter would soon have come.

Already the gales were singing: »Good night, good-night! There goes a leaf, there goes a leaf! We're plucking, we're plucking! Now then, go to sleep. We'll sing you to sleep, we'll ruffle you to sleep, but that does the old branches good, doesn't it? Makes them groan in sheer enjoyment! Sleep well, sleep well! This will be your 365th 'night' – you're only a one-year-old really, – sleep well! The clouds are sprinkling snow; there'll soon be a regular sheet and a cosy blanket for your toes. Sweet sleep and pleasant dream!«

And there was the oak tree, stripped of all its leaves, ready to go to bed the whole long winter through and in it to dream many a dream, always of some adventure just as in human dreams.

It, too, had once been small – yes, with an acorn for its cradle. After our reckoning it was now over three hundred years old. It was the largest and finest tree in the forest, its top towered above all the other trees and could be sighted far out at sea, a landmark for ships; but it never gave a thought to all the eyes that were on the look-out for it. High up in its green summit the woodpigeons built their nests and the cuckoo kept calling;

331

and in autumn, when the leaves glowed like slabs of beaten copper, the migrant birds came and rested there before they flew away across the sea. But now winter had come, and the tree stood leafless; it was easy to see how bent and rugged were its outstretched branches. Crows and jackdaws came and settled there in turn and chattered of the hard times ahead and how difficult it was to get food in winter.

It happened to be the holy time of Christmas and it was then that the tree dreamt its loveliest dream. We really must hear that.

The tree had a clear impression that it was a season of festivity and that, round about, it could hear all the church-bells ringing; and, moreover, it was as soft and warm as on a lovely summer's day. The tree spread out its mighty crown, so fresh and green; sunbeams played among leaves and branches; the air was full of the fragrance of herbs and undergrowth. Gay butterflies were playing »touch last«, and the day-flies were dancing as though everything existed merely for them to dance and enjoy themselves. All that the tree had been through and seen around it for years past went trailing by like a regular pageant. It saw old-time knights and their ladies on horseback, with plumes in their hats and hawks at their wrists, riding through the wood. It heard the sound of the huntsman's horn and of hounds in full cry. It saw enemy troops with gleaming weapons and glittering uniforms, with spears and halberds, pitch their tents and then strike them; there were watch-fires blazing, and song and sleep beneath the spreading branches of the tree. It saw lovers meeting in silent happiness here in the moonlight, cutting the initial letter of their names in the grey-green bark. Zither and Æolian harp had once – so many years ago – been hung in the branches of the oak by gay, wandering prentices; now they were hanging there again and twanging there again so charmingly. The wood-pigeons cooed as if to describe what the tree was feeling, and the cuckoo called out how many summer days it had to live.

Then it seemed as if a fresh current of life went rippling right through it down to the lowest roots and up to the topmost branches out into the very leaves. The tree could feel itself spreading and spreading – feel, too, at its roots that also down in the earth there was life and warmth. It felt itself getting stronger, as it grew taller and taller. The trunk shot up without a pause, more and more it grew, its crown spread more lustily, outward and upward .. and as the tree grew, so grew its vigour, its blissful longing to come higher and higher, right up to the bright warm sun.

Already it had grown high up above the clouds that trailed away below it like dusky troops of migrants or great snowy flocks of swans.

And every one of its leaves could see, as though it had eyes. The stars became visible by day, great shining stars, that winked at one like human eyes, so dear and gentle. They made it think of kind eyes that it had known, children's eyes, lovers' eyes where they met under the tree.

It was a joyful, delicious moment. And yet in the midst of all this joy the tree felt that it longed for all the other forest-trees down there, the bushes and herbs and flowers, to be able to soar with it and to share its gladness and splendour. The mighty oak, in all the glory of its dream, was not completely happy until the others came with it, all of them, big and little; and this feeling quivered through leaves and branches as deeply and strongly as in a human breast.

The tree-top stirred as if looking for something that it missed. Then, glancing back, it caught the scent of woodruff and, after that, the even stronger scent of violets and honeysuckle. It fancied it could hear the cuckoo answering back.

Yes, through the clouds peeped out the green summit of the wood. Down below it saw the other trees growing and rising up beside it. Bushes and herbs shot high into the air; some tore themselves loose, root and all, and flew more swiftly up. Swiftest of all was the birch. Like a pale streak of lightning its slim trunk went hustling upward, and the branches swayed like green gauze banners. The whole woodland scene, even the brown-plumed reeds, went up with it, and the birds joined in and sang, while there on its blade of grass that fluttered and flowed like a long green silk ribbon sat the grasshopper fiddling on his shinbone with his wing. »Boom!« went the cockchafers, »zoom!« went the bees, the birds all raised their beaks and sang. From every side flowed joyful songs right up to heaven.

»But the small red flower beside the brook, that must come, too,« said the oak tree; »and the blue bell-flower, and the little daisy« – yes, the oak wanted them all to come.

»Here we are, here we are!« came the echoing answer.

»But last summer's sweet woodruff – and the year before we had glorious lilies-of-the-valley – and the wild apple tree, how lovely it looked! – and all the beauty of the woods for years and years and years – if only it had gone on living till now, then that too could have joined us.«

»Here we are, here we are!« came the echoing answer from yet higher up, just as though they had flown on ahead.

»Oh, but it's all too wonderful to be true!« was the happy cry of the old oak. »Why, I've got them all here, big and little – not one has been forgotten. How ever can all this happiness be possible and imaginable?«

»Possible and imaginable in God's heaven,« came echoing back. And the tree, while still it grew, felt that its roots were loosening in the earth.

»This is the best of all,« said the tree. »Now there is nothing to keep me back. In light and splendour I can fly up to the Most High, and all those dear ones with me. Big and little, all of them with me.«

»All!«

That was the oak tree's dream and, while it was dreaming, a violent gale swept over land and sea that holy Christmas Eve. The sea flung heavy breakers on to the shore; the tree cracked, crashed and was torn up by the roots just as it dreamed that its roots were loosening. Down it fell. Its 365 years were now like a day for the day-fly.

When the sun came out on Christmas morning, the gale had gone down. The church-bells were ringing merrily; and from every chimney, on even the smallest cottage roof, the smoke rose blue as from the altar at a Druid's feast – the incense of gratitude. The sea turned calmer and calmer, and on a large vessel out there, which had weathered the storm in the night, every flag was being hoisted with a fine air of Christmas.

»The tree's gone!« cried the sailors. »The old oak – our landmark – it's come down in last night's gale. Who can find us such another? No one!«

That was the funeral sermon, short but well-meant, that the tree was given, as it lay stretched out upon the carpet of snow beside the beach; and away over it from the ship came the sound of a hymn, a song of Christmas joy and the saving of men's souls through Christ and the life eternal:

> Let hymn on hymn to heav'n succeed.
> Now man has all that man can need,
> great joy beyond comparing.
> Alleluia! Alleluia!

So ran the ancient hymn, and everyone there in the ship was uplifted in his own way by the hymn and its prayer, just as the old tree was uplifted in its last, its loveliest dream on Christmas Eve.

The Sprinters

There was a prize offered – in fact, two were offered, a big one and a small one – for the greatest speed shown, not in a single race but really for running all the year round.

»I got first prize,« said the hare. »There's bound to be fair play, if your own family and friends are judging. All the same, for the snail to get second prize – I take that as almost a personal insult.«

»Not at all,« maintained the gate-post, who had been present at the prizegiving. »A number of respectable people declared that hard work and determination must also be considered, and I too thought the same. It's true, the snail took six months to get across the doorstep, but he broke his leg in going so fast. He lived for nothing but his race, and he raced with his house on his back .... All this is very creditable, and so he got second prize.«

»I really can't see why *I* was left out of it,« said the swallow. »I don't believe there's anyone quicker at flying and swerving than I am, and just think how I travel about –far, far, far!«

»Exactly. That's the worst of you,« said the gate-post. »You gad about too much. You always have to be off somewhere, right out of the country, as soon as it gets cold here. You've no love of the land you were born in. There can be no question of *you* for a prize.«

»Well, but suppose I stayed back in the marsh all the winter,« said the swallow, »and slept the whole time away, should I then be considered for a prize?«

»Get a certificate from the marsh-woman that you've slept half the time in your mothercountry, and then you shall be considered.« »I really deserved first prize,« said the snail, »not second. As a matter of fact, I know the hare only sprinted from cowardice, every time he thought there was danger about. On the other hand, my running was a wholetime job, and it made me a cripple. If the first prize was to go to anyone, surely it was me – though I'm not making a fuss; I'd scorn to do that.« All it did was to spit.

»I am ready to pledge my word that every prize – or at any rate my vote for it – was awarded on fair grounds,« said the old boundary-post, who was a member of the judging committee. »I always proceed with method, deliberation and care. On seven previous occasions I have been privileged to take part in awarding the prize, but today is the first time I have got my way. At each distribution I have gone on a definite plan. I have always gone forward in the letters of the alphabet for the first prize, and backwards for the second. Now will you kindly notice that, going forward, the 8th letter from the beginning is H; there we have the Hare, so I voted for the Hare to have first prize. And the 8th letter from the end is S, so I voted for the Snail for second prize. Next time the letter I will get first prize, and R second ... There must always be method in everything; you must have something to keep to.«

»I should have voted for myself, you know, if I hadn't been one of the judges,« said the donkey, who was also on the committee. »You have to consider, not only the question of speed, but other qualities as well – a thing you see, like the size of the load you're pulling, though I wouldn't have stressed that on this occasion, nor the hare's shrewdness in escaping: the clever way in which it dodges to one side in order to throw pursuers off the track of its hiding-place. No, but there still remains one thing that many people think highly of and should never be forgotten: it's what is called 'the beautiful'. That's what I had an eye for in this case. I had an eye for the hare's beautiful, well-developed ears; it's a pleasure to see how

long they are. I felt I was looking at myself when I was small, and so I voted for him.«

»Hush!« said the fly. »No, I won't talk; I only want to say something. I know there's more than one hare that I've overtaken. The other day I broke the hind legs of one of the youngest. I was sitting on the engine in front of a railway train; I often do that, because in this way you get the best idea of your own speed. A young hare was running a long way in front of us; he had no idea that I was there. At last he had to swerve away, but in doing that he had his hind legs broken in two by the engine because I had settled there. The hare was left lying, while I dashed further ahead. Surely that's the same as beating him? Still, I don't want the prize.«

»Well, it seems to me,« thought the wild rose, only it didn't say so, for it isn't its nature to speak out, though it might have been a good thing if it had. »It seems to me that the sunbeam ought to have got first prize – and second prize too. It flies in a moment that enormous distance from the sun down to us and comes with such strength that all nature wakes up; and it has such beauty that we roses all blush and smell sweet because of it. That's something that the honourable adjudicators never seem to have noticed. If I was a sunbeam, I'd give each of them a good sunstroke – though that would only make them mad, which they may become anyhow. No, I won't say a thing,« thought the wild rose. »I prefer peace in the woods. It's wonderful to flower, to smell sweet, to be so refreshing, and to live in legend and song. Still the sunbeam will outlast us all.«

»What's the first prize?« asked the earth-worm, who had overslept and only just turned up.

»Free entrance to a kitchen garden,« said the donkey. »I suggested the prize. The hare was dead certain to win it; and so, as an active, thoughtful member of the committee, I paid due regard to how useful it might be to the winner. Well, now the hare's provided for. The snail's entitled to sit on the stone wall and lick off the moss and bask in the sun and, moreover, will in future be included as one of the chief judges in the sprint. It's a good thing to have one expert on what the humans call a committee. I must say, I'm extremely hopeful of the future, now that we've made such a good beginning.«

The Wicked Prince

(A legend)

There was once a wicked, arrogant Prince, whose one thought was to conquer every country in the world and strike terror with his name. On he swept with fire and sword. His soldiers trampled down the corn in the fields; they set farmhouses on fire, so that the red flames licked the leaves from the trees and scorched the fruit as it hung from its charred blackened branches. Many a poor mother hid with her naked nursling behind the smoking wall; and the soldiers searched for her and, if they found her with her baby, then their devilish game began – no evil spirits could have acted more shamefully ... Yet the Prince felt that all this was exactly as it should be. Every day his power increased; his name was dreaded by all, and fortune followed him in everything he did. From the captured cities he carried away gold and endless treasure; in his royal capital there were heaped up riches without parallel anywhere else in the world. And now he built magnificent palaces, churches and cloisters; and everyone who saw all this splendour used to say, »What a mighty Prince!« None gave a thought to the misery he had brought to other countries, none heard the wailing and lamentation that rose up from the burnt-down cities.

The Prince looked at his gold, looked at his sumptuous buildings, and thought, as the rest did, »What a mighty Prince! But I must have more, much more. No power must be named equal to mine, let alone greater.« And he went to war with all his neighbours and conquered them every one. He had the defeated Kings chained with gold shackles to his chariot, as he drove through the streets; and when he sat at table they had to lie at his feet and at the feet of his courtiers and eat the scraps of bread that were thrown to them.

The Prince now had his statue set up in the public squares and in the royal palaces. He even wanted it to stand in the churches before the holy altar; but the priests said, »Your Highness, you are great, but God is greater. We dare not do it.«

»All right!« said the wicked Prince. »Then I'll conquer God as well.«
And in the pride and foolishness of his heart he caused a fantastic ship to
be built, in which he could sail through the air. It was as gaily coloured
as a peacock's tail and seemed to be studded with a thousand eyes; but
every eye was a gun-barrel. The Prince sat amidships. He had only to press
a spring to fire a thousand bullets, and there were the guns ready loaded
again as before. Hundreds of lusty eagles were harnessed to the bows of
the ship, and in this way he now flew up towards the sun. The earth lay
far below. At first it looked, with its mountains and forests, merely like a
ploughed-up field, where a green plot peeps out from the turf that has
been rolled back; next, it resembled a plain ordnance map, and soon it
was completely veiled in mist and clouds. Higher and higher up flew the
eagles. Then God sent out a single one of his countless angels, and the
wicked Prince fired a thousand bullets at him; but the bullets fell back
like hail from the angel's shining wings. A drop of blood, only one,
dripped down from the white feathers, and this drop fell on the ship
where the Prince was sitting. It burnt itself fast into the ship; it was as
heavy as a thousand hundredweight of lead and sent the ship crashing
headlong towards the earth. The powerful wings of the eagles were

snapped in two; the wind whizzed about the Prince's head; and the clouds
all around, created no doubt from the cities he had burnt, massed themselves in threatening shapes like enormous crabs stretching their great
claws out after him, or like tumbling boulders, or fire-breathing dragons.
Half dead he lay in the ship, which at last was left hanging among the
stout branches of a wood.

»I *will* get the better of God!« cried the Prince. »I've sworn to do it; my
will shall prevail.« And for seven years he was building fantastic ships for
sailing through the air. He had thunderbolts forged from the toughest
steel, for he meant to blast a way into the fortress of heaven. From all his
lands he collected huge armies; ranged man to man, they covered a circuit
of many miles. They went on board their fantastic ships and just as the
Prince was approaching his, God sent out a swarm of gnats, a single little
swarm of gnats that buzzed about the Prince and stung his face and
hands. In his fury he drew his sword, but the empty air was all he slashed;
he couldn't get at the gnats. Then he ordered precious carpets to be
brought; these were to be wrapped round him, so that no gnat could
penetrate with its sting. And they did as he commanded. But a single gnat
found its way into the innermost carpet, and it crept into the Prince's ear

and stung him there. It burnt like fire, the poison flew to his brain. He wrenched himself free, flung off the carpets, tore his clothes to pieces and danced naked in front of his coarse brutal soldiers, that now jeered at their mad Prince who was bent on storming the gates of heaven and was mastered in a moment by one little gnat.

The Wind Tells the Story of Valdemar Daa* and His Daughters

When the wind sweeps over the grass, it ruffles it like water; and when it sweeps over the corn, it goes surging like the sea. That's the dance of the wind. But listen to it telling a story, singing it out so that it sounds quite differently in the forest trees from what it does through the holes and cracks and crevices of a wall. Look how the wind goes chasing the clouds up there like a flock of sheep! Hark how the wind down here howls through the open gates, like a watchman blowing his horn! That curious whistling down the chimney and into the fireplace, it makes the fire blaze and sparkle and shine all over the room, and how cosy and snug it is to sit listening here. Come on! Let the wind tell us a story. It knows more stories and fairy tales than the rest of us put together. Listen now to the way it begins.

»Hu-woosh! Let's be off!« That's the burden of the song.

»By the shore of the Great Belt stands an old country-house with thick red walls,« said the wind. »I know every brick in it; I saw it in the old days when it was part of Marsk Stig's estate on the headland. It had to be pulled down, but the bricks were put up again to make new walls for a new house on another spot; this was Borreby Manor, which is still standing.

I have seen and known the noble lords and ladies, the successive families, who have lived there; and now I'll tell you about Valdemar Daa and his daughters.

Full high he carried his head, for he was of royal descent. He could do

* pronounced DAW

more than just hunt a stag or drain a tankard. It will all come right, he used to say.

His wife walked stiffly in gold brocade across her polished parquet floor; the hangings were magnificent, the furniture costly and elaborately carved. She had brought gold and silver ware to the house; what beer there was in the cellar was German beer; fiery black horses neighed in the stables. They were well off at Borreby Manor – in their prosperous days.

And there were children: three fine young ladies, Ida, Joanna and Anna Dorothea – yes, I still remember their names.

They were rich people, society people, born in luxury and brought up in it. Huwoosh! Let's be off!« sang the wind, and went on with its story.

»I never saw here, as in other old manors, the high-born mistress sitting at the spinningwheel in the great hall with her maids. No, she would play on the sounding lute, and sing to it – yet not always the old Danish songs, but ballads in a foreign tongue. Here was life and hospitality, distinguished visitors from far and near. The music clanged, the glasses clinked, I couldn't drown the sound of them,« said the wind. »Here was pride, with boasting and bragging; goodliness, but not godliness.

And then – it happened to be the evening of May Day,« said the wind. »I was coming from the west; had seen ships founder and crash on the west coast of Jutland; had raced over the moors and the wooded coastline, away over the fields of Fyn; and now, panting and blowing, I crossed the Great Belt.

There I lay down to rest on the coast of Zealand near to Borreby Manor, where the woods were still standing with their splendid oaks.

The young farm-hands from the district came out and collected twigs and brushwood, the biggest and driest they could find. These they took into the town, piled in a heap and set fire to, and men and girls circled it with song and dance.«

»I lay still,« said the wind, »but softly I stirred one twig – the one that had been put on the fire by the handsomest youth. His wood blazed up, blazed highest; he was the chosen one to be given the name of honour, to become the May King and to have first choice among the girls for his May Queen. They had more fun and merry-making there in the town than there was up at the rich manor of Borreby.«

»Towards the manor, riding in a gilded coach drawn by six horses, came the great lady and her three daughters, three such fine graceful young blossoms: rose, lily and pale hyacinth. The mother herself was a flaunting tulip; not a single greeting did she return to the whole flock, as they stopped their play to cringe and curtsey before her. Her ladyship gave the impression of a flower decidedly stiff in the stalk.

Rose, lily and pale hyacinth – yes, I saw them all three. Whose 'queen'

will they be one day, I wondered. Their 'king' will be some haughty knight, maybe a prince. Huwoosh Let's be off! Let's be off!

And the coach carried them off, and the country folk carried on with their dancing. The coming of summer was fêted in Borreby, in Tjereby and all the villages around.«

»But at night, as I got up again,« said the wind, »the noble lady of the manor lay down, never to rise again; it befell her even as it befalls all mankind; there's nothing new in that. Valdemar Daa stood solemn and thoughtful a while. The proudest tree may bend and yet not break, he said to himself. The daughters wept, and at the manor all of them wiped their eyes; but the Lady Daa had gone her way – and I went mine. Huwoosh!« said the wind.

———————

»I came again, yes, often again, across the fields of Fyn and the waters of the Belt, and settled by Borreby Strand, by the glorious oak wood. There the osprey built its nest, and the wood-pigeons and the blue ravens and even the black stork. It was early in the year; some of the birds had eggs, and some already had young. My! How they fluttered and screamed at the sound of the axe, blow upon blow! The oaks were to be felled. Valdemar Daa meant to build a fine ship, a three-decker warship, that the King would be sure to buy; that's why the wood – a landmark for sailors, a home for the birds – must be felled. The shrike flew up in panic; its nest was destroyed. The osprey and all the woodland birds were losing their homes with nowhere to fly to, and they screamed in fear and anger. I understood them so well. Crows and rooks squawked loudly in mockery, 'Awa'! Awa'! Far! Far!'

In the middle of the wood, amongst a crowd of workmen, stood Valdemar Daa and his three daughters, laughing together at the frantic screaming of the birds. But the youngest daughter, Anna Dorothea, pitied them in her heart and, when they were also going to cut down a half-dead tree on whose naked branches the black stork had built its nest with the little young ones poking out their heads, she pleaded for it, pleaded with tears in her eyes. So the tree with the black stork's nest was allowed to stay; it wasn't much of a tree, anyhow.

There was hewing, there was sawing – and a three-decker was built. The architect was a man of humble origin, but of excellent parts. Eyes and forehead spoke of how clever he was, and Valdemar Daa enjoyed listening to him; so did little Ida, the eldest daughter, now fifteen. And as he built a ship for the father, he built a castle in the air for himself in which he and little Ida sat as man and wife; and this might have happened, too, if his castle had been made of bricks and mortar with moat and rampart, garden and wood. But with all his cleverness the architect hadn't any money, and what can a sparrow do among hawks? Hu-woosh!

I flew off and he flew off, for he didn't dare to stay. And little Ida got over it, because she had to.«

»The black horses neighed away in the stables; good they were to look at, and looked at they were. The admiral was sent straight from the King to see over the new man-of-war and go into the question of her sale. He spoke in great admiration of the fiery horses. I heard it all distinctly,« said the wind. »I went with the gentlemen through the open door and scattered straw like bars of gold before their feet. Valdemar Daa wanted gold, the admiral wanted the black horses; that was why he praised them so much. But the point was missed, and so the ship wasn't sold either. There she lay gleaming on the shore, covered in with planks, a Noah's Ark that never took the water. Hu-woosh! Let's be off! Let's be off! What a pity!«

»In wintertime,« said the wind, »when the fields were covered with snow and the Belt was full of drift-ice that I pressed up against the coast, then ravens and crows came in large flocks, each one blacker than the other. They perched on the lifeless, deserted, lonely ship on the shore and croaked in hoarse cries of the vanished wood and the many fine bird's-nests that had been laid waste and of the old and young ones that were now homeless – all this for the sake of that rubbishy great vessel, the proud ship that would never go to sea.

I whirled up a blizzard, and the snow piled like heavy seas around and over the ship. I let her hear my voice – hear what a gale has to say. I did what I could, I'm sure, to teach her navigation. Hu-woosh! Let's be off! Let's be off!

And winter whirled along; winter, and then summer, they whirled along – and still whirl, as I whirl, as the snow drifts, and the appleblossom drifts, and the leaves fall. Let's be off, off, off!' And mankind with us!

But the daughters were still young, and Ida a rose as lovely to look at as when the architect used to see her. Often I would take hold of her long brown hair as she stood by the apple tree in the garden so lost in thought that she never noticed I was sprinkling blossoms on her flowing hair, while she gazed at the red sun and the golden space of sky between the dark shrubs and trees in the garden.

Her sister Joanna was like a lily, straight and elegant; full of airs and graces and 'stiff in the stalk', like her mother. She liked walking in the great hall, where the family portraits hung. The ladies were shown in velvet and silk, with a tiny little hat embroidered with pearls on their braided hair. They were fine-looking women. Their husbands were there in steel or a valuable cloak lined with squirrel's fur and the blue ruff; they wore the sword strapped to the thigh, not buckled at the hip. Where would Joanna's portrait one day hang on the wall? And what would her noble husband look like? Yes, those were her thoughts and the things she muttered to herself; I heard them, as I rushed through the long gallery into the hall and then turned back.

Anna Dorothea, the pale hyacinth, a child of only fourteen, was quiet and thoughtful. There was a wistful look in her pale-blue eyes, though a child's smile still hovered round her lips; I couldn't blow that away, and I didn't want to either.

I used to meet her in the garden, the sunken lane and in the fields, as she gathered herbs and flowers. She knew her father could use these for the potions and drops that he knew how to distil. Valdemar Daa was haughty and cocksure, but he was also skilled and experienced. That was obvious enough and was the cause of some murmuring. Fire burnt in his stove even in summertime; the door of his room was locked, and this went on for days and nights together; but he said little about it. The forces of nature must be mastered in silence; soon enough he meant to discover how to make the best thing of all – the red gold.

That's why the chimney was always smoking, the reason for the roaring and the flaming. And I was there, too,« said the wind. »'Give over! Give over!' I sang down the chimney. 'It will all end in smoke, vapour and ashes. You'll burn yourself up. Hu-woosh! Give over! Give over!' But Valdemar Daa did not give over.

The splendid horses in the stables – what became of them? What became of the gold and silver ware in cupboard and chest, the cows on field, estate and farm? Yes, they could melt, melt in the crucible, and yet no gold come.

It was empty in barn and pantry, in cellar and loft. Fewer servants, but more mice. One window would crack, another break; no need for me to go in by the door,« said the wind. »Where the chimney's smoking the dinner's cooking. Yes, the chimney smoked, but it gobbled up all the food – for the red gold.

I blew through the manor gate like a watchman blowing his horn, but there was no watchman,« said the wind. »I turned the weathercock on the tower, and it grated like the snoring of the watchman; but there was no watchman – only rats and mice. Poverty laid the table, poverty sat in the wardrobe and the larder. The door came off its hinges, cracks and crevices appeared, and in and out I went,« said the wind, »so I know what I'm talking about.

Smoke and ashes, sorrow and sleepless nights turned his hair grey on beard and forehead, his skin yellow and muddy-looking. His eyes peered greedily after gold, the longed-for gold.

I puffed smoke and ashes into his face and beard; instead of gold came debts. I sang through the broken panes and the gaping crevices, blew in to where the daughters' clothes lay faded and shabby on their folding beds, because now their clothes had to last. That song was never sung at the cradle of these children. A lowly life became a life of misery. I was the only one to sing out loud at the manor,« said the wind. »I snowed them up; people say that keeps you warm. They had no firewood, and the forest they might have fetched it from had been cut down. There was a hard frost. I danced through loopholes and galleries, over gable and wall, to keep myself nimble. They were lying in bed because of the cold, Valdemar's noble daughters; their father huddled under his leather counterpane. Not a thing to bite or burn – there's a lordly life for you! Huwoosh! Give over! But that's just what Sir Valdemar couldn't do.

'Spring follows winter', he said. 'Good times follow bad – though they do keep you waiting, waiting ... Now my whole manor is mortgaged, the eleventh hour has come, and gold will be here – at Easter!'

I heard him mumble into the spider's web, 'You clever little weaver, you've taught me to keep going. Your web may be torn to pieces, you start all over again and remake it entirely. Once more it's demolished – and undismayed you set to work again from the beginning, from the beginning. That's the way to do it – and it pays.'

It was Easter morning. The bells were ringing, and the sunshine was playing in the sky. In a fever-heat he had sat up, boiling and cooling, mixing and distilling. I heard him sigh like a soul in despair, I heard him pray, I saw how he caught his breath. The lamp had gone out, but he never noticed it. I blew on the embers and they shone into his ashen face, giving it a tinge of colour; his eyes, shrunk into their deep sockets, now grew larger and larger as though they would burst.

There, look at the alchemist's glass! There's a gleam inside it, a pure and heavy glow. With quaking hand he raised it, with quivering tongue he shouted. 'Gold! Gold!' and grew dizzy – I could have blown him over,« said the wind; »but I only blew on the glowing coal and followed him in

through the door to where his daughters sat and shivered. His coat was covered with ashes; they clung to his beard and his matted hair. He stood up straight and lifted his precious treasure in the brittle glass. 'Gold! Gold! Found at last!' he shouted, held up the glass as it glittered in the sunlight ... and it fell from his trembling hand to the floor and burst into a thousand pieces. Burst, too, was the last bubble of his hoped prosperity. Huwoosh! Let's be off! ... And away I flew from the alchemist's manor.

Late in the year, when the days are shortening and the mist comes with its sponge to squeeze out drops of moisture on the red berries and the leafless branches, I came back cheerfully with a breath of fresh air and swept the sky clean and snapped off the rotten branches. That's not very hard work, but it has to be done. There was also a clean sweep of a different kind, at Valdemar Daa's inside Borreby Manor. His old enemy, Ove Ramel of Basnæs, was there with a mortgage he had purchased on the house and furniture. I drummed on the cracked panes, slammed the ramshackle doors, whistled through the cracks and crevices – Hu-ee! Ove Ramel must not be encouraged to stay there. Ida and Anna Dorothea cried bitterly, Joanna stood erect and pale, biting her thumb until it bled – but what was the good of that? Ove Ramel agreed to Valdemar Daa's staying on at the manor as long as he lived, but he got no thanks for the offer. I was listening, and I saw the homeless nobleman hold up his head and toss it more proudly; and I loosed a squall against the house and the old lime trees, so that the thickest branch snapped, though it wasn't rotten. It lay in front of the gate like a broom, in case there was any sweeping out to be done; and a sweeping out there was. I thought it would come.

It was a stern day, a hard time to hold out; but their mood was stern, their hearts were hard.

They had nothing they could call their own but the clothes they were wearing. Well, yes, there was the alchemist's glass that had lately been bought and filled with the wasted bits scraped up from the floor – the treasure of so much promise that was not fulfilled. Valdemar Daa put it away in his bosom, took his stick in his hand, and the one-time wealthy squire walked with his three daughters out of Borreby Manor. I blew cold on his burning cheeks, I stroked his grey beard and his long white hair, I sang at full blast – hu-woosh! Let's be off! Let's be off! ... That was the end of their wealth and splendour.

Ida and Anna Dorothea walked on either side of him. Joanna turned round in the gateway. What was the point of that? There was no chance of their luck turning. She looked at the red-bricked walls of what had once been Marsk Stig's castle – was she thinking of his daughters?

'The eldest took the youngest's hand,
and forth they fared to a distant land.'

Was she thinking of that old ballad? Well, here they were three, and their father with them. They walked along the road where they had once driven in their coach; they walked like beggars with their father to Smidstrup Common, to the mud-and-wattle house which was let to them for ten pounds a year. This, with its bare walls and bare cupboards, was their new mansion. Crows and jackdaws flew above them, squawking as though in mockery, 'Get awa'! Get awa'! Far! Far!' just as the birds did in Borreby Wood, when the trees were being cut down.

Valdemar Daa and his daughters heard it of course; but I blew in their ears – it was better for them not to listen.

So they moved into the mud-and-wattle cottage on Smidstrup Common ... and I tore away over marsh and meadow, through naked hedges and leafless forest, to open waters and other lands, Hu-woosh! Let's be off! Let's be off! – for years and years.«

How did it go with Valdemar Daa? How did it go with his daughters? The wind will tell us.

»The last I saw of them – yes, the very last – it was Anna Dorothea, the pale hyacinth. By now she was old and bent; it was fifty years later. She lived longest, and she knew the whole story.

Across the heath, by Viborg town, stood the Dean's handsome new deanery with red bricks and stepped gables; a thick smoke was rising from the chimney. His gentle wife sat with her pretty daughters in the bay-window, looking out over the box hedge in the garden across the brown heath. What was it they were looking for? They were looking for the stork's nest out there on that tumble-down cottage. The roof – what there was of it – was all moss and house-leek; it was the stork's nest that did most of the roofing and gave the only help there was, for the stork himself kept it in repair.

That's a better house to look at than to touch; I must go gingerly,« said the wind. »For the stork's sake the house was allowed to remain, though of course it was an eyesore on the heath. The Dean and his family didn't want to drive away the stork, and so the hovel was left standing, and the poor creature who lived there was allowed to stay. She had the Egyptian

bird to thank for that; or was it gratitude for her having once upon a time pleaded for his frantic black brother's nest in Borreby Wood? Poor thing, she was then a young child, a delicate pale hyacinth in nobility's garden. She remembered it all, did Anna Dorothea.

»'Heigh-ho!'« – yes, humans can sigh, just as the wind does in the reeds and rushes. »'Heigh-ho! There were no bells rung for your burial, Valdemar Daa, no poor schoolboys to sing when Borreby's one-time lord of the manor was laid to earth. Heigh-ho! Everything ends in time, even misery. Sister Ida became the wife of a peasant; that was the sorest trial for our father. His daughter to be married to a miserable serf, whom his lord and master could order astride the wooden horse. Now I suppose he's dead and buried. And you too, Ida? ... Ah, yes, but it isn't all over yet. Poor me! There's still poor old penniless me. Call me home, rich Christ!'«

That was Anna Dorothea's prayer in the miserable hut that was left standing for the sake of the stork.

»I looked after the strongest of the sisters,« said the wind. »She cut her clothes according to her cloth. She went on board as a fellow who was hard-up and signed on for the voyage with the skipper. She was a creature of few words, rather sulky-looking, though a willing worker. But she couldn't climb; so I blew her overboard before they found out that she was a woman, and no doubt it was just as well that I did,« said the wind.

»It was an Easter morning – as it was when Valdemar Daa imagined he had discovered the red gold – when I heard a hymn being sung within the rickety walls below the stork's nest; it was Anna Dorothea's last song.

There was no window, but only a gap in the wall, into which the sun came and settled like a nugget of gold – what brilliance! Her eyes grew dim, her heart gave out, as indeed they must have done, even had the sun not shone on her that morning.

The stork gave her a roof to die under. I sang at her grave,« said the wind. »I sang at her father's grave; I know where it is and where hers is, but no one else does.

New times, different times! Old roads merge in enclosed fields, hallowed graves become busy highways; and soon we shall have steam with its row of carriages roaring along over the graves, now as forgotten as the names they bear. Hu-woosh! Let's be off!

Well, there's the story of Valdemar Daa and his daughters. Tell it better, you others, if you can,« said the wind, and turned – and was gone.

The Girl Who Trod
on the Loaf

I expect you've heard of the girl who trod on the loaf so as not to dirty her shoes, and of how she came to a bad end. The story's been written, and printed too.

She was a poor child, proud and vain; there was a bad streak in her, as the saying is. When quite a little child she enjoyed catching flies and pulling off their wings, so making creeping things of them. She would take a cockchafer and a beetle, stick each of them on a pin, and then place a green leaf or a little bit of paper up against their feet. The poor creature would hold on tight to it, turning and twisting it to try and get off the pin.

»Now the cockchafer's reading,« said little Inger. »Look how it's turning over the page.«

As she grew older, she got worse rather than better; but she was very pretty, and that was her misfortune, for otherwise she'd have been slapped a good deal oftener than she was.

»It'll need a desperate remedy to cure *your* disease,« said her own mother. »Often, when you were little, you trod on my apron; now you're older, I'm afraid you'll end by treading on my heart.«

And, sure enough, she did.

She now went out to service with a good family who lived in the country. They treated her as if she was their own child and dressed her in the same way; she was very goodlooking, and she grew vainer than ever.

After she had been with them for a year, her mistress said to her. »Don't you think you ought to go some time and see your parents, Inger dear?«

So she went, though it was only to show herself off and let them see how fine she had become. But when she got to the outskirts of the town and saw some girls and young fellows gossiping together by the pond

and her mother, too, resting on a stone with a bundle of faggots she had gathered in the wood, she felt ashamed that she who was so finely dressed should have a mother who went about in rags collecting sticks. She wasn't in the least sorry at having to turn back; she was only annoyed.

And now another six months went by.

»You really ought to go home one day and see your old father and mother, Inger dear,« said her mistress. »Look – here's a big white loaf; you can take that with you. They'll be so glad to see you.«

So Inger put on her best things and her new shoes, and she caught up her skirt and looked well where she was going, so as to keep her shoes nice and clean; and of course she couldn't be blamed for that. But when she came to where the path led across marshy ground and there was a long strip of puddles and slush, she flung the loaf down into the mud, so as to tread on this and get across without wetting her shoes. But as she stood with one foot on the loaf and lifted the other, the loaf sank down with her deeper and deeper, and she disappeared altogether, till there was nothing to be seen but a black bubbling swamp.

That's the story.

What became of her? She came down to the marsh-woman, who goes in for brewing. The marsh-woman is aunt to the elf-maids; they are well enough known – they've had ballads written about them and pictures drawn of them. But all that people know about the marsh-woman is that, when the meadows are steaming in summer, that's the marsh-woman brewing. It was down into her brewery that Inger sank, and that's not a place you can stand for long. A cesspit is a gay palatial apartment compared with the marsh-woman's brewery. Every vat stinks enough to make a man faint and, besides, the vats are all pressed up against each other; and if there is somewhere a little gap between them through which you might squeeze yourself out, you can't do it because of all the slimy toads and fat snakes that get entangled here together. This was where Inger sank down. All that nasty living mess was so icy cold that she shuddered in every limb, and it made her more and more stiff and numb. The loaf still clung to her feet and dragged her on, just as an amber button may drag a bit of straw.

The marsh-woman was at home; the brewery that day was being inspected by the Devil and his great-grandmother, an extremely venomous old female who is never idle. She never goes out without her needlework, and she had it with her now. She had her pin-cushion with her, so as to give people pins and needles in their legs. She embroidered lies and did crochet from rash remarks that had fallen to the ground – anything, in fact, that could lead to injury and corruption. Oh yes, she knew all about sewing, embroidery and crochet work did old great-granny.

She caught sight of Inger, put on her spectacles and then had another look at her. »That's a girl with talent,« she said. »I'd like her as a memento of my visit here. She will do very well as a statue for my great-grandson's entrance-hall.«

And she got her. In this way Inger came to hell. People can't always go straight down, but they can get there by a roundabout way if they have talent.

It was an entrance-hall that never seemed to end. It made you giddy to look ahead and giddy to look back. And then there was a forlorn crowd waiting for the door of mercy to be opened; they might have to wait a long time. Great fat waddling spiders spun a thousand-year web over their feet, and these toils cut into the feet like screws and clamped them like copper chains; and, added to this, there was a never-ending disquiet in every soul, a disquiet that was itself a torment. Among them was the miser who had lost the key of his safe and now remembered he had left it in the lock. But there – it would take too long to go through all the different pains and torments that were felt there. Inger felt that it was ghastly to be standing as a statue; she was just as though riveted from below to the loaf.

»This comes of taking care to keep your shoes clean,« she said to herself. »Look how they're staring at me« – and, it's true, they were all looking at her. Their evil passions gleamed from their eyes and spoke silently from the corners of their mouths; they were a horrible sight.

»I must be delightful to look at,« thought Inger. »I have a pretty face and nice clothes,« and then she turned her eyes – her neck was too stiff for that to be turned. Goodness, how dirty she had got in the marsh-woman's brewhouse! She hadn't thought of that. Her clothes seemed to be smeared over with one great blotch of slime; a snake had got caught in her hair and was dangling down her neck, and from each fold in her dress a toad peeped out with a croak like the bark of a wheezy pug-dog. It was most unpleasant. »Still,« she consoled herself, »the others down here really look just as dreadful.«

Worst of all was the terrible hunger she felt. Couldn't she at least stoop down and break off a bit of the loaf she was standing on? No, for her back had stiffened, her arms and hands had stiffened, her whole body was like a stone pillar; all she could turn were the eyes in her head, turn them right round, so that they could see backwards – and that was a ghastly sight, that was. Then the flies came and crawled over her eyes, to and fro. She blinked her eyes, but the flies didn't fly away; they couldn't, because their wings had been pulled off and they had become creeping things. That was torment for her, and as for her hunger – well, at last she felt that her innards were eating themselves up, and she became quite empty inside, so appallingly empty.

»If it goes on much longer, I shan't be able to bear it,« she said; but she had to bear it, and it still went on.

Then a burning tear fell on her head. It trickled down her face and breast right down to the loaf. Another tear fell – and many more beside. Who was it crying over Inger? Well, hadn't she up on earth a mother? Sorrowing tears that a mother sheds for her child will always reach it, but

they don't set it free; they burn, they only make the torment greater. And now this unbearable hunger – and not to be able to get at the loaf she was treading with her foot! At last she got a feeling that everything inside her must have eaten itself up. She was like a thin hollow reed that drew every sound inside it. She could hear distinctly everything up on earth that concerned her, and what she heard was harsh and spiteful. Her mother, to be sure, wept in deep sorrow, but she added, »Pride goes before a fall – that was your misfortune, Inger. How you have grieved your mother!«

Her mother and all the others up there knew about her sin, how she had trodden on the loaf and had sunk down and disappeared. The cowherd had told them, for he had seen it all himself from the slope.

»How you have grieved your mother, Inger!« said the mother. »Yes, and I always felt you would.«

»I wish I had never been born,« thought Inger. »It would have been far better. What's the good now of my mother snivelling like that?«

Inger heard how her master and mistress were speaking, those two good-natured people who had been like father and mother to her: »She was a wicked child,« they said. »She had no respect for God's gifts, but trod them underfoot; the door of mercy will be hard for her to open.«

»They should have corrected me more often,« thought Inger, »cured me of my bad ways if I had any.«

She heard that a whole ballad about her had been brought out – *The proud young girl who trod on the loaf to save her pretty shoes* – and it was sung all over the country.

»To think of being blamed so much for it and suffering so much for it,« thought Inger. »Why aren't the others punished for what they've done? Yes, and what a lot there would be to punish! Ooh, how I'm tormented!«

And her heart grew even harder than her shell.

»I shall never get any better while I'm down here in this company, and I don't want to get any better. Look how they're glaring.«

And she felt angry and vicious towards all mankind.

»Now I dare say they'll have something to talk about up there – ooh, how I'm tormented!«

And she heard them telling her story to the children, and the little ones called her Wicked Inger. »She was so horrid,« they said, »so nasty, she deserves to be well punished.«

There were nothing but hard words against her in children's mouths.

And yet one day, as hunger and resentment were gnawing deep in her hollow shell and she heard her name mentioned and her story told to an innocent child, a small girl, she noticed that the little one burst into tears at the story of the proud Inger and her love of finery.

»But won't she ever come up again?« asked the small girl. And she was told, »No, she'll never come up again.«

»Yes, but if she will ask to be forgiven and promise never to do it again?«

»But she won't ask to be forgiven,« they told the child.

»Oh, I do wish she would,« said the little girl, and refused to be comforted. »I'll give up my doll's house, if they let her come up. It's so horrible for poor Inger.«

These words went right down into Inger's heart; they seemed to do her good. It was the first time anyone had said »poor Inger« without adding the least thing about her faults. An innocent little child cried and pleaded for her; it gave her such a queer feeling that she would like to have cried herself, but she couldn't cry, and that too was a torment.

As the years passed by up there – there were no changes below – she heard sounds from above less often and there was less talk about her. Then one day she heard a sigh, »Inger, Inger, what sorrow you have

brought me! I always said you would.« It was her mother dying.

Sometimes she heard her name mentioned by her old master and mistress, and the mildest remark was when the housewife said, »I wonder if I shall ever see you again, Inger, There's no knowing what may become of one.«

But Inger knew well enough that her honest mistress never could come where she was.

In that way another long and bitter time went by. Then Inger again heard her name spoken and saw above what seemed to be two bright stars shining. They were two gentle eyes that were closing on earth. So many years had passed since the time when the small girl cried inconsolably for »poor Inger« that the child had now become an old woman, whom God would soon be calling to himself; and at that very moment, when the thoughts of her whole life were rising before her, she also remembered how as a little child she couldn't help crying bitterly when she heard the story about Inger. That time and the impression it made on her stood so vividly before the old woman in her hour of death that she burst out aloud, »Lord, my God, haven't I too, like Inger, sometimes trodden thoughtlessly on the blessings you gave? Haven't I, too, gone with pride in my heart? And yet you, in your mercy, did not let me sink, held me up. Do not abandon me in my last hour.«

And her old eyes closed, and the soul's eyes opened to what lies hidden; and as Inger was there so vividly in her last thoughts, she saw Inger – saw to what depths she had been dragged down – and at the sight of her the

saintly soul burst into tears. She stood like a child in the kingdom of
heaven and wept for poor Inger; her tears and prayers rang like an echo
down into the hollow empty shell that hemmed in the imprisoned tormented soul, and it was overcome by all this undreamed affection from
above. To think that an angel of God should be weeping for her! Why
was she granted this favour? The tortured soul seemed to gather up into
its thoughts every deed it had ever done in its life on earth, and it shook
with weeping; Inger could never have wept like that. She was filled with
sorrow for herself, and she felt that never could the gate of mercy be
opened for her. As in her contrite heart she realized this, at that moment a
beam of light flashed down into the bottomless pit – a beam stronger
even than the sunbeam that thaws the snowman made by the boys in the
yard. Then, far quicker than the snowflake falling on a child's warm lips
melts away to a drop, Inger's stiffened stony figure evaporated; a little
bird soared like forked lightning up towards the world of men. But it was
timid and shy of everything near; it felt ashamed of itself in the sight of
all living creatures and hurriedly looked for shelter in a dark hole, and
found it in a crumbling wall. Here it perched cowering and trembling all
over without uttering a sound, for it had no voice. It stayed there a long
while before it felt calm enough to see and appreciate all the beauty that
lay before it. Yes, indeed, beauty there was. The air was so fresh and
genial, the moon shone so bright, trees and shrubs smelt sweet; and then
the spot where it perched was so cosy, its feather coat so clean and delicate. What a revelation of love and splendour in all created things! All
the thoughts stirring in the heart of the bird strove to find utterance in
song, but the bird didn't know how. It would have liked to sing as the
cuckoo and nightingale do in spring. God, who also hears the worm's
silent song of praise, hearkened now to the song of praise that rose in har-
monies of thought, just as a psalm used to ring in David's heart before it
found words and music.

For days and weeks these noiseless songs grew and grew; surely they must break out at the first beat of wings in a good deed; such a deed must now be done.

The holy festival of Christmas was here. The farmer put up a pole close against the wall and tied on it an unthreshed bundle of oats, so that the birds of the air might also have a merry Christmas and a cheerful dinner at this season of the Saviour's.

And the sun rose up on Christmas morning and shone on to the sheaf of oats, and all the twittering birds flew round the dinnerpole. Then, too, a »tweet, tweet!« sounded from the wall. The swelling thought turned into sound; the feeble chirp became a whole paean of joy. The idea of a good deed had awakened, and the bird flew out from its hiding-place. In heaven they knew well enough the kind of bird it was.

Winter began in earnest, the waters were frozen deep, and birds and forest animals were often pinched for food. The little bird flew along the high road and there in the tracks of the sledges it managed to find, in places, a grain of corn. At coaching inns it might come across a few breadcrumbs, but would only eat one of these and then let all the other famishing sparrows know that here they could find food. It also flew to the towns, scouted around, and wherever a kind hand had scattered crumbs from the window for the birds, it ate only a single crumb itself and gave the rest to the others.

In the course of the winter the bird had collected and given away so many crumbs that the weight of them all would have equalled that of the whole loaf that Inger had trodden on so as not to dirty her shoes; and when the last crumb had been found and given away, the bird's grey wings turned white and spread themselves out.

»Look! There's a tern flying off across the lake,« cried the children who saw the white bird. First, it dipped down on to the lake, then it rose into the bright sunshine; the bird was so dazzling white that there was no chance of seeing what became of it. They said that it flew straight into the sun.

The Butterfly

The butterfly wanted to find himself a sweetheart. Of course, one of the nice little flowers was what he wanted. So he had a look at them. Each sat so quietly and modestly on her stalk, just as a young lady should sit, when she's not yet engaged. But what a lot there were to choose from! This was a difficulty the butterfly didn't know how to get over, and so he fluttered off to the daisy. The French call her Marguérite, for they know she can tell fortunes – and she does, too. Lovers pick off her petals one by one, and with each of them they ask a question about their sweetheart: »She loves me – she doesn't – she may do – she won't – she would if she could, but she can't« – or something like that. Everyone asks in his own language, and so the butterfly also came to ask. He didn't pull off the petals, but gave each of them a kiss, his idea being that kindness pays best in the long run.

»Chère Marguérite,« he said, »you are the wisest woman among all the flowers. You can tell fortunes. Please tell me – which am I to have? This one, or that one, or which one? Directly I know, I can fly straight along to her and begin courting.«

But the daisy never answered a word. She couldn't bear him to call her a woman; for, you see, a woman would be a 'Mrs', and she was a 'Miss'. He asked her a second time and he asked her a third time; and as he couldn't get a single word out of her, he gave up asking her any more, but flew off courting again.

It was early spring; there were masses of snowdrops and crocuses. »They're very pretty,« said the butterfly. »Sweet little things who have just come out, though rather colourless.« Like all young men, he had an eye for older girls. Then he flew away to the anemones, but found them a trifle bitter in their outlook; the violets rather too romantic; the tulips too showy; the daffodils too suburban; the lime blossoms too small – and, besides, they had such a lot of relations. The apple blossoms certainly looked like roses, but they were here today and gone tomorrow at the least breath of wind; he felt that would be too short a marriage altogether. The sweet pea was the one he liked best; she was red and white, and so delicate and refined. She was one of those domesticated girls who are both good-looking and good in the kitchen. He was just going to propose her, when suddenly close by him, be caught sight of a pea-pod with a dead flower hanging on the end of it. »Who's that?« he asked. »It's my sister,« said the sweet pea.

»Oh, I see. So that's what you'll look like later on, is it?« This rather scared the butterfly, and so off he flew.

There was some honeysuckle hanging over the fence, with a lot of those girls that have long faces and sallow complexions. They weren't at all his type. Well, but what sort did he like? You'd better ask him yourself.

Spring passed, summer passed, and now it was autumn. He was no nearer making up his mind. And the flowers now put on their loveliest dresses, but what was the good of that? The fresh fragrance of youth had all gone. Fragrance it is that the heart's in search of, as the years go by; and it can't be said there's much of that in dahlias and hollyhocks. So the butterfly flew down to the mint.

»She hasn't any blossom, I know, but she's a whole flower in herself, scented from root to crown, with fragrance in every leaf. She's the one I'll choose.«

And so at last he proposed.

But the mint stood stiff and silent, and at last she said. »Friendship, but nothing more! I am old, and you are old. I dare say we might live for one another, but marry – no! Don't let's make fools of ourselves at our time of life.«

So the butterfly got no one at all.. He had been too 'choosy', and that doesn't do. The butterfly remained a bachelor, as they're called.

It was late autumn, wet and gusty. The old willows creaked as the wind sent shivers down their backs. This was no time to gad about in summer clothes – you might be sorry you did, as they say – but the butterfly wasn't out of doors. He happened to have come inside, where there was a fire burning; proper summertime warmth it was. Yes, here he could live. But, »just living is not enough,« he said. »One must have sunshine, freedom and a little flower.«

Then he flew against the window-pane, where he was seen, admired and stuck on a pin in a box of curios. Could more have been done for him?

»Well, here I am on a stalk just like the flowers,« said the butterfly. »I can't say it's altogether comfortable. I expect it's like being married: you're certainly pinned down then!« And the thought consoled him.

»Rather a poor consolation,« said the pot-plants in the parlour.

»Still, pot-plants aren't always to be trusted« thought the butterfly. »They have too much to do with human beings.«

Dad's Always Right

Now listen! I'm going to tell you a story I heard when I was a boy. Since then the story seems to have become nicer every time I've thought about it. You see, stories are like a good many people – they get nicer and nicer as they grow older, and that is so pleasant.

Of course you've been in the country, haven't you? You know what a real old farmhouse looks like, with a thatch roof all grown over with moss and weeds and a stork's nest perched on the ridge – we can't do without the stork – and crooked walls and low-browed windows, only one of which will open. The oven pokes out its fat little stomach; and the elder-bush leans over the fence, where there's a little pond with a duck or some ducklings, just under the wrinkled willow-tree. Yes, and then there's a dog on a chain that keeps barking at all and sundry.

Well, that's just the sort of farmhouse there was out in the country, and two people lived in it, a farmer and his wife. They had little enough of their own, and yet there was one thing they could do without: that was a horse which used to graze along the roadside ditch. Father would ride it into town, the neighbours would borrow it, and of course one good turn deserved another; and yet they felt it would pay them better to sell the horse or to change it for something else that might be still more use to them. But whatever was it to be?

»You'll know best, Dad!« said his wife. »It's market-day today, so you just ride into town and get some money for the horse or else change it for something good. What you do is always right. Now ride along to market!«

And then she tied on his necktie – she knew how to do that better than he did – and she tied it in a double bow; it did look smart. And she brushed his hat with the flat of her hand and gave him a nice warm kiss, and then away he rode on the horse that he was either to sell or exchange. Yes, depend upon it, Dad knew.

There was a burning sun and not a cloud in the sky. The road was full of dust, there were such a lot of people driving and riding to market or going there on Shanks' pony. It was scorching hot, and there wasn't a scrap of shade on the road.

A man came along driving a cow – you couldn't imagine a finer cow. »I'll bet she gives lovely milk,« said the farmer to himself, thinking what a good exchange it would make. »I say, you with the cow,« he called out, »I'd like to have a word with you. Now look here, I suppose a horse is really worth more than a cow. But, never mind, I've more use for a cow. Will you change over?«

»You bet I will!« said the man with the cow. And so they changed over.

Well, now the deal was done, and the farmer might just as well have turned back. After all, he had done what he wanted; but then, you see, he had made up his mind to go to market, and so to market he would go, if only to have a look at it. So on he went with his cow. He quickened his pace, and so did the cow, and presently they found themselves walking alongside a man who was driving a sheep. It was a good sheep, in good condition and with a good fleece.

»I could do with that sheep, I could,« thought the farmer. »It would find plenty of grazing at the side of our ditch, and in the winter we could bring it into the house. Really, when you come to think of it, we'd do better to keep a sheep than a cow. Shall we do a swop?« he asked.

Yes, the man who had the sheep was quite ready to do that; and so the bargain was struck, and the farmer went on with his sheep down the road. There, by a stile, he saw a man with a big goose under his arm.

»That's a plump 'un you've got there!« said the farmer. »It's got both feathers and flesh; that'd look well if we kept it by our little pond. It'd be something Mother could save her scraps for. She's often said: 'If only we had a goose!' Well, now she can have one – and she *shall* have one! Will you do a swop? I'll give you the sheep for the goose – and a thankee as well.« The other man said yes, he didn't mind if he did, and so they made the exchange; the farmer got the goose.

As he neared the town, the traffic on the road got bigger and bigger; there was a swarm of people and cattle, stretching over road and ditch right up to the toll-keeper's potatoes, where his hen was kept shut in so as not to take fright and go astray and get lost. It was a bob-tailed, good-looking hen, that winked with one eye. »Cluck, cluck!« she said. What her idea may have been, I can't say; but the farmer's idea, when he saw her, was: »she's the finest hen I've ever seen; she's finer than Parson's broodhen. I could do with that hen, I could. A hen will always find a bit o' corn; she can almost take care of herself. I reckon it's a good exchange if I get her for the goose. »What do you say to a swop?« he asked. »Swop?« answered the other. »Why, yes, that's not at all a bad idea.« And so they

changed over; the tollkeeper got the goose, and the farmer got the hen.

He had done such a lot of things on his way to town, and it was a warm day and he was tired. He felt he could do with a drop to drink and a morsel to eat. He had now reached the inn and, just as he was about to enter, there was the ostler coming out, and he met him right in the doorway carrying a bag that was brimful of something.

»What's that you've got there?« asked the farmer.

»Rotten apples,« answered the ostler. »A whole sackful for the pigs.«

»Why, what a tremendous lot! I do wish Mother could see that. Last year we only had one solitary apple on the old tree by the coal-shed. That apple had to be kept, and it lay on the chest of drawers till it burst. 'That looks so prosperous', said Mother. Well, here's a prosperous sight for her – how I wish she could se it!«

»What'll you give me?« asked the ostler.

»Give? I'll give you my hen in exchange.«

And so he gave him the hen, got the apples in exchange and went into the taproom straight up to the bar. His sack with the apples he leaned against the stove, without noticing that the fire was alight. He found a number of strangers in the room - horsedealers, cattle-dealers and two Englishmen; these two were so rich that their pockets were bursting with gold. And the way they bet – you just listen to this.

S-s-s! S-s-s! What was that they could hear beside the stove? The apples were beginning to roast. »Whatever is it?« they asked. Well, they very soon heard. They were given the whole story of the horse which was changed for the cow, and so on right down to the rotten apples.

»Well, well! Your missus'll warm your ears for you, when you get home!« said the Englishmen; »there'll be a fine set-out.«

»No, she won't, she'll give me a kiss,« said the farmer. »She'll say: Dad's always right!«

»Shall we have a bet?« they asked. »Golden sovereigns by the barrel – a hundred pounds to the hundredweight!«

»Make it a bushel – that'll be enough,« said the farmer; »I can only put up a bushel of apples, with myself and the missus thrown in. After all, that's more than full measure – that's heaped measure.«

»Done!« they answered, and the bet was made.

The innkeeper brought out his cart; the Englishmen got in, the farmer got in, the rotten apples got in, and soon they all came to the farmer's house.

»Good evening, Mother.«

»Good evening, Dad!«

»Well, I've done the deal.«

»Ay, you're the one for that,« said the wife and, heeding neither bag nor strangers, she gave him a hug.

»I exchanged the horse for a cow.«

»Thank goodness for some milk!« said the wife; »now we can have milkpuddings and butter and cheese to eat. What a lovely exchange!«

»Well, but I swopped the cow again for a sheep.«

»There, that's better still,« she replied; »You think of everything. We've got plenty of grazing for a sheep. Now we can have ewe's milk and cheese and woollen stockings, yes, and woollen night-clothes – the cow couldn't give us that; it sheds its hair ... You really are a considerate husband.«

»But I swopped the sheep for a goose.«

»My dear Dad, do you mean to say we shall have Michaelmas goose this year? You're always thinking how you can give me pleasure. What a lovely idea of yours! We can tether the goose and fatten it up for Michaelmas.«

»But I swopped the goose for a hen,« said the husband.

»A hen? That was a good exchange,« said the wife. »The hen will lay eggs and hatch them out; we shall get chicks and a fowlrun. That's just what I've always wanted.«

»Yes, but I swopped the hen for a bag of rotten apples.«

»Why, now you must have a kiss,« said the wife. »Thank you, dear husband o' mine. And now I've got something for you to hear. While you were away, I thought of a really nice meal to cook you when you got back: omelette flavoured with onion. I had the eggs, but no onions. So I went across to the schoolmaster's; they grow chives there, I know. But his

wife's stingy, the mealymouthed vixen! I asked her to lend me - 'Lend?'
she repeated. 'Nothing grows in our garden, not so much as a rotten
apple. I couldn't even lend you that.' Well, now I can lend her ten – in
fact, a whole bagful! What a lark, Father!« And then she gave him a kiss
right on the mouth.

»I do like that,« cried the Englishmen together. »Always going down-
hill and never downhearted. It's worth the money.« And with that they
counted out a hundredweight of gold coins to the farmer who was not
scolded but kissed.

Yes, it always pays for the wife to admit freely that 'Dad' knows best
and that what he does is right.

Well, what do you think of that for a story? I heard it as a child and
now you have heard it, too, and realize that Dad's always right.

The Naughty Boy

There was once an old poet – such a kindhearted old poet, he was. One evening that he was sitting at home, the weather outside got worse and worse. The rain came pouring down, but the old poet had a nice cosy seat beside his fire where the flames were blazing and the apples were sizzling.

»I'm afraid they won't have a dry stitch on them,« he said, »the poor creatures who are out in this weather;« for he was such a kindhearted old poet.

»Oh, let me in! I'm so cold and wet,« shouted a little child out in the street. It was crying and hammering away on the door, as the rain poured down and the wind rattled all the windows.

»You poor child!« said the old poet, and he went and opened the door. There stood a little boy; he was quite naked, and the water streamed from his long yellow hair. He was shivering with cold and, if he hadn't come in, he would certainly have perished in such terrible weather.

»You poor child!« repeated the old poet, taking his hand. »Come in here, and I'll soon help you to get warm. You must have some wine and an apple, a lovely boy like you.«

And he was, too. His eyes were like two shining stars and, although the water was running down his yellow hair, yet he had such pretty curls. He looked like a little angel-child, but he was quite pale with cold and trembling all over his body. He had a fine bow in his hand, but this was badly spoilt by the rain; all the arrows' pretty colours had run into each other because of the wet.

The old poet sat down by the fireside, took the little boy on his lap, wrung the water from his hair, warmed his hands in his own, and heated

369

up sweet wine for him. After that the boy was quite all right and got rosy cheeks; he jumped down on the floor and began dancing round the old poet.

»You're a merry boy!« said the old man. »What's your name?« »My name's Cupid,« he answered. »Don't you know me? That's my bow; you bet I can shoot with that! Look, now the weather's clearing up; there's the moon.«

»Yes, but your bow is all spoilt,« said the old poet.

»I say, that's dreadful,« said the little boy and picked it up and looked at it. »Oh, but it's dry already; there's nothing at all the matter with it. The string's as tight as anything; I'll just try it.« And then he bent it, put an arrow in the bow, took aim and shot the kind old poet clean through the heart. »There, now you can see that my bow isn't spoilt,« he said, and off he went laughing gaily ... What a naughty boy! To go and shoot the old poet who had let him into his nice warm room, been so kind to him and given him the delicious wine and the best apple.

The kind-hearted poet lay on the floor and wept. Yes, he had been shot clean through the heart, and he said, »For shame! what a naughty boy Cupid is! I shall tell all good children about it and warn them not to play with him, for he does them harm.«

All the children, girls and boys, that he told about it kept a kind of look-out for the naughty Cupid, but he tricked them all the same, for he's so artful. As the students come out of lectures, he runs alongside them with a book under his arm and a black gown on. They never can tell who he is, and they take him under the arm, thinking that he is a student like themselves, and then he sticks the arrow into their breast. At Confirmation time, when the girls are going home from the parson's and when they are standing in church at the service, then he is after them again. Yes, he's always running after people. He sits in the big chandelier at the theatre and blazes up so that people think it's a lamp, but they notice later that it's something else. He goes in the King's Garden and on the Ramparts. Once upon a time he shot your father and mother in the heart. You've only to ask them, and you'll hear what they say. Oh, yes, he's a bad lad, this Cupid; you mustn't ever have anything to do with *him*. He's after everybody. Just fancy – he even shot an arrow at old Granny; but that's a long time ago, that's past history – though she'll never forget a thing like that. For shame! You rascally Cupid!

Well, now you know him and realize what a naughty boy he is.

The Hill of the Elves

Some lizards were scuttling about in the crevices on an old tree. They could understand each other all right, because they spoke the lizard language.

»Goodness! What a rumbling and mumbling is going on in the old Elf Hill,« said, one lizard. »For two nights together I haven't closed my eyes for the clatter they're making. I might as well be lying with toothache for all the sleep I get.«

»There's something going to happen in there,« said another lizard. »The Hill's been standing on four glowing pillars right away till cockcrow; and it's been thoroughly aired, and the elf girls have been learning new dances – dances with stamping in them. Yes, there's something going to happen.«

»And I've had a talk with an earthworm I know,« said a third lizard. »He was just coming up from the Hill, where for nights and days he had been rummaging in the ground, and he had overheard a great deal. Of course, he can't see, poor creature, though he knows how to feel his way and to listen. They're expecting visitors in the Elf Hill, distinguished visitors, but the earthworm wouldn't say who – or perhaps he didn't know. All the will-o'-the-wisps are summoned to attend for the torchlight procession (as it's called), and the silver and gold, of which there's plenty in the Hill, are being polished and set out in the moonlight.«

»Who ever can the visitors be?« asked all the lizards. »I wonder what's going to happen. Just listen to the humming and the drumming!« At that very moment the Elf Hill opened and an old Elfwoman, who had no back but was otherwise very respectably dressed, came tripping out; she was the old Elf King's housekeeper, distantly connected with his family and wearing an amber heart on her forehead. She knew how to get about. Trip, trip! My word, she was quick on her pins – how she could run! And she made straight for the marsh, to the night-raven.

»You are invited to the Elf Hill – it's for tonight,« she said. »But will you first do us a favour and see to the invitations? You must do your bit, you know, as you don't yourself have to keep house. We are having some very distinguished guests, trolls of great importance, and so the Elf King means to be there.«

»Who are to be invited?« asked the night-raven.

»Well, to the grand ball anybody may come, even humans, as long as they can talk in their sleep or manage to do something more or less in our line. But for the first banquet the guests are to be very carefully chosen; we will only have the most select. I have battled for this with the Elf King, because I don't consider we can even let ghosts in. The merman and his daughters must first be invited, though I dare say they are not very keen on coming ashore; still I'll see that each of them gets a wet boulder or something better to sit on, so I rather fancy they won't say no this time. All old trolls of the first class with tails must be asked, and the river-sprite and the goblins; and then I don't see how we can leave out the grave-pig, the death-horse and the church-lamb. It's true that they really rank among the clergy, who don't belong to our people, but those are just their duties; they are nearly related to us, and they pay us regular calls.«

»Brah!« croaked the night-raven and flew off to do the inviting.

Elf girls were already dancing on the Elf Hill; they were dancing in shawls woven of mist and moonlight, which looks charming for people who like that sort of thing. In the middle of the Elf Hill the great hall had been properly smartened up: the floor had been washed with moonlight and the walls rubbed down with witches' lard until they shone like tulip petals with the light behind them. The kitchen was crammed with frogs on the spit, snake-skins stuffed with little children's fingers and salads of toadstool seeds, moist mouse-noses and hemlock, beer from the marsh-woman's brewery, sparkling saltpeter wine from the burial vault – all very substantial. Rusty nails and bits of stained-glass window were for nibbling in the sweet course.

The old Elf King had his gold crown polished with powdered slate-pencil – it was top form slate-pencil, and it's very difficult for the Elf King to get top form slate-pencil. In his bedroom they hung up curtains and made them fast with snake spittle. Yes, there was a tremendous hurrying and scurrying.

»Now we must fumigate with horsehair and pig's bristles, then I think I shall have done my share,« said the old housekeeper.

»Daddy darling,« said the smallest of the daughters; »mayn't I hear who the grand visitors are to be?« »Well, I never!« he said. »Then I suppose I shall have to tell you. Two of my daughters must hold themselves in readiness to get married. Yes, two of them will certainly be married off. The old Troll up in Norway, the one who lives in the old Dovre mountain and owns a number of granite castles and a gold mine which is better than people think, he's coming down to us with his two boys – they're each looking for a wife. The old Troll is a real genuine old Norwegian greybeard, merry and openhearted. I know him from olden days, when we drank to eternal friendship with each other. He was down here to fetch his wife; she's dead now – she was a daughter of the King of the Moen chalk cliffs; she had been chalked up to be his wife, as the saying is ... Oh, I am longing to meet the old Norwegian Troll again. They say his boys are a couple of pert, ill-mannered young cubs, but it may of course be that people are not being fair to them, and that they'll improve with keeping. Now let me see you girls lick them into shape.«

»And when are they arriving?« asked one daughter. »That depends on wind and weather,« said the Elf King. »They're travelling on the cheap. They're coming down whenever there happens to be a ship. I wanted them to come by way of Sweden, but the old buffer hasn't any leanings yet in that direction. He doesn't keep up with the times, and that's a thing I can't bear.«

Just then two will-o'-the wisps came hopping in, one faster than the other, and therefore he came in first.

»Here they are, here they are!« they shouted.

»Give me my crown, and let me stand in the moonlight,« said the Elf King. His daughters raised their shawls and bowed low to the ground.

There stood the old Troll from Dovre in his crown of stiff icicles and polished fircones, wearing, too, bearskin and sleighboots. The two sons, on the other hand, went open-necked and without braces, for they were lusty fellows.

»Do you call that thing a hill?« asked the younger of them, pointing to the Elf Hill. »Up in Norway we should call it a cave.«

»Come, boys!« said the old Troll. »Caves go inward, hills go upward. Haven't you any eyes in your head?«

The one thing that surprised them down here, they said, was the way they could straight away understand the language.

»Now, stop showing off, you two!« said the old Troll. »Anyone might think that you were only half-baked.«

And then they went into the Elf Hill, where there certainly was a distinguished company assembled, and all in a hurry, too – almost as if they had been blown together – and the arrangements for everyone were all so neat and attractive. The sea folk sat at table in large water-jugs; they felt completely at home, they said. They all minded their table manners except the two young Norwegian trolls, who put their feet on the table; but then they were so cocksure in everything they did.

»Feet out of the food!« cried the old Troll, and they obeyed, though they didn't do so at once. They tickled the lady sitting next them with fircones they had brought in their pockets, and then they took off their boots to be comfortable and gave them to her to hold. But their father – the old Troll from Dovre – his behaviour was completely different. He told wonderful tales of the splendid Norwegian mountains and of the foam-white waterfalls that came rushing down with a roar like peals of thunder or of organ-music. He told of the salmon that leapt from the rushing waters, when the water-sprite played on his gold harp. He told of the glittering winter-nights, when sleighbells jingled and the youngsters ran with blazing torches away over the shining ice which was so transparent that they could see the fish panicking under their feet. Yes, he could tell a tale so that you saw and heard what he said; it was just as if the sawmills were going, as if lads and lassies were singing songs and dancing the Hallinge dance.

All at once the old Troll gave the old Elf maid a smacking uncle's kiss – yes, a real proper kiss – and yet they were in no way connected.

Now the elf girls had to do some dancing, both the simple kind and the kind with stamping, and it just suited them. Then came figure dancing or, as it's called, »stepping in free style.« Goodness me, how they could foot it! You couldn't tell end from beginning; you couldn't tell arms from legs; they wound in among each other like shavings from a saw; and then they did a toe-spin that quite upset the death-horse and he had to leave the table. »Prrrrr!« said the old Troll. »What fun to cut capers like that! But what else can they do besides dancing, high kicks and toe-spins?«

»All right, you shall see,« said the Elf King; and then he called up the youngest of his daughters. She was slender and as radiant as moonshine, the most delicate of all the sisters; she could take a white peg in her mouth and, there! she had vanished. That was her secret.

The old Troll said he didn't want his wife to have a trick like that, and he didn't suppose his boys would either.

The second daughter was able to walk beside herself as if she had a shadow , and trolls don't go in for shadows.

The third was quite another type. She had been taught in the marsh-woman's brewery, and she was the one who knew how to lard alder-stumps with glow-worms.

»She'll make a good housewife,« said the old Troll, and he drank to her with his eyes, for he didn't want to take so much liquor.

Now it was the turn of the fourth elf girl. She had a big gold harp to play and, as she plucked the first string, they all raised their left legs, because trolls are left-legged; and, when she plucked the second string, they all had to do what she wanted.

»She's a dangerous woman,« said the old Troll, but both his sons walked out of the Hill, for by now they were tired of listening.

»And what can the next daughter do?« asked the old Troll.

»I have grown so fond of Norwegians,« she said, »and never shall I marry, unless I can come to Norway.«

But the youngest of the sisters whispered to the old Troll: »It's only because she has heard of a Norwegian folk-song that, when the world comes to an end, the crags of Norway will stil stand as monuments; and that's why she wants to go there, for she's so afraid of coming to an end.«

»Aha!« said the old Troll, »so that's it! But what can the seventh and last do?«

»The sixth comes before the seventh,« said the Elf King, for he could do arithmetic. But the sixth held back. »I can only tell people the truth,« she said; »no one bothers about me, and I have enough to do stitching my own winding-sheet.«

Now came the seventh and last, and what could she do? Well, she could tell stories – as many as she liked.

»Look,« said the old Troll, »here are my five fingers. Tell me a story about each of them.« And the elf girl took him by the wrist, and he gurgled with laughter. When she came to the ring-finger, which had a gold ring round its waist, as if it knew there was to be an engagement, the old Troll cried out: »Hold tight what you've got, the hand is yours. You shall be my own wife.«

The elf girl said there was some more about the ring-finger and about little Peter Playboy.

»We'll hear more about them in the winter,« said the old Troll, »and we'll hear about the fir and the birch and the presents from the wood-nymphs and the crisp ringing frost. You'll come and tell us stories, won't you, because there's no one up there yet who can do that properly. And then we'll sit in the stone chamber, where the pine chips blaze, and drink mead out of the gold horns of the ancient Norwegian kings; the water-sprite has presented me with one or two. And as we sit like that, the Garbo brownie will pay us a visit, and he'll sing you all the dairymaids' songs. We'll have a merry time. The salmon will leap in the torrent and beat against the stone wall, but they'll never come in ... Yes, you may take my word for it – it's wonderful in dear old Norway. But where are the boys?«

Yes, where were the boys? They were running about in the fields and blowing out will-o'-the-wisps who had come so kindly to make a torch-light procession.

»All this gadding about!« the old Troll said to them. »I've just taken a mother for you, now you two can each take an aunt.«

But the lads said that they would much rather make a speech and drink toasts; as for getting married, they had no desire to. So then they made speeches and drank toasts and turned their glasses upside down to show that they were empty, took off their coats and lay down on the table to sleep, for they didn't care what they did. But the old Troll went dancing round the hall with his young bride and exchanged boots with her, because that's smarter than exchanging rings.

»There's the cock crowing!« said the old elfin housekeeper. »Now we've got to close the shutters to save us from being burnt to death by the sun.« And with that the Hill was closed for the day ...

But outside the lizards were still scuttling up and down the crevices on the tree, and one of them said to the other: »Oh, I *did* enjoy the old Norwegian Troll!«

»I prefer the boys,« said the earthworm; but of course he couldn't see, poor creature.

The Snow Man

Ooh! I'm creaking all over in this lovely cold weather,« said the snow man. »I must say the wind knows how to sting life into you. And that goggle-eye over there – how she does stare!« – it was the sun he meant, which was just going down – »she won't get me to wince; I can hold on to my bits all right.« These were two large three-cornered bits of roof-tiles that he had for eyes; the mouth was part of an old rake, and so he had teeth.

He had been born amid shouts of glee from the boys, and saluted with jingling of bells and cracking of whips from the sledges.

The sun went down and the full moon rose, round and huge, clear and lovely in the blue sky. »There she comes again from another direction,« said the snow man. He imagined it was the sun appearing once more. »I have cured her of staring. Now she can hang there and light me up to see myself. If I only knew how one sets about moving! I should so like to move. If I could, I would go straight away and do some sliding on the ice, as I saw the boys doing. But I don't know how to run.«

»Be-off-off!« barked the old watchdog from his chain. He was a bit husky; he had been like that ever since he had lived indoors and lain close to the fire. »The sun will teach you to run all right! I saw that happen last year to the snow man before you, to the one before him, 'be-off-off' – and off they've gone.«

»I don't follow you, mate,« said the snow man. »Will that creature up there teach me how to run?« (He was referring to the moon.) »Well, yes, she ran fast enough just now, when I stared back at her; now she's creeping up from another direction.«

»You don't know a thing,« said the watchdog; »but, there, they've only just stuck you up. What you're looking at is called the moon; the other, who disappeared, was the sun. She'll come back tomorrow and show you well enough how to run – right down into the pond. There'll soon be a change in the weather, I can feel it in my left hind leg – such twinges! yes, the weather's going to change.«

»I can't make him out,« said the snow man, »though I've a feeling that it's something unpleasant he's getting at. The one who stared and went down – he calls her the sun – she isn't my friend either, I feel sure of that.«

»Be-off-off!« barked the watchdog, turned round three times about himself and lay down inside his kennel to sleep.

There really was a change in the weather. A thick clammy fog settled down in the early morning over the whole neighbourhood. At break of day there was a light breeze; the wind was so icy cold that the frost got a firm grip. But what a sight there was when the sun rose! All the trees and bushes were covered with hoar-frost; it was like a whole forest of white coral; it was as if all the boughs had been smothered with glittering white blossoms. Thousands of delicate twigs, that in summer are not to be seen because of all the leaves, now stood out, every one of them. It all looked just like lace and so dazzling white that a white radiance appeared to stream from every branch. The weeping birch stirred in the breeze, with life in it you might see in a tree in summer. You never saw such loveliness; and as the sun shone out, goodness! how everything sparkled as if it had been sprinkled over with diamond dust, and the whole snow-covered earth was a glitter of big diamonds – or you might also suppose they were thousands of tiny candles, even whiter than the snow itself.

»How perfectly beautiful!« said a girl, as she stepped with a young man out into the garden and paused alongside the snow man, looking at the glistening trees. »You couldn't see anything lovelier even in summer,« she said with sparkling eyes.

»Nor a fellow like this one here – you'd never come across him,« said the young man and pointed at the snow man. »He's splendid!«

The girl laughed and gave the snow man a nod; then she tripped off with her friend across the snow, which crunched under them as if they were walking on starch.

»Who were those two?« the snow man asked the watchdog. »You've been here longer than I have; do you know them?«

»Indeed I do,« replied the watchdog. »She sometimes pats my back, and he has given me a bone. I'll never bite *them*.«

»But what are they doing here?« asked the snow man.

»They're swee-eethearts!« said the watchdog. »They are to move into a kennel of their own and gnaw bones together. Be-off-off!«

»Are these two just as important as you and I?« asked the snow man.

»Well, you see, they belong to the family,« said the watchdog. »It's true, no one can be expected to know much if he was born yesterday. That's clearly the case with you. Now, I possess age and knowledge; I know everyone here at the house. There was a time when I didn't have to stand chained up here in the cold. Be-off-off!«

»But cold is delightful,« said the snow man. »Do go on with your story! But don't keep rattling your chain; that upsets me.«

»Be-off-off!« barked the watchdog. »I was a puppy then; a sweet little thing, they said I was. There I lay indoors on a velvet chair, curled up on my lady's lap. I was kissed on the nose and had my paws wiped with an embroidered handkerchief; they called me »the beautifullest«, »ducky-ducky-darling« ... But soon I grew too big for them, and they gave me to the housekeeper. I came down to the basement; you can see into it from where you're standing. You can see down into the room where I was lord and master, for that's what I was with the housekeeper. I dare say they were humbler quarters than upstairs, but it was more comfortable here: I wasn't pawed and lugged about by children as I had been upstairs. I got just as good food as before, and much more of it. I had my own cushion, and then there was a stove. That's the most glorious thing in the world at this time of the year. I used to crawl right in underneath it, till I was out of sight. Oh, I still dream of that stove. Be-off-off!«

»Is a stove really so nice to look at?« asked the snow man. »Is it at all like me?«

»It's just the opposite of you. Coal-black, and has a long neck with brass collar. It feeds on logs, so that flames shoot out of its mouth. You can keep beside it, close up, or right under; it is such a comfort. You must be able to see it through the window from where you are.«

And the snow man looked and, sure enough, he saw a shiny black-polished object with a brass collar; fire was gleaming out from below. The snow man had a strange sensation, a feeling he couldn't himself account for. Something came over him that was quite new to him, though people all know it who are not snow men.

»And why did you leave her?« asked the snow man, for he felt that the stove must be one of the female sex. »How could you desert such a spot?«

»Well, the fact is I had to,« said the watchdog. »They turned me out and chained me up here. I had bitten the youngest son of the house in the leg, because he had kicked away the bone I was gnawing; a bone for a bone, I thought. But they didn't like it, and from that day I've been

chained up and have lost my clear voice; listen how hoarse I am – be-off-off! That was the end of it all.«

The snow man gave up listening. He still went on staring into the housekeeper's basement, down into her room where the stove stood on its four iron legs and looked about the size of the snow man himself.

»There's a queer creaking inside me,« he said. »Am I never to come into that room? It's an innocent wish, and surely our innocent wishes ought to be granted. It's my greatest wish, my one and only wish; and it would be hardly fair if it weren't satisfied. I must come in, I must nestle up against her, even if I have to smash the window.«

»You'll never come in there,« said the watchdog; »and if you did reach the stove you'd soon be off, off!«

»I'm as good as off already,« said the snow man. »I feel I'm breaking up.«

All day long the snow man stood looking in at the window. At dusk the room became still more inviting. The stove shone so kindly in a way that neither moon nor sun can ever shine – no, but as only a stove can shine, when there's something in it. When the door was opened, the flame shot out; that was its habit. The snow man's white face went flaming red, and the pink glow spread right up his chest.

»It's more than I can bear,« he said. »How pretty she looks when she puts out her tongue!«

The night was very long, but not for the snow man. He stood there with his own beautiful thoughts, and they froze till they crackled. In the early morning the basement windows were frozen over; they had the loveliest ice-ferns any snow man could ask for, but they hid the stove. The panes refused to thaw, so he couldn't see her. There was crackling and crunching, it was exactly the kind of frosty weather to delight a snow man; but he was not delighted. He might and ought to have felt so happy, but he wasn't happy; he had 'stove-sickness'.

»That's a serious complaint for a snow man,« said the watchdog, »I've had it myself, but I've got over it – be-off-off! There's a change in the weather coming.«

And there was a change in the weather; it turned to a thaw. The thaw increased, the snow man decreased. He didn't say anything, he didn't complain, and that's a sure sign.

One morning he collapsed. Where he had been standing there was something like a broom-handle sticking out; it was round this the boys had built him up.

»Now I understand about his 'stove-sickness',« said the watchdog. »The snow man has a stove-rake in his body; that's what upset him, and now he's done with it. Be-off-off!«

And soon winter was done with too.

»Be-off-off!« barked the watchdog; but the little girls at the house sang:

»Sweet woodruff, now's the time to sprout,
and, willow, hang your mittens out.
Come, lark, and cuckoo, when you sing
then winter's gone and here is spring.
I'll join you both – twit-twit! cuckoo! Come, darling sun, we long for you!«

After that, nobody gave a thought to the snow man.

The Silver Shilling

There was once a shilling that came fresh from the mint; he jumped and jingled - »Hurrah! now I'm off to see the great big world!« And away he went.

Children would clutch tight hold of him in their warm hands, and the miser ind his cold clammy hands. Older folk would twist and turn him over and over, while the younger ones immediately let him run away. The shilling was made of silver, with very little copper in him and had already been out in the world for a whole year – that's to say, round about in the country where he was coined. But then he went on a journey abroad; he was the last of his country's coins to be left in the purse that his master had on his travels - the man didn't himself realize that he had got the coin till he felt him between his fingers.

»Why, I've still got a shilling here that I brought from home,« he said. »He can travel along with me.« And the shilling jingled and jumped for joy, as he was put back into the purse. There he lay together with foreign companions who came and went; one gave way to another, but the shilling from home always stayed in the purse; that was an honour.

By now several weeks had gone by, and the shilling had come far out into the world without exactly knowing where. He heard of the other coins being French or Italian; one explained that now they were in this town, another that they were in that. But the shilling couldn't possibly tell, because you don't see the world if you're always inside a purse; and that's where the shilling was. But one day, as he lay there, he noticed that the purse wasn't shut, and so he crept up to the opening to take a little peep outside. Of course, he oughtn't to have done that, but he was inquisitive; and that seldom pays. He slid out into the trouser-pocket and, when at night the purse was put on one side, the shilling remained where he was and came with the clothes out in the passage. There he at once fell on the floor; nobody heard it, nobody saw it.

First thing in the morning the clothes were brought in, the gentleman put them on and continued his journey; but the shilling didn't go with him. Somebody found him; he was put into service again and went out with three other coins.

»Anyhow, it's nice to travel about in the world,« thought the shilling; »to come across other people and other ways of doing things.

»What sort of a shilling is this?« said someone just at that moment.»It's not one of ours; it's bad money; no good!«

Well, this is where the shilling's story begins, as he told it later on.

»'Bad money!' 'No good!' The words went right through me,« said the shilling. »I knew I was good silver, rang true and bore a genuine stamp. There was no doubt they were making a mistake; they couldn't mean me. But they did mean me! I it was they called bad, no good.« »I must pass this off in the dark,« said the man who had him.« »So I was passed off in the dark and then, in the daylight, was again called 'bad', 'no good' – 'we must get rid of this somehow!'«

And the shilling trembled in the owner's fingers every time he had to steal out on the sly and pass as a coin of the country.

»Wretched shilling that I am! What's the good of my silver, my value, my stamp, if they don't stand for anything. For the public you're simply what the public thinks you are. All the same, it must be terrible to have a bad conscience, to find yourself sneaking along the wrong path when I, who am so completely innocent, can feel uncomfortable at the very sight of wrongdoing ... Every time I was taken out of the purse, I'd cringe before the eyes that looked at me; I knew that I should be refused, flung on to the table as a cheat and swindler.

One day I came to a poor wretched woman who was given me as pay for her drudgery. But, no, she couldn't get rid of me; not one would have me; I was a piece of real bad luck for her.

'I'm afraid I'll be forced to take somebody in with this coin,' she said. 'I can't afford to keep a bad shilling. The well-to-do baker shall have it; he's the one who can best put up with it. Still, I feel I'm doing wrong, all the same.'«

»Now I'm going so far as to burden the woman's conscience,« sighed the shilling. »Has really such a change come over me in my old age?«

»The woman went to the well-to-do baker, but he knew perfectly well what a geniune shilling looked like. I wasn't allowed to lie where I was; I was flung in the woman's face. She got no bread in exchange for me, and I felt utterly miserable at having been coined just to get others into trouble – I, who in my young days had been so bold and confident, so certain of my value and my genuine stamp. I felt as down in the mouth as a poor shilling can be, when nobody will have him. But the woman took me home again and looked at me very closely, even gently and kindly. 'No,' she said, 'I can't cheat anyone with you. I'll punch a hole in you, so that everybody can see that you're not genuine ... and yet, it suddenly occurs to me, perhaps you're a lucky shilling – yes, I'm sure you are. The idea has just struck me: I'll make a hole in the shilling, thread a string through the hole and give it to my neighbour's little girl to wear round her neck as a lucky shilling.'

And she punched a hole in me. It's never very pleasant to have a hole knocked into you, though when the intention is good you can stand a good deal. I had a string put through me and became a sort of medal to wear. I was hung round the little child's neck, and she smiled at me and kissed me, and I lay all night on the child's warm innocent breast.

Early next morning the mother took me between her fingers, looked at me and mean-while thought her own thoughts. I soon learnt what they were. She got out some scissors and cut the string.

'Lucky shilling!' she said. 'We'll soon see about that.' And she put me in salts till I turned green; after that, she puttied up the hole, rubbed me a bit and then went off at dusk to the lottery agent in order to get a lottery ticket that was to bring good luck.

How uneasy I felt! I was in such a tight corner that I thought I should break in two I knew I should be called bad and thrown out, right in front of a lot of shillings and coins with inscription and face to be proud of; but I got through. There were so many people at the agent's, and he was so busy, that I was sent tinkling into the drawer among the other coins.

Whether, later on, anything was won on my ticket I don't know, but I do know that already the following day I was found to be a bad shilling, laid on one side and sent out to swindle someone else – always to swindle. Really it's more than anyone can stand, when he's honest and trustworthy; and I can't deny being that.

In the course of time I was bandied about like this from hand to hand, from house to house, always abused, always distrusted. No one believed in me, and I didn't believe in myself nor in the world; I had a hard time of it.

Then one day a traveller turned up. Of course they passed me off on him, and he was simple-minded enough to take me for legal tender. But when the time came for him to spend me, once more I heard the cry of 'It's a bad shilling – no good!«

'It was given to me as genuine,' said the man; and he had a good close look at me. Then he smiled all over his face; no other face had ever done that after examining me. 'Why, what on earth's this?' he exclaimed. 'Here's a coin from our own country, a good honest shilling from home, which they've made a hole in and called counterfeit. Well, that *is* funny! I'm jolly well going to save you up and take you home with me.'

A thrill of joy went through me. To be called a good honest shilling, and to be going home where everyone would recognize me and know that I was good silver with a genuine stamp – I could have sparkled for joy, only I don't go in for sparkling; steel can do that, but not silver.

I was wrapped up in delicate white paper, so as not to get mixed with the other coins and get spent. Only on festive occasions, when we came across fellow-countrymen, was I brought out and spoken tremendously well of. They found me interesting. That's funny, isn't it? - to be able to be interesting without uttering a single word!

And at last I came home. All my troubles were over, and my joy was beginning. You see, I was good silver, I had the genuine stamp, and no harm whatever had been done to me by the hole knocked into me as a bad coin. That doesn't matter as long as you're not lead. You've got to stick it out. Everyone comes into his own in time. Well, anyhow, that's my belief,« said the shilling.

The Teapot

There was a proud teapot, proud of its porcelain, proud of its long spout, proud of its broad handle. It had something in front, something behind – the spout in front and the handle behind – and that's what it liked to talk about. It never talked about its lid, for that was cracked, that was riveted; the lid had a defect, and we don't care to talk about our defects – others will see to that. Cups, cream jug and sugar basin, the whole tea-set would of course much more easily bear in mind the frailty of the lid and gossip about that rather than about the good handle and the excellent spout. The teapot was well aware of all this.

»I know them,« it said to itself. »And I also know my own defects well enough and admit them. That's where my humility, my modesty, come in. We all have our failings, though we also have gifts, don't we? The cups have a handle, the sugar basin has a lid; but I have both, as well as one thing in front which they've never got: I have a spout, and that makes me Queen of the tea-table. The sugar basin and the cream jug are privileged to be the handmaids of taste, but I am the giver, the mistress. I pour out a blessing for thirsting humanity; in my inside the Chinese tea-leaves are brewed in boiling, tasteless water.«

All this was said by the teapot in the confident days of its youth. It stood on the teatable, it was lifted by the most delicate hand; but the most delicate hand was clumsy, and the teapot was dropped. The spout broke off, the handle broke off, and the lid – well, the lid isn't worth mentioning; it's been talked about enough already. The teapot lay fainting on the floor with the boiling water running out of it. It was a hard blow that it got, and yet the hardest blow was the way they laughed; they laughed at the teapot, and not at the clumsy hand.

»That's something I shall never forget,« said the teapot, when it afterwards turned over in its mind the story of its own life. »They said I was done for. I was put aside in a corner and, the day after, given away to a woman who had come to beg for dripping. I was reduced to poverty; I couldn't say a word, whether outwardly or inwardly. Yet, as I stood there, a better life began for me. First, you're one thing, and then you become something quite different. Earth was put into me. That means burial for a teapot, but in the earth there was placed a bulb. Who put it there, who gave it, I have no idea; but given it was - a substitute for the Chinese tea-leaves and the boiling water, a substitute for the handle and spout that broke off.

The bulb lay in the earth; the bulb lay in me and became my heart, my living heart, such as I'd never had before. There was life in me, there was strength and energy. My pulse beat, the bulb sprouted till it almost burst with thoughts and feelings; it broke out into flower. I saw it, I carried it; I forgot myself in its loveliness - a wonderful thing it is to forget yourself in others. It never thanked me, never gave a thought to me .... It was praised and admired. All this made me so glad; how glad it must have made the bulb! Then one day I heard someone saying that it deserved a better pot. They broke me across the middle, which hurt like anything. But the flower was moved into a better pot - while I was thrown out into the yard, to lie there like an old potsherd ... But I have my memories; I can't be robbed of those.«

Twelve by the Mail-Coach

There was a sharp frost, a clear starry sky, not a breath of wind. »Cro-omp!« – that was a jar they hurled at the door. »Bang!« – they were shooting the New Year in. It was New Year's Eve; the clock was striking twelve.

»Taran-tara!« There came the mail. The big mail-coach halted outside the town gate; it brought twelve passengers. There was no room for more; every seat was taken. Cheering and singing could be heard inside the houses, where people were keeping New Year's Eve and had just stood up with their glasses filled to toast the coming year.

»Here's health and happiness in the New Year!« they cried. »A pretty wife! Lots of money! No more troubles!«

Yes, that's what they wished each other, as they clinked glasses – and the mail-coach halted at the town gate with twelve unknown travellers.

What sort of people were they? They had passports and luggage with them – yes, and presents for you and me and everybody in the town. Who were the strangers? What did they want and what were they bringing?

»Good morning!« they said to the sentry at the gate.

»Good morning!« he replied, for 12 o'clock had already struck. »Your name and profession?« asked the sentry of the first to step out of the coach.

»You'll find it on the passport,« said the passenger. »I am I.« He certainly was no end of a fellow, wearing a bearskin coat and sleigh-boots. »I'm the man on whom so many people pin their hopes. Come tomorrow and you shall have your Christmas box. I scramble pennies and shillings, give away presents, yes, and I give balls too, as many as thirty-one; that's as many nights as I have to give away. My ships are icebound, though it's nice and warm in my office. I'm a merchant; my name's January. I've got nothing but bills on me.«

The next passenger to come was a gay spark. He ran plays, fancy-dress balls and every kind of entertainment you can think of. His luggage consisted of a big barrel. »We'll knock a lot more out of that at Shrovetide than just the cat,« he said. »I mean to amuse others as well as myself, because I have the shortest life in the whole family. I shall never be more than twenty-eight ... Well, perhaps one day may be tacked on, but it makes no difference. Cheerio!«

»Don't bawl out so loud,« said the sentry.

»That's just what I will do,« he replied. »I'm Prince Carnival, and I travel under the name of Februarius.«

Now came the third passenger. He looked the very image of fasting, but he held his head high because he was connected with »The Forty Knights« and was a weather prophet, though that's not a very fat job; that's why he thought so much of Lent. He sported a bunch of violets in his buttonhole, but they were very small ones.

»Quick march, Mr. March!« cried the fourth passenger, giving the third a push. »March, Mr. March, into the guard-house. They've got some punch there, I can smell it!« But there wasn't any; he only wanted to make an April fool of him – that was how the fourth chap began. He looked to be in good spirits. He didn't do much work, it's true, but went in for so many holidays. »My spirits go up and down,« he said. »Rain and sunshine, moving out and moving in. I'm a house-agent, I'm an undertaker, I can both laugh and cry. I've got a summer suit in my trunk, but it would be sheer madness to put it on. Here I am! When I'm in full fig, I put on silk stockings and carry a muff.«

Now it was a lady who got out of the coach. »Miss May!« she said. She wore a summer dress with goloshes. She had on a silk gown of beech-leaf green, with anemones in her hair, while the scent of her sweet woodruff was so strong that it made the sentry sneeze. »Bless you!« she said – that was how she greeted him. She was charming, and a singer too – not at the theatre, but in the woods; not in booths, but she liked to sing in the fresh green glades for her own enjoyment. In her work-bag she had poems such as Christian Winther's »Woodcuts«, for they are like the beech wood itself, and Richardt's »Short Poems«, which are like sweet woodruff.

»Here comes my lady, our youthful mistress,« they called out from inside the coach. And there she came, young and slender, queenly and attractive. She was born lackadaisical; you could see that at a glance.

She always gave a party on the longest day in the year, so as to allow time to eat the many different courses. She could afford to drive in her own carriage, but preferred to come by coach with the others; she wanted in this way to show that she wasn't proud. She wasn't anyhow travelling alone, for with her she had her younger brother Julius.

He was stout, and wore a summer suit and a Panama hat. He took very little luggage with him; it was so tiring in the heat. He had nothing but swimming trunks and a bathing cap; that's not very much.

Now came Mother August. She was a fruitdealer on a large scale, owner of a good many fish-tanks, and also a farmer in petticoats. She was buxom and hearty; she took part in all that was going on and even went

round with kegs of beer to the people out working in the fields. »In the sweat of the face shalt thou eat bread,« she said; »that's what it says in the Bible. There'll be plenty of time afterwards for dancing in the meadow and harvest home.« Yes, she was Mother August.

Next came another man, a printer by profession, a colourist who let the forest know when its leaves had got to have a change of colour, though this could be lovely if he wanted, splashing red, yellow and brown all over the woods. The colour master could whistle like a blackbird, and he was a clever workman who twined the brownish green hop-bine round his beer-mug; this was very effective, and he always had an eye for effect. There he stood with his box of paints, which was all the luggage he had.

Now came the gentleman farmer, whose mind was on the month for sowing, on ploughing and working the soil and – well, yes – also on the pleasures of sport. He had dog and gun with him, and he had nuts in his game-bag – crack, crack! He brought all sorts of things with him, including an English plough. He talked agriculture, but what with the coughing and wheezing he was difficult to follow ... for here was November arriving.

November had a cold, a violent cold, so that he had to use a sheet instead of a pocket handkerchief; and yet he was obliged, he said, to go with the maids to their new place. However, he'd be sure to get rid of his cold when he started chopping firewood, and he was ready to do that because he was chief sawyer to his guild. He spent the evenings in making wooden skates, as he knew that in a very few weeks there would be a demand for this enjoyable footwear.

And now came the last passenger of all, a little old grandam with her brazier. She was cold, but her eyes shone like two bright stars. She was carrying a flowerpot with a little fir tree in it. »I will tend it and take care of it so that it grows tall enough by Christmas Eve to reach from the floor right up to the ceiling, with lighted candles, gilded apples and cut-out paper figures. The brazier will give warmth like a stove; I'll take the storybook out of my pocket and read aloud from it, so that all the children in the room keep still. But the dolls on the tree will come alive, the little wax angel at the top of the tree will shake her tinsel wings and fly down and kiss big and little ones in the room – yes, even the poor children that stand outside singing their christmas carol about the star of Bethlehem.«

»Very well,« said the sentry. »Now the coach may drive on; that makes the dozen. Let a fresh mail-coach be brought up.«

»Right you are. But first I want the twelve passengers to come in here,« said the captain of the guard. »One at a time! I shall keep your passports, which are each valid for one month. At the end of that time I shall write on them how each of you has behaved. Now then, Mr. January, will you kindly step in?«

And so in he went.

»When a year's up, I'll tell you what the twelve travellers have brought you and me and all of us. At present I don't know, and of course they don't know themselves either, for these are strange times that we live in.«

The Cripple

There was an old country-house with a splendid young squire and his wife living there. They had wealth and all they wanted; they liked to enjoy themselves, and they did good to others. They wanted everybody to be as happy as they were themselves.

On Christmas Eve a beautifully decorated Christmas tree stood in the old baronial hall, where the fire was burning on the hearth and the old pictures were hung with branches of fir. Here the master and mistress and their guests were assembled, and there was singing and dancing.

Earlier in the evening there had already been Christmas merriment in the servants' hall. Here, too, stood a large Christmas tree with lighted red and white candles, small Danish flags, swans and fishing-nets cut out of coloured paper and filled with »sweeties«. The poor children from the village were invited, each one with its mother, though the mothers never took much notice of the tree but kept their eyes on the Christmas tables laden with woollens, linen, dress material and stuff for trousers. Yes, these caught the attention of the mothers and their older children; only the very little ones stretched out their hands to the candles, the tinsel and the flags.

They had all arrived early in the afternoon and got their Christmas pudding as well as roast goose and red cabbage. Then, when the Christmas tree had been looked at and the presents given round, each got a small glass of punch and doughnuts stuffed with apples.

When they came home to their own humble parlour, there was gossip about »the good way of living«, that's to say, good things to eat; and they had a proper look once more at their presents.

Now there were a couple called Garden Kirsten and Garden Ole. They were married and had their house and daily bread for weeding and digging in the manor garden. Every Christmas party brought them a generous share of presents. They had five children, and all five got their clothes from the squire and his wife.

»They're kind-hearted folk at the manor«, they said. »But then they can afford it, and it gives them pleasure.«

»Well, here's some good clothes for the four children to wear out,« said Ole; »but why isn't there something for the cripple? They don't generally forget him, even though he doesn't come to the party.«

It was the eldest of the children whom they called »the cripple«; otherwise his name was Hans. When he was small, he was the quickest and liveliest child, but then he suddenly went »groggy« in the legs – unable to stand or walk, and now for five years he had been bedridden.

»Oh, but I did get something for him as well,« said the mother, »through it's nothing much; it's only a book for him to read.«

»A fat lot of use that'll be to him,« said the father.

But Hans was pleased with it. He was a very intelligent boy, who enjoyed reading; yet he also used his time in working, as far as he, who always had to lie in bed, could make himself useful. He was neat with his fingers and used his hands to knit woollen stockings and even counterpanes; the lady at the manor had praised them and bought them.

It was a story-book Hans had been given. There was lots to read in it, lots to think about.

»Not much use for that sort of thing in this house,« said the parents. »Still, let him read; it'll make the time go, and he can't always be knitting stockings.«

Spring arrived. Flowers and greenery began to sprout – also weeds, as no doubt the nettles may be called, although the hymn speaks so well of them:

> »No king there be nor royal chief,
> with all his might and mettle,
> could ever bring the smallest leaf
> to grow upon a nettle.«

There was plenty to do in the manor garden, not merely for the gardener and his assistants, but also for Kirsten and Ole.

»It's a tough job«, they said; »and, soon as we've raked the paths and got them to look really nice, they go and get all messed up again; there's forever o' visitors coming here to the manor. Think what that must cost! Still, they're rich people, the master and mistress.«

»That's a queer kind o' share-out,« said Ole. »Parson says we're all God's children. Then why's there so much difference?«

»That all comes of the Fall,« said Kirsten.

They went on with their talk in the evening, while Cripple Hans lay reading his story-book.

Poverty and daily grind had hardened the parents' hands – and also their judgment and their minds. They couldn't make things out, they weren't equal to it, and now they talked themselves still sulkier and angrier.

»Some people are well off and happy, others are always hard-up. Why should we have to suffer because Adam and Eve were disobedient and inquisitive? We'd never have gone on like those two.«

»Oh, yes, we should!« said Cripple Hans all of a sudden. »It's all down here in this book.«

»What does the book say?« asked the parents.

So Hans read them the old tale of *The Woodcutter and his Wife*. They too came to words over the inquisitiveness of Adam and Eve, which was the cause of their misfortune.

Just then their King went by. »Come home with me,« he said, »and you shall live just as I do: seven courses for dinner, and a show-dish. That will be in a closed tureen; you mustn't touch that, or it will be the end of your fine living.« »I wonder what is in the tureen,« said the wife. »That's no business of ours,« said the husband. »Well, but I'm not inquisitive,« said the wife; »I'd only like to know why we mayn't lift up the lid; it must be something tasty.« »As long as it's not some infernal machine,« said the husband; »Some kind of pistol-shot that goes off and wakes the whole house.« »Gracious me!« said the wife and didn't touch the tureen. But in the night she dreamt that the lid raised itself, and there came a whiff of the finest punch such as you get at weddings and funerals. There was a big silver shilling with the inscription:

»Drink of this punch and you shall be the richest couple in the world, and the rest of mankind shall be beggars« – and at that point the wife woke up and told the husband her dream. »You're thinking too much about the thing,« he said. »We could of course raise it cautiously,« said the wife. »Yes, cautiously!« he replied; and very gently she raised the lid ... Out sprang two nimble little mice and disappeared into a mouse-hole. »Good night!« said the King. »Now you may go home and lie in your own bed. Don't find fault any more with Adam and Eve; you've been just as inquisitive and ungrateful yourselves.«

»I wonder where the book got that story from,« said Garden Ole. »You might have thought it was aimed at us. It gives you plenty to think about.«

On the following day they went to work again. They were scorched by the sun and drenched to the skin by the rain; and they were filled with grumpy thoughts, which they brooded over.

The evening was still light when they got home and had eaten their milk-porridge. »Read us that story again about the woodcutter,« said Garden Ole.

»There are so many nice ones in this book,« said Hans, »such a lot you don't know.«

»Well, I don't mind about them. I want to hear the one I know.«

And he and his wife listened to it again. On more than one evening they came back to that story.

»It still doesn't make everything quite clear to me,« said Ole. »It's the same with people as with milk that curdles; some of it makes fine curd-cheese, but it may also turn to thin watery whey. Some folks are lucky in everything, always given the place of honour and know nothing of sorrow or want.«

Cripple Hans heard that. Though weak in the legs, he was wise in the head. So he read them another tale from his book, one about *The Man free from Sorrow or Want*. Where ever was he to be found – and found he must be!

The King was ill and could only be cured by putting on a shirt worn threadbare on the back of a man who could truly be said never to have known sorrow or want.

»But *I* haven't!« cried a swineherd who sat in the hedge, laughing and singing. »I'm the happiest!«

»Then give us your shirt,« said the King's messengers. »You shall be paid half-a-kingdom for it.«

But he hadn't got a shirt, and yet he claimed to be the happiest man.

»Well, that was a grand chap!« shouted Ole, and he and his wife laughed as they hadn't laughed for years.

Just then the schoolmaster went by.

»What a gay time you're having!« he said. »That's quite a novelty in this house. Have you drawn a lucky number in the lottery?«

»No, nothing of that sort,« said Ole. »You see, Hans has been reading to us from his story-book. He read about *The Man free from Sorrow or Want;* that chap, he had no shirt. It makes you laugh till you cry, to hear that sort of thing, especially out of a printed book. I reckon each one of us has his troubles to bear; we're none of us alone in that. Well, that's always a comfort.«

»Where did you get the book?« asked the schoolmaster.

»Hans was given it over a year ago at Christmas; it was a present from the manor. You know how fond he is of reading – fancy, a cripple like him! At the time we'd rather he had got a couple of canvas shirts. But the book's extraordinary; it seems to kind of answer your thoughts.«

The schoolmaster took the book and opened it.

»Let's have the same story over again,« said Ole. »I haven't yet taken it all in. And then he must also read us the other one about the woodcutter.«

Those two tales were quite enough for Ole. They were like two sunbeams coming into that humble parlour, into that stunted mind which could be so sullen and surly.

Hans had read the whole book over and over again. The tales carried him out into the world, where of course he couldn't go, because his legs wouldn't take him there.

The schoolmaster sat by his bed; they talked together, and that was jolly for both of them.

From then on, the schoolmaster came more often to see Hans, while his parents were out at work. It was quite a treat for the boy every time he came. How eagerly he listened to what the old teacher told him of the size of the earth and its many countries, and how the sun was yet nearly half a million times bigger than the earth and so far away that a cannon-ball would need a good twenty-five years to travel from the sun to the earth, whereas the sun's rays could reach the earth in eight minutes.

Of course, every schoolboy knows all this, but to Hans it was new and even more wonderful than what was in his story-book.

Every now and then the schoolmaster used to go and dine at the manor, and on one such occasion he told his host and hostess how much the story-book had come to mean to that humble household, where two stories alone from the book had proved an inspiration and a blessing. With his reading the weakly, shrewd little boy had brought happiness and food for thought into the house.

As the schoolmaster was leaving the manor to go home, the lady pressed a couple of golden sovereigns into his hand for little Hans. »They'll be for Dad and Mum,« said the boy, when the schoolmaster brought him the money. And Ole and Kirsten said, »Our cripple boy, after all, is a boon and a blessing to us.«

A few days later, while the parents were out working at the manor, the squire's carriage stopped outside. It was the kind-hearted mistress, who had come, delighted that her Christmas present had brought such comfort and enjoyment to the boy and his parents. With her she had brought fine bread, fruit and a bottle of sweet syrup; but, what was even nicer, she carried, in a gilt cage, a little blackbird which could whistle delightfully. The cage with the bird was placed up on the old chest of drawers some distance from the boy's bed, where he could see the bird and hear it; in fact, even people right out in the road could hear it singing.

Ole and Kirsten didn't get home till the lady had driven away. They noticed how pleased Hans was, and yet they felt it would only mean more trouble for them, this present he had been given.

»Rich people don't look at a thing all round,« they said. »Have we now got this to mind as well? Poor Hans can't do that, of course. It'll end by the cat getting it.«

A week passed, and then another week. During that time the cat had often been in the room without frightening the bird, let alone hurting it. Then an astonishing thing happened. It was afternoon. The parents and the other children were away at work; Hans was left quite alone. He had the story-book in his hand and was reading about the fisherman's wife, who had all her wishes granted. She wished to be an emperor, and she was. But then she wished to be God – and she found herself sitting again in the muddy ditch she had come from.

That story had nothing whatever to do with the bird or the cat, but it happened to be story the boy was reading when the incident took place; he remembered it ever after.

The cage stood on the chest of drawers; the cat stood on the floor with its greeny-yellow eyes fixed on the bird up there. There was something in the cat's face that seemed to say to the bird, »How lovely you are! How I would like to eat you!«

Hans realized that; he read it plainly in the cat's face.

»Go away, cat!« he shouted. »Get out of the room, will you!« It looked as if it was just going to jump.

Hans couldn't get at it, hadn't anything to throw at it but his dearest treasure, the story-book. He threw that; but the binding was loose, it flew to one side, and the book itself with all its leaves flew to the other. The cat slowly backed a little way in the room and looked up at Hans as much as to say, »Don't you meddle in this affair, Master Hans! I can walk and I can jump, but you can't do either.«

Hans kept his eye on the cat and was very much alarmed, and the bird was also frightened. There wasn't a soul to call out to. The cat semed to know this and again got ready to spring. Hans waved his counterpane at it, for he could use his hands; but the cat took no notice of the counterpane, and when this too had been thrown at it in vain, it hopped on to a chair and then on to the windowsill, where it was nearer to the bird.

Hans could feel his own warm blood inside him, but he had no thought of that; he thought only of the cat and the bird. The boy couldn't of course manage to get out of bed; he couldn't stand up on his legs, much less walk. His gorge seemed to rise inside him, when he saw the cat spring from the window straight on to the chest of drawers and crash into the cage so that it overturned. The bird fluttered about wildly inside.

Hans gave a shriek, his legs twitched and, without a thought of what he was doing, he jumped out of bed towards the chest of drawers, knocked the cat off it and caught hold of the cage with the terrified bird inside it. With the cage still in his hand he ran out of the door and right into the road.

The tears were now streaming from his eyes; he shouted for joy, crying out loud, »I can walk! I can walk!« He had got back the use of his legs. Such things can happen, and it happened with him.

The schoolmaster lived near by. The boy ran to him in his bare feet, wearing nothing but a shirt and jacket, and with the bird in the cage.

»I can walk!« he cried. »God in heaven!« and he burst into sobs of sheer joy.

And there was joy at home with Ole and Kirsten. »We shall never live to see a happier day than this,« they both said. Hans was sent for to the manor; he hadn't been that way for many years. It seemed as though the trees and hazels that he knew so well were nodding to him and saying, »Good day, Hans! Glad to see you out here.« The sun shone into his face, right into his heart.

At the manor the kind young master and mistress made him sit with them and looked as delighted as if he had been one of their own family.

And yet most delighted was the lady, who had given him the story-book, given him the songbird. This, it is true, had now died – died of fright – but it had been, in a way, the means by which he was cured; and the book had proved an inspiration to him and his parents. He had it still and meant to keep it and read it, however old he became. And now he could make himself useful at home. He wanted to learn a handicraft, become a bookbinder for choice; »because«, he said, »then I can get all the new books to read!«

Later in the afternoon the lady at the manor sent for the two parents. She had had a talk with her husband about Hans; he was a good intelligent boy, quick and eager to work; and Heaven helps those who help themselves.

That evening the parents went home very happy from the manor, especially Kirsten; but a week later she was in tears, for their dear Hans was leaving them. He had been given good clothes and was a good boy, but now he was to go across the salt water, a long way off, to a grammar school, and it would be many years before they saw him again.

He didn't take the story-book with him; his parents wanted that as a keepsake. And his father often read it, though nothing but the two stories that he knew so well.

They got letters from Hans, each happier than the last. He was boarding with very nice people and was well looked after. Most of all he enjoyed going to school; there was so much to learn and to know. He only wanted now to live to be a hundred and one day be a schoolmaster.

»If only we could live to see that!« said the parents, and they pressed each other's hands, as at communion.

»Think of all that's happened to Hans!« said Ole. »God doesn't forget the poor man's child. But fancy our cripple being the one to prove it! Why, it's just as if Hans was to read it to us out of the story-book.«

Auntie Toothache

Where the story comes from – you want to know that, do you? We got it from the butter cask, the one with the old papers in it.

Many a good and rare book has gone to the grocer's and the provision dealer's, not for reading, but as something that may come in handy. They must have paper to make bags for starch and coffee-beans, paper to wrap up bloaters, butter and cheese. Handwritten documents can also be used.

Things often go into the tub that oughtn't to go into the tub.

I know a grocer's boy who's the son of a provision dealer. He has risen from the store-room to the front shop; a young man well up in paper-bag literature, whether printed or in manuscript. He has an interesting collection, including several important documents from the waste-paper basket of some bewildered overworked official; secret notes between lady friends; bits of scandal that mustn't go further or be mentioned to a soul. He's a walking salvage store for a large range of literature; and he has a big field to work in, for he has the shops of his parents and of his employer. He has rescued many a book or page of a book that might well deserve a second reading.

He has shown me his collection of printed and written things from the tub, chiefly from the grocer's. There were a few pages from a biggish exercise book, and the particularly fine clear handwriting at once caught my attention.

»That was written by the student,« said the young man; »the student who lived just opposite and died a month ago. He must have suffered a lot from toothache. It's well worth reading. There's only a little left here of what he wrote – originally a complete book and some more besides. My parents gave half a pound of green soap for it to the student's landlady. Here's what I manage to rescue.«

I borrowed it and read it, and now I'll pass it on to you. The title was:

Auntie Toothache
I

My aunt used to give me sweets when I was small. My teeth held out and weren't ruined. Now I'm older and have left school. She still spoils me with sweets and says I'm a poet.

There is something of the poet in me, though not enough. Often, as I walk through the streets of the town, I feel as if I was in a large library. The houses are bookcases, every storey a shelf with books. Here is a tale of everyday life, there a good old play and scientific works on every subject, and there again reading pleasant and unpleasant. All that literature is for me to dream and philosophize over.

Yes, I've got something of the poet in me, but not enough. Lots of people must have just as much as I have - and yet have no badge or title to the name of poet.

To them and to me is given a gift from God, a boon big enough for oneself, but far too small to be parcelled out again among others. It comes like a ray from the sun, filling mind and soul; it comes like the scent of a flower, or a melody one has heard but cannot remember where.

The other evening, as I sat in my room longing to read, but without book or paper to look at, all at once a fresh green leaf dropped down from the lime tree, and a puff of air blew it in to me through the window.

I was looking at all the branching veins on the leaf, when a little insect crawled across it, just as though it wanted to make a close study of the leaf. That set me thinking about human wisdom. We, too, crawl about on a leaf, knowing nothing but that, and then proceed to give a lecture on the whole great tree - root, trunk and summit - the whole great tree, that's to say, God, the world and immortality ... And all we know of the whole thing is on a little leaf.

As I sat there, I had a visit from Auntie Millie. I showed her the leaf with the insect, told her what had come into my mind, and her eyes shone.

»You're a poet!« she exclaimed. »Perhaps the greatest we have. If I should live to see that, I would go happy to my grave. You have always, ever since Brewer Rasmussen's funeral, astonished me by your tremendous imagination.«

So said Auntie Millie and kissed me.

Now, who was this Auntie Millie, and who was Brewer Rasmussen?

II

Mother's aunt was always called »Auntie« by us children; we had no other name for her.

She gave us sugar and jam, although this was very bad for our teeth, but she was weak with the dear children, she said; it was so cruel to deny them the little bit of sweet stuff they were so fond of.

And that made us very fond of Auntie. She was an old maid – always old, as far back as I can remember. Her age stood still.

In earlier years she suffered a lot from toothache and was always talking about it; that's why her friend, Brewer Rasmussen, called her for a joke »Auntie Toothache«.

He didn't do any brewing in his later years, but lived on his dividends; he often came to see Auntie and was older than she was. He had no teeth at all, only a few black stumps.

As a child he had eaten too much sugar, he told us children, and that's what happened to your teeth. Auntie can't ever in her childhood have eaten sugar; she had the loveliest white teeth. She saved them, too – said Brewer Rasmussen – by not sleeping with them at night!

We children knew that was very naughty of him, but Auntie said he didn't mean anything by it.

One morning, at breakfast, she told us of a nasty dream she had had in the night: one of her teeth had fallen out. »That means I shall lose a true friend,« she said. »Was it a false tooth?« asked the brewer with a chuckle. »Then it may only mean that you'll lose a false friend!«

»You're a rude old gentleman,« said Auntie, more angry than I've ever seen her before or since.

But later on she said that her old friend was only teasing; he was the most generous man on earth and, when he came to die, he would become one of God's little angels in heaven.

I puzzled a lot over this tranformation and wondered whether I should ever be able to recognize him in his new shape.

When Auntie was young and he too was young, he proposed to her. She hesitated too long, was slow in making up her mind, was *much too*

slow in making up her mind; and so she always remained an old maid, yet always a faithful friend.

And then Brewer Rasmussen died.

He was driven to his grave in the most expensive hearse and was accompanied by a large number of people in uniform and decorations.

Dressed in mourning, Auntie stood at the window with all of us children – except for the little brother that the stork had brought a week before.

When the hearse and all the mourners had gone by and the street was empty, Auntie wanted to leave, but I didn't want to. I was waiting for the angel, Brewer Rasmussen; for, of course, he had now become a little winged child of God and must show up.

»Auntie,« I said, »don't you think he'll come now, or maybe when the stork brings us another little brother he'll bring us Angel Rasmussen?«

My imagination quite took Auntie's breath away, and she said, »That child will be a great poet«; and she kept on saying this all through my schooldays, even after I was confirmed, right down to my present years as a student.

She was and is my most sympathetic friend both in the throes of writing and the throes of toothache. You see, I have attacks of both.

»Write down all your thoughts, that's all,« she said, »and then put them away in a drawer. Jean Paul did that, and became a great writer, who as a matter of fact I'm not very fond of. He doesn't thrill. You must thrill – and you will thrill!«

The night after this conversation I lay in longing and agony with a deep desire to become the great writer that Auntie could see in me. I was aching to be a poet. But there is a worse ache than that – toothache. It smashed me and hashed me; I became a writhing worm with a hot poultice and blistering Spanish beetles.

»Yes, I know all about that!« said Auntie.

There was a sad smile about her mouth; her teeth shone so very white.

But here I must begin a new chapter in my aunt's history and in my own.

III

I had moved into new lodgings and had been living there for a month. I was chatting with Auntie about this.

»I'm living (I said) with a quiet family. They don't worry about me, even when I ring three times. Otherwise, it's a regular house of din with all the hubbub of wind and weather and people. My room is right over the entrance; every cart that comes out or in sets the pictures swinging on the wall. The banging of the gate shakes the house as if there was an earthquake. If I'm lying in bed, the shocks go right through me, though it's all supposed to strengthen the nerves. If it's windy - and it's always windy in this country – then the long window-catches outside swing to and fro and knock against the wall. The gate bell to the yard next-door peals with every gust of wind.

The lodgers in our house come home in driblets, late at night, well into the small hours. The lodger immediately above me, who by day gives lessons on the trombone, is the last home, and before he gets into bed he has a little midnight walk up and down, with heavy steps and hobnailed boots.

There are no double windows, but there is a broken pane which the landlady has stuck paper over; all the same, the wind blows in through the crack and produces a sound like a buzzing hornet. That's my lullaby. When I do at last fall asleep, I'm soon woken up by a cock crowing. Both cock and hen announce from the cellarman's chicken-house that it will soon be morning. The little Norwegian ponies, which have no stable but are tethered in the cubby hole under the stairs, kick on the door and skirting as they stretch their legs.

The day dawns. The concierge, who sleeps with his family in the attic, goes stamping downstairs; the clogs clatter, the door slams, the house trembles and, when that's all over and done with, the lodger overhead begins to do his morning exercises, lifting with each hand an heavy dumb-bell which he cannot hold on to - it keeps falling. Meanwhile the young people of the house, who are off to school, come rushing screaming downstairs. I go to the window and open it to get some fresh air – and it *is* refreshing, as long as I can get it and the young woman in the backhouse isn't washing gloves in her chemicals, which is how she gets a living. Otherwise, it's a nice house and I'm living with a quiet family.«

Well, that's the account I gave Auntie of the place where I lodged. Only I made it livelier, for a description by word of mouth is more vivid than it is in writing.

»You're a poet!« cried Auntie. »Only write your talk down, and you'll be as good as Dickens. In fact, you interest me much more. You paint, when you talk. You describe your house so that one sees it, and shudders! Go on writing – about something that's alive – about people; best of all, about unhappy people!«

As for the house, I really did write it down, with all its din and drawbacks, but only with myself in it. There was no action; that came later.

IV

It was during winter, late in the evening, after the theatre; with terrible weather – a snowstorm – so that you could hardly get along.

Auntie had been at the theatre, and I was there to take her home; but it was hard enough to get along yourself, let alone take others with you. The cabs were all engaged. Auntie lived a long way out, whereas my lodgings were close to the theatre; but for that we might have stood sheltering till further notice.

We stumbled ahead in the deep snow with the snowflakes whirling around us. I lifted her, I supported her, I pushed her forward. We only fell twice, but we fell softly.

We approached my gate, where we shook ourselves. Again, on the steps, we shook ourselves, and even then we took in enough snow with us to cover the floor of the entrance-hall.

We took off overcoats and undercoats and any other things that could be taken off. The landlady lent Auntie dry stockings and a dressing-gown; this was necessary, said the landlady, and added - truly enough - that auntie couldn't possibly go home that night. She invited her to make shift with her sitting room; she would make up a bed for her on the sofa in front of the permanently locked door into my room. And this was done.

The fire was burning in my stove, the tea things were laid on the table, and it was very cosy in the little room – even though hardly as cosy as at Auntie's, where in the winter there are thick curtains on the door, thick curtains on the windows, double carpets on the floor with three layers of thick paper underneath. You sit there as if you were in a well-corked bottle with warm air; and yet, as I said just now, it was also very cosy in my room, with the wind whistling outside.

Auntie talked and talked. Her young days came back to her; the brewer, too, came back, and old memories.

She could remember me cutting my first tooth and how delighted the family was.

The first tooth! The tooth of innocence, shining like a little white drop of milk: the milk tooth.

There came one, there came several, a whole row, side by side, above and below, the loveliest child's teeth; and yet these were only the advance troops, not the real ones that must last right through life.

Then they too arrived and the wisdom-teeth as well, fuglemen in the ranks, born in pain and great trouble.

They leave you again, everyone of them. They go before their period of service has run out; even the last one goes, and that's no day of rejoicing; it's a day of sadness.

And then you're old, even if your heart is young.

Conversation and thoughts like that are hardly amusing, and yet we came to talk of all that; we came back to the years of childhood, talked and talked, and the clock struck twelve before Auntie retired to rest in the room next to mine.

»Good night, my dear child,« she called out. »Now I shall sleep as if I lay in my own chest of drawers!« And she settled down to sleep in peace.

But no peace was to be found either in the house or outside. The gale shook the windows, flogged the long dangling window-catches, rang the neighbour's door-bell in the yard behind the house. The lodger overhead had come home; once more he took his little nightly stroll up and down, then he flung his boots on to the floor and laid himself to rest. But his snoring is so loud that it can easily be heard through the ceiling.

There was no rest or peace for me, and the weather didn't settle down either; it was abominably active. The wind whizzed and sang in its own way; my teeth also began to be active, and whizzed and sang in their own way. It was the signal for a full-dress toothache.

There was a draught from the window. The moon shone in across the floor. The glimmer came and went as the clouds came and went in the gale. There was a restless light and shadow, but at last the shadow on the floor began to look like something. I stared at this moving object ... and I felt my blood run cold.

On the floor sat a figure, long and thin, just as when a child draws with a pencil on its slate something resembling a person. A single thin stroke makes the body, another and another are the arms; the legs are also each done in one stroke, and the head is a polygon.

Presently the shape grew more distinct, wearing some sort of drapery, very thin and delicate; but this showed that it belonged to one of the female sex.

I heard a droning sound. Was it her, or was it the wind humming like a hornet through the window-crack?

No, it was Madame Toothache herself, her infernal Satanic Frightfulness – heaven preserve us from a visit from her!

»It's good to be here,« she droned. »This is a good neighbourhood: marshy, boggy ground. The mosquitoes have buzzed here with poison in

their sting; now I have the sting. It must be sharpened on human teeth. They're shining so white on this fellow in bed. They have defied sweet and sour, hot and cold, nutshells and plum stones; but I'll take them and shake them, nourish their roots with draughts, let the cold in their stumps.«

This was a terrible speech, from a terrible visitor.

»Dear, dear, so you're a poet, are you?« she said. »Very well. I'll compose tortures for you in every metre. I'll give you iron and steel in your body, new fibres in all your nerves.«

I felt as if a red-hot gimlet was piercing my cheekbone; I writhed and squirmed.

»A capital toothache!« she said. »Quite an organ to play on. Concert on the Jew's harp – magnificent – with trumpets and kettledrums, piccolos, and a trombone in the wisdom-tooth. Great poet – great music!«

And she struck up – no doubt about that – and her appearance was frightful, even though you could hardly see more of her than her hand, that shadowy ice-cold hand with the long skinny fingers. Each of them was an instrument of torture. Thumb and first finger had forceps and screw, the second finger ended as a sharp-pointed awl, the ring finger was a gimlet and the little finger squirted mosquito poison.

»I'll teach you metrics!« she said. »A big poet must have a big toothache, a little poet a little toothache.«

»Please let me be little,« I begged. »Don't let me be anything! I'm no poet, I only have fits of writing, like fits of toothache. Do go away!«

»Will you admit, then, that I'm more powerful than poetry, philosophy, mathematics and all music?« she asked. »More powerful than all those impressions in paint and in marble? I'm older than the whole lot of them. I was born near the Garden of Eden, just outside, where the wind blew and the damp toadstools were growing. I got Eve to wear clothes in the cold weather, and Adam too. Believe me, there was strength in the first toothache.«

»I believe everything you say,« I replied. »But do go away!«

»Very well. If you will give up being a poet, never write down a single verse on paper, slate or any other kind of writing material, then I'll leave you. But I shall come back, if you start writing.«

»I swear!« I answered. »All I ask is never to see you or meet you again.«

»But you *shall* see me, only in an ampler form, one dearer to you than mine is at present. You shall see me as Auntie Millie; and I shall say, 'Write, my dear boy! You're a great poet, maybe the greatest we have'. But, believe me, if you start writing I shall set your poems to music and play them on your Jew's harp, you darling child! Remember me, when you see Auntie Millie.«

And she vanished.

As a parting gift I got a red-hot stab in the cheekbone, but it was soon lulled. I seemed to glide on smooth water and to see the white water-lilies with their broad green leaves give way and sink beneath me, then wither and dissolve, and I sank with them and faded away in rest and peace ...

»Die, melt away like snow,« came the sound of singing in the water. »Vanish in the cloud, sail away like the cloud...«

Down to me through the water came shining large luminous names inscribed upon floating banners of victory, the patent of immortality written on the may-fly's wings.

I slept deeply, a sleep without dreams. No longer I heard the whistling wind, the banging door, the clanging bell at the neighbour's entrance, nor the clumsy exercises of the lodger.

How heavenly!

Suddenly there came a gust of wind, and the locked door into Auntie's room flew open. Auntie jumped up, slipped on clothes and shoes, and came in to me.

I was sleeping like an angel, she said, and she hadn't the heart to wake me.

I awoke of my own accord, opened my eyes and had quite forgotten that Auntie was in the house. But then presently I remembered it, remembered my toothache apparition. Dream and reality became mingled together.

»I suppose you didn't write something last night, after we had said good-night?« she asked. »If only you had! You are my poet, and you'll always be that.«

Her smile seemed to me so crafty. I wasn't sure whether it was the good-natured Auntie Millie who loved me, or the terrible one I had given my promise to last night.

»Have you written anything, dear child?«

»No, no!« I cried. »You *are* my Auntie Millie, aren't you?«

»Who else?« she said. And it was Auntie Millie. She kissed me, got into a cab and drove home.

I wrote down what is written here. It's not in verse and it shall never be printed ...

Well, that's where the manuscript stopped. My young friend, the future grocer's apprentice, couldn't lay his hands on the part that was missing; it had gone out into the world as paper to wrap up bloaters, butter and green soap. It had fulfilled its destiny.

The brewer is dead; Auntie is dead; the student is dead, the sparks of whose spirit went into the tub. That's the end of my story – the story of Auntie Toothache.

The Flea and the
Professor

There was once a balloonist who came to grief. His balloon burst, and the man tumbled out and was dashed to pieces. Two minutes earlier he had sent his boy down by parachute. That was lucky for the boy; he was unhurt and was left with plenty of knowledge how to sail a balloon, but he had no balloon and no means of getting one.

He had got to live, and so he went in for conjuring and learnt to talk with his stomach, which is called being a ventriloquist. He was young and good-looking, and when he grew a moustache and was well-dressed, he might have been taken for a nobleman's son. The ladies thought him handsome, and one young woman was so carried away by his charm and his conjuring that she went along with him to cities and countries abroad. There he called himself Professor, which was the least that would do.

His one thought was still to get hold of a balloon and to go up with his dear wife, but so far they hadn't the wherewithal.

»It'll turn up,« he said.

»I do hope so,« she replied.

»Well, we're both young, and I'm now a professor. Half a loaf is better than no bread.«

She helped him faithfully, for she sat at the door selling tickets for the performance, and that was a chilly pastime in winter. There was one trick, too, in which she helped him. He used to put his wife into the drawer of a table – a large one. There she crept into a drawer at the back, and so was invisible in front. It was a kind of optical illusion.

But one evening, when he opened the drawer, she had vanished. She wasn't in the front drawer, or in the back drawer, or anywhere in the building; she was not to be seen or heard. That was *her* conjuring trick. She never came back; she was tired of it, and it bored him too – he lost his spirits and ceased to laugh and make jokes, and so nobody came. The takings grew worse, and so did his clothes. At last he owned nothing but a large flea, an inheritance from his wife, and therefore especially dear to him. So he began training it, taught it some good tricks, taught it to present arms and fire a cannon – a little one, of course.

The Professor was proud of the flea, and the flea was proud of itself. It knew a thing or two and had human blood in its veins and had been in the largest cities; it had been seen by princes and princesses and had won their royal applause. It was billed in the newspapers and on posters. It knew it was a celebrity and could support a professor and, in fact, a whole family.

Yet, proud as it was and famous as it was, when the Professor travelled by train they went third class; that gets there just as quickly as first class. There was an unspoken promise between them that they would never be parted, never get married; the flea would stay a bachelor and the Professor a widower. That would make them all square.

»Where you've once had a great success,« said the Professor, »don't chance your luck a second time.« He was a judge of character, and that too is an art.

At length he had toured every country but the land of the savages; and so to the land of the savages he made up his mind to go. The Professor knew of course that they eat Christian people there; but he wasn't really a Christian and the flea wasn't really a person, so he thought they might as well risk a tour there and earn good profits.

They went by steamer and by sailing ship. The flea went through his tricks, and so their voyage cost them nothing and they came to the land of the savages. This was governed by a little Princess; she was only eight, but still she governed. She had seized power from her father and mother, for she had a will of her own and was so marvellously pretty and naughty.

Directly the flea presented arms and fired the cannon, the Princess was so taken with him that she cried, »Him or nobody!« She fell quite wildly in love, and she was already wild enough before.

»My dear, darling, sensible child,« said her father, »if only it could first be turned into a man!«

»Leave that to me, old thing!« she said. Not a very nice way for a little princess to speak to her father, but she was wild.

She placed the flea on her little hand.

»Now you're a man, reigning with me. But mind you do what I want, or I'll kill you and eat the Professor.«

The Professor was given a large room to live in. The walls were made of sugar cane, which he might go and lick, only he hadn't a sweet tooth. He got a hammock to sleep in. It reminded him of sleeping in a balloon, which was what he had always longed for and couldn't get out of his thoughts.

The flea stayed with the Princess, sitting on her little hand and on her soft neck. She pulled a hair out of her head, and the Professor had to tie this round the flea's leg; in this way she kept it fastened to the large piece of coral she wore in the lobe of her ear.

What a lovely time for the Princess – and also for the flea, she thought.

But the Professor was not at all pleased; he liked to keep on the move and wander from town to town, to read in the papers about his perseverance and skill in teaching a flea to do everything a man can do. Day in, day out, he lolled in his hammock and was given good food: fresh bird's-eggs, elephant's eyes and giraffe steaks. Cannibals don't only live on human flesh; that's a delicacy. »Shoulder of child with piquant sauce,« said the Princess's mother, »is the most delicious.«

The Professor was bored and wanted very much to get away from the land of the savages, but the flea must come with him; it was his prodigy and his bread-and-butter. How could he catch it and keep it? That was not so easy.

He racked his brain to think of a way, and then said to himself, »I have it!«

»Princess's father! Please let me have something to do. May I train your inhabitants in the proper way to salute? That's what the greatest countries call culture.«

»And what can you teach me?« asked the Princess's father.

»My finest trick«, said the Professor, »is to fire off a cannon, so that the whole earth trembles and all the tastiest birds of the air fall down ready cooked. There's no end of a bang.«

»Come on – let's see that cannon!« said the Princess's father.

But in the whole country there wasn't a cannon to be found, except the one the flea had brought, and that was too small.

»I'll make a bigger one, « said the Professor. »All I want are the materials. I must have fine silk, needle and thread, ropes and cords, together with balloon's stomach medicine. This will inflate, lighten and heave it up; it's what gives the bang to the stomach of the cannon.«

He got all that he asked for.

The whole country gathered to see the big cannon. The Professor didn't give the word till he had the balloon quite ready to fill and go up.

The flea sat on the Princess's hand and looked on. The balloon filled, bellying so much that it could scarcely be held – it was so hard to control.

»I must take it up to cool it off,« said the Professor and took his seat in the basket that hung below. »But I can't manage to steer it all by myself. I must have an expert with me to help. There's no one here that can do it except the flea.«

»I don't like to allow that,« said the Princess. All the same, she passed the flea over to the Professor who set it on his hand.

»Slip cords and cables!« he cried. »Now then off she goes!«

They thought he meant the cannon.

And the balloon went higher and higher, away above the clouds, away from the land of the savages.

The little Princess, her father and mother, and the whole population with them, stood and waited. They're waiting still; and if you don't believe it, then go to the land of the savages, where every child talks about the flea and the Professor and thinks they will both come back when the cannon has cooled off. But they won't. They're at home here with us; they're in their mother country, travelling by train, first class, not third. They earn good money and have a large balloon. Nobody asks how they got the balloon or where it comes from. They are well-to-do, highly respected people, the flea and the Professor.

The Beetle*

The Emperor's horse was given gold shoes, a gold shoe to each foot ... Why should he have gold shoes?

He was a most beautiful animal: he had good legs, intelligent eyes, and a mane that hung from his neck like a silk veil. He had carried his master through gunpowder fumes and a hail of bullets, and had heard the bullets sing and whistle past him. He had snapped and kicked and joined in the fighting, when the enemy surged forward; with the Emperor on his back he had leapt clean over the fallen horse of the enemy and saved his Emperor's crown of red gold, saved his Emperor's life, more precious than red gold – and for that the Emperor's horse was given gold shoes, a gold shoe to each foot.

Then the beetle came crawling out.

»First the big ones, then the little ones,« he said: »And yet it isn't size that does it.« With that he stretched out his thin legs.

»What do you want?« asked the smith.

»Gold shoes,« replied the beetle.

»Why, you must have gone off your head,« said the smith. »Do you mean to say *you* want gold shoes, too?«

»Yes, gold shoes,« said the beetle. »Am I not just as good as that great brute who has to be waited on, rubbed down, looked after, fed and watered? Don't I also belong to the Emperor's stables?«

»Yes, but why is the horse being given gold shoes?« asked the smith. »Don't you understand?«

»Understand? I understand that I'm being treated with contempt,« said the beetle. »It's an insult – and so now I'm going out into the wide world.«

»Be off with you!« said the smith.

»Ill-mannered brute!« said the beetle, and he went outside, flew a little way, and there he was in a pretty little flower-garden where there was a delicious smell of roses and lavender.

»Isn't it beautiful here?« said one of the tiny ladybirds that were flying about with black spots on their red scaly wings. »Doesn't it smell nice, and isn't the garden lovely!«

»I'm accustomed to something better,« said the beetle. »Do you call this beautiful? Why, there isn't even a manure heap.«

And so he went a bit further on, till he reached the shade of a large stock on which a caterpillar was crawling.

* Suggested by an Arabian proverb quoted by Dickens.

»What a nice world it is!« said the caterpillar. »The sun's so warm, everything's so delightful; and when I one day fall asleep and die, as they call it, then I shall wake up and be a butterfly.«

»Where did you get that idea from?« said the beetle. »We're flying about like butterflies already. I come from the Emperor's stables; but nobody there – not even the Emperor's own charger, though he wears my cast-off gold shoes – has ideas like that. Get wings? Fly? Yes, let's fly straight away.« And the beetle flew off. »I don't like getting annoyed, but I *am* annoyed all the same.«

Then he dropped down on to a large patch of grass and lay there a while; and then he fell asleep.

Bless my soul, how it rained! It was coming down in sheets. The beetle was woken up by all this pelting and at once tried to go into the ground, but couldn't. He toppled over; he tried swimming on his stomach and then on his back. Flying was out of the question; it looked as if he would never get away from this spot alive. He lay where he lay, and went on lying there.

When it cleared a little and the beetle had blinked the water out of his eyes, he caught a glimpse of something white; it was some linen left to bleach. He came up to it and crept into a fold of the soaking fabric. This was certainly quite a different thing from lying on a warm heap in the stable; still, here there was nothing better to be had, and so he stayed where he was for a whole day and night, and the rain stayed too. In the morning the beetle crept out; he was furious with the weather.

Two frogs were squatting on the linen; their eyes shone bright from sheer enjoyment. »What glorious weather!« said one of them. »How refreshing it is! And the linen holds the water so splendidly. My hind legs are simply itching to swim.«

»I should very much like to know«, said the other, »whether the swallow – that gadabout creature – on its many journeys abroad has ever found a better climate than ours, with all its drizzle and damp. It's just as if you lay in a soaking wet ditch. If you don't revel in that, you can't really love your native land.«

»Then I suppose you've never been in the Emperor's stables, have you?« asked the beetle. »The moisture there is both warm and spicy. That's what I'm used to; that's my climate, but you can't take it with you when you travel. Isn't there a hotbed anywhere in the garden, where people of some standing like myself can put up and feel at home?«

But the frogs couldn't make head or tail of him – or they didn't want to.

»I never ask a second time,« said the beetle, when he had already asked three times without getting an answer.

Then he went on further and came across a bit of broken flower-pot. It oughtn't to have been there but, lying like that, it offered shelter. Several earwig families were living here; they don't need a lot of space, but they do like company. The females have a great gift for mother love, and so of course each one's child was the nicest-looking and the cleverest.

»Our son has just got engaged,« said one mother. »The little innocent! His great ambition is to be able one day to creep into a parson's ear. He's such a dear childish boy; his engagement will keep him out of mischief, and that's such a comfort for a mother.«

»Our son,« said another mother, »he was at it directly he came out of the egg; he's all fizzle and splutter; he's sowing his wild oats. That's a great relief to a mother, don't you think, Mr. Beetle?« They could tell the stranger by his shape.

»You're both right,« said the beetle; so then he was invited in – as far he could manage to get – under the broken flower-pot.

»Now let me show you *my* little earwig,« said a third mother and a fourth. »They're the dearest children and so amusing. They're never naughty unless they have stomachache, though that's easy to get at their time of life.«

And each mother talked about her young ones, and the young ones joined in and used the little fork they have on their tails to pull the beetle's moustache.

»They're always up to something or other, the little rogues!« said the mother earwigs, dribbling over with motherliness; but the beetle was bored, and so he asked how far it was to the hotbed.

»It's a tremendous way off on the other side of the ditch,« said the earwig. »I hope no child of mine will ever go so far away, for if it did I should never get over it.«

»All the same, that's where I mean to try and get,« said the beetle and went off without saying goodbye, as they do in the best circles.

By the ditch he came across several of his own kind, all beetles.

»This is where we live,« they said. »We're very snug. May we invite you to join us in this fertile spot? You must have had a tiring journey.«

»Yes, I have,« said the beetle. »I've been lying on linen in the rain, and too much washing always takes it out of me. I've also got rheumatism in the wing-joints from standing in a draught under a broken flower-pot. It's a great relief to find yourself among your own people.«

»Do you happen to come from the hotbed?« asked the oldest of them.

»Higher up than that,« said the beetle. »I come from the Emperor's stables, where I was born with gold shoes on. I'm travelling on a secret errand, but you mustn't pump me about that, for I shan't say a word.«

And with that the beetle crawled down into the rich mud, where three young she-beetles sat and giggled, for they didn't know what to say.

»They're none of them engaged,« said their mother, and they giggled again, though this was from bashfulness.

»They're as pretty as any I've seen in the royal stables,« said the beetle traveller.

»You mustn't turn my daughters' heads! And please don't speak to them unless you have honourable intentions ... but I feel sure you have, and I give you my blessing.«

»Splendid!« cried all the others, and the beetle then became engaged. First betrothal, then marriage – what else was there to wait for!

The following day went off well enough, the day after was so-so, but the third day there was food to be thought of for wife and maybe little ones.

»I've let myself be caught by surprise,« he said. »Well, the only thing to do is to surprise *them*.«

And he did. He was gone: gone all day, gone all night, and his wife was left a widow. The other beetles said it was nothing but a tramp they had taken into their family, and now they had his wife on their hands.

»Then she can be a spinster again,« said her mother, »and be with my other children. What a shame! Such a caddish trick to go and leave her like that!«

In the meantime he was on the move and had sailed across the ditch on a cabbage leaf. Later in the morning two people came along, who caught sight of the beetle, picked him up and turned and twisted him about; they both knew all about insects, especially the boy. »'Allah sees the black beetle in the black stone in the black mountain' – isn't that what it says in the Koran?« he asked. Then he translated the beetle's name into Latin and gave an account of its species and their habits. The elder expert was against taking him home with them; they had, he said, just as good specimens already. This wasn't very polite of him, thought the beetle; and so he flew off his hand, flew a good way – for his wings had dried out – and in this way reached the greenhouse. As it happened, one of the windows had been pushed open, so he was able to slip in and dig himself down in the fresh manure.

»Ooh, this is delicious!« he said.

Presently he fell asleep and dreamt that the Emperor's horse had had a fall and that Mr. Beetle had been given its gold shoes and the promise of two more. That was a pleasant dream, and when the beetle woke up, he crawled out and looked around. How gorgeous it was in the greenhouse! Huge palms spread themselves like fans up in the roof, and the sun shone right through their leaves, while below them grew a wealth of greenery and a blaze of flowers that were red as fire, yellow as amber, and white as new-fallen snow.

»Did you ever see such vegetation!« exclaimed the beetle. »Won't it taste lovely when it all goes bad! This is a fine larder they've got; I dare say some of my family are living here. I'll try and track them down and see if I can find any I can mix with. I have my pride, and I'm proud of it.« And he fell to thinking of his dream about the dead horse and the gold shoes he had won.

Suddenly a hand caught hold of the beetle; he was squeezed, twisted and turned.

The gardener's small son was in the greenhouse with a friend; they had seen the beetle and meant to have some fun with him. Wrapped in a grape-vine leaf, he was put into a warm trouser-pocket, where he wriggled about until he got another squeeze from the boy, who was running off to the big lake at the bottom of the garden. Here the beetle was put into an old broken wooden shoe with the instep missing. A little peg was stuck in as a mast, and the beetle was tied up to this with a wool thread. He was to be skipper, and now he was going for a sail.

The lake was so big that the beetle thought it was the ocean and was so astonished that he fell over backwards with his legs kicking in the air.

The wooden shoe sailed off with the current, but when the boat got too far out one of the boys immediately rolled up his trousers and went out and fetched it back; but next time it went adrift the boys happened to be wanted – wanted at once – and so off they ran, leaving the wooden shoe to its fate. Away it drifted, further and further from the shore. This was dreadful for the beetle, and he couldn't fly because he was lashed up to the mast.

Then a fly came to see him.

»Delightful weather we're having,« said the fly. »This is just the place for me to take a rest and bask in the sun. You've found a cosy spot.«

»What nonsense you're talking! Can't you see that I'm tied up?«

»Well, I'm not tied up,« answered the fly and promptly flew away.

»So *that's* the kind of world it is,« said the beetle. »It's a mean low-down world. I'm the only respectable creature in it. First, I'm refused gold shoes; then I have to lie on damp linen and stand in a draught; and

after that they saddle me with a wife. Next, I stride boldly out into the world to see something of life and how I ought to live it, and up comes a human puppy and sets me tethered on the raging sea. And all this time the Emperor's horse is going about in gold shoes! That's what gets my goat ... But you can't expect sympathy in this world. I've had a most interesting career, though what's the good of that if nobody knows about it? No, and the world doesn't deserve to know about it either, or it would have given me gold shoes in the royal stables that time the Emperor's charger stretched out its legs and was shod. If I'd been given gold shoes, I should have been an honour to the stables. Now they've lost me, and the world has lost me. It's all over.«

But it wasn't all over yet, for a boat came along with two young girls in it.

»Look, there's a wooden shoe floating,« said one of them.

»It's got a little creature tied up in it.« said the other.

They were just alongside the wooden shoe, so they lifted it out of the water and one of the girls took out a small pair of scissors and cut through the wool thread without doing any harm to the beetle; and as soon as they landed she put him down in the grass.

»Now then, crawl, crawl – fly, fly – if you can!« she said. »It's lovely to be free.«

And the beetle flew straight in through the open window of a large building – and sank down exhausted in the beautiful, long mane of the Emperor's charger, which was standing in the stable they both belonged to. The beetle held on tight to the mane and sat for a while trying to pull himself together: »Here I am, sitting on the Emperor's own charger – riding like a horseman ... What was that I said? Ah, yes, now I'm beginning to understand. What a good idea, and quite correct too. Why was the horse given gold shoes? He asked me that as well, the smith did. Now I realize. It was because of me that the horse was given gold shoes.«

That put the beetle into a good humour again. »Travelling helps one to see things more clearly,« he said.

The sun shone in on him, shone very beautifully. »The world isn't so bad considering,« said the beetle, »only you've got to learn how to take it.« Yes, the world was beautiful now; for, you see, the Emperor's charger had been given gold shoes because the beetle was to be the rider.

»Now I'll dismount and tell the other beetles how much has been done for me. I'll tell them of all my pleasant adventures abroad, and I shall explain to them that now I'm going to stay at home till the horse has worn out his gold shoes.«

Soup from a Sausage-Stick
I
Soup from a sausage-stick

»That was an excellent dinner we had yesterday,« said an old she-mouse to one who hadn't been at the party. »I sat twenty-first from the old Mouse-King; that wasn't bad, when you come to think of it. Now would you like to hear the different courses? They were extremely well put together. There was mouldy bread, bacon rind, tallow candle and sausage – all with second helpings. It was as good as having two meals. There was a pleasant atmosphere of cheerful nonsense, such as you get in a family circle. Not a crumb was left except the sausage-sticks and, while

we were talking about these, the question cropped up of making soup from a sausagestick. Everyone, of course, had heard about it, but nobody had tasted such soup, much less knew how to make it. A charming toast was proposed to the inventor: he deserved (said the speaker) to be master of a workhouse. Wasn't that witty? And the old Mouse-King got up and promised that the young mouse who could turn out the tastiest soup of the kind mentioned should become his Queen; they should have a year and a day to think it over.«

»That's not so dusty!« said the second mouse. »But how do you make soup from a sausage-stick?«

»Yes, how's it made?« asked all the she-mice, young and old. They all liked the idea of being Queen, but they didn't fancy the bother of going out into the wide world in order to learn how to make the soup – which of course they would have to do. After all, it isn't everyone who is ready to leave their family and the old nooks and corners; away from home, you don't run across cheese-rind and sniff bacon-rind every day. No, you may starve sometimes – and even perhaps be eaten alive by a cat.

These no doubt were the thoughts that scared most of them out of sallying forth in search of knowledge, and only four mice – young, nimble, but poor – turned up at the start. They were each of them ready to go to one of the four corners of the earth; the result would then have to be left to chance. Each one took a sausage-stick with her as a reminder of why they were going; it would do for a pilgrim's staff.

Early in May they set out, and early in May the following year they came back ... but only three of them. The fourth one didn't report, nothing was heard of her, and today was the day of decision.

»There always has to be a touch of sadness clinging to our gayest entertainments,« said the Mouse-King. Still, he ordered invitations to be sent out to every mouse for many miles around; they were all to assemble in the kitchen. The three mice who'd just come back stood lined up by themselves; and for the fourth one, who was missing, a sausage-stick had been brought wound about with black crape. Nobody dared to say what he thought until the three had spoken and until the Mouse-King had announced what might be said after that.

Now we're going to hear all about it.

II

What the first little mouse had seen and learnt on her travels

»When I set out into the wide world,« said the little mouse, »I imagined, like so many of my age, that I knew all there was to know. Well, I didn't; it takes a year and a day for that to happen. I went straight away to sea; I joined a ship bound for the north. I had heard that at sea a cook has got to know how to make things do; but it's easy enough to make things do; when you've plenty of sides of bacon, barrels of salt meat and mitey flour. You can live like a fighting-cock – but you don't learn how to make soup from a sausage-stick. For days and nights we sailed along, rolling and drenched. As soon as we came to the port we were making for, I left the vessel; it was far up in the north.

It's a curious feeling to leave your own little hole at home, sail in a ship (which is also a kind of hole) – and then suddenly find yourself hundreds of miles away, standing in a foreign country. There were trackless forests with trees of spruce and birch; they smelt so strong - I don't like that – and the wild herbs smelt so spicy that it made me sneeze, and I thought of sausages. There were forest lakes with water that looked quite clear from close by, but inky black from a distance. White swans were floating there; they lay so still that I mistook them for foam, though when I saw them fly and saw them walk I knew what they were. They belong to the goose family; once you see them waddle, there's no getting away from their relationship. I stuck to my own sort; I made friends with fieldmice, who as a matter of fact know precious little, especially on the subject of good food, and that was just what I went abroad for. The very idea of making soup from a sausagestick was to them so extraordinary that it was immediately passed through the whole wood, but that it could actually be done they regarded as quite hopeless; least of all did I imagine that here this night I should be let into the secret. It was midsummer and that, they said, was why the perfume of the woods was so strong and the herbs so spicy, why the lakes were so clear and yet showed so dark against the white swans.

At the edge of the wood, among three or four houses, a pole as tall as a mainmast was put up, and from the top of it hung wreaths and ribbons. It was the maypole. Girls and boys danced round and round it, and their singing vied with jigging of the fiddler. It was a merry party at sunset and in the moonlight, though I didn't join in – imagine a little mouse at a dance in the woods! No, I stayed in the velvety moss and held on to my sausage-stick. The moon shone on one spot especially, where there was a tree covered with moss as delicate – yes, I make bold to say, as delicate as the coat of the Mouse-King; but it was of a green colour that was most refreshing to the eyes. Then all at once there came tripping forward the sweetest little people not more than knee-high to me. They looked like human beings, though better proportioned. They are called elves and are elegantly dressed in flower-petals trimmed with the wings of flies and gnats: really quite smart. It was soon clear that they were looking for something, I couldn't make out what. But then a few of them came up to me, and the chief one pointed to my sausage-stick and said, »That's just the very thing for us. It's cut the right length; it'll be top-hole« – and he got more and more delighted, as he eyed my pilgrim's staff.

'You may borrow, but not keep,' I said.

'Not keep,' they all repeated. They took over my sausage-stick, as I let go of it, and they danced away with it to the beautiful mossy bit of ground; there they set up the sausage-stick in the middle of the glade. They, too, wanted to have a maypole, and the pole they now had might have been cut specially for them! Then it was dressed, and it looked an absolute picture.

Tiny spiders spun a thread of gold round and round it, hung up fluttering veils and pennants, so finely woven, so bleached and snowy in the moonlight, that my eyes were dazzled. The elves took colours from the butterfly's wings and sprinkled them over the white linen and, with flowers and diamonds glittering there, I didn't know my sausage-stick any longer. A maypole such as this had become was surely not to be found

anywhere else in the world. And now at last came the arrival of the really important elves. They wore no clothes, which gave them an air of great distinction, and I was invited to look on at the show, but from some way off, as I was too big beside them.

Now the music began. It was like the deep clanging of a thousand glass bells. I thought it was the swans singing; I even fancied I could hear the cuckoo and the thrush. At last it was as if the whole wood joined in: the voices of childen, the ringing of bells and the singing of birds, the most delicious melodies. And all that loveliness rang out from the maypole of the elves; it was a complete chime, and it came from my sausage-stick. Never had I dreamt that so much could come from it, but no doubt it all depends on who handles it. I was tremendously moved; I cried, as a little mouse can sometimes, tears of pure delight.

The night was only too short, but they always are up there at that time of the year. A breeze got up at dawn and ruffled the surface of the lake; all the delicate, hovering veils and pennants flew off into the air; the swaying kiosques of gossamer, suspension bridges and balustrades (or whatever they're called) which had been flung across from leaf to leaf, vanished into nothingness ... Six elves came and brought me my sausage-stick, asking whether I had any wish they could grant me. So I begged them to tell me how you make soup from a sausage-stick.

'How we do it?' said the principal elf, laughing. 'Well, you've just seen. I expect you could hardly tell your sausage-stick, could you?'

'Oh, you mean in that way,' I said, and told him straight out why I had come abroad and what was expected of me when I got back. 'What use,' I asked, 'will it be for the Mouse-King and the rest of our great empire to know that I've seen all this beauty? I can't shake it out of my sausage-stick and say, Look, here's the stick, now comes the soup – though it might do, all the same, as a kind of dessert when you'd had enough.'

Then the elf dipped his tiny finger down into a blue violet and said to me, 'Now, mind! I'll rub your staff with magic, and then, when you get back to the Mouse-King's palace, touch your King's warm breast with the staff. At that, violets will come out all over the staff, even on the coldest days in winter. There, that's something for you to take home, and a bit extra as well ...'«

But before the little mouse said what this was, she turned her staff towards the King's breast and, sure enough, the loveliest bunch of flowers burst out, smelling so strong that the Mouse-King ordered the mice who stood next to the fireplace to put their tails at once into the fire, so as to cause a slight smell of burning; for the scent of the violets was unbearable, and not at all the kind that the mice cared for.

»But what was the bit extra you spoke of?« asked the Mouse-King.

»Well, you see,« said the little mouse, »it's what's generally known as the 'effect'.« And then she turned the sausage-stick round, and there were no flowers left. She simply held the bare stick and raised it like a conductor's baton.

426

»Violets are for sight, smell and touch – that's what the elf told me; but there must still be something for hearing and taste.« So she began to beat time. It wasn't the music she heard in the wood at the festival of the elves – no, it was the kind you can hear in the kitchen ... Well, well! What a hotch-potch! It came suddenly, as though the wind was roaring down all the chimneys: kettles and saucepans boiled over, the coal-shovel banged against the brass kettle – and then, just as suddenly, it quietened down. You could hear the faint song of the tea-kettle, so curious that you couldn't possibly tell if it was stopping or beginning. Then the little pot boiled, and the big pot boiled – they didn't take any notice of each other – it was as if a pot never had any brains. And the little mouse waved her baton more excitedly than ever, till the saucepans foamed and bubbled and boiled right over, the wind whistled and the chimney whined ... Phew! it got so terrific that the little mouse even dropped her stick.

»That was a stiff soup!« said the old Mouse-King. »What about the next course?«

»There isn't any more,« said the little mouse, and curtseyed.

»No more?« exclaimed the Mouse-King. »Very well; then let's hear what the next one has to say.«

III

What the second little mouse had to tell

»I was born in the Castle library,« said the second mouse, »I as well as several of my family, who never had the luck to go into the dining-room, let alone the larder. Not until I left home and came here today did I ever see a kitchen. We were often positively starving in the library, but we got to know a great deal. Report reached us up there of the prize offered by the King for making soup from a sausage-stick, and then if my old grandmother didn't go and rout out a manuscript! She couldn't read herself, but she had it read to her – in which it said, 'If only you've a poet, you can make soup from a sausage-stick.' She asked me if I was a poet. I couldn't claim to be this, and she said that in that case I must set about becoming one. 'But what's wanted to become one?' I asked; for it was just as hard for me to find this out as to make the soup. However, Granny had listened to what others read; she said that three things were required, 'common sense, fantasy, and feeling; if you can only get these into you, then you'll be a poet and you'll manage all right with the sausage-stick'.«

And so I went westward out into the wide world, in order to become a poet.

Common sense, I realized, is the most important thing of all; the other two don't seem to matter so much. So I began by searching for common sense. Now, where's it to be found? 'Go to the ant and become wise,' said a great king in Palestine; I knew that from my library, and I didn't stop till I got to the nearest big ant-hill, where I lay in wait watching for wisdom.

They're a highly respectable people, the ants; they're common sense itself. Everything with them is like a correctly done sum that comes out right. To work and to lay eggs, they say, is to live for the present and provide for the future; and that's just what they do. They divide up into clean ants and dirty ants, and they're numbered according to rank. The queen ant is number one, and what she thinks is always right, for she knows all there is to know, and this was an important thing for me to grasp. She spoke so much, and so cleverly, that it seemed to me nonsense. She said that their ant-hill was the highest thing in the world; but close by stood a tree that was taller, much taller. This couldn't be denied, and so the subject was allowed to drop. One evening an ant had strayed off in that direction, crept up the trunk, not as far as the top, and yet higher than any ant had ever been before; and when it turned round and found its way back, it told them in the ant-hill of something much higher, further off. But the ants all found this statement insulting to the whole community, and the ant was condemned to wear a muzzle and to serve a long term of solitary confinement. Then, not long after, another ant went to the tree and made the same climb and discovery, but its account (they felt) was given in a quiet level-headed way; and as, besides that, it was a much respected ant and one of the clean ones, they believed what it said and when it died they put up an egg-shell to its memory, for they always paid respect to knowledge. I noticed,« said the little mouse, »that the ants frequently ran along with their eggs on their backs. I saw one of them drop hers, and she was making great efforts to get it up again, but she couldn't manage it. Then two others came and did all they could to help – in fact, they nearly dropped their own eggs – and this made them at

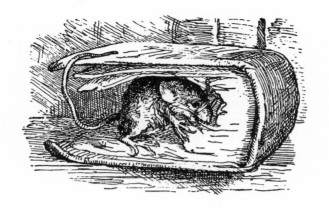

once give up helping, for you have to look after number one; and the queen ant's comment was that it had been a good example of kindness and intelligence. 'These,' she said, 'are two qualities that set us ants highest among rational beings. Intelligence must and should outweigh everything, and it's I who have most of that.' With that she rose on her hind legs; she was so easy to recognize, I couldn't mistake her – and I swallowed her. 'Go to the ant and become wise?' I'd now got the queen.

I then went nearer to the big tree I've been speaking about. It was an oak of great age, with a tall trunk and a gigantic crown. I knew there was a living creature dwelt here, a woman called a dryad, who is born with the tree and dies with it. I had heard about this in the library, and now I was seeing such a tree, such an oak-nymph, with my own eyes. She gave a terrible scream when she saw me so near, for like all women she was very frightened of mice, though as a matter of fact she had more excuse than the rest of them because I could gnaw right through the tree, on which of course her life depended. I spoke to her in a friendly cordial way, and she got back her courage and took me on her delicate hand. And when she heard why I had come out into the wide world, she promised me that perhaps that very evening I might come by one of the two treasures I was still looking for. She explained to me that Fantasus was a very good friend of hers, that he was as beautiful as the god of love, and that he often took a rest under the leafy boughs of her tree, which then rustled more than ever above their heads. He called her his dryad (she said) and the tree his tree; the oak – all gnarled, gigantic and beautiful – was just after his own heart, with spreading roots going deep down into the earth and with trunk and crown that rose high into the cool air and knew the drifting snow, the bitter winds and the warm sunshine as they should be known. 'Yes (she went on), the birds sing in the tree-top and tell of foreign lands, and there on that one dead bough the stork has built his nest; it looks very well and we get to hear something of the land of the Pyramids. All this appeals very much to Fantasus, though it isn't really enough for him. I myself have to tell him about life in the woods ever since the time when I was small and my tree was so tiny that a nettle could have hidden it, until now when it's grown so huge and majestic. Sit down there, will you, under the woodruff, and mind! as soon as Fantasus comes, I shall be sure to get a chance to pluck at his wing and nip out a little feather. Take that – no poet ever had a better – then you'll have all you need.'

And Fantasus came, the feather was twitched off, and I seized it,« said the little mouse. »I held it in water till it was soft ... It was still difficult to digest, but I managed to nibble it up. It isn't at all easy to nibble yourself into being a poet; there's such a lot you must get inside you. Well, anyhow, now I'd got two things, common sense and fantasy, and through them I now realized that the third was to be found in the library, for a great man once said and wrote that there are novels which are written solely that people may be relieved of their unnecessary tears; in fact, they're a kind of sponge to mop up feeling with. I called to mind a few of these books, which had always seemed to me so tempting; they looked so used and greasy, they must have soaked up no end of feeling.

I went home to the library and immediately devoured pretty well a whole novel - that's to say, the soft part, the real book, whereas the crust, the binding, I left alone. Once I had digested this novel and another like it, I soon noticed their effect inside me; I ate part of a third and, lo and behold, I was a poet! I said so to myself – and to the others, too. I had head-ache, stomach-ache, and goodness knows what other aches. And when I thought of all the stories that might be associated with a sausage-stick, my mind became full of sticks; the queen ant must have had a wonderful head. I thought of the man who put a white stick in his mouth, so that he and the stick both became invisible. I thought of a dry old stick, who was goldstick-in-waiting, and a stick-in-the-mud who wasn't; and of drumsticks and fiddlesticks. My whole mind seemed to run on sticks; and surely they would all make poems, if you were a poet, and I *am* a poet – I've worn myself out to become one. So, you see, any day of the week, sir, I shall be able to treat you to a stick – a story. There, that's the soup I'll make.«

»Now let us hear the third one,« said the Mouse-King.

»Pee-pee!« There was a squeak from the kitchen door, as a little mouse – the fourth of them, the one they thought was dead – came scurrying in and knocked over the sausagestick with the black crape on it. She had run night and day, travelling on the railway by goods train when she had the chance, and even then she had nearly come too late. She pushed herself forward, looking rumpled and ruffled; she had lost her stick, but not her voice. She at once began speaking, as if she was the only one they were waiting for – the only one they would listen to – and as if nothing else in the world mattered to the world but herself. She began at once and said her say. Her arrival was so unexpected that no one had time to object to her or what she had to say, as long as she was saying it. Well, now let's listen.

IV

What the fourth mouse, who spoke before the third one had spoken, had to say

»I went straight to the largest town,« she said. »I can't remember its name; I never can remember names. From the railway I went, along with some goods that had been seized by the Customs, to the town-hall, and there I called on the gaoler. He talked about his prisoners, especially about one who had been making rash speeches; and these had been quoted and quoted till he had to be made an example of. 'The whole thing's just soup from a sausage-stick,' said the gaoler, 'but soup may well cost him his napper'.«

»That aroused my interest in the prisoner,« said the little mouse, »and I seized the opportunity to slip into his cell; there's always a mousehole behind every locked door. The prisoner looked pale; he had a long beard and big flashing eyes. The lamp smoked, but the walls were used to that and could hardly become blacker. The prisoner scratched both pictures and verses on them, white on black, but I didn't read them. I fancy he was bored, and so I was a welcome visitor. He coaxed me with bread-crumbs, with whistling and gentle words. He was very fond of me, I came to trust him, and so we were soon friends. He shared his bread and water with me, and gave me cheese and sausage. I lived in grand style, and yet it was more than anything our familiar intercourse (if I may put it that way) that appealed to me. He let me scamper on his hand and arm and even up his sleeve; he allowed me to creep into his beard and called me his little friend. I grew tremendously fond of him, and of course that sort of thing is mutual. I forgot my errand out in the wide world, forgot my sausagestick that I left in a crack in the floor; it's still there. I only thought of staying where I was. If I went away, then of course the poor prisoner would have had no one left, and that's much too little in this world! So I stayed – but he didn't. He spoke to me so mournfully on our last day, gave me a double helping of bread and cheese-rind, kissed his fingers to me, and then he went and never came back. I don't know what happened to him. 'Soup from a sausage-stick,' said the gaoler; and to him I went, but I never ought to have trusted him. It's true, he took me on his hand, but then he shut me in a cage, on a treadmill. It's terrible! You run and run and you get no farther; you're just a laughing-stock.

The gaoler's grandchild was a sweet little thing with golden curls, merry eyes and a laughing mouth. 'Poor little mouse!' she said, peeping into my horrid cage. Then she drew back the catch ... and I jumped down on to the window sill and out into the gutter. Free! Free! That was all I thought of, not what I had come away to find out.

It was dusk, and night was coming on. I found lodging in an old tower, where a watchman lived, and also an owl. I didn't trust either of them, least of all the owl. Owls are like cats and have one serious drawback, that they eat mice. You're bound to make mistakes sometimes, and that's what I did. She was a respectable old owl, most ladylike, who knew more than the watchman and just as much as myself. The young owls kept grumbling about one thing and another. 'Don't make soup out of a sausage-stick!' the old owl would tell them. That was the harshest thing she could say to them, so deeply attached was she to her family. I came to have such confidence in her that I said 'peep!' to her from the crack where I was, She seemed pleased with this trust and promised me her protection: no creature should be allowed to do anything to me – she would see to that herself next winter, when they were on short commons.

Yes, she was a downy old bird. She explained to me that the watchman couldn't hoot without a horn that hung loose from his shoulder. 'He fancies himself no end with that; he thinks he's an owl in the tower – thinks a big splash can be made by a small stone. Soup from a sausage-stick!' I begged her to jot down the recipe, and this is what she told me: 'Soup from a sausage-stick,' she said, 'is just a phrase among human beings; it can be taken in various ways, and every one thinks his way is the right way, though it's really nothing at all.'

»'Nothing at all!' I repeated. It gave me quite a shock. The truth's not always pleasant, but truth's the highest thing we know – the old owl agreed to that. I thought it over and realized that, if I brought back the highest thing we know, I should be bringing a good deal more than soup from a sausage-stick. So I hurried away to get home in good time, bringing with me the highest and best, namely, truth. Mice are canny folk and the Mouse-King is the leader of them all. He's in a position to make me Queen for the sake of truth.«

»Your truth's a lie!« said the mouse who hadn't yet got leave to speak. »I can make the soup, and I shall.«

V
How the soup was made

»I didn't go away,« said the fourth mouse. »I stayed in this country; that's the right thing to do. There's no point in going abroad. You can get all you want just as well here. I stayed at home. *My* knowledge hasn't come to me from elves and dryads; I haven't nibbled my way to it, nor gossiped with owls. I've got mine by thinking things out for myself. Now please let's have the kettle on. Fill it up with water – right up. Light the fire, and let it burn till the water is brought to the boil – it must boil till it bubbles. Now throw in the stick. Next, will your Majesty please dip your tail into the seething pot and stir it round. The longer the stirring, the richer the soup. It costs nothing; no need of flavouring; just stir round.«

»Can't someone else do the job?« asked the Mouse-King. »No,« said the mouse. »Only the King's tail makes the right kind of stock.«

The water boiled right over, and the Mouse-King came close up, almost dangerously near. And he whisked out his tail in the way that mice do in the dairy when they skim the cream from a bowl and then lick their tails. But his tail came no further than the hot steam before he jumped quickly down.

»Why, of course, you shall be my Queen,« he said. »The soup can wait till our gold wedding; then our poor will have something to look forward to – and plenty of time to do it.«

So the wedding took place. But a number of the mice, when they got home, said, »You could hardly call that soup from a sausage-stick; it was more like soup from a mouse's tail.« One or two of the stories, they thought, weren't half bad, though the whole might have been better done. »For instance, I should have said - so on and so forth!«

That was criticism, which is always so clever - afterwards.

The story went round the world. Opinion on it might differ, but the story itself remained entire. And that's just as it should be in things great or small, even in soup made from a sausage-stick – though you mustn't expect to be thanked for it.

The Puppet Showman

On board the steamer there was an oldish-looking man with such a contented face that, unless you were mistaken, he must surely be the happiest being on earth. And that's just what he said he was; he told me himself. He was a Dane, a countryman of mine, and a travelling theatre manager. He had his entire company with him in a large box; he was a puppet showman. His natural cheerfulness, he said, had been put to the test by a Bachelor of Science, and through this experiment he had become completely happy. I didn't understand him, to begin with; but presently he came out with the whole story, and here it is.

»It happened in the town of Slagelse,« he said. »I was giving a performance at the coaching inn there and had a splendid audience – all of them quite young except for a couple of old ladies. But then a fellow in a dark suit, who looked as if he might have been a university student, came in and sat down. He always laughed in the right place and clapped correctly – he was quite an unusual playgoer! I was curious to know who he was, and then they tell me he's a bachelor-of-arts sent out by the Scientific Institute in Copenhagen to instruct people in the provinces. By eight o'clock my show was over; children must of course go to bed early, and the convenience of the public must be borne in mind.

At nine o'clock the bachelor-of-arts began his lecture and experiments, and this time it was my turn to listen to him.

It was extraordinary what he had to tell us and to set before our eyes. Most of it went over my head and into the parson's, as the saying is, but I couldn't help thinking: if mankind can discover so much, surely we must be able to last out longer than we do before being put underground. They were positive small miracles that he showed us, and yet it was all done as easily as kiss your hand, straight from nature. In the time of Moses and the prophets a young man like this would have become one of his country's Wise Men, and in the Middle Ages he would have been burnt at the stake.

I lay awake all night, but when on the following evening I gave another performance and the bachelor-of-arts was there again, I was soon in high spirits. I was once told by an actor that, when playing the part of a lover, he used to fix his thoughts on a single one of his audience; for *her* he played – and forgot all the rest of the house. The bachelor-of-arts was my 'her', my one spectator, for whom I performed.

When the show was over, all the puppets were called before the curtain, and then I was invited by the bachelor-of-arts to come in and have a glass of wine. He spoke about my plays, and I spoke about his science, and I fancy they both gave us equal enjoyment, though really I got the best of it; there was so much in what he did that he himself couldn't explain - as, for instance, that a bit of iron that is put through a coil becomes magnetised. Well, what is the explanation? The spirit comes over it, but where does it come from? It seems to me just as it is with people of this world: God sends them hurtling through the coil of time, the spirit comes over them, and there you have a Napoleon, a Luther, or someone like that. 'The whole world is a series of miracles,' said the bachelor-of-arts, 'but we are so accustomed to them that we take them as a matter of course.' And he went on talking and explaining, till at last he seemed to be prizing open my brain and I frankly admitted that, if I weren't such an old'un, I'd go at once to his Scientific Institute and learn to examine the world most carefully, even although I was one of its happiest creatures. 'One of its happiest?' he repeated, as if rolling it round on his tongue. 'Are you happy?' he asked. 'Yes', I said, 'and I'm welcomed in every town to which I bring my puppets. Still, it's true there is one wish that sometimes comes over me and haunts my good humour like a nightmare. I should like to have a real live troupe, to be manager of a genuine company of men and women.'

'I see. You want your puppets brought to life,' he said, 'you want them to be turned into real live actors, and yourself to be their manager. Then you would be completely happy, you think?'

Well, he didn't think so, but I did; and we argued it backwards and forwards and at the end of it were no nearer to agreeing. Still, we clinked glasses, and the wine was excellent – though there must have been magic in it, otherwise the whole thing would simply mean that I got drunk. But I didn't; my eye was perfectly clear. There was a kind of sunshine in the room, beaming out of the face of the bachelor-of-arts. He made me think of the ancient gods in their eternal youth, when they still went about on this earth. I told him so, and he smiled, and I could have sworn he was a god in disguise or one of their kinsmen. And he was too, or the dream of my life was to be realized: my puppets were to come alive, and I was to be the manager of a living company. We drank to the success of this; and he packed all my puppets into the wooden box, which he tied on to my back, and then he sent me hurtling through a coil. I can still hear how I crashed, and there I was, lying on the floor – it's as true as true – and the whole company jumped out of the box.

The spirit had come over them all. The puppets had all become splendid artists – they said to themselves – and I was their manager. Everything was ready for the first performance. The whole company wanted to speak to me, and so did the audience. The lady dancer said that, if she didn't stand on one leg, the house would come down; she was the leading spirit of the whole show and wished to be treated as such. The puppet who played the Empress wanted to be treated as Empress off the stage as well, or else she'd get out of practice. The man who had to come on with a letter did it with all the assurance of a No. 1 lover; for the small and the great, he added, are of equal importance, when looked at as an artistic whole. Then the hero insisted that his part should have nothing but exit lines, because they always got a clap. The leading lady would only play under pink lights, as they suited her; no blue lights for her! They were like flies in a bottle, with me in the middle of the bottle, for I was manager. I could scarcely breathe; my head went round; I was just as miserable as anyone can be; it was a new type of humanity I had around me; I did so wish I had them all in the box again, and that I had never become their manager. I told them straight out that, when you came to think of it, they were really only puppets. And so then they killed me...

I was lying on my bed in my room. How I had reached there from the bachelor-of-arts, well, perhaps he knows, because I don't. The moon

shone through on to the floor, where the puppet-box lay overturned and the puppets thrown all over the place, big ones and little ones, the whole gang of them! I lost no time; I jumped out of bed and bundled them all into their box, some on their heads and some on their feet. I slammed down the lid and sat on the top of the box. What a picture to paint! Can't you see it? I can. 'Now you've got to stay there,' I said, 'and never again shall I want to see you as flesh and blood.'

I was in high spirits; I was the happiest of mankind. The bachelor-of-arts had put my cheerfulness to the test. There I sat in utter bliss and fell asleep on the box. In the morning I was still sitting there; happy, because I had learnt that my one great wish of former days had been a foolish one. I asked after the bachelor-of-arts; but he had gone, like the old Greek and Roman gods. And from that time I've been the happiest man alive. I'm a happy manager, my company don't argue, nor my audience either; they enjoy themselves to the top of their bent. I'm free to concoct my pieces just as I like. I pick out what I think is the best part of any play, and nobody minds. Pieces that the big theatres have no use for nowadays, but thirty years ago the public crowded to and cried over, these I now take up and give to the children, and the children cry just as Daddy and Mummy used to; only I shorten the pieces, because the little ones don't care for a lot of rubbishy love-making; sad, but soon over, is what they prefer. By this time I've been all over Denmark, up and down, this way and that; I know and am known by everyone. Now I'm off to Sweden and, if all goes well and I earn good money, I shall become a Scandinavian – but not otherwise. I can say that to you, as you're a countryman of mine.«

And, being a countryman of his, I have naturally told the story all over again, just for the pleasure of telling it.

Something to Write About

There was a young man who was studying to be a writer. He wanted to be one by Easter and then marry and live by writing. That, he knew, only meant hitting on something to write about; the trouble was, he couldn't hit on anything. He had been born too late; every idea had been used up before he came into the world, everything had been thought of and written about.

»Lucky creatures who were born a thousand years ago!« he said. »They could easily become immortal. Even one who was born a hundred years ago was lucky, for after all there was still something to write about. Now the world is written out – what is there left for me to write about?«

He studied the question till he was quite ill, poor fellow. No doctor could help him, though maybe the »wise woman« could. She lived in the cottage by the gate leading into the fields, which she opened to people out driving or riding. Yes, and she could direct people further than just through the gate; she was wiser than the doctor who drives in his own carriage and pays high taxes.

»I must go and see her,« said the young man.

The house she lived in was a nice little cottage, though in dull surroundings without a tree or a flower. Outside her door stood a beehive, which came in very useful, and a small potato patch, also very useful. Likewise, a dike with a blackthorn which had ceased flowering and now produced berries that give your mouth a twist, if you taste them before the frost has been on them.

»Here we have a graphic picture of the unpoetic age we live in,« thought the young man; and that was at least a thought, a grain of gold that he came upon at the wise woman's door.

»Write it down!« she said. »Half a loaf is better than no bread. I know why you've come. You can't hit on anything to write about, and yet you want to be a writer by Easter.«

»Everything's been written already,« he said. »Our days are not the old days.«

»No,« said the woman. »In the old days the wise women were burnt, and the poets went about with empty stomachs and were out at elbows. These are good times, the very best of all. But you don't look at things in the right way. You haven't sharpened your hearing, and I don't suppose you ever say your prayers at night. There's plenty these days of every kind to write poems or tales about, if you can do it. You can draw it from the plants and produce of the earth, scoop it out of the running brooks and the stagnant pools; but you must know its meaning, know how to catch a sunbeam. Now have a try with my glasses, put my ear-trumpet to your ear, then pray to God and stop thinking about yourself.«

The last was of course very difficult, more than a wise woman could expect.

He took the glasses and the ear-trumpet, and she stood him up in the middle of the potato patch. She handed him a big potato, and it gave out sounds. It was a song, with words to it, yes, the interesting story of potatoes – a domestic story in ten parts; ten lines would have been enough. And what did the potato sing about?

It sang about itself and its family, about the coming of potatoes to Europe, about all the lack of appreciation they had met and endured before they were recognized, as they now are, to be a greater boon than a nugget of gold.

»By royal decree we were given out at the town-hall in every city. A proclamation was made about our great importance, but people didn't believe in it; they didn't even understand how to plant us. One person would dig a hole and throw his whole bushel of potatoes down into it; another put his potatoes singly into the ground, one here, one there, and expected each one to shoot up as an entire tree, from which you could shake potatoes. And, in fact, plant, blossoms, watery fruit did appear, but it all withered away. No one thought of what lay beneath the ground: the boon, the potatoes. Yes, we've been through trials and suffering – that's to say, our forefathers have, we and they, it comes to the same thing. What tales we could tell!«

»Well, that'll do for the present,« said the woman. »Now take a look at the sloes.«

»We, too,« said the sloes, »are closely related to the homeland of the potatoes, but further north than they were growing. Northmen came from Norway, steering west through mist and gales to an unknown land. There, behind ice and snow, they found plants and vegetables and bushes with the blue-black berries of the vine – sloes; they froze to ripe grapes like ourselves. And the country was called 'Vineland' – 'Greenland' – 'Sloeland.'«

»That's a wonderfully romantic tale,« said the young man.

»Well, now come along with me,« said the wise woman, and led him to the beehive. He peeped inside it. What a bustle and stir! Bees in all the passages, fluttering their wings to make a healthy draught through the whole great factory – that was their job. Now came bees from outside, born with baskets on their legs to carry pollen from the flowers; this was shaken out, sorted and made into honey or wax. In and out they flew. The queen bee also wanted to fly, but then they would all have to go with her, and it wasn't yet time for that. But fly she would; so they bit off her Majesty's wings, and then she had to stay.

»Now get up on to the dike,« said the wise woman. »Come and have a look at the highroad, where people are to be seen.«

»What an enormous crowd!« said the young man. »One story after another! Such a purring and whirring! It's getting too much for me, it'll knock me endways!«

»No, you must go straight ahead,« said the woman. »Go in and mix with the crowd, have a sight of them, lend them an ear, give them your heart. Then you'll soon hit on something to write about. But before you go, I must have my glasses back and my ear-trumpet;« and she took them both from him.

»Now I can't see a thing,« said the young man, »and I can't hear now either.«

»Very well, then you can't be a writer by Easter,« said the wise woman.

»No? But when can I?«

»Neither by Easter nor by Whitsuntide. You'll never learn to hit on anything.«

»Then what ever shall I do to earn a living by writing?«

»You can do it as early as Shrovetide*. Knock the poets out of the barrel! Slash at their writings; that's as good as slashing at themselves. Only don't let them get the better of you; slash away for all you're worth, then you'll get buns enough for yourself and your wife.«

»Something to have a cut at!« cried the young man; and then he knocked every other poet out of the barrel, since he couldn't become a poet himself.

We have all from the wise woman; she can tell you what to have a cut at.

---

* At Shrovetide in Denmark the »cat« is knocked out of the barrel at carnival time. Also, at dawn, children awaken their parents with a switch or »teaser« and demand buns.

The Toad

The well was deep, and so the rope was long; the windlass had scarcely room to go round when a bucket of water was to be hauled up over the edge of the well. The sun could never reach down far enough to be reflected in the water, however clear that was; but as far as it did manage to shine, there was green of some sort growing between the stones.

It was there that a family of toads were living. They had immigrated; actually they plunged headlong down into the well after old Mother Toad, who was still living. The green frogs, who had settled there much earlier and used to swim about in the water, recognized that they were cousins and called them »our well-guests«. But these quite intended to stay there; they thoroughly enjoyed living on dry land, as they called the wet stones.

Mother Frog had gone travelling once. She had been in the bucket when it was drawn up, but the light proved too strong for her and she had trouble with her eyes. Luckily she managed to get out of the bucket and tumbled with a fearful splosh into the water and lay for three days afterwards with a pain in the back. She hadn't much to tell about the world up above, though she did know – in fact they all knew – that the well was not the whole world. Mother Toad should have been able to tell them a thing or two, but she never answered when she was asked, and so they never asked her.

»She's fat, ugly and loathsome,« said the young green frogs. »Her brats will be just as loathsome.«

»Quite possibly,« said Mother Toad, »but one of them has a jewel in its head, or else I have.«

The green frogs glared when they heard this and, as they didn't like it, they made faces and dived to the bottom. But the young toads stretched their hind-legs in sheer pride; each one thought he had the jewel. Then they squatted with their heads quite still, though finally they began asking what they were proud of and what this jewel thing really was.

»It's something so fine and precious,« said Mother Toad, »that I can't describe it. It's a thing you wear to please yourself, and that the others go and get annoyed about. But no more questions! I shan't answer.«

»Well, I haven't got the jewel,« said the smallest toad, which was as ugly as could be. »Why should I have anything so fine? And if it annoys others, then it can't give me any pleasure. No, all I want is just to be

allowed to go up to the edge of the well and look out. That must be grand.«

»Much better stay where you are,« said Mother Toad. »You're at home here; you know your way about. Mind the bucket, or it'll squash you. And, remember, if you do find your way into it, you may tumble out. Not everyone falls as luckily as I did, with no damage done to legs or eggs.«

»Ko-eks!« said the little toad, as though it were trying to talk.

It did so want to go up to the edge of the well and look out. It felt such a longing for the green things growing up there; and when the next morning it happened that the bucket, filled with water, was being hauled up and stopped for a moment in front of the stone where the toad was squatting, the little creature quivered all over, jumped into the full bucket and sank to the bottom of the water, which was then drawn up and emptied out.

»Ugh!« said the fellow who saw it. »That's as ugly as ever I see'd, that is.« And he gave a kick with his clog at the toad, which came near to being badly hurt, though it just managed to get away in among some tall stinging nettles. It saw masses of stalks. It also looked overhead and saw the sun shining on the leaves, which were quite transparent. It was the same for the little toad as it is for us when we suddenly go into a big wood where the sun comes shining through between boughs and foliage.

»It's far nicer here than down in the well,« said the little toad. »I should like to stay here all my life.« It stopped there for an hour; it stopped for

442

two. »I wonder what there is outside,« it said. »Having come so far, I may as well go a bit further.« Then it hopped along as quickly as it could and came out on to the road, where it had the sun on its back and was sprinkled with dust as it marched across the highway.

»This really *is* dry land,« said the toad. »For me, it's almost too much of a good thing; it tickles.«

Now it reached the ditch. Here grew forget-me-not and meadow-sweet and, close by, a quickset hedge with bushes of may and alder; here, too, was convolvulus, growing as bindweed; masses of colour, and a fluttering butterfly. The toad thought this was a flower that had broken loose in order to have a better look at the world, which was of course so likely.

»If only I could speed along like that,« said the toad. »Ko-eks, ko-eks! What fun!«

It stayed on for eight nights and days in this ditch and never went short of food. On the ninth day it thought:»Time to be moving!« ... And yet what ever could be more delightful? Possibly a little toad or some green frogs. There had been sounds on the wind last night as if there were »cousins« not far away.

»It's wonderful to be alive, to come up out of the well, to lie among stinging nettles, to crawl across the dusty road, to have a good rest in the wet ditch! But on we go! Look out for frogs or a little toad – they're a thing no one can do without. Nature is not enough.« So it continued to ramble.

Going through the field, it came to a large pond with rushes round it and made straight for them.

»This is rather too damp for you, isn't it?« said the frogs, »though you are very welcome. Are you a 'he' or a 'she'? Not that it makes any difference. You will be just as welcome.«

Then the toad was invited to a concert in the evening, a family concert: lots of enthusiasm, but thin voices – we've met that before. No refreshments; only free drinks – the whole pond if they liked.

»Now I must be getting on,« said the little toad. It still felt a desire for something better.

It saw the stars twinkling, so far and so clear; it saw the new moon shining; it saw the sun rising higher and higher.

»I see I'm still in the well, in a larger well. I must go up higher; I'm so restless and full of longing.« And when the moon was full and round, the poor creature thought, »I wonder if that's the bucket being trundled down for me to jump into, in order to go up higher. Or is the sun the great bucket? How huge, how gorgeous it is! It has room for us all. I must look out for a chance. Oh, how my head's shining! I don't believe the jewel can shine brighter. Still, I haven't got that, and I'm not sorry. No, higher up into splendour and joy! I feel confident, and yet anxious. It's a difficult step to take, but it's got to be done. Forward! Straight on towards the main road!«

And it stepped out – as far as a crawling animal like that can step out – and soon found itself on a public highway where people lived; there were both flower-gardens and kitchen-gardens. It came and rested by a cabbage-patch.

»Good heavens!« it said; »what a lot of different creatures there are whom I've never known! And how lovely and big the world is! But I must have a look round it and not stay squatting in one place.« With that, the toad hopped into the cabbage-garden. »How green it is here, how beautiful!«

»Yes, of course,« said the caterpillar on its leaf. »My leaf is the biggest of the lot. It covers up half the world, but that's the part I can do without.«

»Cluck, cluck!« was heard, and some chickens came tripping into the garden. The leading hen had very quick eyesight; she spied the caterpillar on the curly leaf and pecked at it, so that it fell twisting and turning to the ground. The hen peered first with one eye, then with the other, not knowing what might come of all this wriggling.

»It's not doing that because it wants to,« thought the hen and drew back its head to strike. The toad became so frightened that it crawled straight towards the hen.

»So it has troops in support,« said the hen. »Filthy vermin!« And it turned away. »I don't want that tiny green morsel; it only makes my throat tickle.« The other hens thought the same, and off they went.

»I wriggled away from it, « said the caterpillar. »It's a great thing to have presence of mind, though the hardest job is still left, namely, to get up on my cabbage-leaf again. Where is it?«

The little toad came along to show his sympathy and say how glad it was that its ugliness had frightened the hens away.

»What ever do you mean by that?« asked the caterpillar. »Why, I wriggled away from them myself. You're a hideous sight. Kindly allow me to go back to where I was ... I smell cabbage! Here's my leaf! There's no place like home. But I must go higher up.«

»That's it – higher up,« said the little toad, »higher up. It feels just as I do, but today it's not in the mood because of the fright it had. We all want to go higher up,« and it looked up as high as it could.

The stork was in its nest on the farmer's roof. He was clacking his beak, and Mother Stork was clacking too.

»Fancy living so high up,« thought the toad. »If only I could come up there!«

In the farmhouse lived two young students. One was a poet, the other a naturalist. The first sang and took delight in writing about all that God had created and how it was mirrored in his heart; he sang it out, short, clear and rich in melodious verse. The other student tackled the problem itself and split it right up if need be. He considered the works of God as a big sum of subtraction and multiplication; he was determined to get to know it all, inside and out, and to talk intelligently about it. It was all intelligence, and joy and wisdom were in his talk. They were kindly, gay young fellows, both of them.

»I say – there's a good specimen of a toad,« said the naturalist. »I must have it to keep in spirits.«

»But you've already got two others,« said the poet. »Leave it in peace to enjoy itself.« »Yes, but it's so beautifully ugly,« said the other.

»Of course, if we could find the jewel in its head!« said the poet, »then I'd take a hand myself in cutting it open.«

»Jewel!« said the other. »You must be good at natural history.«

»Well, isn't there something rather nice in the popular belief that the toad, the ugliest of all creatures, often has the most precious jewel hidden in its head? Isn't it the same with human beings? Think of the jewel that Æsop had – yes, and Socrates.«

The toad heard no more and didn't understand half of what it did hear. The two friends went away, and the toad escaped being put into spirits.

»They spoke about the jewel, too,« said the toad. »Good thing I haven't got it, or it might have been very awkward for me.«

There was clacking of beaks on the farmer's roof. Father Stork was giving his family a lecture, and they were casting sidelong glances at the two young men in the garden.

»Man is the most conceited of creatures,« said the stork. »Listen what a clatter they make. But their rattle can't compare with ours. They plume themselves on their ready speech and on their language. A fine language, indeed, that slops over into gibberish every day's journey we go; they just can't understand each other. We can speak our language all over the world, both in Denmark and in Egypt. Men can't fly either*. They get speed with a discovery they call 'the railway', but they often break their necks doing that. It gives my beak the shivers whenever I think of it. The world can do without mankind; we don't need them. If only we may keep frogs and earthworms!«

* Written in 1866.

446

»That was a top-hole speech,« thought the little toad. »He's a great man, that stork, and what a lofty perch he's got – I've never seen anything like it – and how he can swim!« it exclaimed, as the stork went speeding through the air with outstretched wings.

Meanwhile, Mother Stork was chattering in her nest all about the land of Egypt, the waters of the Nile and the glorious mud to be found in foreign parts; it sounded so novel and attractive to the little toad.

»I must go to Egypt,« it said. »If only the stork would take me with him – or one of the young ones might. I'd pay him back with a good turn on his wedding-day. That's it; I shall go to Egypt, for I'm so lucky. All this endless longing of mine, it's far better, isn't it, than having a jewel in my head.«

And yet it *had* got the jewel – that endless longing to go up, always up! It gleamed inside it, gleamed with joy, gleamed with yearning.

At that very moment up came the stork. He had seen the toad in the grass, and he swooped down and grabbed the little creature not too gently. The beak squeezed, the wind whistled; it was far from pleasant, yet up it went, up to Egypt, it felt sure – and so its eyes shone, just as though a spark were flying out of them: »Ko-eks, ko-eks!«

The body was dead, the toad killed. But the spark from its eyes, what became of that?

The sunbeam took it. The sunbeam carried off the jewel from the toad's head. Where to?

It's no good asking the naturalist; much better ask the poet. You'll hear it all from him like a fairy tale, bringing in the caterpillar and the stork family, too. Just imagine – the caterpillar is transformed and turned into a pretty butterfly. The stork family flies over the mountains and away across the sea to far-off Africa, and yet finds the shortest way home again to Denmark – to the same spot, the same roof. Yes, it's almost too fantastic, isn't it? and yet it's true. You can ask the naturalist if you like; he'll have to admit it. And you know it yourself, too, because you've seen it.

»But what about the jewel in the toad's head?«

»Have a look for it in the sun. Try if you can find it there.«

The light up there is too dazzling. We haven't yet got eyes that can gaze into all the splendour that God has created, but we shall get them one day; and that will be the finest fairy tale of all, for we shall be in it ourselves.

Auntie

I wish you could have known Auntie – she was charming. Well, that's to say, not a bit charming in the way we generally mean by the word 'charming'; but she was kind and pleasant, even jolly in her way, a good subject for gossip, if there's gossip and fun to be made about someone; she was just the kind to put into a play, if only because she lived for the playhouse and everything to do with it. She was so respectable; but Commissioner Fabb(whom Auntie called Fibb) said she was theatre-mad.

»The theatre's my school,« she said, »my fountain of knowledge, at which I freshen up my history of the Scriptures: 'Moses', 'Joseph and his Brethren' – well, these are operas. From the theatre I get my world-history, my geography, and my knowledge of mankind. From the French pieces I learn about Paris life – improper, yet highly interesting. How I have cried over 'The Riquebourg Family'! To think that man has to drink himself to death in order that she may marry her sweetheart!... Ah, yes, what tears I must have wept during the fifty years I've had a seat at the theatre!«

Auntie knew every play, every stage-property, every actor who was appearing or ever had appeared. She only really lived during the nine months the theatre was open. Summer time, without summer performances, was a time that made her feel old; whereas an evening at the play that went on past midnight was a lengthening of life. She never said, as others do, »Here comes the spring, for the stork has arrived,« or »The papers are announcing the first strawberries.« No, this was how she heralded the approach of autumn: »Have you seen? Seats at the theatre are now on sale; the season's just beginning.«

She worked out the value of a house and its situation by its nearness to the theatre. It grieved her to desert the narrow little street behind the theatre and to move into the big street rather further away and live there in a house with no opposite neighbour.

»At home,« she used to say, »my window has to be my box at the theatre. It's no good sitting wrapped up in yourself; you must see people. But here I'm livng as if I had moved out into the country. If I want to see people, I have to go out into the kitchen and climb on to the sink; only there have I an opposite neighbour. And yet, when I was living in my narrow little street, I could see straight into the grocer's shop and at the same time I was only three hundred steps from the theatre; now I'm three thousand guardsman steps away.«

Auntie might be unwell, but however poorly she felt, she never missed the play. Her doctor ordered her one evening to have her feet poulticed with sour dough, and she did as he said; but then she drove off to the theatre and sat there with her feet in poultices. If she had died there, she would have been delighted. Thorvaldsen died in the theatre, and she called that a »wonderful death.«

It's certain she couldn't imagine the kingdom of heaven without a theatre. Of course, we were never promised one; and yet it was natural to suppose that the many illustrious actors and actresses who had gone on ahead should have a continued sphere of activity.

Auntie had an electric wire between the theatre and her room; the telegram came every Sunday at breakfast time. Her electric wire was Mr. Sivertsen, one of the stagemanagers, the man who signalled curtains up or down and scenery on or off.

From him she received an advance notice, brief and to the point, of the various plays. Shakespeare's *Tempest* he called »a dreadful play – far too many scene changes – it starts off with water right down to the first wings.« Which is to say, the rolling waves came right down to the foot-lights. On the other hand, if one and the same interior set was to serve through all five acts, then (he said) the play was sensible and well-constructed, an 'easy' piece that played itself without a lot of scene-shifting.

In earlier days – as Auntie used to call the period of some thirty years ago – she and the said Mr. Sivertsen were younger. He was just a stage-hand then, but was already her »benefactor«, as she christened him. The fact is, that in those days, for an evening performance at the town's one large theatre, it was the practice to admit spectators up in the flies. Every stage-hand had a pass or two at his disposal. The flies were often crammed with quite a distinguished company, including (it was said) the wives of generals and Government officials. It was so interesting to look down behind the wings and to notice what everybody did when the curtain was down.

Auntie had been up there several times, both for tragedies and ballets, since the pieces with the greater number of performers were the most interesting to see from the flies. You sat pretty well in the dark up there, and most of you had brought along some supper. Once three apples and a large sausage-sandwich fell straight down into Ugolino's prison, where the man was supposed to be starving, and this made people guffaw. That sausage was one of the chief reasons that led the management to do away altogether with places for the public in the flies.

»But I was there thirty-seven times,« said Auntie, »and I shall always remember Mr. Sivertsen for that.«

It happened to be the very last night that the flies were open to the public. They were playing *The Judgment of Solomon;* Auntie remembered so well. Through her benefactor, Mr. Sivertsen, she had secured a ticket of admission for Commissioner Fabb, although he didn't deserve it, as he was always teasing her and making fun of the theatre. All the same, she had got him a pass to the flies. He was anxious to see this play-acting nonsense the wrong way round – those were his own words, and it was just like him, said Auntie.

So he saw *The Judgment of Solomon* from above and fell asleep. You might have thought he had come from a big dinner where a lot of toasts had been drunk. He slept and got shut in, sat and slept through the darkness of night in the flies above the stage; and he told Auntie (though she didn't believe him) that when he awoke, *The Judgment of Solomon* was over, lamps and candles were out, all the people, from balcony to stalls, had gone. But it was not till then that the real comedy began: *Epilogue.* This was the best, said the commissioner. Everything came alive. It wasn't *The Judgment of Solomon* they were giving; no, it was *Doomsday at the Theatre.* Commissioner Fabb had the impudence to try and make Auntie believe all that; this was his way of thanking her for having got him a seat in the flies.

What the commissioner had to tell – that was no doubt funny in its way, though at bottom it was just spitefulness and teasing.

»At first all was dark up there,« said the commissioner. »But then the magic began, the great performance: *Doomsday at the Theatre.* The attendants stood at the doors, and every member of the audience had to show by his good conduct book whether he might go in with his hands tied or free, and his mouth gagged or no. Gentlepeople who arrived late, after the show had already begun, and also young folk who never can keep time, were tethered outside and given felt soles under their feet to go in

with at the beginning of the second act, besides being gagged. And so they made a start with *Doomsday at the Theatre.*«

»Just spitefulness!« said Auntie. »God has nothing to go with that.«

The scene-painter, if he wanted to go to heaven, had to go up by a stairway he had painted himself, but which no one on earth could clamber up. That was of course merely a sin against perspective. All the plants and buildings that the stage-carpenter had carefully set up in countries to which they didn't belong had to be shifted by the poor man to their right place – shifted, too, before cockcrow if he wanted to get to heaven. Mr. Fabb should have made sure that he could get there himself; and his tales about the actors, whether in comedy or tragedy song or dance, were some of Mr. Fabb's wickedest. Fabb's fibs! He didn't deserve to be allowed backstage. Auntie wouldn't soil her lips by repeating what he said – such impertinence! It was all written down, he had said (fibs!), and was to be put into print when he was dead and gone, not before. He didn't want to be flayed alive by the critics.

Only once had Auntie been in fear and trembling at her temple of bliss, the theatre. It was a winter's day, one of those days when we have two hours of drab daylight. It was cold and snowy, but Auntie couldn't stay away from the theatre. They were doing *Herman von Unna,* and also a short opera and a long ballet, a prologue and an epilogue. It would go on till past midnight. Auntie was determined to go; her lodger had lent her a pair of sleigh-boots with fur both inside and out; they came half-way up her legs.

She came to the theatre, came to her box. The boots were warm, so she kept them on. Suddenly there was a cry of 'fire!' Smoke was coming from one of the wings, smoke from the flies. There was terrible alarm; people stampeded out. Auntie was the last in her box –« second tier, left side, the scenery looks best from there,« she used to say, »it's always placed so as to look most effective from the side of the royal box« – and she wanted to get out. But the panicking people in front of her had thoughtlessly slammed the door behind them. There sat Auntie, unable to get out or in – that's to say, into the next box; the rail was too high. She called out, but no one heard. She peered down into the tier below her. It was empty, it was low, and not far away. In her alarm Auntie felt quite young and nimble. She wanted to jump down, and she did get one leg over the balustrade, the other off the seat; there she sat astride, nicely draped in her flowered skirt, with one leg dangling right out, a leg wearing an enormous sleigh-boot. What a sight to see! And when it was seen, Auntie was also heard – and saved from being burnt to death; for, as a matter of fact, the theatre wasn't really on fire at all.

That, she said, was the most memorable evening in her life; but she was glad she hadn't been able to see herself, for then she would have died of shame.

Her benefactor from among the stage-staff, Mr. Sivertsen, always came on Sunday to see her, but it was a long while from Sunday to Sunday. So she had lately, in the middle of the week, had a little child in to 'left-overs' – that is, to eat up what was left over from yesterday's dinner. It was a small child from the ballet, who needed more to eat. She was appearing both as a fairy and as a page; her most difficult part was as hind-legs of the lion in *The Magic Flute*, but she grew to be the lion's front paws. It's true she only got three shillings for this, whereas the hind-legs earned her four; but for that she had to walk with a stoop and also to miss the fresh air. Auntie thought all this was most interesting to hear about.

She had deserved to live as long as the theatre itself, but she didn't manage to last it out. Nor did she die there but nicely and properly in her own bed. Incidentally, her last words were full of meaning: she asked, »What are they playing tomorrow?«

When she died she left, I suppose, about five hundred pounds; we infer that from the interest, which comes to twenty pounds. This sum Auntie had directed to be paid to a deserving old maid without relatives; it was to be expended yearly on a subscription to a seat in the second tier, left side, on Saturdays, for it was then they put on the best plays. There was only one condition for the person who benefited by this legacy: every Saturday, in the theatre, she was to think of Auntie who lay in her grave.

That was Auntie's religion.

The Rags

Outside the factory were stacks of rags piled up in heaps, gathered in from far and wide. Each rag had his history, each could tell his own tale; but we can't listen to them all. Some were domestic rags, others came from foreign countries. Now, here was a Danish rag up against a Norwegian rag; the one was out-and-out Danish, the other as Norwegian as possible; and that was the amusing thing about these two, as every sensible Norwegian and Dane will agree.

They could tell each other, of course, by the way they spoke, although the Norwegian maintained that their two languages were as different from each other as French and Hebrew. »Our tongue draws its strength from the craggy heights, while the Dane makes up a namby-pamby gibberish of his own.«

The two rags talked on, and rags are rags in every country; they only really count in a rag-heap.

»I'm Norwegian,« said the one from Norway; »and when I say that I'm Norwegian, I reckon that's enough. I'm tough in every fibre, like the oldest rocks in ancient Norway – the land that has a constitution, like free America. It makes my thread quiver to think what I am and to feel my thoughts clang out in words of granite.«

»But we have a litterature,« said the Danish rag. »Do you understand what that is?«

»Understand!« echoed the Norwegian. »Dweller in a flat country, shall I lift him up to the hills and bathe him in Northern Lights, rag as he is? When the ice thaws in the Norwegian sun, then Danish apple barges sail up to us with butter and cheese, such a tasty cargo! And, as ballast, there comes with them – Danish literature! We don't need it. And we'd sooner go without that stale beer, here where the fresh spring gushes forth, and the well has not been bored, nor boosted into European fame by newspapers or the travels of Oddfellows and authors abroad. I speak right out

453

from the lungs, and the Dane must get used to the sound of freedom. He'll learn to do that from his Scandinavian attachment to our proud rocky land, Earth's earliest clod.«

»Well, well! A Danish rag could never talk like that,« said the Dane. »It isn't our nature to. I know myself, and all our Danish rags are like me; we're so amiable and modest, we've too little faith in ourselves, and that really doesn't get you anywhere. But it's a temperament I quite like; I find it charming. Otherwise, I assure you, I'm well aware of my own good qualities, though I don't talk about them. That's a failing no one shall have the chance to accuse me of. I'm weak and yielding. I put up with everything, I envy no one and speak well of everybody, even though there isn't much to be said for most of the others; still, that's their look-out. I treat it all as a joke, being so talented myself.«

»Don't talk to me in that flat country's paste-pot language; it makes me sick,« said the Norwegian, and managed in the wind to get away from the heap and go over to another.

In the end they were both turned into paper; and, as luck would have it, the Norwegian rag beame paper on which a Norwegian wrote a faithful love-letter to a Danish girl, while the Danish rag became the manuscript of a Danish ode written in praise of Norway's power and splendour.

So some good can come even out of rags, once they leave the rag-heap and are transformed into truth and beauty. Then a close understanding is kindled, and that is a blessing.

There's the story. It's quite amusing and can't possibly offend anyone – except the rags.

The Most Incredible Thing

The one who could do the most incredible thing was to have the King's daughter and half the kingdom.

The young men – and the old ones, too – strained every thought, muscle and sinew: two of them killed themselves by overeating, and another drank himself to death, trying, each according to his lights, to do the most incredible thing. But that wasn't how it was to be done. Little street-boys practised spitting on their own backs; they considered that the most incredible thing.

On a fixed day a display was to be given of what each one had to show as the most incredible thing. The judges appointed ranged from children of three up to people in their nineties. There was a whole exhibition of incredible things, but everyone soon agreed that the most incredible was a huge clock in its case, most cunningly contrived both in and out. At every hour living pictures appeared, showing which hour had struck; altoge-

ther, there were twelve representations with moving figures that sang or spoke.

»Yes, that was the most incredible thing,« people said.

The clock struck one, and Moses stood on the mountain and wrote down on the Tables of the Law the first Commandment: »Thou shalt have none other gods but me.«

The clock struck two, and the Garden of Eden was seen, where Adam and Eve met, both happy without so much as a wardrobe; they didn't need one.

On the stroke of three the three Wise Men appeared, one of them was coal-black, but he couldn't help that – he had been blackened by the sun.

On the stroke of four came the four seasons: spring with the cuckoo in the fresh foliage of a beech tree, summer with a grasshopper on the ripe ear of corn, autumn with an empty stork's nest from which the bird had flown, winter with an old crow who could tell stories in the chimney-corner, memories of the past.

As it struck five, there came the five senses: sight as an optician, hearing as a coppersmith; smell sold violets and sweet woodruff, taste was a cook, and feeling an undertaker with mourning cape down to his heels.

The clock struck six. There sat a gambler, throwing dice; the die showed its highest face, and it was »six'.

Then came the seven days of the week – or the seven deadly sins – people couldn't agree about that, for they went together and weren't easy to tell from each other.

Next, a choir of monks came and sang eight o'clock matins.

On the stroke of nine appeared the nine Muses, one engaged in astronomy, another as a keeper of historical documents, while the others belonged to the theatre.

On the stroke of ten Moses stepped forward again with the Tables of the Law, on which were all the commandments of God, and they were ten.

The clock struck again, and little boys and girls came skipping out; they were playing a game, at which they sang:

»Three, four, five, six, seven –

the clock has struck eleven«.

Finally, the clock struck twelve, and the watchman stepped forward with fur cap and halberd; he sang the old song of the watchman:

»Twas at the hour of midnight

our Saviour he was born«.

and, as he sang, roses sprang up and turned to angel-heads borne on rainbow-coloured wings.

It was charming to hear, and delightful to see. The whole contrivance was a matchless work of art; everyone declared that *this* was the most incredible thing. The artist was a young man, kind-hearted and happy as a child, a faithful friend and good to his badly-off parents. Yes, he deserved the Princess and half the kingdom.

The day of decision had arrived. It was a fête day for the whole city, and the Princess sat on the royal throne, which had been newly stuffed with horsehair but wasn't any more comfortable for that. The judges all round looked knowingly across at the likely winner, who stood there confident and happy; his success was certain, for he had done the most incredible thing.

»No, no! I shall do that« suddenly shouted a gaunt, lanky giant of a fellow. »I am the man for the most incredible thing.« And he swung a great axe at the work of art.

»Crash! Bash! Bang!« -- there lay the whole contrivance. Wheels and

springs flew all over the place. Everything was dashed to pieces.

»That was what I could do,« said the man. »My deed has beaten his and beaten you all. I have done the most incredible thing.«

»To destroy such a work of art!« said the judges. »Yes, that was the most incredible thing.«

All the people said the same, and so the man was to have the Princess and half the kingdom; for a law is a law, even if it is the most incredible thing.

From the ramparts and all the towers in the city it was proclaimed by trumpet that the wedding was to take place. The Princess wasn't at all pleased; still, she looked charming and was gorgeously dressed. The church was ablaze with candles; late at night they are seen at their best. The noble young girls of the city sang and led the bride forward; the knights sang and escorted the bridegroom, who strutted as though *he* could never be broken in two.

Now the singing stopped, and the church became so silent that you could have heard a pin fall. But, in the midst of the silence, with rolling and rumbling the great churchdoor flew open and boom! boom! all the works of the clock came marching up the middle aisle and stood in between bride and bridegroom. Dead men can't walk again – we know that well enough – but a work of art can. The body had been dashed to pieces, but not the spirit. The spirit of great art haunted the place; there wasn't the ghost of a doubt about that:

The work of art stood there exactly as it was when it was new and untouched. The clock struck the hours, one after the other, up to twelve, and the figures came swarming out. First, Moses; flames of fire seemed to blaze from his forehead, as he hurled the heavy stone Tables of the Law on to the bridegroom's feet and pinned them to the floor of the church.

»I cannot lift them up again,« said Moses. »You have knocked off my arms. Stand as you are!«

Next came Adam and Eve, the Wise Men from the east and the four seasons; each told him unpleasant truths – »shame upon you!«

But he felt no shame.

All the figures that had to appear at the stroke of each hour now stepped out of the clock and all increased terribly in size, till there hardly seemed room for the real people. And when at the stroke of twelve the watchman stepped out with fur cap and halberd, there was a rare to-do. The watchman went straight up to the bridegroom and bashed him on the head with his halberd.

»Lie there!« he cried. »Measure for measure! Now we're avenged, and our young master, too. We vanish.«

And then the whole contrivance disappeared. But the candles all over the church turned into great flowers of light, the gilded stars under the roof threw out long luminous beams, and the organ played of itself. All the people said that this was the most incredible thing they had ever known.

»Then please to summon the right one!« said the Princess. »He that made the work of art – let him be my lord and husband.«

And he stood in the church with all the people around him. All rejoiced and wished him well. There wasn't one who was jealous – and that was the most incredible thing of all.*

* This tale, first published in 1871, was thought to be an allegory of the Franco-Prussian War; and its publication in Denmark, like that of »The Wicked Prince«, was forbidden by the Nazis during the occupation of 1940-45, though it was nevertheless circulated by the Underground Movement.

The Gardener and the Squire

About four miles from the capital stood an old manor-house with thick walls, turrets and stepped gables. Here lived, though only in the summer, a rich nobleman and his wife; this house was the best and handsomest of the various houses they owned. Outside, it looked as if it had only just been built, but inside it was as cosy and comfortable as possible. The family arms were carved in stone over the entrance, beautiful roses climbed round arms and oriel window, and a large grass lawn spread out in front of the house; there were may trees, both pink and white, and there were rare flowers even outside the greenhouse.

The squire had also a clever gardener; the flowers, the orchard and the kitchen-garden were a treat to see. Up against this part of the garden there was still some of the old original garden left with box hedges clipped in the shape of crowns and pyramids. Behind these stood two massive old trees which were nearly always leafless, and you might well suppose that a gale or a waterspout had spattered great lumps of manure over them; but every lump was a bird's nest.

Here, from time out of mind, a swarm of screaming rooks and crows had built; it was an absolute colony of birds, and the birds were the masters, the landed proprietors, the oldest family on the estate, the real lords of the manor. None of the people down below meant anything to them, but they put up with these crawling creatures in spite of their sometimes banging away with their guns, so that the birds got their spines tickled and each of them flew up with frightened cries of »Caw! Caw!«

The gardener often spoke to his master and mistress about cutting down the old trees; they didn't look well (he said) and, once they were gone, the place would most likely be rid of the screaming birds, which would go in search of new quarters. But the squire was unwilling to give up either the trees or the swarms of birds; they were something the manor couldn't be without, something from the old days, and these should not be altogether lost to mind.

»Those trees have now become the birds' inheritance. Let them keep it, my good Larsen.«

Larsen was the gardener's name, but we needn't bother any more about that.

»My dear Larsen, haven't you enough room already? With your flower-garden, glasshouses, orchard and kitchen-garden?«

Yes, he had all these, and he tended and looked after them with great keenness and skill. His master and mistress admitted this, and yet they couldn't hide from him the fact that at other people's houses they often ate fruit or saw flowers that were better than anything in their own garden. The gardener was sorry to hear this, for he did his best that the best should be done. He was good at heart and good at his job.

One day the squire sent for him and told him, as friend and master, that, on the previous day, at the house of some distinguished friends, they had been given apples and pears so rich in juice and flavour that they and all the guests were filled with admiration. The fruit was obviously not home-grown, but it ought to be introduced into this country, if it could stand the climate. The fruit was known to have been bought in the town at the leading fruiterer's, and the gardener should go in and find out where these apples and pears had come from and then order cuttings.

The gardener knew the fruiterer well, for it was to him that he sold for the squire the surplus fruit growing in the manor garden.

So the gardener went to town and asked the fruiterer where he had got these apples and pears that were so much admired.

»They come from your own garden,« said the fruiterer and showed him both apples and pears, which he soon recognised.

Dear me, how pleased the gardener was! He hurried to the squire and explained to him that both apples and pears came from his own garden.

The squire and his lady could simply not believe this. »It's not possible, Larsen. Can you produce a written assurance from the fruiterer?«

Yes, he could; and he brought along a written certificate.

»How very odd!« said the squire.

And now every day at the manor huge bowls of these magnificent apples and pears from their own garden appeared on the table. Bushels and barrels of the fruit were sent to friends in and out of town, and even abroad, bringing no end of pleasure. Still, they had to admit that of course there had been two unusually good summers for fruit-trees; these had done well all over the country.

Time passed. The squire and his wife went and dined at Court. The day after, the gardener was sent for by his master. At the royal table they had had melons so full of juice and flavour from their Majesties' green-house.

»You must go to the royal gardener, my good Larsen, and get us some of the seeds of these delicious melons.«

»But the royal gardener got the seeds from us,« said the gardener, quite delighted.

»Then the man has known how to improve the fruit in some way,« answered the squire. »Every melon was excellent.«

»Well, that does make me feel proud,« said the gardener. »I must explain to you, sir: the royal gardener has had no luck this year with his melons, and when he saw how fine ours were and tasted them, he ordered three of these to be sent up to the castle.«

»Larsen, don't tell me that those melons were out of our garden!«

»I fancy so,« said the gardener; and he went to the royal gardener and got out of him a written certificate saying that the melons on the King's table had come from the manor.

This was indeed a surprise for the squire, and he made no secret of the incident, but showed people the certificate and even had melons sent out far and wide just as previously the cuttings had been.

Then news came back that the seeds were striking and setting admirably and the plant was called after the squire's manor, so that in this way its name could now be read in English, German and French. That was something never dreamed of before.

»I do hope the gardener won't begin to think too much of himself,« said the squire.

But the gardener took it in a very different way. His great ambition now was to establish his name as one of the leading gardeners in the country, and to try every year to produce something first-rate in garden-ing; and he did this. But, all the same, he often heard it said that his very first fruit, the apples and the pears, were really his best; all that came after was much inferior. The melons were no doubt extremely good, but they were of course something quite different. His strawberries might be cal-led excellent, and yet no better than those to be found on other estates; and when one year the radishes were a failure, it was only the unfortunate radishes that they talked about and not a word about anything else that turned out well.

It was almost as though the squire felt relieved to be able to say, »Well,

Larsen, rather a poor year, eh?« They quite enjoyed saying, »Rather a poor year.«

Twice a week the gardener brought fresh flowers up to the house, always most tastefully arranged. The colours seemed to be heightened by the way they were grouped.

»You have taste, Larsen,« said the squire. »That's a gift, not of your own, but of God.«

One day the gardener brought in a big crystal bowl with the leaf of a waterlily lying inside. On this had been laid, with its long thick stalk in the water, a brilliant blue flower as large as a sunflower.

»An Indian water-lily!« exclaimed the squire and his wife. They had never seen such a flower; by day it was carefully placed in the sun and, when evening came, in a reflected light. Everyone who saw it thought it very lovely and most unusual; even the highest young lady in the land, said so, and she was a princess, kind and sensible.

The squire and his lady were only too proud to present her with the flower, and she took it with her back to the castle. Then they both went down into the garden to pick a similar flower themselves, if such a thing was still to be found; but it wasn't. So they called the gardener and asked him where he'd got the blue water-lily from.

»We can't find it anywhere,« they said. »We've been through the greenhouses and right round the flower-garden.«

»Well, but that's not where it is,« said the gardener. »It's only a humble flower from the kitchen-garden. Still, it is beautiful, isn't it? It looks like a blue cactus, and yet it's only the blossom on an artichoke.«

464

»You should have told us that straight away,« said the squire. »We couldn't help thinking it was a rare foreign flower. You've made us look ridiculous in the eyes of the young Princess. She saw the flower at our house and found it so beautiful. She didn't know what it was – though she's well up in botany - but that science has nothing to do with vegetables. How on earth, my good Larsen, could you think of sending such a flower up to the house? It will make us a laughing-stock.«

And the pretty blue flower that had been brought from the kitchen-garden was taken away from the room at the manor, where it was quite out of place; and the squire sent an excuse to the Princess, explaining that the flower was nothing but a vegetable which the gardener had taken into his head to display, and for this he had had a good talking-to.

»What a shame! How unfair!« said the Princess. »Why,he has opened our eyes to a splendid flower we had never noticed; he has shown us beauty where we never dreamed of looking. Every day, as long as the artichokes are in flower, the royal gardener is to bring me one up to my room.«

And this was done.

The squire sent word to the gardener that he might again bring them a fresh artichoke blossom.

»It's really quite handsome,« he said; »altogether remarkable.« And the gardener was praised.

»That's what Larsen enjoys,« said the squire. »He's a spoilt child.«

In the autumn there was a tremendous gale. It sprang up in the small hours and was so violent that numbers of big trees on the fringe of the wood were torn up by the roots, and to the great sorrow of the squire and his wife – sorrow for them, but joy for the gardener – the two massive trees were blown down, together with all the bird's-nests. The cries of rooks and crows could be heard through the gale, as they beat their wing on the windows, said the servants at the manor.

»Now, Larsen, I suppose you're happy,« said the squire. »The gale has brought down the trees, and the birds have taken to the woods. So it's goodbye to the dear old days; not a sign or hint of them is left. To us it is a great grief.«

The gardener said nothing – but he thought of what he had long had in mind – how he could best make use of the fine sunny space he had never before had at his disposal. It should grow to be an ornament to the garden and a joy to the squire.

The big trees that had been blown down had crushed and flattened the venerable boxhedges with all their cut-out patterns. Here he put up a thicket of shrubs, native plants from field and wood. Things that no other gardener had thought of putting in at all abundantly in the garden near the house, he now planted in their proper soil and in the shade and sunshine required by each sort. He tended in love, and they grew into splendour.

Junipers from the heaths of Jutland were raised, with the shape and colour of Italy's cypress; the glossy prickly holly, green alike in winter cold or in summer sunshine, was a delight to the eye. In front grew ferns of every species, some looking as if they were children of the palm tree, and others as if they were parents of that lovely delicate plant we call maidenhair. Here was the despised burdock that when freshly picked is so beautiful that it can look fine in a bunch of flowers. The burdock was on dry soil, but on lower damper ground there grew the common dock, also a despised plant and yet with its height and its tremendous leaf wonderfully picturesque. Six foot high, with flower upon flower like a huge many-branched candlestick, rose the great mullein, transplanted from the fields. And here were sweet woodruff, primroses and lilies-of-the-valley, arum lilies and the delicate three-leaved wood sorrel... All most beautiful to look at.

In front, with steel wire supports, there grew rows of little French pear trees. They got plenty of sun and attention, and they soon bore large juicy pears, as they had done in the country they came from.

To take the place of the two old leafless trees, a tall flagstaff was put up flying the Danish flag, and, near by, another pole round which the hops twined their sweet-smelling clusters in summer and at harvest-time. But in winter according to ancient custom a sheaf of oats was hung from this pole, so that the birds of the air might have something to eat at happy Christmas time.

»Our good Larsen is getting sentimental in his old age,« said the squire. »But he's faithful and devoted to us.«

With the New Year there appeared in one of the capital's illustrated papers a picture of the old manor-house, showing the flagstaff and the sheaf of oats for the birds at Christmas, and emphasis was laid on the happy idea of keeping up a time-honoured custom in this way – an idea so very characteristic of the old place.

»They beat the big drum for every mortal thing that Larsen does,« said the squire. »He's a lucky man. I suppose we ought almost to be proud of having him.«

But they weren't in the least proud of it. They felt that they were the master and mistress and could give Larsen a month's notice if they liked, but they didn't do that. They were kind people, and there are so many kind people of that sort. What a good thing that is for all the Larsens!

Well, that's the story of *The Gardener and the Squire*... Now you can think it over.

What the Thistle Found Out

Adjoining the stately manor-house lay a beautifully-kept garden with rare trees and flowers. Friends who visited the house were enchanted by these; people from the country round and from neighbouring towns would come on Sundays and public holidays and ask for leave to see over the garden, and even whole schools arrived on similar visits.

Outside the garden, close by the fence against the road through the fields, stood a huge thistle. It was so large that, spreading from the root in several branches, it could almost be called a thistle-bush. No one gave it a thought except the old donkey that drew the milkmaids' milk-cart. He put out his neck full stretch and said, »You're lovely! I could eat you!« But the tether-rope wasn't long enough for the donkey to reach out and eat it.

There was a large party at the manor, including a well-known family from the capital with some nice-looking girls and, among these, a young lady from a very long way off; she came from Scotland and was of good birth with plenty of means and property – a bride worth having, said more than one young gentleman, and their mothers said the same.

The young people amused themselves on the lawn and played croquet. They strolled among the flowers, and each of the girls picked a flower and put it in one of the young men's buttonhole. But the Scottish girl spent a long time looking around and would have none of the flowers; none of them seemed quite to her liking. Then she looked over the fence ... There stood the big thistle-bush with its sturdy purple blooms. She saw them and smiled, and she begged the son of the house to pick her one of them.

»It's the flower of Scotland,« she said. »It waves proudly on my country's shield. Do get me one!«

So he fetched her the finest bloom and pricked his fingers, as if it were the most prickly rosebush that it grew on.

She put the thistle bloom in the young man's buttonhole, and he felt highly honoured. Each of the other young men would gladly have given up his own splendid flower to have worn this one, from the fair hands of the young lady from Scotland. And if the son of the house felt honoured, think what were the feelings of the thistle-bush! It was just as though she were bathed in dew and sunshine.

»I'm more important than I thought,« the thistle said to herself. »My real place is inside the fence, and not outside. One's position in the world is indeed surprising. To think that I've now got one of my bairns on the other side of the fence and even in a buttonhole!«

Every bud as it came out and unfolded was told what had happened; and not many days went by before the thistle-bush heard, not from people or the chirping of birds, but from the air itself which keeps and sends out sounds far and wide (right from the most secret walks of the garden and through the open doors and windows of the manor) that the young gentleman, who was given the thistle bloom by that fair Scottish hand, had now won hand and heart as well. They made a handsome pair, a splendid match.

»It was I who fixed that up for them,« thought the thistle-bush, and her mind turned to the flower she had given for the buttonhole. Every flower that came out was told about this.

»I expect I'll be moved into the garden,« she said to herself, »or perhaps be put in a pot that squeezes; still, that's the greatest honour of all.« And the thistle-bush pondered so deeply on this that she declared with absolute certainty, »Yes, I shall be put in a pot.«

She promised every little thistle bloom that came out it should also be put in a pot, possibly in a buttonhole, which was the highest one could hope for. But none of them was put in a pot, let alone a buttonhole; they drank in light and air, basked in the sun by day, lapped up the dew by night, came into full flower, were visited by bees and hornets searching for a dowry of honey in the flowers – and the honey they took but let the flower alone. »Set of robbers!« murmured the thistle-bush. »If only I could stab them! But I can't.«

The flowers hung their heads and drooped, but fresh ones came in their place. »You're just what I wanted!« said the thistle-bush. »Every minute I'm expecting us to get across the fence.« A group of innocent daisies and plantains stood listening in deep admiration and believed every word she said.

The old donkey from the milk-cart stole a glance by the roadside over to the flowering thistle-bush, but its tether-rope was too short to reach her.

And the thistle thought so long about Scotland's thistle, to whose family she felt she belonged, that at last she really believed she came from Scotland and that her own parents had grown into the Scottish shield. That was a big thought, but big thistles can of course have big thoughts.

»Sometimes one comes of so distinguished a family that it makes you tremble to think of it,« said the nettle growing near by, which also had a kind of feeling that it might turn into »nettle-cloth«, if it were treated in the right way.

Summer passed, and autumn passed. The leaves fell off the trees, the flowers grew deeper in colour and fainter in smell. The gardener's boy sang in the garden, the other side of the fence:

»Up we go, sir, down we go, sir,
that is all we need to know, sir!«

The young fir trees in the wood were beginning to long for Christmas, but it was still a far cry to Christmas.

»Here I am – still here!« said the thistle. »It's just as though nobody gave me a thought, and yet it was I who arranged the match. They got engaged, and now they're married – married a week ago. Well, there's nothing I can do, for I can't move a yard.«

Several more weeks passed, and the thistle was now left with her last solitary bloom, large and full-blown. It had shot out near the root; the wind blew cold across it, till the colours were gone, the splendour gone, and the calyx – big as the bloom on an artichoke – had all the appearance of a silver sunflower.

Then the young couple, now man and wife, came into the garden. They strolled along the fence, and the young wife looked over it.

»The big thistle's still there,« she said; »but she hasn't a flower left.«

»Yes, she has. Look, there's the ghost of the last one,« he said, pointing to the silvery remainder of the flower, itself a flower.

»Oh, yes, it's lovely,« she said. »We must have one like that carved into the frame round our picture.«

So once more the young man had to climb over the fence and break off the calyx of the thistle. It pricked his fingers; that came of calling it a »ghost«. It was brought into the garden, up to the manor and into the drawing-room, where there was a painting of the married couple. In the bridegroom's buttonhole a thistle had been painted. They talked about this, and they talked about the calyx they had brought in – the last thistle bloom, now shining like silver, which was to be copied and carved on the frame.

And their talk was carried out, far away, by the wind.

»What a lot we may live to see!« said the thistle-bush. »My first-born came to a buttonhole, my last-born has come to a frame; where shall I come?«

The donkey stood by the roadside and glanced at her. »Come to me, my yum-yum thistle. I can't come to you; my tether isn't long enough.«

But the thistle-bush didn't answer. She grew more and more thoughtful; she went on thinking right up to Christmas time, and then her thought came into flower.

»As long as one's children come inside the fence, a mother can put up with staying outside.«

»That's a beautiful thought,« said the sunbeam. »You, too, shall be given a good place.«

»In a pot or in a frame?« asked the thistle.

»In a fairy tale,« said the sunbeam.

And here it is.

Old Johanna's Tale

(Andersen's last)

The wind sighs in the old willow tree. It's as though you heard a song; the wind sings it, the tree tells the story. If you don't understand it, then ask old Johanna in the almshouse; she knows all about it, for she was born and bred in the parish.

Years back, when the highway still ran along here, the tree was already tall and striking. It stood, where it still stands, outside the tailor's white-washed half-timbered house close to the pond, which was at that time so big that cattle were watered here, and where in a hot summer the little boys of the village ran about naked and splashed in the water. Close under the tree was a milestone of hewn granite, but this has now fallen over and brambles are growing across it.

On the far side of the rich farmer's house the new highway had been made, while the old one became a lane and the pond a mere pool choked with duckweed. When a frog plopped into it, the green surface parted and you saw the black water; round about it grew cat's-tails, buck-beans and yellow irises.

The tailor's house was now old and leaning on one side, the roof a hotbed for moss and house-leek. The dovecote had fallen in, and the starlings were building there; the swallows hung nest after nest on the gable of the house and away under the roof, just as if it was a lucky spot to live in.

It was once; but now it had become lonely and silent. »Poor Rasmus« (as they called him) lived in it, solitary and weak-willed. He was born here, had played here, bounded over fields and fence, paddled as a child in the village pond, clambered in the old willow tree.

In glorious beauty it raised its long branches, as it raises them still; but gales had already twisted the trunk a little, and time had given it a crack; now wind and weather had blown earth into the crack so that grass and greenstuff are sprouting there, and even a little rowan has planted itself there.

When the swallows returned in spring, they would fly about tree and roof, and would daub and repair their old nests. But poor Rasmus allowed his nest to stand or fall as it liked; he neither daubed nor propped it. »What's the good?« was his watchword, and his father's before him.

He stayed in his home. The swallows flew away, but they came back again, the faithful creatures. The starlings flew off, and came back and whistled their songs. There was a time when Rasmus could whistle with the best of them, but now he neither whistled nor sang.

The wind sighed in the old willow tree; it's sighing still. It's as though you heard a song; the wind sings it, the tree tells the story. If you don't understand it, then ask old Johanna in the almshouse; she knows all about it. She's an old hand – almost a Book of the Chronicles – full of wise saws and ancient memories

When the house was first built, the village tailor, Ivar Gossage, moved in with his wife Maren – honest, hard–working folk, both of them. In those days old Johanna was a child; she was the daughter of the man who made clogs, one of the poorest men in the parish. Many a titbit did she get from Maren, who was never short of food. Maren was well in with the squire's wife, always smiling and happy; she kept in good heart and, while busy with the tongue, she was also busy with her hands – her needle was as nimble as her tongue – and at the same time she looked after her house and her children; there were nearly a dozen of them: eleven anyhow, for the twelfth didn't turn up.

»The poor always have the nest full of young ones,« growled the squire. »If you could drown them like kittens and only keep one or two of the lustiest, there wouldn't be much harm done.«

»Goodness gracious me!« said the tailor's wife. »Why, children are a blessing from heaven; they're the joy of the house. Every child is one more prayer to God. When times are hard and there are many mouths to feed, then you exert yourself more and more to find out ways and means in all honesty. God doesn't let go, as long as we don't let go.«

The squire's lady agreed with her, nodded kindly and patted Maren's cheek. She had done that many a time – yes, and kissed her, too – but she was a little child then, and Maren her nursemaid. They were both very fond of each other and that sentiment still held.

Every year at Christmas time supplies for the winter were sent over from the manor to the tailor's house: a barrel of flour, a pig, two geese, a cask of butter, cheese and apples. This was a great help to the larder. And Ivar Gossage actually looked quite pleased, though he soon came back to his familiar byword, »What's the good?«

It was clean and tidy in the house, with curtains in the windows and flowers, too, both pinks and yellow balsam. A sampler hung in a picture-frame; and close beside it a little knitted poem, which Maren Gossage had written herself, for she knew how to make up rhymes. She was really rather proud of the name »Gossage«; it was the only word in the language to rhyme with sausage. »After all,« she said with a laugh, ».that's an advantage we always have over other people.« She was always in good spirits and never said like her husband, »What's the good?« Her motto was, »Have faith in yourself and in God!« That's what she did, and it

kept everything together. The children were healthy, outgrew their nest, went ahead and were well-behaved. Rasmus was the youngest. He was such a lovely child that one of the best artists from the capital borrowed him to do a painting of him – as naked as when he first came into the world. That picture was now hanging in the King's palace, where the lady of the manor had seen it and recognized little Rasmus, although he had no clothes on.

But after that came hard times. The tailor got rheumatism in both hands; they became all knotted. No doctor could do anything, not even the wise Stine, who went in for »doctoring«.

»We mustn't lose heart,« said Maren. »Never say die! Now we've no longer got Dad's two hands to help us, I must get all the busier with mine. Little Rasmus also knows how to use a needle.« He was already squatting on the table, whistling and singing; he was a merry boy. But his mother didn't want him to sit there all day; that wouldn't be fair on the child. He must also run about and play. The clog-maker's Johanna was his best playfellow; she came of even poorer parents than Rasmus. She wasn't pretty, and she went bare-legged; her clothes hung in tatters. She had no one to help with them, and it didn't occur to her to mend them herself. She was a child, happy as a bird in God's sunshine.

Rasmus and Johanna were playing together by the granite milestone under the big willow tree.

Rasmus had great ideas. He meant to be a fine tailor one day and live right in the town, where there were master tailors who had ten men working together; he had heard about that from his father. He would begin as a worker by the day, and then he would grow to be a master, and then Johanna was to come and see him; and if she could cook, well, she should cook dinner for them all and have a parlour of her own.

Johanna hardly dared to believe in all this, but Rasmus believed that it could happen all right.

There they sat under the old tree, and the wind sighed in the leaves and branches; it was as though the wind sang and the tree told the story.

In the autumn every single leaf dropped off, and the rain dripped from the naked branches.

»They'll grow green again,« said Mother Gossage.

»What's the good?« said her husband. »New year means new worry to earn a living.«

»The larder's full,« said his wife. »We can thank the squire's good lady for that. I'm in good health and full of energy. It's wicked of us to complain.«

The squire and his family spent Christmas at their house in the country; but early in the New Year they moved into the capital, where they passed the winter in a round of pleasure and fun. They were invited to balls and parties even by the King himself.

The lady had got two expensive dresses from France; their material, cut and needlework were so fine that the tailor's Maren had never seen anything like it before. So she asked the squire's wife if she might bring her husband up to the manor, so that he too could see the dresses. It was certain, she said, that no country tailor had ever seen dresses to compare with them.

He saw them and hadn't a word to say till he got home, and then what he said was only what he came out with each time: »What's the good?« and this time there was some truth in what he said.

Master and mistress went to town. Balls and gaiety were just beginning; but in the middle of everything the old squire died, and his wife never put on her gorgeous clothes. She was bowed down with sorrow and was dressed all over in black, in the deepest mourning, not a shred of white to be seen. All the servants were in black, and even the state coach was draped in fine black cloth.

It was a night of sharp frost, the snow glittered and the stars were shining. The melancholy hearse came with the body from the capital to the private chapel of the manor, where it was to be laid in the family vault. The agent and the head of the parish council were waiting on horseback with torches at the churchyard gate. The church was lighted up, and the priest stood at the open church-door and received the body. The coffin was carried up into the chancel, and all the people of the parish followed it in. The priest gave an address, and a hymn was sung. The widow, too, was in church; she had driven there in the black-draped state coach, black inside and out. Nothing like it had ever been seen before in the parish.

This funeral pomp became the talk of the whole winter, which always came back to »the squire's funeral«. »You could see there just what the man stood for,« said the country folk. »He was high-born at birth, and he was borne high at his funeral.«

»What's the good of that?« said the tailor. »Life and property are both lost to him now. We've at least got one«.

»You mustn't talk like that « said Maren. »He has eternal life in the kingdom of heaven«.

»Who told you so, Maren? « said the tailor. »Dead men are good manure. But this man was of course too well-connected to bring benefit to the soil; he's to be buried in a vault.«

»Don't talk so wicked,« said Maren, »I tell you, he has eternal life.«

»Who told you so, Maren?« repeated the tailor. But Maren threw her apron over little Rasmus; he mustn't hear such talk. She carried him across to the peat shed and wept.

»Those words you hear over there, little Rasmus, they weren't your father's. It was Satan who went through the room and used your father's voice. Say 'Our Father' – we'll both say it.« And she folded the child's hands.

»Now I'm happy again,« she said. »Have faith in yourself and in God!«

The year of mourning had ended, the widow went into half-mourning, but there were no half-measures about her happiness.

There was a rumour that she had a suitor and was thinking of marrying again. Maren knew something of this, and the parson knew a bit more.

On Palm Sunday, after the sermon, the banns of marriage were to be published between the widowed lady and her betrothed. He was a stone-carver or sculptor – there was some uncertainty as to what his occupation was called, for at that time the name of Thorvaldsen and his art were hardly yet talked about. The new squire was not of noble birth, though certainly a fine figure of a man. He was one, they said, who was something nobody could understand: he carved figures, was clever at his job, and was young and handsome.

»What's the good of that?« asked the tailor.

On Palm Sunday the banns were published from the pulpit, after which came hymnsinging and communion. The tailor was in church with his wife and little Rasmus. When his parents went up to the altar, Rasmus stayed in his pew, for he was not confirmed. They had lately been running short of clothes in the tailor's house; the old ones had been turned and turned, sewed and patched, but now all three of them were in new clothes, though they were black ones as if for a funeral because their clothes were made from the covering used on the funeral coach. The man had got a coat and trousers from it, Maren a high-necked dress , and Rasmus a whole suit to grow in until he was confirmed. The cloth from both inside and outside the funeral coach had been used. No one need have known what it had previously been used for; but, all the same, people did soon get to know: the wise woman, Stine, and one or two other equally »wise« women who didn't make a living out of their wisdom, said that these clothes would bring plague and pestilence to their home, for »none may get his clothes from a hearse without driving to his grave.«

The clog-maker's Johanna wept when she heard this said; and, as it happened that from that day the tailor's health grew worse and worse it would soon be revealed who was to be the victim.

And revealed it was.

On the 1st Sunday after Trinity tailor Gossage died. Now Maren would have to keep everything going by herself and she did; kept faith in herself and in God.

The following year Rasmus was confirmed. Next, he had to go to town and be apprenticed to a big tailor – not, it's true, with twelve daily assistants, but with one; and little Rasmus might count as another half. He was happy and looked very pleased, but Johanna wept, for she was fonder of him than she realized. The tailor's widow stayed in the old house and carried on the business.

It was about this time that the new highway was opened. The old one, running past the willow tree and the tailor's house, became a lane. The pond grew full of weeds; the mere puddle that was left got covered with duckweed; the milestone gave way – there was nothing for it to stand for – but the willow tree held on, turdy and beautiful. The wind still sighed in the leaves and branches.

The swallows flew off, the starlings flew off, and yet they came back in the spring and, when they now returned for the fourth time, Rasmus too came back home. He had finished his apprenticeship and was now a good-looking, though slight, young man. Now he meant to pack up his knapsack and see foreign parts; his heart was set on that. But his mother kept him back; after all, home was the place! The other children were all scattered about; he was the youngest, and the house was to be his. He could get plenty of work, if he would go about the district and be a travelling tailor; work, say, two weeks at one house and a couple more at another. That could also be called travelling. And Rasmus followed his mother's advice.

So he once more slept in the house where he was born, sat again under the old willow and heard it sigh.

He was nice-looking, he could whistle like a bird and sing songs new and old. He was welcome at the big farms, especially at Klaus Hansen's, the second richest farmer in the parish.

The daughter, Elsa, was like the loveliest flower, and she was always laughing. In fact, there were people who were unkind enough to say that she only laughed to show her pretty teeth. She loved to laugh and was always ready to play pranks; nothing came amiss from her.

She fell in love with Rasmus, and he fell in love with her, but neither of them said it in so many words.

Then he took to having fits of depression; he had more of his father's temperament than his mother's. His spirits only rose when Elsa turned up; then they would both of them laugh and joke and play pranks but, although there were plenty of chances, he never hinted a word about his love. »What's the good?« he thought to himself. »Her parents are hoping to find her someone who's well off, and I'm not that. The wisest thing would be for me to clear out.« But he couldn't desert the farm; Elsa had him fast on a string. With her he was like a bird trained to sing and whistle at her will and pleasure.

Johanna, daughter of the clog-maker, was merely a servant at the farm, given humble jobs. She drove the milk-cart out to the fields, where with the other maids she milked the cows, and she even if need be had to cart manure. She never came up to the parlour, and she saw little of Rasmus or Elsa, though she did hear that the two were as good as engaged.

»Yes, Rasmus will soon be well off«, she said. »I don't grudge him that.« And tears came into her eyes, though there wasn't anything here to cry about!

It was market-day in the town. Klaus Hansen drove in, and Rasmus went too. He sat beside Elsa both going there and coming back. He was head over ears in love, but he didn't say a word about it.

»Well, he'll surely say something to me on the subject,« thought the young woman, and that was natural enough. »If he doesn't speak, bless me, I'll give him a fright.«

Soon it was being said at the farm that the richest farmer in the parish had proposed to Elsa, and so he had; but no one knew what answer she had given him.

Rasmus' brain was in a whirl.

One evening Elsa put a gold ring on her finger and asked Rasmus what that stood for.

»You're engaged,« he answered.

»And who with, do you think?« she asked.

»With the rich farmer,« he said.

»You've hit it!« she nodded, as she slipped away.

And he too slipped away; rushed home to his mother's house like a man gone crazy, and packed his knapsack. He was off into the wide world; his mother's tears were of no avail. He cut himself a stick from the old willow and began to whistle, as if he were in good spirits. He was starting out to see all the splendours of the world.

»For me,« said his mother, »it's a sad disappointment. But for you I dare say it's wisest and best to go away, so I must put up with it. Have faith in yourself and in God, then I shall soon have you back again, pleased and happy.

He went by the new high road, and there he saw Johanna driving up with a load of manure; she hadn't caught sight of him, and he didn't want her to see him. So he crouched behind the hedge – there he was hidden – and Johanna drove past.

Up he rose and went out into the world, no one knew where. His mother thought to herself: »He'll be sure to come home before the year's out. Now he'll have new things to see, new things to think about, and

then once more take up the old ways that can't be ironed out by any tailor's »goose«. He's got rather too much of his father's temperament; I'd rather see him with mine, poor child. But he'll come home all right; he can't turn his back on us altogether, me and the house.«

The mother was ready to wait for ages; Elsa only waited a month. At the end of that time she paid a secret visit to the wise woman, Stine, who went in for »doctoring«, told fortunes from cards or tea leaves, and knew a thing or two besides. For instance, she knew where Rasmus was; she read that from the coffee grounds. He was in a foreign town, but she couldn't make out the name of it. It was a town with soldiers in it and charming young ladies. He wasn't sure whether to go for a soldier – or one of the young ladies.

Elsa couldn't bear to hear this. She would gladly give up her savings to buy him off, but no one must know it was her.

Old Stine promised he should come back. She knew a magic art, dangerous for the one who came under its spell, but it was the last resort. She would put on her cauldron to boil for him, and then he would have to come away wherever he might be; he would have to come home to where the pot was boiling and his sweetheart awaited him. It might be months before he came, but come he must – if there was still breath in his body.

Night and day he must keep on the move – without stop or stay, over lake and mountain, be the weather fair or foul, be he ever so footsore. No help for it, he should and must come home.

The moon was in its first quarter – as it had to be for this bit of magic, said old Stine. There was a gale blowing, so that it creaked and groaned in the old willow tree. Stine cut off a twig and twisted it into a knot; this would help recall him to his mother's home. Moss and house-leek were taken from the roof and put into the pot where it stood on the fire. Elsa had to tear a leaf out of the hymn-book and, as it happened, she tore out the last page – the one that gave the misprints. »It makes no odds,« said Stine and threw the leaf into the pot.

Lots of different things had to go into the broth, which had to boil and keep on boiling till Rasmus came home. The black cock in Stine's room had to part with his red comb; it went into the pot. Elsa's heavy gold ring went in as well, and she would never see it again, Stine warned her in advance. She knew so much, old Stine. Many things that we couldn't put a name to went into the pot; and all the time it stood on the fire, or on glowing embers, or on hot ashes. Only she and Elsa knew what was in it.

The moon waxed, and the moon waned. Each time Elsa came and asked, »Can't you see him coming?«

»Much do I know,« said Stine, »and much do I see, but how far he still has to travel I cannot see. Now he is over the first mountains, now he is at sea in bad weather. The way is long, through great forests; he has blisters on his feet, he has fever in his body; but he must keep moving.«

»Oh, no!« said Elsa. »I'm so sorry for him.«

»He mustn't be stopped now; for if we do that, then he'll fall down dead on the road«...

A long time had passed. The moon was shining round and huge, the wind was sighing in the old tree, and in the moonlight a rainbow appeared in the sky. »That is a sign to confirm that he's coming,« said Stine.»Rasmus will soon be here.«

And yet he didn't come.

»It's been a long wait,« said Stine.   »Yes, and I'm tired of waiting,« said Elsa. Now she came less often to Stine and brought her no more presents. She grew more cheerful, and one fine morning everyone in the parish heard that Elsa had said yes to the richest farmer.

She went over to look at the house and the land, the cattle and the furniture. Everything was in good order; there was nothing for the marriage to wait for.

It took place with great festivities, which lasted for three days. There was dancing to clarinet and fiddles. Nobody in the parish was forgotten in the invitation. Mother Gossage was there too; and when the whole thing was over, and the caterers had said thank you to the guests, and the trumpets had sounded the retreat, she went home with left-overs from the feasting.

She had only fastened the door with a latch; this had been raised, the door was open, and there in the living-room sat Rasmus. He had come home – yes, just come home. Heavens above, what a sight he was! Nothing but skin and bone, pale and sallow.

»Rasmus!« exclaimed his mother. »Is that really you? How poorly you look! But how glad I am to have you!« And she gave him some of the good food she had brought away from the wedding-feast, a piece of the roast and some of the wedding-cake.

He told her how in recent times he had often thought of his mother, his home, and the old willow tree. It was strange how often in his dreams he had seen that tree and Johanna with her bare legs.

He made no mention of Elsa. He was ill and had to go to bed. But we mustn't suppose that the cauldron had anything to do with this, or that it had cast a spell over him. Only old Stine and Elsa believed that, but they said nothing about it.

Rasmus lay in a fever; it was infectious. And so no one called at the tailor's house except Johanna, the clog-maker's daughter. She wept to see Rasmus looking so wretched. The doctor gave him a prescription at the chemist's but he refused to take the medicine. »What's the good?« he said.

»Yes , but that's the way to get better,« said his mother. »Have faith in yourself and in God. If only I could see you put on weight, hear you whistle and sing, then I would gladly give up my own life.« And Rasmus got over his illness, but his mother caught it. God called her away, not him.

It was lonely in the house, and conditions grew poorer. »He's worn out,« they said in the parish. »Poor Rasmus!«

He had led a reckless life on his travels; it was that, and not the black pot on the boil, which had sapped his strength and made him feel so restless. His hair had turned thin and grey; he had no desire to do any real work. »What's the good?« he said. He betook himself to the inn rather than the church.

One autumn evening, in wind and rain, he was struggling along the muddy lane from the inn to his house; his mother had long ago been laid in her grave. The swallows and starlings had also gone, the faithful creatures. But Johanna, the clog-maker's daughter, had not gone; she overtook him on the road and went along a little way with him. »Pull yourself together, Rasmus,« she said.

»What's the good?« he replied.

»That's a bad saying of yours,« she said. »Remember what your mother used to say – 'Have faith in yourself and in God.' You don't, Rasmus, but you should and must. Never say, 'What's the good?' for, if you do, you root up all power of action in yourself.«

She went with him to his door, and there she left him. He didn't stay in the house, but made his way under the old willow tree and sat down on a block of the fallen milestone.

The wind sighed in the branches of the tree; it was like a song, it was like a story. Rasmus answered it; he spoke out loud, but no one heard him – no one but the tree and the sighing wind.

»I feel so cold. I dare say it's time I went to bed. Sleep, sleep!« And he went, not towards the house, but towards the pond; there he stumbled and fell. The rain was pouring down, and the wind was icy cold, though he didn't notice it. But when the sun got up and the crows flew away over the reeds, he awoke half-dead. Had he laid his head where his feet were lying, he would never have got up again; the green duckweed would have been his shroud.

Late in the morning Johanna went to the tailor's house. She was his help; she got him to hospital. »We've known each other since we were children,« she said. »Your mother gave me meat and drink; I shall never be able to repay her. You'll get your health back; you'll be one to go on living.«

And God willed that he should live on. But his health and his spirits went up and down.

The swallows and starlings came and went and came again. Rasmus grew old before his time. All by himself he sat in the house, which fell more and more into decay. He was a poor man, worse off now than Johanna.

»You've no faith,« she said, »and without God what have we left? I tell you what - you should go to communion,« she said. »I don't suppose you've been since you were confirmed.«

»Yes, but what's the good?« he said.

»If that's your answer and that's your faith, then don't! God wants no unwilling guest at his table. Still, think of your mother and the time when you were a child. In those days you were a nice good boy. May I say a hymn to you?«

»What's the good?« he said.

»I always find it such a comfort,« she answered.

»What a saint you've become, Johanna!« And he looked at her with tired listless eyes.

Johanna went through the hymn, but she didn't read it out of a book, for she hadn't one there; she knew it by heart.

»Those were beautiful words,« he said, »Though I couldn't follow all the way through. My head feels so heavy.«

Rasmus had become an old man, but neither was Elsa any longer young, if we may venture to name her. Rasmus never mentioned her. She was now a grandmother. A pert little girl, who was her grandchild, was playing with some other children in the village. Rasmus came along, leaning on his stick; he stood still and looked smiling at the children's play, with memories of old times shining through his thoughts. Elsa's grandchild pointed at him – »poor Rasmus!« she called out. The other little girls followed her example: »poor Rasmus!« they shouted and ran screaming after the old man.

It was a grey gloomy day, followed by several more, but after days that are grey and gloomy comes one also with sunshine. It was a beautiful Whitsunday morning. The church was decorated with green sprays of birch, and a smell of the woods had come inside while the sun shone across the pews. The big altar-candles were alight, for there was communion, and Johanna was among the kneelers – but not Rasmus. That very morning he had been called away... With God were mercy and compassion.

Many years have passed since then. The tailor's house is still there, but no one lives in it. The first gale in the night may sweep it away. The pond is choked with reeds and marsh trefoil. The wind sighs in the old tree. It's as though you heard a song; the wind sings it, the tree tells the story. If you don't understand it, then ask old Johanna in the almshouse.

There she lives and sings her hymn that she sang for Rasmus. She thinks of him and prays to God for him, faithful soul that she is. She can tell of the times that are gone, of the memories that sigh in the old tree.

About the Author

Hans Christian Andersen, the son of a poor shoemaker, was born in the slums of Odense, Denmark, in 1805. At the age of fourteen he moved to Copenhagen, "in order to become famous." He worked for a time with the Royal Theater, and then, in 1828, entered Copenhagen University. Andersen's first book was published in 1822, but it was not until 1835 that his first four tales for children were published. Andersen's tales were an almost immediate success, and he continued to write fairy tales and stories until 1872, completing 156 altogether. He died in 1875 at the age of seventy.

The Pantheon Fairy Tale & Folklore Library

Abbey Lubbers, Banshees & Boggarts:
An Illustrated Encyclopedia of Fairies
by Katharine Briggs

America in Legend
by Richard M. Dorson

British Folktales
by Katharine Briggs

Chinese Fairy Tales and Fantasies
translated and edited by Moss Roberts

The Complete Grimm's Fairy Tales
introduced by Padraic Colum

Eighty Fairy Tales
by Hans Christian Andersen

An Encyclopedia of Fairies: Hobgoblins, Brownies,
Bogies, and other Supernatural Creatures
by Katharine Briggs

Gods and Heroes: Myths and Epics of Ancient Greece
by Gustav Schwab

Italian Folktales
selected and retold by Italo Calvino

Nine Lives: Cats in Folklore
by Katharine Briggs

The Norse Myths
introduced and retold by Kevin Crossley-Holland

Norwegian Folk Tales
collected by Peter Christen Asbjørnsen and Jørgen Moe

Russian Fairy Tales
collected by Aleksandr Afanas'ev